The Confessions of Sherlock Holmes

THE THEOLOGICAL ODYSSEY OF THE GREAT DETECTIVE

Volume 6

The Secrets of Sherlock Holmes

Thomas Mengert

BLUE FORGE PRESS

Port Orchard, Washington

The Secrets of Sherlock Holmes
Copyright 2024
by Thomas Mengert

First eBook Edition December 2024
First Print Edition December 2024

ISBN 979-8-89439-029-1

For information about film, reprint or other subsidiary rights, contact: blueforgegroup@gmail.com

Blue Forge Press is the print division of the volunteer-run, federal 501(c)3 nonprofit company, Blue Forge Group, founded in 1989 and dedicated to bringing light to the shadows and voice to the silence. We strive to empower storytellers across all walks of life with our four divisions: Blue Forge Press, Blue Forge Films, Blue Forge Gaming, and Blue Forge Records. Find out more at www.BlueForgeGroup.org

Blue Forge Press
7419 Ebbert Drive Southeast
Port Orchard, Washington 98367
blueforgepress@gmail.com
360-550-2071 ph.txt

Acknowledgements

The Confessions of Sherlock Holmes has, for all of its primary theological intent, a subtext that emerged in the course of the writing. That subtext is the decline and fall of the British Empire and of the imperial family structures that once supported it. The three Holmes brothers each manifest the end result of the system of primogeniture and the conflict present between art and reason in their blood. Each brother in his own way manifests the conflict entailed in finding a place and an identity in opposition to their father and his estate.

The character of the Holmes father remains distant and perhaps finally indecipherable. As the reader will discover in the course of reading the book the parental figure looks beyond his own sons in order to find an image of a substitute son that would meet the requirements and the pattern that the father needed each of them to represent. Unfortunately, each son manifested instead a diluted solution of traits that drew more from their artistic mother and her French heritage than from their stern father and his code. The individuality and character of the brothers manifests a freedom from convention that the father perhaps wished that he could have claimed for himself, but to see it present in his sons seemed both indulgent and a betrayal of his own strict principles. He valued rebellion, but not within his own house and among his own progeny. For this reason both Mycroft and Sherlock are comparative exiles, while Sherringford is saddled with maintaining Sigerside, the Holmes estate. If the Christian religion can be seen as the process of overcoming exile from God as Father through the sacrifice of a Son, the parallels will be immediately apparent.

I doubt that I would have been able to compose this book if it were not present as a reflection of the dynamics of my own family. So for this reason I dedicate this book as with all my efforts in life to my parents and grandparents and especially to my two grandmothers who each nurtured my early love for literature with their deep love and affirmation.

The support of my parents made my life possible in every way imaginable.

To my Father's mother, Tilly, who read me Longfellow's poetry on sunny afternoons.

To My Mother's mother, Gerda, who gave me the Doubleday Edition of The Complete Sherlock Holmes.

To my Father's father, Otto, who shared his library with me and taught me the value of family heritage.

To my Mother's father, Fred, who instilled in me a love of the sea and for his humor and love of stories.

To all of these my everlasting thanks.

"What is the meaning of it, Watson?" said Holmes, solemnly, as he laid down the paper. "What object is served by this circle of misery and violence and fear? It must tend to some end, or else our universe is ruled by chance, which is unthinkable. But what end? There is the great standing perennial problem to which human reason is as far from an answer as ever."

—From *The Adventure of the Cardboard Box*

"There is nothing in which deduction is as necessary as in religion," said he, leaning with his back against the shutters. "It can be built up as an exact science by the reasoner. Our highest assurance of the goodness of providence seems to me to rest in the flowers. All other things, our powers, our desires, our food, are really necessary for our existence in the first instance. But this rose is an extra. Its smell and its color are an embellishment of life, not a condition of it. It is only goodness which gives such extras, and so I say again that we have much to hope from the flowers."

—From *The Adventure of the Naval Treaty*

"The greatest schemer of all time, the organizer of every deviltry, the controlling brain of the underworld, a brain which might have made or marred the destiny of nations – that's the man!"

"Barker beat his head with his clenched fist in his impotent anger. 'Do not tell me that we have to sit down under this? Do you say that no one can ever get level with this king devil?' 'No, I don't say that,' said Holmes, and his eyes seemed to be looking far into the future. 'I don't say that he can't be beat. But you must give me time—you must give me time.' We all sat in silence for some minutes while those fateful eyes still strained to pierce the veil."

—From *The Valley of Fear*

Introduction

As the author of The Confessions of Sherlock Holmes series I would like to take this opportunity thank those dedicated and intrepid readers who have climbed this "Mount Everest of a work" from base camp to ever higher latitudes of critique and speculation on the nature of religion in general, and of Catholicism in particular. As is the case with any literary endeavor of substance this book, complex and comprehensive as it was my intention to make it, cannot act as a substitute for proper religious catechetical instruction conducted under the auspices and with the approval of those persons with ecclesiastical authority. The present book is a drama meant to highlight many of the issues confronting church and state in the late Victorian era and in the 20th century with residual relevance for today where these questions are even more urgent.

The appeal of the character, Sherlock Holmes is well-nigh universal. Few if any other fictional characters have so deeply engaged the imagination of readers ever since the original stories were published in The Strand Magazine. They are not mere entertainments. Sir Arthur Conan Doyle was obsessed by the deeper meaning of human life and it has been the purpose of this series to probe even more deeply where the originator first indicated a path waiting for further speculations.

Entire societies of aficionados of the great detective developed as the years passed. In America these scholars were termed "Sherlockians," whereas in the home country of England they are known by the more formal appellation of, "Holmesians." One of the first to point the way forward after the last tales were written was the author, Vincent Starrett, whose early book in 1933, entitled *The Private Life of Sherlock Holmes*, led to an avalanche of later books seeking to untangle the web of allusions left behind to stimulate thought by the often incomplete hints left by Doctor Watson. My own series of books on Sherlock Holmes has been composed with this background of scholarship in mind to serve as an inspiration for my own synthesis that I hope may hereafter provide the equivalent of a unified field theory to later Sherlockians.

The question of the meaning of human existence provides the high-stakes arena where Holmes and Moriarty meet to discuss matters that continue to divide the world to this very day. It is important at the outset to realize that in European history religion preceded the national state system that prevails today. Geopolitics in its present form would once have been seen as inconceivable. Even our sense of stable geography is different from what prevailed in the former disputed regions of Europe. Repeated local wars decided the fate of the people living in zones that were contentious and in dispute. The carefully delineated borders we presume to encounter today did not exist. Even the loose class structure characteristic of capitalist economies is a latter-day phenomenon, one that would have been meaningless in the feudal system where religion provided the undergirding of all social distinctions and the basis of sovereignty, of the right to rule. These former organizational principles no longer exist; when social conditions change perceptions of ultimate reality change as well. Religious questions deal with ultimate reality. The encounter with religion today comes from many directions. In our individualistic culture religion is often seen as an appendage to life rather than as its source and basis. Yet a concern with religious questions still plays a central role if one that is sometimes in conflict with the demands of secular life in our fast-paced world.

The first major work of apologetics was written by St.

Augustine and entitled *The City of God.* Its purpose was to explain and to justify the Christian religion by showing that Christian belief contributed to social virtue and good citizenship in the Roman Empire. Unfortunately even the city of Rome was in peril at the time, threatened by various invaders such as the Vandals and other invading northern tribes. The need for new works of apologetics, even if they take fictional form, is never more necessary than in times of social upheaval. The religious instinct takes various forms from laconic tolerance to zealous advocacy. No religion can be properly understood if removed from the communal setting where it flourishes. Christianity and Catholicism in particular depend upon liturgical and sacramental means to convey belief through proclamation and encounter. Theological concepts look odd when transplanted outside the environment where alone they can be comprehended and found to be compelling towards adopting a religious way of life.

Religious belief once seemed impervious to any historical reappraisal; but the 18th and 19th centuries began a reassessment of the role of religion in public life. The effort to rationalize religious doctrines distorted their actual claims and denied their unique nature. Many of the ideas in this book stem from major philosophers of late 19th century that still cast their shadows for good or ill as we penetrate ever deeper into the 21st century without major intellectual figures of like stature to influence and to guide us. Early modern philosophers like John Locke, Georg Hegel, Ludwig Feuerbach, Ernest Renan, Herbert Spencer, and Karl Marx began to dislodge Christianity and particularly Catholicism from the position of power and authority that had existed for centuries to provide an ultimate explanation and answer for every question.

Already the advent of the secular nation-state at the Peace of Westphalia in 1649 had led inevitably to the end of residual feudalism and finally led over the course of centuries to the fall of the great monarchical empires after the First World War. The period of history that has followed that watershed event has been collectively influenced by various modernist movements inspired by writers in multiple fields such as Freud, Husserl, Einstein, Heidegger, Bergson, Proust, Joyce, Sartre, Keynes, Merleau-Ponty, Wittgenstein, Gide, Camus, and countless others.

The Modernist Movement in turn has been supplanted since the 1970's by an emphasis on structuralism, systems theory, and by the influence of significant post-modern thinkers and critics such as Derrida, Foucault, Baudrillard, Lyotard, and Deleuze. There has also been an overlapping influence from authors addressing the particular issues raised by hitherto neglected minority communities formerly marginalized by the dominant culture. Astute readers will be able to trace some of these voices prefigured in the battle of wits between Sherlock Holmes and Professor Moriarty in this work where even the devil is given his due at times, because faith emerges out of and must contend with the times and conditions of each age. As is the case with any comprehensive world-view, prior patterns and assumptions are at first resistant to new ideas. This is particularly true when, as is the case with theology, the established institutional framework is determined to protect and to look with suspicion on any supposed additions or clarifications to subject matter that has proven to be both necessary and sufficient for ages past and been definitively communicated by God and entrusted to the Catholic Church. The Catholic Church moreover regards itself as more than a mere benevolent institution; it is the living body of believers in Jesus Christ assembled under the successors to the Apostles engaged in completing the work of Jesus on earth while preparing for a Second Coming of Christ that will initiate the new order of all things in what has been traditionally called, The Kingdom of God.

As part of the cohesive synthesis formerly provided by Catholicism, theology was considered to be the Queen of all the sciences, one superior even to philosophy in its explanatory scope. However, as the particular disciplines of human knowledge began to carve out separate areas of expertise and new methodologies to add to the sum total of human knowledge, the former comprehensive synthesis provided by Catholicism became marginalized and reduced to privatized religious observances with little influence upon the unfolding of history. Naturally this was a cause for dismay and even outrage in the higher institutional fabric of the Roman Catholic Church and resistance to these trends became more determined with time.

The rear-guard action of the papacy after the fall and annexation of the Papal States during the past two centuries in order to safeguard the Catholic faith in tradition and to heal European culture as a whole from the effects of two world wars has been a troubled one. Atheism and the appeal of other religious traditions in the newly independent colonies, no longer under European domination, combined with the fragmented denominational groupings of Christianity have only added to the difficulties of maintaining a religion that is meant to provide the single and definitive basis for all human communities and to each individual human life in the form of eternal salvation.

The result of all of this is that we stand today on the edge of a moral and political watershed and even possibly upon the brink of some final apocalyptic event. As an author I share this general concern, but I refuse to surrender to an easy pessimism or worse still to some last-ditch effort to restore a golden age of mythical tranquility by force. Religious questions are never easy ones and no age has ever been immune from the twin evils of religious fundamentalism and of its opposite, religious indifferentism. The Confessions of Sherlock Holmes attempts within a fictional setting to balance these opposing positions in search of a middle-point where our currently beleaguered world can catch its breath before forging on into the uncertain future with hope and understanding of our common destiny as human beings.

It is that common destiny that is in question whenever one encounters religious belief systems that presume that the purpose of all that we see about us is to provide a setting for a cosmic drama enacted between opposing ethical systems that owe their origin to a supernatural order presided over by God and a host of spiritual beings that either aid or detract from human moral progress and the ultimate destiny of souls. However fantastic or mythological these claims may appear to the unbeliever, they are no less startling than the ordinary and ready acceptance by the general populace of the formulations of science from general relativity to quantum theory. Similar to the case with scientific theories formulations of religious language must be adapted by using concepts that can be understood within the culture that is meant to receive the religious message. History, understood as the teleological development of God's intentionality plays a major thematic role in The Confessions of Sherlock Holmes.

At the present time various political and religious groupings share a preoccupation with values and would readily demand institutional as opposed to merely speculative support to advance their particular values. Philosophical discussions of contending values may be animated, but they should not descend into violence or be considered adequate in isolation to provide the structural support for entire societies. Sociology, psychology, and economics may explore human behavioral patterns, but they usually maintain an attitude of academic distance and emotional neutrality that leads to clarity of description rather than to proscriptive norms for human behavior. Even the term, "ego functionality," for instance is a vague term resting upon uncertain pragmatic grounds. In the absence of widely accepted and definitive norms any number of substitute ideologies, social theories, world-views, and stylized liberation movements vie for supremacy and together create an atmosphere of incommensurable narratives with no overriding principle of verifiability to differentiate among them. In such a stifling atmosphere conflicts, perceived betrayal of principle and general confusion reign.

The overheated contemporary historical environment may make the very idea of the sort of reasoned debate similar to that waged between Sherlock Holmes and Professor Moriarty a luxury proper to another age but of little value today. We have collectively come to a point where we are willing to abandon the quest of finding some grounding in rationality and a basic appreciation for the great traditions of the past. Religion in particular is menaced by such an intellectual environment as that which prevails at the present time. Any discussion of a transcendent reality demands that a common theological language should exist. Even the effort to arrive at a definition of Divine Being is likely to be distorted today by an influx of other associations. Here is a brief example taken from the beginning of the ancient Nicean Creed to clarify an essential point—what does it mean in the language and prevailing cosmology of today to affirm our faith at the most basic level in words such as these?

I believe in one God, the Father almighty, maker of heaven and earth, of all things visible and invisible. I believe in one Lord Jesus Christ, the only begotten Son of God. Born of the Father before all ages. God from God, Light from Light, True God from True God, begotten not made, consubstantial with the Father; through Him all things were made...

These sentences and dogmatic assertions lose their true meaning without a theological context to provide the historical background and an awareness of the prevailing cultural assumptions of the times when certain essential theological definitions were made. Absent this effort these dogmatic assertions are deprived of their full resonance and appear arbitrary to the person aspiring to believe. Are the definitions and connotations in the basic creedal text clear and meaningful to us without appending some further commentary and clarification? A proper approach to theology requires insight into the text so that it acquires the same sense it possessed when these distinctions were made so as to arrive at a formula of faith at the Council of Nicaea when arriving at the closest possible definition of the relations existing between two of the three equal members of the Holy Trinity. To make this essential point even clearer I ask the reader to consider how we are to understand the word "light" in the creed: is God merely a form of electromagnetic energy and are "invisible" angels tenants of a spiritual realm or are they only beings existing beyond the visible spectrum of human eyesight. We cannot appreciate the analogical character of the formula of basic belief arrived at by the council fathers if we apply an overlay of modern scientific theory to the text.

Many theologians today that might have been considered to be heretical as recently as a century ago are therefore actually engaged in preserving the insight of faith by applying proper hermeneutical methods to the prior understanding of concepts formerly thought to have a one to one relationship with the transcendent realm. Analogical thinking in contrast to this naïve approach to reading a text realizes that there exists a sort of "step-down gear ratio" between what God actually is and how we are able to capture that mysterious reality in linguistic formulations.

For this reason the gospels and the Old Testament writers speak in forms that are more experiential and poetic than those using the philosophical distinctions inherited from the Greek tradition that was utilized by the early Christian Fathers of the Church and later by St. Thomas Aquinas and the scholastic philosophers of the Middle Ages. Any methodology that has been long in use appears to be natural and exclusive; our own age is no less limited by our own customary ways of looking at the world. Language is always the great transport system of ideas so that each age must, while respecting the parameters set by divine revelation, adapt the language in which it is expressed in order to conserve its meaning and make it comprehensible in a changing world.

I mention this problem in order to place any theological speculations that I have made in this book occurring between Sherlock Holmes and Professor Moriarty in their proper perspective as mere elements of dramatization rather than official Church teaching. A fictional work like this may raise interesting questions, but it is incapable of acting as a substitute for the official magisterium of the Catholic Church. The role of the literary artist is even more differentiated than that of the theologian in that art creates its own world of interrelationships through mimesis. Whether art can ever be judged for its morality is a vexed question, but many artists have been persecuted and even executed for failing to adhere to supposedly universal norms and it has been no defense for them to claim that art is an airy nothing. Writers have always been held in suspicion by any absolutist system because the artist's loyalty is always to his craft even more than to its content as viewed from an outside perspective. Any true reading of a text creates a common ground of mutual understanding, which may be more valuable from being analogical than from being literal. The goal of a "correct reading" of a text may more harmful than simply allowing the text to speak and to inspire the recipient.

The tendency to view "the word of God" in absolutist terms has a tendency, particularly in ecclesiology, to freeze "the word of God" into a "deposit of faith" analogous to a bank balance presided over by a set of trustees that scrutinizes any applicant for a loan to see if he or she is reliable and will retain what has been withdrawn in the same form and manner that it was issued to the receiver. The underlying fear is that otherwise a sort of theological drift may set in, a rip tide of sorts that will draw the recipient into error. The ability to give a correct rendition of the message, even if imperfectly understood, is held to be the essence of salvation. This is why heresy has been seen as the greatest danger to orthodox belief from the very beginning when the very survival of Christianity was at stake. The paradox is that this fear is more likely to have been inspired by a latent Platonism in the early church and a mistrust of the human element present in all religion.

A more recent theological position operating from a hermeneutical perspective suggests that a better image of Catholic tradition is one of proclamation and confession. The good news of Christian redemption arrives according to the mode of the receiver and in a form that brings the unconvinced into relation with the Living Triune God. How God manages this encounter is for God alone to determine. The response of the one seeking God (even when he or she does not know that this is what he or she has been doing) is as personal as the account given in the Gospel of St. Luke of the invitation of Jesus to the tax-collector Zacchaeus who had climbed a sycamore tree in order to catch a glimpse of Jesus. He is startled to be told by Jesus to come down because Jesus wishes to eat with him that very day! The impact of this encounter is both great and decisive; an act of recognition takes place.

Conversion is a response to love. Divine Love elicits love in return in the form of confession that Jesus is Lord; not in a distant way of power employed to elicit submission, but of joyful acceptance at finding that for which one has been seeking. Jesus constantly reminds his followers that the Kingdom of God is now, within you, and among you. This is also the constant proclamation for which the Catholic Church was instituted so as to draw all things to God. The Confessions of Sherlock Holmes took its inspiration and motivation with the end in view of serving this process of recognition by bringing people close enough that their remaining questions can be answered by those in a better position to clarify any misconceptions that remain after wrestling with the drama presented here and in the other volumes of the series. I ask only that my readers bear in mind that a literary work must speak for itself; while the artist as James Joyce once said must stand outside of it paring his fingernails. I wish to emphasize once again that this series contains theological speculations by fictional characters meant to appeal to a broad audience by pointing out that these questions are of ultimate concern particularly at the present time.

The conclusions in the book are those of the characters and do not in all respects represent the teachings of the Catholic Church and should not be relied upon as if they were. At the same time I hope that persons whose station in life allows them to clarify these issues because of their clerical status will find the assertions suggestive and useful. It has been my experience in writing that the characters speak, while the author merely takes down dictation and colors in the margins. I believe that most writers have experienced this same odd sensation of being a mere conduit and only recognize what they have written after it stands naked before them in print. Execution forms the thought that is only discernible after it has already been expressed. It is the joy of writing to enter upon this process. The rest lies with the reader as he or she sits down to read.

Bon appétit!

The Secrets of Sherlock Holmes

THOMAS MENGERT

Book Fourteen

The Duel of the Masters

Preface by Dr. Watson

The myth of a golden age seeds the ground for slaughter and the young are offered up on a funeral pyre to appease and to satisfy the guilt of the vanished dead.   —Anonymous

The sorrows of the child are never wholly erased by time; they become part of his very being, structured into not merely the child's expectations of what is possible, but as the undertone resonating in every experience, bludgeoning whatever melody the child wishes to create into silence.   —Anonymous

If you seek me here, I will be over there; if you seek me over there, I will be here. If you seek me still, you will not find me. If you find me I will escape you. If you turn away from me, I will come to you; and if I come to you, I will never leave you.   —Anonymous

The quotations above struck me forcibly when I read them the other day in a book of memoirs of an unnamed soldier who died fighting in the Punjab campaign in Northern India. Where he obtained them is a mystery. Each of these quotations seemed to call forth a sense of some primordial desolation, the very essence of original sin. Each quotation in its own way reveals the vanity of a sought after salvation. The dread of loss and abandonment haunts our every waking hour and disturbs our dreams. I have received over the years a charming correspondence from my readers assuring me that their own anxieties were lessened and their confidence renewed in imagining that they too might, if the necessity arose, climb the seventeen steps of 221B Baker Street and be ushered into the presence of the great detective. As my readers know, it was upon my return from Afghanistan that I first met Sherlock Holmes.

I was wounded and upon arriving back in England on a small pension I was in need of lodgings and my friend Stamford introduced me to an odd fellow who was doing work in the morgue of the hospital at the University of London. I have always thought it strange that my association with Sherlock Holmes began in a morgue and now as I write these words, in what are hopefully the last years of the Great War, all of Europe has become one great charnel house of a generation of young men who have gone to their deaths in order to preserve the great European empires. As my own story moves swiftly to its close I cannot help but reflect that the book of history is a serial production where every end is a new beginning and where every beginning is an end.

The image of life as a stream is a common one, but the most significant salient of this image is the indifferent quality displayed by fate to the individual lives that have so little effect on the course of the events that sweep them up into diverse and conflicting currents and whisk them swiftly out of sight. We honor the noble dead and promise to remember them and the reasons that justified their sacrifice, but their obsequies are scarcely finished before the attention of the surviving multitudes is drawn away to some other spectacle of the perennial fatality of man. The idea of finding the meaning of life through the death on a cross of Jesus of Nazareth would appear as a startling incongruence if it was not for the fact that this sacrifice is a sign of a covenantal relationship with God that plays such a vital role in the Hebrew Scriptures. Death and purification rituals play a role in many religions, perhaps naturally because to be reduced to non-existence, often accompanied by pain, is the worst punishment or affliction imaginable. To take a person's life even more than slavery is the ultimate exercise of power and supremacy so that many wars in the most primitive eras were followed by mass deaths exacted as a form of revenge and retribution.

A question arises however when we consider death to be a source of food and of renewed life in the sinner so that the death of Jesus, a unique historical occurrence, becomes the basis for our idea of the Holy and a timeless and transcendent event with decisive implications for all of humanity. No prior religion has ever claimed so much or tested the parameters of human credulity in precisely this manner. There is something brutal in the idea of the death of an innocent man as atonement from evils for which he is not responsible—the act of Godly justice appears to be at face value to be a supreme act of injustice. If Jesus did not deserve to die, then something or someone should have prevented it but no one did.

On the other hand, if Jesus rushed forward to embrace His own destruction, a natural feeling arises that He must have been misled in some way into making personal the metaphoric language found in Holy Scripture referring to a suffering servant as in Isaiah. Perhaps these passages were meant to refer to Israel as a whole rather than to any individual human being however well-intentioned He might be. Then there is the observation that European history that for all of its overtly Christian pretentions, has been one long succession of wars many of which were waged over doctrinal disputes left irresolvable even by the authoritative Church of Rome unless by recourse to arms.

Colonel Sebastian Moran and his role model Professor Moriarty in contrast presume that no meaning to events is ever available. Terrible things simply happen without reason or pattern and any search for regularities is as pointless as assigning a center to a universe consisting of countless galaxies all moving away from each other at the speed of light. When placed against what we know of physical reality, any supposed transcendent theory appears on its face to be terrible reductionist: that human lives matter and that any lasting truth is ever obtainable. Instead our lives appear to be playthings of chance with occasional instances of beauty and harmony to tempt us into assigning an overall meaning to events. Is religion simply a byproduct of language, particularly a religion that is based upon a God contained within a text? The interwoven texture of theology might be thought of as one long commentary resting upon an initial category error, that mankind and God have anything to do with each other. When we affirm simultaneously that there is one God in Three Divine Persons and rest that belief upon the composite history of the Christian conquest of Europe we can only hope that other cultures are willing to accept such an assertion and consequently prepared to forsake their own belief systems and willing to concur with our assessment or not well-armed and ready to resist.

If we choose though to look at religion only as a cultural phenomenon or as a reflection of the growth into consciousness of the human mind we will be biased from the start against entertaining the possibility that something really startling is at play in Christianity. The problem with any truly unique or startling event, and what can be more startling than for God to become man and then after entering into history suffering death at our hands on a cross only to rise again, is that a process of oxidation and intellectual rust begins to form about the event over time in order to explain that event to ourselves.

As Christianity became more intelligible and explainable, formulaic rather than utterly unique, and above all else less proclamation than indoctrination, Christianity became more of an example of what human beings might devise by themselves independently from God. If we add to this incipient tendency all the encumbrances that flow naturally from various institutional imperatives, religion as such is transformed into merely one more instance of social control or human expressiveness and any residual element of the divine that remains is reduced to magic. As we gain control of the mystical element in revealed events we revert to practicality, the single greatest temptation of human beings, to manage our own affairs while paying only lip-service to God.

Education for instance was once thought of as a bringing forth of the capacity of the student to learn; it was in all truth an awakening to full consciousness. But when education is less a matter of posing questions and discovery and is proportionately reduced to memorization and the regurgitation of information, the human mind becomes only another blank sheet of paper on which anything at all may be written.

Medicine might be chosen as a similar example of this same process. When medicine began in the time of Hippocrates it was more dedicated to restoration of health by any means available rather than to artifice and to intervention. The human body was a mystery rather than merely a complicated mechanism to be engineered into greater efficiency. As practitioners of medicine grew to understand first anatomy and later physiology the balance began to shift and the body, rather than being a mysterious conduit of the life-force, became something in our control and any conception that life is a result and example of a truly momentous event, an explosion if you will, an indwelling of the Holy Spirit from conception to death, yielded to seeing human life as an arbitrary process no different than any other process and one equally subject to our manipulation and control.

Similarly the gap between the private and the public tends to disappear as the individual person is reduced to occupying an institutional existence. Any ecclesiology that absorbs the individual in the name of collective ritual forgets that Jesus encountered each individual in the gospel accounts in their particular life situation. The apostolic nature of the Church must proceed in a similar manner if it is to be in any way Christ-like in character. When Christianity becomes a mass-phenomenon it is no longer Christianity but rather a monstrous octopus-like creature dedicated to power and indifferent to the fate of the person other than as one more cell in an amorphous spiritual conglomeration of organic matter.

For Catholicism to be really Catholic then it must be universal and individual simultaneously. The canonized saints are examples for us of what the Holy Spirit actually manifests in individual people when they encounter the living God. At that point Christianity emerges collectively as precisely what it claims to be, the one unique and sufficient communication of God to the entire human race in order to answer the need that we feel within ourselves as we encounter evil, for salvation and for eternal life.

The duel to be fought between Sherlock Holmes and Professor Moriarty was like most duels a private affair, but the stakes and meaning of their encounters implicate wider interests than their own; I cannot but reflect upon the short advice of Jesus to the young man who asked if before following Jesus he could at least complete a final filial task and bury his father as Judaic Law commanded him to do. To this request Jesus gave the curt and abrupt answer, to let the dead bury their dead. It is advice that the world has yet to follow. The desire to restore the past and to recapture even our own youth is a futile one. Even the assumptions and the hardened presumptions that congeal into dogma over time found in religion are not immune to the desire to freeze everything into place and always in the name of reaching eternal truths that we can at best intuit rather than define.

Any ongoing project exercised in time and space and projected upon an idealized future dishonors the demands of the present hour where alone we can hope to meet the living God; in that moment of shared humanity and divinity that the sacred authors dreamt of recording we arrive at a true religious revelation. In a similar manner only lovers occasionally manage to glimpse beyond their separate bodies to where the walls that divide our separate souls become translucent for a moment and we can peer within and see the outline of a face and body not very different from our own, one with all of our hopes and fears before this vision too vanishes once again and all is left in the darkness of our solitude.

When we turn and look back upon our lives from a certain vantage point it is easy to lose the connecting thread that unites our past to our present self. Who was the person that made those choices long ago? What inscrutable fate has kept us alive until the present moment when at any number of points in any number of places a single link in the chain might have been broken so that even to be alive and able to reflect backwards in time is already to occupy a sort of God-like perch? We may ask ourselves, "Who am I that I should be able to contemplate my own life as a whole?" Is this question due to the fact that we already begin to draw away from life as we age long before that final hour when suddenly we are plucked forth while the world and its history go on like a speeding coach while we remain behind locked and encased in a past formerly shared but now ours alone? Any further power or agency remaining within us has been abstracted from us and at best lingers in the written word.

To be dead is to cease being a part of ongoing time and space and to be frozen forever in the only true democracy that exists, one where all are equal in having once been and are now no more. The present volume is entitled, *The Secrets of Sherlock Holmes,* which is really no more than saying that the man called Sherlock Holmes is still alive and was alive in 1893, a year now long ago but frozen forever in the words of his journal, when after coming home at last to reclaim his place in the key relationships that played a determining role in his life, he dared to journey forth again into those troubled regions of definition where great minds struggle to unravel the essential clues to life's great mystery: to find a solution to the problems posed by being human at all in a world where even our most fundamental axioms remain in dispute.

To say that our life is a journey is a commonplace expression, but to say that this journey even within a single soul is a composite and even cosmopolitan journey may sound strange at first to those who assume that we are a single person. Our sense of stability and assignment of responsibility is predicated on the idea that such and such a person holds title to the body that he or she inhabits. What marriage could ever take place if the one taken in wedlock might be an entirely different character year by year and even season by season? But I suggest that our usual assumption of a univocal identity is contradicted by our experience in daily life.

We are the product of what happens to us and through us each day. The will is compromised and deflected by whatever currents are manifest moment by moment in the cerebral storms existing in that enclosed sea we call the human mind. This is why death and life are in fact so intertwined that some part of us is dying each day to make room for new occupants of the soul that is itself customarily assumed to be monolithic and immortal. No person is ever so self-possessed that an eternity of reflection, if accompanied by new information, might not lead to different conclusions. This is why any duel waged between opponents is in reality one waged first of all in the individual consciousness of each combatant and even then provisionally and contingently as events will reveal. Palingenesis or the rebirth and recapitulation of what has gone before means that the past is never dead. The gestation process takes us from fish to reptile to mammal. Some part of us still swims in ancient seas and breathes with gills, remnants of a tail are still visible, and our brain is a synthetic organ with successive functional layers of cells piled one upon another seeking harmony. What exists now has been before and what is new will be passed along to whatever follows us. Only language is ever really new, because it is conditioned by immediate circumstances and formed into constantly new phrases, metaphors, and analogies.

The human mind is a symphony of images and language filtered by emotion and perception. Our highest conceptions, of which religion is one, are webs of assertions, extended metaphors intertwined with historical events condensed into the formation of doctrines and rituals. Meaning is the application of general rules to particular instances. The mind is attracted by symmetry, but intrigued by dissonance and dissent, which are the root and inspiration of all cultural progress. Politics in contrast is the science of making self-interest and oppression look as though they serve higher ends or grow logically out of accepted norms of conduct and are thus acceptable. Revolution and restoration are the twin poles around which all historical events circle in an irregular orbit.

And finally there is God, at once the most unique and the most general of all concepts; one that embraces all things, yet is utterly severed and set aside as the source rather than the composite reproduction of all that exists. We speak with such certainty of God as though God was really a part of our cognitive apparatus, an essential part indeed, but still something that can be objectified and spoken for in addressing other human beings, those whom we seek to convert so that they will in turn apply whatever net we are currently using to fetch God up like a squirming fish from the sea before being stowed aboard and brought home to market.

Religion daily greases the wheels of commerce and industry, enables wars, subsidizes funerals, and funds the endless sanctuaries of mortal remains. The numbers of the dead grow daily so that no birthrate, however growing or vital, can supplant those who daily fall away from us to swell the numbers of those who rest in sepulchers or lie unknown beneath the heaving swell of the sea. I am scandalized daily by the very faith that I profess, yet I still believe. The only prayer that seems worthy of the name is that of silence.

The attempt of Sherlock Holmes to answer the great why and the attempt of Professor Moriarty to minimize and deny any metaphysical reality has been the subject of this book—a most daring venture; while I as that mythical figure, Everyman, have wandered through these pages not so different from my readers, pressed forward by events and falling into sleep each night hoping that they will greet the dawn still breathing and be granted another day. May all these labors not be in vain!

In any case it is not to my account here that anyone should look for salvation. Perhaps the search for God is itself the problem. Abraham encounters God by chance. Perhaps this is also the meaning of the second quotation included above from an anonymous source: that God appears precisely where we do not look for God because our very act of looking for God is pragmatic and even instrumental in nature.

We often look for God in the same way that we look for a saw or a hammer, for their utility to us, to serve us in some way. We use God as a stepping-stone to obtain paradise while forgetting that paradise is God Himself! God stands outside of any gradient of utility that we may wish to apply to Him—God is neither subject nor object, because as the transcendent, God embraces both objectivity and subjectivity, while going beyond even these fundamental categories of thought.

God must stoop down in order to enter the world of being. If God chooses to dwell among us, He chooses the modality by which He does so. Anything else may be theology or even Holy Scripture, but it is not God—to use the Bible as a tool is to misunderstand the nature of the Bible, which has far more to do with reaching up than being a definitive and complete limit imposed upon God in reaching down and within human history. Religion might best be conceived as what remains in accounts of the sacred after the sacred is frozen, dried, condensed, and reduced to whatever will best mesh with what we need God to be. A pure theology will therefore never be written, because God cannot be reduced to an object of study. Nor can God be considered as a mere subject either, because God sets the grounds for subjectivity and therefore must exceed our ability to encompass God as a single entity manifesting subjectivity as we understand subjectivity. The Mystery of God then is that before which we can only surrender and wait; it is that of which we cannot speak.

As this volume begins it is appropriate to locate this narrative in time and circumstance. It is being written long after the events recounted here, just as the gospels were written many decades after the Ascension, when after the events that purchased for humanity as a whole eternal salvation Jesus returned to where he was before while promising to return in the fullness of time. I of course intend to provide no such authoritative theological witness in these humble pages, but I consider it of the utmost importance to remind the reader that any narrative is fixed at the time of its composition and within certain parameters of intentionality in the author. To say that I know more now than I did when the events recounted here took place is simply to admit that a constant re-working of events may draw out meanings that were not fully evident at the time when those events occurred.

As my story continues it is essential therefore to set down the conditions that prevailed in 1898 when Holmes and I set out to influence the course of history. To any serious student of history the search for a nexus of events is necessary if any story element is to be discerned. This nexus sets the basic pattern out of which history is woven. Once that process begins it becomes difficult if not impossible to imagine that events might have led to different results or that any later reconstruction by historians might have been woven into a different narrative and arrived at different conclusions. It is essential that my story shall continue to stress that historical determinism is a fallacy; in fact the opposite is the case, history is an arbitrary creation meant to advance a specific narrative in the same way that fiction does. History is not a science; rather, history is an art. For anyone who doubts this thesis a reading of Herodotus or Thucydides will prove my point; the creative element can be easily discerned.

The war of America with Spain was nothing other than a constructed narrative pressed into service to justify America in joining the imperial march of the European nations in order not to fall behind them in conquest and trade. Nations compete with nations for national survival not for the immediate benefit of their citizens. Indeed the immediate cost of that competition is a detriment in treasure and in lives in which the individual is only one more item on a balance sheet.

History in its inception is identical with imagination projected forward into time. At any given moment the national consciousness is in a process of being formed by various leaders. A balance must be reached between memory and projected possibilities; when these two come together the result is national strategy. At any given point of time an assessment could theoretically be made of which narratives will collide with opportunity so that a war will break out somewhere in the world; when it does so a duel can be said to begin. The concept of a duel is aligned with theater; indeed armed conflict begins and ultimately ends at two terminal points: the first is when fear gives way to resolution and the second is where exhaustion leads to a reassessment of possibilities.

Before a war begins hopes run high that an adventitious outcome is attainable at a reasonable cost. A war ends when one party or both conclude that the cost and uncertainty of continuing to fight is simply too high to undertake the risk of an even more inglorious defeat. The same people who began the war usually survive to take part in its termination. Whatever personal guilt they may feel for the lives that they have sacrificed is ameliorated by the thought that they have now arranged a peace that will endure (until the thought of relative advantage once again raises its serpent's head). The process of weaving history begins almost immediately, at first chastened and subdued, but later on forthright and triumphant. The resolution of the leaders is vindicated, their instances of foolishness are forgotten, and the national honor is burnished in preparation for a new conflict of arms.

A question now arises: if the above observations apply to all nations why should we make an exception for Israel in the process of its formation? Are we so willing to do this because God mandated the slaughter of the Hittites and the Amorites because their religions embraced a multitude of Gods so even now several millennia later are willing to give the refugees from Egypt an ethical pass? Is our own later adoption of the God of Israel sufficient justification for this latitude? Do we not clothe our own subsequent intentions in a similar righteous anger?

What was *The Battle Hymn of the Republic* sung by the union troops but an effort to portray the American Civil war as an effort designed to defeat the idea of slavery, an institution accepted as an acceptable aspect of life in the Old Testament? What was Sherman's fiery march through Georgia but a latter-day recapitulation of the vengeance of the winning armies of God over a supine and defeated populace? Why above all else is the history of Israel the origin of a religion that still endures while the gods of the Greeks and Romans are of only literary interest? Why, considering the role of sin in the history of Israel is the Bible spoken of as "the good book?" Can any ethical system emerge intact from such a blighted history?

Or perhaps the real essence of Christianity was its radical departure from previous religions, because by stepping into history

God demonstrated through the incarnation and in the example of the life of Jesus what no ethical system can ever supply, the mystery of divine love for sinners? The commands of Jesus then are less an exercise of authority than a prediction of what consequences naturally flow from immoral conduct—the death of the innocents; the death of the sinner after all is self-imposed.

The supposed wrath of God therefore is really the wrath of mankind that condemns what it never ceases to do. In this paradox Christianity demonstrates the difference between prophesy and mere fortune-telling. The truth of prophesy does not need to wait to be fulfilled in the future, because the truth of prophesy is a matter of our daily encounter with life. We wake to the sins that lead to death every day. Jesus said that the Kingdom of God is within you, but so is every other kingdom because it is we who create those kingdoms.

The death of Christ merely held up a mirror to history so that history was returned to mere facts without any latitude granted for later interpretation. Even Pontius Pilate managed to acknowledge what prophesy proclaimed when he had this inscription placed on the cross on which Jesus was crucified, "This is Jesus, the King of the Jews." When he was asked by representatives of the Sanhedrin to change this inscription Pilate answered his own question, "What is truth?" by saying, "What I have written, I have written"—the ultimate confession that in this world every fact is engraved into the unforgiving slate of time, never to be erased.

That the biblical narrative has been a sufficient template that it has been applied to such varied circumstances would alone be an indication that it constitutes God's letter to the world, one of constantly renewed hope in the presence of what looks like final defeat. The one overriding theme is that despite the fickle nature of mankind, God keeps his promises. God continues to stand by a covenant that at times only exists in shreds. Figures of great wisdom and splendor fail and beg for just one more chance.

Is God deceived by such repeated promises of amendment only to be followed by renewed offenses? When the promised

Messiah finally shows up only to be crucified is this example evidence of some inadequate preparation on the part of God or of humankind's perpetual adherence to a faulty estimate of the real nature of the glory of God? Is it really true when Jesus assures Philip, in answer to Philip's remarkable demand to Jesus, "Show us the Father and it will be enough for us," that Jesus claims, "He who sees me sees the Father?"

This whole claim of identity went beyond simply claiming to be the long-awaited messiah. Jesus was actually claiming to be Yahweh, the inexpressible name of God! Such an equivalence was simply unthinkable from the within the Jewish mindset and it remains a scandal to Jews and Moslems alike to this very day. These assertions are textually based, for we do not have Jesus before us to submit to cross-examination. One cross was quite sufficient to found the religion that persists to this day. The echoes of circumstance are swiftly dissipated and only witnesses remain. Let us return then to that period when events crowded down swiftly upon us, so swiftly in fact that years needed to elapse before their full import was evident even to me.

During our entire journey to America Holmes had been receiving messages from his brother Mycroft regarding the activities of Baron Maupertuis on the continent. It must be remembered that the schemes of the Baron were not confined to the building of a canal through the Americas in order to open up trade with Japan and China. The deeper levels of his schemes embraced global dimensions and were conducted below the surface of events. His primary obsession, insofar as Holmes was able to make it clear to me, was the role of capital mobility when conducted at a level embracing a view of world affairs that might be considered trans-historical.

To a man like Baron Maupertuis the deaths of thousands or even millions were only factors on a balance sheet and were important merely as indicators of where capital flows might be best directed in order to yield the highest profits. At any given moment it became apparent from the dispatches that we received that Baron Maupertuis received daily reports from every hub of industrialism and commerce from around the world.

Reports came in hourly to his offices from Zurich, Paris, London, Vienna, Brussels, Amsterdam, Moscow, and even from far off San Francisco. Shipping reports, grain prices, stock indexes, and even works of science and philosophy were all directed through an organization where information was received, processed, decoded if necessary, and placed before him in a daily summary while various minions stood by at any hour of the day to receive his instructions. It was reported that his hours of sleep were few and that his energy was more than most men might ever hope to emulate. He was in short the equal in sheer mental capacity to Mycroft Holmes.

To summarize the direction of his thought or to discern the ultimate ends that he hoped to achieve by all this activity was bound to exceed my poor capacity, but as is the case with most men of influence his case was indicative of the spirit of the age. The last decades of the 19th century were an age of expansion and connection and therefore the age of great enterprises. The new century in contrast appears to be an age of general regression to a more primitive level of historical aspirations based upon domination and revenge.

Power is neutral of course until it is attached to a goal. The goal of Sherlock Holmes it became apparent was to answer the question of whether our calculations should embrace a life after death. If this life is a mere prelude and preparation for a life to come it would appear sensible to fill in the substantial gaps left even in the dogma of Catholicism regarding what we may reasonably expect in an afterlife and whether it has any resemblance to what we know and experience on this side of the membrane that separates us from whatever lies beyond.

The Divine Comedy of Dante Alighieri written between the years 1308 and 1321 has had an influence upon the mind of the western church just short of the Bible and has as a result biased and distorted our conceptions and anticipations of what to expect when we must leave this present dispensation of earth behind and as a naked soul come to face to face with God. The few references in Holy Scripture describing hell imply regret and an abiding sense of uselessness as the prevailing attitude of the damned combined with a sense of moral chaos and loss of substance so that we might better conceive of hell as a place of isolation and of endless discontent, a place devoid of community and good fellowship, a place where love has no place, rather than a domain of physical tortures and of vindictive retribution traceable ultimately to God.

The concoction of fiendish tortures says more about the human imagination than about the ultimate destination of lost souls. To the healthy mind the loss of heaven should be adequate punishment without any supplementary need to enhance that loss by painting an inverted world designed by demons and animated by mutual hatred and disgust with no admixture of sympathy or compassion to act as an anodyne to misery. To truly visualize heaven may therefore enhance the probability that one may someday experience it while to do the opposite is to indirectly give honor to the devil as an equal competitor with God.

Of course to avoid either destination by seeking to conceive an idea of nothingness or to imagine one's own absolute extinction at death with no prospect of review or return is intolerable. Only the sustained pain of victimhood or of guilt may so soil our expectations or sap the strength of our will that we may desire total extinction. But even then we may view with horror the thought that one whom we loved and whose presence was once as familiar to us as our own voice and countenance is no more, as celebrated in the great series of poems on mourning by Alfred Lord Tennyson, *In Memoriam*. Even the most complete life, one with the least regrets, should be open to the chance of continuation in some eternal realm, even if a return to traverse a new path in a new life here in our present state may seem insupportable. Human life as we live it is therefore inexplicable without some manner of religious belief to assuage our pain and to vindicate our losses and discontents.

The real question precedent to belief in any religion however is just what status are we as human beings willing to assign to human life as a phenomenon existing parallel to all other events in the cosmos. Religion assigns a centrality to human existence and even relates absolute meaning to our perception and definition of what meaning is. As far as we know the universe does not query itself, unless that function is accomplished by human beings acting as proxies for an inarticulate cosmos. Mathematics may be inherent in the relations that exist between moving bodies in space and through time, but it would certainly appear fanciful to picture rocks and gases on the silent planets engaging in adding up sums or in factoring a quadratic equation. The effort to rescue religion from being a mere human projection upon events and upon substances is essential if we are to use religion as a stepping stone to God.

Of course Christianity proceeds even further by claiming that God has condescended to become one of us. This completely reverses the direction of inquiry in pursuit of God from the vertical to the horizontal. If Jesus is one member of the human race and also of the same substance as God the Father and if we are asked to share that life sacramentally, then we are far more likely to find God in each other than by gazing upwards into the uncomprehending abysses of the numberless galaxies above our heads on a starry night.

A structural analysis of religion though soon reveals that no religion is untainted however by elements that are more political or aesthetic than they are strictly religious in nature. The case could be made for instance that Judaism is tainted by a profound worldliness; the promised Kingdom is political and centered on Jerusalem. Islam promises a garden filled with fleshly delights. Even Christianity has more to say about what happens to unrepentant sinners than it has to say about heaven. Holy Scripture tantalizes us by saying that the reward for our ethical conduct will be the uninterrupted vision of the glorified Christ after we have put aside these mortal bodies and exchanged them for one that is immortal like His and that then we shall see Him as He is and know Him even as we are known.

The promised kingdom will in other words be characterized by a change in our perceptual apparatus so that God will not be distant or obscure, but clear and present to us so that our joy will be full. Any aspersions cast upon our present state of earthly existence then are comparative in nature so as to point out the excellence of the Kingdom of God and to urge us to approach its advent even now by making every effort to adapt our thoughts and behavior so as to approximate that exalted state even in our present condition of exile and alienation. No higher goal has ever been set for humanity than this; but to stand back and to calmly consider its merits is equally beyond human capacity.

No religion can be evaluated from an entirely objective point of view, because the very nature of the transcendent demands a surrender and openness to religious experience that makes it both impossible and disingenuous to pretend to adopt and to proceed from a position towards religion of absolute neutrality and objectivity. In this sense a debate between Holmes and Moriarty regarding religion would be a mischaracterization of what these two men proposed to do when they met again. It is this very indefiniteness that ensured that each of these two great men was as close to considering with the mind alone the question of an ultimate meaning to be found in human life as it is possible to reach.

Of course what we call individual human beings is actually a mere point of convenience. My own experience of life has revealed that individuals are actually part of larger processes of which the individual is a mere epiphenomenon, just as stars are mere components of galaxies, and even galaxies are only organizations in even larger patterns and conglomerations. How strange it is then to posit the God-head, the origin of such complexity, as summed up by the humble number three, the Holy Trinity of Christian belief.

But let us pursue my main point the scope of individual discretion or what psychologists call personality. Anyone who cares to trace the course of human destiny will discover that the family is the primary entity with various members as simply parts of a system that they cannot comprehend any more than the part can ever contain the whole. In the years when countless human problems were presented to us in Baker Street I noticed again and again that the most tragic situations could be traced to familial roots. The Greek Tragedians realized this fact and the Viennese psychologist, Sigmund Freud, has written some books and papers on the matter that are of some interest.

My own conclusions and theories are more limited—they pertain to the rise and fall of family fortunes and the conservation of wealth. Great estates seldom endure beyond four generations. My belief is that the possession of wealth entails guilt, which leads to forgetfulness of the source of that wealth. Excess and carelessness then leads to poverty and decline, at which point the cycle of accumulation must begin anew. I will even go so far as to say that legatees of wealth resent and despise the source of their good fortune, because to receive it is an assault on their pride. This in turn sets in play a dynamic of destruction characterized by the Greeks as nemesis, whereas in the world of secular reality it is really as basic as cause and effect.

Christianity, in spite of its pretense to be supernatural in origin, shows forth in its economy of salvation many all-too-human elements, particularly in the Old Testament. If we imagine the moral universe as manifesting a certain conservation of energy, then in any closed system nothing is ever lost and every deficit must be paid by someone. That payment may take many forms, but within the family as within the society it may be characterized as a will to destruction. That force may be focused upon a single individual or group that is then offered up as a sacrifice. An entire family or nation may manifest a similar and virtually simultaneous decline into shame and oblivion.

Holmes and I witnessed this dynamic again and again in the course of our years at Baker Street—a wife standing over a dead husband with a gun in her hand on an evening that began with delightful smiles earlier that same day at the races at Ascot, or a son lying over his desk with a beaker of poison at his side and a notice of bankruptcy before him. This is the world in which we live and which theology pretends to unravel in the eternal tug-of-war between good and evil. Whether our two dualists could make sense where the contending religions of the world exist in mutual contradiction or temporary truce and equilibrium these pages must reveal.

I have asked myself whether families, nations, and even confederations show patterns that can first be descried and only then altered in some way so that evil may be minimized if not eliminated so that whatever innocence remains to the human race may be preserved, so that at last the new generations may escape the cycles of misery and pain that characterize our lives on this side of eternity?

If we conceive of the human race as a whole, religion must serve as the great and primary source of unity. Unfortunately historically that has not been the experience of mankind. Religion has as often been a source of divisions as of unity. The advances in communication and transportation have brought the world into closer physical proximity. Trade now spans both nations and alliances. An upset in any quarter of the globe now resonates through the various fractionated regions that hover constantly on the edge of open hostilities. The desire to vindicate religious sensibilities bestows moral justification on the actions of nations and on the moral choices of groups and of individuals. The very concept of an all-abiding God or gods as the guarantor and originator of all things gives an absolutist cast to any problem where interests and passions are involved.

The certainties of faith are resistant to any sort of correction based upon human experience. Christianity at the time that this writing has occurred has not been able to avoid or to resolve a degree of slaughter that calls into question any pretence that Europeans can boast of having a civilization worth preserving. These reflections in turn have been bound to exert their influence on this volume of my immense work and it would be disingenuous of me not to express before my readers my doubts as well as my convictions. Supernatural faith is not something attained once and for all. It requires constant reflection and renewal if it to be anything other than pretence sustained by lethargy.

In order to answer these questions and many others I

return now to the journal kept by Sherlock Holmes that I continued to read whenever time permitted as we sauntered through autumnal America seeking clues to the character of that astonishing republic. Others have attempted to define the American character. My task is a more humble one of recording as best I can those events that led to America being a rising power in world affairs, a status that both the nation and its citizens may live to regret. The chains of empire are heavy and the manacles of power are not easily discarded.

From the Journal of Sherlock Holmes

July 5, 1893
Kings Pyland

I traveled by dog-cart over the rough roads that intersect the moor to the Professor's estate at Kings Pyland after sending him a wire that I would come. I reflected that the pending absence away from Grimpen would give me time to consider how best to protect Sir Henry and Lady Beryl from any threat posed by the man, Roger Baskerville. The wet incursions of winter had dried at last to give a rock-like solidity to the road now baking in the summer sun. I still preferred to travel slowly though since the dog-cart rocked from side to side after every curve. Soon I left behind the vale of Grimpen and after climbing a ridge that led to a broad plateau, I descended again after awhile into the dell beyond.

The estate of Kings Pyland is an extensive one with broad pastures and a flat racing course perfect for training racehorses. However, there is no nearby village such as Grimpen so supplies must be brought from a distance. The stables of Kings Pyland act as a sort of commissary for the few tenant farmers who tend the Professor's pastures and service the horse breeding farm. I drove up to the great Georgian house of the attached estate by a long drive bordered with tall poplars that help to break the force of the bitter winter gales that are common here and pulled up at the entrance.

A groom was awaiting me on the broad front steps. He

helped me to unload my small amount of baggage and rang the bell for me before leading my horse and cart away to the barns. The door was opened by perhaps the most taciturn butler I have ever met, who took my few belongings in hand and with a motion signed to me that I should accompany him upstairs where I was soon installed in a spacious room equipped to meet my every need. I was then told that after I had made myself comfortable that the Professor who was out at the racetrack would be happy to have me join him downstairs at my convenience upon his return. The butler then closed the door and I found myself alone.

How strange to find myself in the lion's lair at last. I carry about with me the experience of a lifetime, the wisdom of some of the greatest cultures of the world as they attempt to account for human existence, and I know my adversary as well as any man alive, yet I am unprepared to joust with him. At times I feel unprepared for life itself! I wake to consciousness each day, yet know that I shall die someday and join those ordinary items that I see about me in their insensate nature. At my burial a man may point at me and say there is Sherlock Holmes in the same manner that he would say look at that table-lamp. But will I be there? Will I be anywhere at all?

The mystery of death is truly the mother of religion. If we might live forever, even in this sorry state of earthly affairs in which we find ourselves, we might treat centuries as we now treat decades or as artists speak of the epics of their creative lives, "Ah, that was my blue period. I was obsessed then with all things blue!" Just so would we speak of the fleeting centuries, but as it is now we die inexplicably and too soon! A man must consider himself fortunate to live even to the age of seventy. He no sooner reaches maturity when he is plucked forth out of this life like a ripe grape.

Those who manage by the largess of fate or careful living to further extend that time grow in the end to fail to recognize even their own image in the looking-glass, seeking there always for the youth that is no longer there; thus do we die to ourselves before we die to the world. Tiny bits of ourselves are lopped away daily by the great cleaver of time. If we still persist in life and approach the centennial of our birth, it is only an airy distillation of ourselves that remains to greet us when we celebrate that centennial. Even the skeletal framework that supports our flesh shrinks so that the bones, when finally exposed by the soft ministration of decay, will be only poor brittle things: stooped, dry, and withered like dead leaves. The skull that once housed the greatness of the mind, lately tenanted by an organ that withers its way into senility, will remain an empty cauldron. In our youth we are heirs to the great folly of believing that we have endless time before us; we keep something always in reserve and tell ourselves that there is still time to accomplish the great works of our lives.

What is my great work? I pondered this question as I gazed from the window of my room? Even if I manage somehow to lay Moriarty up by the heels, will that be enough? I have often wondered at the course that my life has taken, spent largely to defeat a single opponent. Professor Moriarty has always been my test case, the standard that I applied to my arts of detection. I have applied that standard to him for so long that I begin to doubt if his final defeat would not plunge me into despair. A man must always have a task before him if he is to live. Moriarty is my canvass. If I can prove that there is a God and a moral purpose to human actions to his satisfaction, might I not then turn and find my own proofs inadequate, not to Moriarty but to myself! Perhaps I use this man, Moriarty, merely to deny my own nature, my own dreadful need of certainty, my own fear that the sphinx of existence will not speak to me but lie forever in its mute and mocking silence.

I realize that these doubts are an ill preparation for my immediate task, so I place them aside for now. I lock them up within those catacombs of the mind where we bury thoughts that have become insupportable. I take up again my own flawed nature in what Walter Pater has called 'this short day of frost and sun,' the eternal present moment, which is all that we ever possess. I splashed some water in my face and dried it with a towel, combed my hair, shook from my head the cobwebs of my fears, and went out into the sun of the summer day to meet my great foe.

s I mentioned I had been informed at the time of my arrival that Professor Moriarty was at the racetrack as he was every day for the time trials for the Wessex Cup and other training sessions. It appears that he enjoys seeing his horses go through their training. I crossed the lawns and gardens and took the path through the woods that had been indicated to me. After passing the rhododendron hedges that surround the house I saw before me through a clearing a large open ground that had been fenced in to make a racetrack. At the finish line I saw Professor Moriarty standing and leaning forward on his cane in excitement as three horses crossed the finish line. As I came up he was speaking to the jockey who had ridden the winning horse.

"She always favors the rail. You have to bring her to the outside. I do not want her to win only when she has the favored place. If she is going to be entered in the Wessex Cup Race, she is going to face stern competition and I don't want her to be injured by being driven into the rail. Still she ran well. Take her for a cool-down and give her some oats; she has earned them today. She may run free later in the north pasture."

Professor Moriarty suddenly became aware of my presence behind him. The jockey, who had been looking down nodding as he received his instructions, looked up at me as well as I approached them.

"Ah Holmes, you have arrived. Did you see her finish? Two lengths and Alfred wasn't even pressing her. She may well carry the field in the Wessex Cup. But then you are here for another purpose than to see my beauties at their paces, isn't that so? I trust that my staff has made you comfortable up at the house? Splendid! You look surprised to see my smiling and at ease. It is a luxury that you perhaps inadvertently provided. You are no doubt thinking of the old days in London. But I was myself in harness then and deeply engaged in managing a great enterprise, an octopus with many arms, while here at last I can pursue my own interests. I think that will be enough today Alfred. Are you prepared for a walk-about, Holmes? Or perhaps you are here only on business. Well you must allow me my little enthusiasms. Come let me show you the stables at least. That will be all, Alfred. Cool her down gently."

The next hour was spent touring the training camp for it was far more than a mere stable. The work that Professor Moriarty has done here, in the short years of my absence from England, is quite remarkable. He has poured money into the facility at Kings Pyland and from the line of Silver Blaze, the great racing stallion, who had once made the name of this stable famous in racing circles throughout the whole of England, the Professor had bred the filly that had demonstrated its speed by winning the training race that I had just observed. The Professor hopes that she in turn might be a valuable breeding mare after a racing career beginning with a Wessex win. The Professor explained his training methods to me as we walked about; they were scientific in nature and spared the horses many of the risks of injury of traditional training methods. He seems to have an instinctive knowledge of the horses and he immediately surprised me by his astonishing gentleness with his thoroughbreds and their evident recognition of him. He seemed to notice my surprise today when he caught my reflective gaze resting upon him.

"There is nothing remarkable in my attitude to my horses, sir. They are after all marvelous creatures. I quite prefer them, as did the great author Jonathan Swift, to the sorry run of humankind. Who can observe their swiftness, their pride, or look into their great and gentle eyes and not agree with my relative assessment of the two species. But then, your theology would deny them souls would it not? But let us not enter prematurely into our deeper discussions. I merely wished you to see what I have accomplished here while you have been running about the world and writing travel journalism. You see I do not spend all of my time on my little criminal plots. My great nefarious brain, as you would have it to be, spends only its more idle hours in the pursuit of crime. Illicit profit and mischief were always a mere pastime for me. I now reserve my true efforts for my beauties and for my research in physics. Crime is after all a sordid affair, is it not? Are you not also glad to have moved on to better things? I must admit that if it had not paid me as well as it has, I would never consider crime worth a single idle hour."

"Are you then perhaps being paid by someone to fulfill your present threat against the British Empire?" I pointedly inquired.

"Oh yes, Holmes. I am being paid very well." He pointed to his scooped and hollowed chest cavity. "I am being paid here. The fall of that bloated empire will liberate the world. I expect to be quite a hero in my way, although secret and unacknowledged, not that that is my motivation."

"What is your motivation, then," I inquired further as we walked on.

"You do not yet know? Dear me, you have grown more obtuse then in the course of your travels. I expected more from you, Sherlock Holmes. I thought that you alone knew my mind in all of its sinuous twists and turnings. You have always seen me as evil incarnate have you not? Oh well, I will give you one hint then right now regarding my plans. It is your need to see me as evil that has always blinded you to what I was really doing in the course of my career. I think that your father understood me far better than you ever could, perhaps more than all three of his natural sons. Your father was a true Viking in blood, while yours has been watered down and diminished by its French admixture from your mother's side. In men as in horses, breeding is everything! Oh, do not take offense sir. I do not blame that good lady, your mother, for she was always kind to me. I speak merely of the French as a nation. They enjoy life too much to ever become true conquerors and to maintain an empire. It takes a bleak outlook on life, one that is only bred in the great northern forests of Scandinavia or Germany, for a man to become a wolf. Your father was of that sort. Even my own violent and depraved father feared him; yes even my father, that great brute, feared him. For that reason I honored your father above all men, for it is said that the man that is the enemy of my enemy is my friend."

could still recall Professor Moriarty's father, a great drunken lout of a man, and of how he had customarily beaten his son, whose feeble constitution had been an embarrassment to a man who still had pride in the ancient Irish name of Moriarty. He no doubt felt that the stooped and twisted body of his son was a comment upon his own heredity and that it impugned his status as a man. In any case he had often abused the boy until my father put a stop to it by personally threatening to horsewhip the senior Moriarty, who was also named James Moriarty, should he ever attempt it again. By then of course the damage to his son's soul had been done.

A year later the elder Moriarty was found dead. He had been drinking at a pub in the village and had missed his way walking home on a January night and fallen over a precipice. He was found the next day frozen and twisted on the footpath across the moors as he attempted to walk back to Sigerside. He had frozen all alone in the bleak snows of a hard Yorkshire winter's night. The frozen ground would not admit his body and it was a month before the ground had thawed sufficiently to permit his interment. I recall that I had the misfortune at the time to view his upturned face and saw within its death grimace the remains of surprise and horror which, when added to his usual brutal features, had left an indelible impression that long afterwards haunted my dreams. Shortly after that event the young James Moriarty was sent away to school.

I did not see him again for many years until he entered my rooms in Baker Street shortly before I departed for the continent with Watson in 1891. During all of that time I was aware of the Professor and of his probable crimes after a brief period as a Professor of physics at one of our smaller colleges. I could never until the end trace his many crimes to him as their source. My relations with the Professor have therefore always been characterized by supposition rather than certainty. I might have brought him to heel earlier had I been consulted by one of his victims, but they were invariably dead or too intimidated to speak so that I could prove nothing against him. Finally, it was a mere slip on the part of the Professor that allowed me to trace a multitude of unsolved mysteries to their causal agent and to weave a web of accusation and proof that would eventually destroy his vast criminal organization.

Even at that penultimate hour, I could not bring the case home against him in a court of law, nor could I trace his evident wealth to the crimes that had filled his coffers. Even the British tax-authorities had been helpless to solve the complexities of his private financial structure. The result was that Professor Moriarty stood before me today as a free man, free to pursue his planning of the destruction of England unless I could turn him from his predetermined course.

I was silent as I walked up to the house with the Professor, limping and leaning upon his walking stick heavily for support. He proceeded to serve me an excellent lunch during which he spoke of his plans for his breeding stables while I listened quietly. At last he inquired after Watson. I told him that Watson was currently engaged in charitable medical work in America, but was due home within the year.

"Good, you may of course go to him upon his return and resume your consulting practice as a detective if you wish with no interference from me. I assure you that I will keep you informed as my plans progress. I intend no surprise. When the trap is about to spring beneath the feet of England and its great bloated body lies swinging from my hangman's noose you will be at my side to watch the execution. After all, what I intend still requires some preparation and I admit to a certain lethargy in the past several years without you on the scene to stimulate my best efforts. I must get to work now because I hope to have all in readiness by, hmmm, let us say 1897. I will wire you a hint now and again in Baker Street and you can pace the rug before your fire, smoke your pipe, and posture and preen before the admiring eyes of Dr. Watson, whose pen will no doubt be itching to finally record a great volume, one which he will no doubt entitle, 'The Death of Moriarty.'"

He smiled grimly, "Of course should my health worsen suddenly I may need to speed matters along, but I am as healthy as

I have ever been and all in all I believe I shall see the century out. No, I think that 1897 will do quite well. Besides, I am surely not your only foe. Just before your departure on your great odyssey you were even engaged if I recall correctly in developing an extension of your practice to the continent. I followed with great interest your handling of Hurat the French boulevard assassin. You handled that quite nicely I thought. Evidently the French thought so also, for you were awarded the Legion of Honor at the time. Perhaps your own country may someday show its appreciation for your labors by a similar honor ... should you be so fortunate as to defeat me that is. Well, if you are quite through with lunch I believe we may adjourn to the library. I have there an excellent claret for you to sample or port if you prefer, and we may discuss matters philosophical or theological or even the price of camel fodder in Mecca or Khartoum at your pleasure." We arose and passed from the great oak-paneled dining room to the damask-shrouded library of Professor Moriarty. His subtle mockery was not ill-spirited and I did not take offense. Indeed, I was surprised at the Professor's assumption of a genial approach to what I had always imagined would be a duel to the death between us. I could not be anything but aware though of the deadly seriousness that lay behind the threats of the Professor, but the very honesty of his exposition of those threats had convinced me that he intended our duel, if I may term it so, to be a battle between gentlemen and according to a code of a sorts. This is a luxury that evil seldom presents to one who would defeat it.

The Professor had provided me with a valuable clue when he told me that he at least does not view himself or his works as evil. I did not ask him then if he viewed my efforts to defeat him as evil, but he must view it as at least misguided. Is the Professor attempting to tutor me, to bring me along to a higher conception of the good? Is he playing Zarathustra or Socrates and addressing me as a pupil? If that should be the case, then I shall allow him to chart the way forward, while always remaining on my guard against a trap. He began at once this afternoon with an extended lecture much like the one that I had already heard in the medical theater lecture hall in Exeter. The habit of lecture for a Professor is one not easily set aside. I will here reproduce his narrative as well as I can recall it.

The ancients understood that wine is the joy of life. I have always thought that the real contributors to mankind have not been the philosophers, the priests, or the great generals and kings but rather those practical and technical folk who have learned the arts of the vintner and the art of the making of cheeses. Please try the *Kaltbach le crème*, a splendid dry cheese that is allowed to mature in caves. It is rather like old book bindings in texture is it not, but it sets the proper taste on the palate for the claret. You will also find in the bowl at your elbow some roasted almonds from the south of France. It is in combination that we assemble those flavors and textures that give life gusto and variety. Is that not what we mean by the good life Holmes? Has anyone improved upon the formula of Epicurus? You look somewhat disapprovingly at my paean to self-indulgence. You would no doubt bring forth the question of how these goods of life are to be obtained for the many in a world of scarcity. You would pose the problem that has beset mankind from the beginning of its existence: that our wants always exceed our means and that for some to enjoy the good things of life is inevitably to accept deprivation elsewhere. To this problem the religions of the world have posed various solutions, but they all add up to the same thing: a hunger for a condition foreign to all that we know on earth, a state of blessedness where all of our needs and wants will be fulfilled. To some this is the Kingdom of Heaven to others the Gardens of Allah, while to the humble Buddhist his only desire is simply the hope for extinction and to be spared even the burden of existing even if it be in paradise."

"Meanwhile, the ever practical Chinese imagine no other realm but this varied and extravagant earth. Their culture has elected for centuries to simply follow Confucius and to create an orderly state or empire in honor to their illustrious ancestors. You see Sherlock Holmes that I have done a bit of reading in the various religious traditions; but I have found them all to be unsatisfactory because they are so clearly designed to remedy the irremediable condition of man. They take their origin from our unfulfilled desires and our disappointed hopes. Each in its way bids us to waste the little time that we have here on earth in hope of a general solution that will render everyone, or at least the most worthy ones, simultaneously and eternally both happy and satisfied. It does this by subsuming the individual into the mass of mankind; that great seething cauldron of fears and hatreds, ever-ignorant and ever-divided, always at odds with itself and this hoping for a God to set all things right at last. Virtues are for the few, not the many. To expect men and women to exist in charity does violence to the endless greed of humankind. What are the gods but a projection of our own outrageous demand that the world should meet our desires in every particular?"

He sipped from his glass of claret with satisfaction before continuing, seeing that I made no objection to the train his thought thus far.

"It is impossible to think of man or woman and not to think first of hunger and desire. One need only look at the young of every species and what does one see but an open mouth! The first development of the embryo is formed about the alimentary canal. Of what use is the brain but as a means to secure food; and why is this but that we may continue to exist. We feed ourselves so that we may endure for another day; and what are those days but suffering. Is anyone ever satisfied with his lot? Yet he must advance along whatever path has brought him satisfaction in the past. We do what we have always done. It is all a matter of habit. Life itself becomes a habit until at last we die. We know our fate, yet even then we protest that we have a right to continue, to muscle aside the others at the great trough of life rather than to gracefully yield up our place here knowing that we have had our day in the sun and that what we have made of life is our own responsibility. If we have been miserable it is no one's fault but our own. If we have looked to the gods to sustain us (and thus wasted our time here in my estimation) we should blame no one but ourselves. We always knew that our time was short. But such is the arrogance of youth that it does not see that what the gods have bestowed they swiftly take away again."

"If we imagine that the gods enjoy our paltry sacrifices made to obtain favors beyond our own efforts, we wrong them and ourselves as well. What divine beings would covet smoking carcasses or sacrificed virgins or for that matter our muttered invocations? Surely such beings would scorn even to deal with us, mere offal that we are while we live and doomed at last to die. If we are obnoxious in life, how much more so are we in death as stinking carcasses! I am you see in the habit of daily reading from Robert Burton's great book *The Anatomy of Melancholy*, which does as good a job as any book to purge us of our illusions."

"Perhaps you have read *The Song of Maldoror* by Compte de Lautreamont or *The Flowers of Evil* by Baudelaire? Those are books that dare to look at the dark visage of life without shrinking. Let us all contemplate together the deaths-head visage of the skull. Let us be like Hamlet gazing at the skull of his friend and seeing his own fate, but still being glad in his inmost heart that it is he who holds the skull of his friend and not the other way around. Which of us does not wish to be the last of our acquaintances to die? We bury our friends and deem ourselves immortal made only stronger by their passing before us. We drink life at the graves of all who die. We are vampires all of us, but we will not admit it! Think of a chapel filled with Christian ladies singing their hymns in cracked and aged voices. What are they but singing cats yowling to a god and taking comfort from the fact that they are not like that fallen woman that they passed on the way to their meeting-house that morning? Yet she is at least a working woman of sorts and she gives at least something for value, a moment of happiness to her paramour, while these hypocrites would purchase heaven with only a hymn and a penny dropped into the plate for offerings to feed a greedy cleric his mutton chop and his glass of ale, while he in return tells them that they are among the elect of God."

Professor Moriarty laughed bitterly. "It is all too preposterous, this stock exchange of the Christian virtues in

England! It only becomes worse when it is the Church of Rome of which we speak. There we take the folly of the London chapel and expand it to the very horizons of the globe. I tell you that the Popes have learned more from Caesar than they ever did from Christ! They have made Rome the tributary center of a religious empire. They have taken that humble fisherman Peter and invented for him a chair, and from that chair they have attempted to subjugate kings and princes, so that a celibate dynasty of priests might rule the world. What is the Papacy but temporal power in disguise? As such the Papal office was coveted by the great families of Italy through most of the history of the Roman Church? All have striven in turn to place a member of their own clan upon the chair of Peter for commercial advantage and political influence. I do not blame them of course. They knew where the true seat of power was to be found—not in armies but in the consciousness of man. What I blame is the hypocrisy of the extortion from ordinary Catholics who must to this very day feed the fat cardinals and other prelates. What do they receive in return but only the empty rituals of the Church and the promise of an unquantifiable and invisible thing called Divine Grace, which will purchase for them their assured place in heaven. Christianity trades on the anxieties provoked by death; it profits from painting heaven in pastels but hell in bold relief. If a dishonest merchant were to sell a bag of goods and the buyer were to take it home and open it to find therein only air, he would rush back and demand a refund from the thief. But the Church makes it a practice century after century to sell the same airy nothings and profit by the selling of what is insubstantial and can never be verified."

"Nor may the teachings of the Church be disproven," I objected quietly.

Professor Moriarty paused before going on confidently, "Perhaps not, but surely the burden of proof rests with those who assert these improbable doctrines and dogmas. What is dogma but mystification rather than mystery! Dogma is the rhetoric of deception that allows a class of clergymen to lie to the lay people and to get a living by speaking those lies."

Professor Moriarty paused as though he was still considering my objection. "The people invite this deception of course, because without it they would be left with just what they have: an unsatisfactory life of scarcity, frustration, and death. The more insupportable are their lives, the more they hunger for religion's vain promises. But if they withhold the penny from the plate, they would at least be a penny richer. They might bestow their trust upon some other sovereign who would better represent their needs. For what does their religion do but condemn the few sources of solace that they have in life? It is not enough that religion takes from the many to feed the few, it must also condemn most normal human aspirations and carnal pleasures as sinful. The seven deadly sins are none other than the most natural inclinations of mankind and the very inclinations that might be used to liberate a man to pursue his own ends upon the earth. These sins lie in the bodily appetites and the natural aspirations of the heart. The Church knows that if it may only turn a man against himself, then it may lead him by the nose anywhere that it pleases. The Church wishes to build a wall around the appetites so that they may only function with the permission of the Church. Not satisfied with territory only, the monks and prelates wished to establish their jurisdiction within the very consciences of men and women the better to practice their extortion. To that end the ecclesiastics claim to have contained the rivers of lust in monasteries and convents so that they might impose a similar control upon the laity, which is taught to admire the supposed virtues of these holy places where the flesh is whipped into submission. The result is the great festering wounds of these very places the vices of which are unnatural and omnipresent. The secrecy of the Church will never reveal them though. What a relief it would be to most men to learn that these model places contain sinners like themselves! What a relief it would be to woman to know that her carnal desires sustain the human race rather than being evidence of her impurity. What a relief to the poor to know that their covetousness and envy is the path of world revolution and the possible advent of a just social order upon the earth. When men and women rise from their knees and demand life from those who already enjoy it at their expense that is when the Kingdom of Heaven will arrive among us."

Professor Moriarty nodded his head, pleased as he was by his own discourse, "Religion has no other function but to delay that day of reckoning between the social classes. The religions of each nation are but the foundations of the unjust social order that we see all about us. If that were not so, then those social orders that enjoy most of the resources of the earth would have long since collapsed before the needs of the majority. The tides of humanity roar about the citadels of the empires of the world, whether they are secular or religious in nature, and they will no longer be denied!"

"The population of the world has doubled in this century. Did you know that Holmes? It will continue to double and then double once again in the next century until this world is awash in a great tide of underserved and penurious humanity. With that growth will come also knowledge, which is the key to liberation. What one knows to be the case requires no faith! Faith on the contrary feeds upon human ignorance and powerlessness. The great river of life is rising and the dam of the illusions of religion will be swept away before it. All general schemata of life, whether religious or political, are the cant of the few to subjugate the many! When there is a free market in ideas, illusions will evaporate like dew drops in the sun."

He raised a bony finger as if in prophesy, "Imagine a million Voltaire's and Nietzsche's my dear Sherlock Holmes! That is the future of the human race. Once mankind accepts the fact that there is no essential difference between a skull and the clam shells to be found along the shore, both mere deposits of calcium, then all men will be free. Once accept irremediable death and one is ready at last to live and to fight back against those who would hold your skull in their hands to add it to their collection of 'saved souls,' the detritus of the catacombs. That is what I am about Holmes. The work that my organization did before your efforts ended its good works was in furtherance of the liberation of the human race."

"But by criminal means, Professor," I reminded him.

He shrugged off my objection scornfully. "It is the oppressor who denies to the weak the very means that are used daily against them by their oppressors. How many murders are committed each day by statesmen and magistrates? Did you never see the great pattern in the laws, Holmes? I ask you to take note— which people did we kill in the name of social order? Which people are slaughtered and imprisoned each day by the courts? Was it not the slave owners of the human race that exist in honor among us that we targeted? Men such as Birdy Edwards, who was later sheltered by the respectable name of Douglas, who once supported the mine-owners of Pennsylvania as they crushed out the lives of the miners in the Pennsylvania and West Virginia coal fields; or that shriveled harpy, Mrs. Stewart of Lauder, who was dispatched by Colonel Moran at my orders; these were not men and women but great corporate institutions. When I think of them and of their deaths I feel the same relish that one would feel when one shoots that poisonous lizard known as the Gila-Monster of the American desert and after prying open its black jaws releases the hand of its victim!"

"We only preyed upon the predators, Holmes. In time we would have even added a few clerics to our game-bag and called it a good day's hunting. What if Pope Urban had been killed before he announced the First Crusade? How many innocent lives would have been spared? What if that sour and embittered man, St. Augustine, had possessed the wherewithal to resist his pious mother Monica and her loathing of male desire? What if he had kept his mistress rather than foisting upon the world the legacy of his own morbid sense of guilt, which led to his preoccupation with original sin? What if Saint Monica had been less of a nagging shrew and left her son to fornicate in peace at his leisure? Would not the world have been better off without his vile ideas? How many un-baptized infants did his teachings deny the joys of heaven so that he might deny the clutches that she retained upon her son? The original Augustine may have been a bronzed Othello of his day, the cincture of the dreams of many a dark beauty in the cities of Carthage and Alexandria. Might not his genius, if perpetuated by the activity of his loins, have been carried on for centuries in a line of fine minds? These minds, rather than defaming mankind by saddling us with primordial sin, might have urged us onwards to embrace our proper dignity as men and as women rather than to consider ourselves flawed by some original sin over which we had no control nor personal responsibility. What did Augustine do but saddle all of mankind with a mortgage upon a home we never wished to purchase? His re-worked Christianity only opened a line of thought that was later embraced by those Protestants who speak of the inherent depravity of man. His version of Christianity, as it diffused into the teachings of subsequent centuries, changed what was meant to be a sign of the liberality of God in the universal salvation offered by Christ and managed to restore scarcity to salvation, which was thereafter seen as a privilege to be enjoyed by an elect group. Instead he was instantly proclaimed a saint and his vile outlook of contempt for the world became normative for the Church."

"Martin Luther tried in his day to loosen the bonds again and to extend the promise of salvation to all, only to discover that once loosed from fear, no man of spirit will return willingly to the slavery of such pernicious doctrines such as those taught by Augustine. Whereas the first breath of freedom only stimulates and inspires further rebellion as you behold in me."

I still said nothing at the time in response, so the Professor continued his discourse. His condemnation now left Catholicism and proceeded to condemn the Protestant Reformation. I took note however that his long diatribe had assumed the nature of a personal defense of his own actions. He seemed less engaged in attacking my position than in vindicating his own actions and by doing so gaining my approval. This surprised me.

Professor Moriarty poured each of us another glass of claret before continuing. "That bitter and twisted French lawyer, John Calvin, of course thought he knew better the direction that the Protestant Reformation should take. He saw how the Catholic Church had treated the early followers of Martin Luther. Any threat to the majority faith had the potential to upset, not merely the authorities of the Church, but of the secular order as well. If the dissenters were not to be executed one by one as heretics, they would require their own state or kingdom to safeguard them from reactionary forces. But if you wish to create a dissenting Christian state or commonwealth the first prerequisite is to inculcate terror in those who do not share the common view of the putative reformers. You need only look at the Calvinist successors in England, the Puritans, to see the result of religious enthusiasm when it is coupled with violence."

"This is true even among those who fled to America to escape persecution at home in England. Their first action upon arriving in New England was to exterminate the members of the Pequot tribe of Indians in Massachusetts (all for the glory of God of course). Once religion has turned a man against himself that enslaved man will hate any free man that he encounters and feel the need to kill him in order to stifle internal opposition at its root. John Calvin knew that if you wish to control a man you must first turn him against his own nature by calling what he already is sinful. A man so convinced will find his own primary guilt to be insupportable and will find ways of feeling holy by destroying others upon whom he has displaced his own guilt."

"What is true of the individual is even more applicable when it is applied to the understanding of whole societies. The history of religion is the history of conquest, of pillage, fire, and sword, all of it done in the name of goodness and to rid the world of evil! So if I am evil, Mr. Sherlock Holmes, if I am a king devil, it is only because I see evil all about me wherever Christian goodness has been allowed to prevail! Christians, as far as I can see, have generally chosen the means of the devil to work for the ends of whatever god there may be."

"I would have abjured following this same course if I could have done so. If I have been violent, it has been because those whom I ordered to be killed sheltered behind their own hired killers. They did so in order that they might remain in repose like vipers in their dens behind the walls of their own devices of security. What is real social peace in contrast to this artificial public peace under law that masquerades as civic virtues and good order? What we have now is but an edifice of injustice imposed upon the great supine mass of humanity. There will come a time of general peace at last, but before that there must be a great bonfire of all that now exists among us. It is coming, Holmes; I tell you it is coming. I may not live to witness it, but things cannot go on forever as they have done heretofore. My small contribution to the great cause will be to bring down the British Empire and I will it Holmes! You know that I have the intellect and the power to do so, for you like your great father have never underestimated me!"

He fell silent then and with a trembling hand poured himself a glass of port which was stronger than the claret which he had been drinking. He held his glass in both hands and drank until the color came back into his cheeks. I could see that he is not well. He was never strong as a lad and the beatings that had once been administered by his father had left some internal damage as well as maiming his back and leaving him with his characteristic stooped appearance. I could not doubt that his crippled body still contained a fiery spirit though and I marveled at his penetration and insight, even while deploring his stated conclusions. I could see that in spite of his earlier bland manner that he is a desperate man and desperate men are the most dangerous of all. But I observed something else during his speech, something that I found at first quite strange and one that has troubled me all day since our discussion.

I realized for the first time that Professor Moriarty respects me after all and that my opinion of him matters deeply. I realize now why he entered into our strange wager in the first place. Professor Moriarty does not desire my death; indeed he has taken every measure to prevent it, even by sending Colonel Moran, who is the most dangerous man that he knew, to guard me. I will even go so far as to say that Professor Moriarty wants to enlist me now as an ally! He wishes first to see me fail in my effort to convert him, but far more than this he wishes to convert me in turn and perhaps through me Mycroft as well to help him in bringing down the British Empire.

If I can be brought over to his side, my conversion will vindicate his own hatred of the English. Now at last I know the path that I must follow if I am to save England and in doing so to save my own faith as well. I must probe the great wound that is Professor Moriarty, to trace its hatred to its source, and quench that ember from the fires of hell that burns brightly within him and will, if it is not healed, destroy his immortal soul at last!

July 6, 1893
Kings Pyland

I continue now to record here my story of my first meeting with Professor Moriarty in his own lair at Kings Pyland. After drinking his claret in silence for a time he resumed his discourse in a calmer tone.

"I should not grow so excited. My doctor informs me that excitement is dangerous to my health. I live a retired and peaceful life here among my horses. I ration out the amount of news of the outer world that I allow to penetrate my consciousness. I am not unaware however that we are at present in a great international period of economic devolution, a profound crisis in public confidence in the economic and political order, and that many people are suffering as a result of an excessive post-war boom in America. A contraction was bound to come. You may be surprised that such fires burn within the soul of an aged and dry mathematics professor. It is one of the misapprehensions of the general public that scientists are not men of passion and conviction. It is assumed that we are indifferent to the results of our experiments and to our own existence as observers of general phenomena. The scientist is held to a standard of so-called objectivity. This conception of science forgets that insight must precede the very structure of any experiment. The scientist constructs experiments to prove what he has already concluded or surmised. He may vary his explanation in the face of contradictory evidence provided by the results of his experiment, but he seldom strays far from his initial insight."

"Science proceeds slowly for the very reason that the insights and intuitions of any given man are limited by his own subjective view of the world. This limited but passionate starting point of the individual is necessary; for without passion and desire no scientist would undertake to face the rigors of his quest in the first place. He would be like most men who are satisfied with the explanations of phenomena that they have received from their fathers. Progress demands that a man shall risk ridicule and rejection and at times even death, imposed by the static social order of any given age. That order usually has a basis in religion, for what is religion but a vast collective intuition that seeks to explain all phenomena at once by positing a cause of all causes, which is to say a god."

"The task of a religion's adherents then becomes that of placating this faith-posited sovereign being by following a manner of life that is imposed upon them by some conception of a revealed divine law. The problem is that the whole thing is backward reasoning. Man assumes that the order that he observes in the cosmos is by design rather than the simple working through of mindless forces. It only becomes design when viewed retrospectively. The man of religion presumes that there might have been another order in the universe instead of the one that is currently seen to prevail and that god or the gods have chosen one particular way for things to be so that the order of things that prevails is said to indicate a divine concern for the fate of man and the world in which he lives. This view is simply an attribution of intention to the unintentional made in virtue of a need to find a pattern within the actually inconsequent and unrelated facts that surround us all. By selecting the metaphor that any given mind will impose upon events, the mind predetermines what facts will be selected and what features will seem paramount in constructing a given version of events. If a celestial purpose is intended to be observed, the universe will be seen as some vast work of art."

"My own mind takes a contrary initial point of departure from which all else emerges in due course. My first postulate is that there is no other way that the universe can be other than the one that I observe. Thus I eliminate from the beginning the need for a celestial engineer or artist to supervise the construction of the universe. It is a reverse of the traditional argument from design as proof for the existence of God. I see the order of the universe as a given substrate of essential Being-as-such, unchangeable and monolithic in itself, but variable (not in itself, but as perceived) depending upon the type of questions that I choose to pose to it by my researches."

"When I find a correspondence between my conceptions and the so-called facts of nature, I simply stop with that correspondence and view it as just one other phenomena of nature of which I am a part. It is true only in the sense of being linked now to a proposition. If I do such and such the following result is obtained. Everything that we know is operational rather than essential. Even mathematical truths are either purely circular in nature and hence matters of definition and interior reference or they are metaphorically applied to that resistant substrate that I am calling Being-as-such."

"As to the freedom of the will, my existence and my knowing are simply part of the whole and thus governed by a type of universal necessity, even when I perceive that I am acting freely. My feeling of freedom is a mere epiphenomenon to the percolating forces of my mind in operation. In any given case there is no other option for the universe than for it to attempt to produce every phenomenon that we observe about us. A vast scroll is unrolling and the writing upon it was produced by a necessity that we can never hope to grasp. Therefore we proceed as though what we see is real and as though we are free to determine events, while from a higher vantage point we might be able to see that these convictions are so short-sighted as to completely miss the essential process of all that is."

"Even if this general theory of mine is wrong and there is no more comprehensive Being-as-such to determine all things from outside of the totality of phenomena, if all phenomena display a pure spontaneity so that it is impossible to trace regular patterns of causality, there is still the chance that in infinite space and infinite time an intelligent being might somewhere evolve and ask the particular questions that I am asking. Throw the dice an infinite number of times and every combination will emerge; still not by design, but by pure chance."

"Above all else in my system of thought there is no god, thus I avoid the absurdity that any god that might exist would care about such worms as we human beings. You will object no doubt that my practice differs from my theory in that I care about the course of events, at least as regards my horses. I answer that though I have a passionate commitment to justice, that passion lies within me and has no basis but in my own will, or since I am a determinist of sorts, in my illusion of having a will. Justice is a prejudice within me, if you wish to put it that way. I cannot prove the dictators and tyrants of this world are wrong; I can only tell them that there exists a man who will oppose them and who has the will and means to do so. These would view me as a rebel, an outlaw, an enemy of the established order, but I tell you that the established world-order is the fruit of murder and rapine. It clothes itself in religion and invokes the gods to approve of what the order of tyranny has itself created. Look about you, Holmes, see the great seething masses of humanity ground under foot generation after generation; see the bodies of the young maimed and twisted, starved into submission to social forces that care nothing for their pain and that provide no lasting solace to their despair! Observe the vast complacency that pervades every source of power on the earth!

Observe this and then think of these words by the great English poet Percy Bysshe Shelley:

> *To suffer woes which Hope thinks infinite;*
> *To forgive wrongs darker than death or night;*
> *To defy power, which seems omnipotent;*
> *To love and bear; to hope till Hope creates*

From its own wreck the thing it contemplates;
Neither to change, nor falter, nor repent;
This, like thy glory, Titan, is to be
Good, great and joyous, beautiful and free;
This is alone Life. Joy, Empire, and Victory.

After this Professor Moriarty fell silent. He summoned his servant to add to the fire that had been burning lower until only a fitful red flame illuminated his haggard countenance. Now that flame grew brighter and some of the shadows of the room retreated backwards before the renewed warmth that soon dispelled the cold that seeped upwards from the hollow hills surrounding the house. For all of the spirit of his animated discourse, he appeared to be renewed and I was loathe to seek respite after my journey, curious as I was to hear finally revealed the courses followed by his intricate and circuitous mind.

"My scorn does not stop with Christianity. Think of those in India who are deemed to be of the caste of untouchables by the Brahmin caste. Are they any different from the strict Calvinist who looks at his possessions and presumes that he is among the elect of God? Does he differ from the Sultan who assumes that Allah wills all things as he takes up the various women from his harem, each of them no doubt presumes that her couch service pleases Allah and is not mere fornication, as any good Christian would conclude of her polygamous service?"

"The religions of the world are doomed to engage in perpetual conflict and they will slaughter their members willingly in order to achieve the world hegemony of belief. Even if a general peace were attainable by law and that all of the greed of mankind could be resolved by contract and treaty, religion would still cause conflicts to break out anew. It is the peculiarity of any ultimate explanation of the universe based upon rival 'revelations' that it may not tolerate rivals. The hunger for truth is in reality ultimately the hunger of men for power and respect. Man does not honor God by his worship, he honors himself! He assumes that a divine being favors his particular sacrifice or prayer and in assuming so he invalidates the worship of every other faith that does not agree with his own. By doing this he insults the believers of that other faith and it cannot be long before they take up arms and storm whatever temple of refuge or of prayer the believer may have sought out to find a moment of peace in his less sanguinary moments. This explains why the Romans persecuted the Christians, because these had dishonored the Roman Gods and by doing so threatened the belief that all Romans shared that they had a divine right to rule the then known world. The rites of religion are nothing more that the means by which a man tries to justify himself in his own eyes and to absolve himself from his own guilt as he destroys those who oppose him. It all comes down then to individual will. Even science, when it becomes a religion and not a mere hodge-podge of unrelated observations about nature, becomes a threat to opposing systems of scientific truth. That fellow Marx was right about this much at least, that there is a dialectic approach that is applicable to all human events, though he was mad if he thought that a terminal state of history would ever really exist.”

“There is no monopoly of virtue in the proletariat! Each economic system (just as is so with every religion) is at war with every other system and it is indeed true that any given system favors one class of men and means of production over others. Trade always invites dishonesty and oppression, to give as little as one can and to obtain as much as one may. Thus all trade aspires to oppression. For this reason England has built a fleet of ships to police the trade routes of the world. For this reason England introduced the opium poppy to China in order to deprave and addict the native population and to restore the balance of trade in tea. The British will not surrender the habit of drinking their tea, so the Chinese must become opium addicts to balance the books of reciprocal trade. For a similar reason the American landlord and financier, John Jacob Astor of New York, sent his whisky to the Indians, the better to debauch them and to decimate their lands of beaver pelts so that the fine statesmen in Europe might wear beaver hats. Show me trade and I will show you the inevitable exercise of political and military power. If England is presently the greatest trading power of the world today, it is so only at the cost of the misery of millions at home and abroad."

"Even within the British Empire the fruits of trade are distributed unequally. How long has it been, Holmes, since you visited Liverpool or Manchester? There you have the image of industrial England! There and in the works of Charles Dickens the true squalor of our vaunted empire is revealed. Dickens is read and esteemed everywhere, yet has England changed in response to his genius? England never shall for all of us are caught up in the great enterprise of empire and cry out 'Rule Britannia, Britannia rules the waves; Britons never, never, never shall be slaves!'"

"Tell that to the miners in Newcastle! Most Britons are slaves today, are they not? Even the members of the middle-class in their boring townhouses or their pubs, gulping down ale and breathing the fumes of London, are they not slaves? Is not the former slave of Georgia or Alabama who picked cotton beneath a clear southern sky more to be envied than a worker in the mills of Lincolnshire in England or of Lowell in Massachusetts for that matter? If then, the established order may not be defended, if its Christianity is mere cant as it is, then am I not justified in doing what I may to destroy that order from the top down, to restore at least the equity of struggle that is known in times of revolution? Violence has this to say for itself, that for one brief moment a man may claim his stature as a man by killing the man who deems himself to be his master. For that brief moment there is equality between them once again!"

"King Louis was no better than any citizen in Paris when the blade of the guillotine fell; he was a citizen of France, soon to be purged of his crimes and the dynasty of his ancestors with him. I tell you that England will be the better for its destruction at my hands. Its present state is manifest in the great bellies of the members of the House of Lords. England is bloated with conquest. It is time for a diet. It will feed for a time on death and such a death as it has not known since the Black Plague of the 14th century. It will find in the commonality of death that men and women are not so different after all. Nothing so levels a man as the contemplation of his own demise. When the body lets forth all of the ghastly fluids that have hitherto sustained it, when it is one vast pustule of corruption, and we hide the corpse in the ground to spare the living, then we can see what we in fact are, mere matter in states of transition. The glorification of man by religion simply allows us to comfort ourselves that death is the wages of sin and for that reason morally appropriate in a God-centered universe. But death is simply the wage imposed by living at all! Death is simply necessity in operation. It is not punishment unless it is imposed by man on man for supposed crimes."

"The universe does not delight in our destruction, it is indifferent to it! The deaths of the innocent will not be avenged by God, but only by man! I will it so; I, Moriarty, will see that justice shall be done! I do not wait for a day of judgment, for such there shall never be. The clock is ticking for England, Holmes. The bell will ring when I decree that it shall. I have the means at my disposal and the will to accomplish my purpose. It will be done ... and in a time of my choosing, and you cannot stop it."

Here professor Moriarty paused. I had followed his reasoning as best I could, yet I remained silent after his long discourse. Silence hung heavy upon the room. What could I say in the face of such a convoluted yet strangely coherent approach to life? I do not know how the Professor interpreted my silence, but in any case he began once again to speak with an air of truculence but also a strange air of hopefulness, if I was not mistaken, that I would contradict him and show forth some flaw in his argument.

"There!" said he at last, "Such is an exposition of my position. I have opened our little game of chess; I hide nothing. No doubt you will soon sally forth with your bishops. You are welcome to challenge my initial presentation if you wish. I assure you that I will listen to whatever you wish to say. You may of course save England by killing me outright. I am sure that Mycroft could arrange to have that done, but that would be admitting your own defeat. I believe that your pride is no less than my own and I doubt if you would be willing to admit to so ignominious a defeat as a direct action to eliminate me would imply. It would invalidate the efforts of a lifetime during which you have elaborated your own convictions. You at least do believe in an objective moral order. If my mind, which you believe to be at least equal to your own, cannot grasp and be forced to yield to your arguments on level ground, well then you may have no hope that lesser minds will be turned by reason and not by mere indoctrination to accept the One True God. You must convince me or doubt your own faith. Since you begin with faith, whereas for me faith is a matter of indifference, I already have you at a disadvantage. You have something to lose, whereas I am quite reconciled to an eternal skepticism."

"Does that frighten you, Sherlock Holmes? It should, because the fall from one who expects to attain all things in God down into utter meaninglessness and insignificance is a long fall indeed. Thus, in one blow, if I prevail, I will destroy England and also its greatest detective, Sherlock Holmes! Dare I say that the opportunity that I offered to you on the brink of the Falls of Reichenbach may have been preferable to facing the exchanges that now stand before us? It would have spared you a long and tiring journey throughout Asia eating the dust of camel dung only to return with whatever notes you may have made, thinking to dish up for me some eastern stew of religious doctrines, or to trot out some old horses from the stable of Thomas Aquinas and beat me in the race to truth."

Professor Moriarty struggled to his feet and grabbed at a cane that had rested alongside his chair.

"Well, that is all that I have to say to you today. You may choose your own hours of repose while you are here. I leave our meetings to you and you are welcome to treat this house as your own. Perhaps a brief walk about the grounds may help to clear your head. Feel free to ring my servant for anything that your require. I desire that you be fresh before offering any rebuttal to the points that I have made tonight. I usually take a nap before teatime and you may wish to do the same. I will leave you now.

Please feel free to peruse any volumes in my library that you wish. I have read them all. You might start with Spinoza, excellent reading for a summer afternoon."

With that he departed with a nod and the great oaken door of the library closed behind his stooped and diminutive figure. I was left alone with my reflections in the great silent room. I saw at once the task that lay before me. Moriarty was above all else a man without hope. The man without hope feels the universe as a great vacuum. If God does not exercise conscious and rational intent with regard to His creation, there remains only necessity, the blind plunging of atoms, force acting upon mass. The study of the scientist then becomes one of being a mere cost-accountant of the universe who records the changes from state to state, from one position to another, the rate of change and transformation. Such a man of science alone is deprived of the simplest right that the philosopher may claim for himself, the right to ask the greatest question of all, the question of why.

July 7, 1893
Kings Pyland

Today I have set time aside to formulate my response to that of Professor Moriarty given last evening. My response is as all embracing as his own and I trust that he will give me a full hearing even as I have done. As a physicist his own speculations are focused on cause and effect relationships; he is incapable of thinking with the expansiveness that philosophy alone can provide. He is locked even there in the mindset of the early pre-Socratics such as Parmenides asking of what fundamental elements the universe consists, whereas true philosophy always begins with teleology, which asks "Why does the universe exist at all?"

To ask that the universe pursue some rational end beyond maintaining its mere mute existence has never seemed a great leap for me. If mankind can pursue some ultimate goal and may even question existence itself by asking why, even while mankind is only part of the whole universe, then surely the whole universe may exercise by proxy a function claimed by what is a mere part. In other words the mere existence of the human intellect demands answers that insensate being is unable to pose; but once those questions are posed a demand is placed on composite being to provide an answer. God emerges from that silence in answer to our query. What we call God is elicited, summoned forth, made real by the questions that we pose.

At the same time the unique feature of Jewish literature is that it reverses the directional flow of questions posed to the philosophical God. The Old Testament has God coming to us before we come to Him. It portrays God as the origin of all being and the direction of mankind as a flight from God in history because once realizing that we are naked human beings realize that they are vulnerable. Humans fear that any subjectivity that is capable of grounding being and morality is also able to dictate and to destroy; therefore human nature fears God even while it invokes God in order to justify humankind's own perceptions. Thus philosophy goes in search for a God to validate its own existence, but lives in fear that it may just possibly find that for which it seeks or alternatively find that it is alone. Both of these elements explain the primal anxiety of human existence. Yet there must be a correlative intelligence somewhere or somehow, a God capable of embodying the whole of our aspirations for transcendental completeness that will answer all of our questions, or we collectively are doomed by what is only an illusion peculiar to our species.

The position of humankind when it engages in philosophy is to assert that the part is greater than the whole in at least our unique capacity to be conscious and to understand. But has the entire universe labored to create a mere particle, which alone is conscious of itself, that may then look about upon the vastness that surrounds it, only to discover that it is quite alone in an empty universe that pulses blindly along, completely unaware of itself, except within the tiny electrical discharges of the mind of the philosopher?

After death will those discharges simply collapse back into unknowing within a brief span of time and join the pointlessness of what Moriarty calls "necessity?" This is the great folly of all determinism which seeks to explain itself by itself, like a dog chasing its own tail. The determinist asserts that all things happen merely because they must happen in just that way, but by stating this position the determinist implies that the opposite of determinism is at least conceivable as an option to be rejected. If we are determined in all things then so is our own decision to defend determinism in which case all apparent options are merely illusory. The choice is in a sense made prior to reflection if all events are determined by prior events. To apply a homely metaphor, the universe in all its elements has no time to scan the menu before some entree is placed before it and that entree is gathered up again by necessity before there is time to even sit down to table and assess what is before it.

To Moriarty's way of thinking necessity allows no intermediate zone of delay between cause and effect wherein reflection might take place or freedom might emerge. Such a universe would be like the unwinding of a great clock; but what hand placed within it such a great potency or force to make possible time and space as we experience them or the capacity for such entropic devolution as the scientist proposes? After all, we make choices every day. Contingent and uncertain events do occur or else the mathematics of probability makes no sense.

But then from being a strict determinist, Moriarty leaps to the other extreme and says that he wills that the British Empire shall be destroyed. This is surely a choice. So Moriarty's entire argument of yesterday becomes, "I alone may will in a will-less universe. All is determined except for me. I shall act with the freedom of a God because there is no God but me!" The whole of his presentation is blatant solipsism! It is the fruit of his own failure to grasp the very idea of another consciousness than his own, which may decide its own fate apart from his will for it. If God may make a space for the sovereign will of man, then surely Professor Moriarty may make a space for contradiction by me, another man like himself.

My first task then becomes a simple one—not to force Professor Moriarty to believe in God, but as a beginning to help him to believe that there is one other person with as much right to live and to choose as he lives and chooses. The beginning of the love of God is the recognition that one's fellow human beings are not alien to oneself, but identical metaphysically to oneself, that all men and women confront the universe that contains them with a similar consciousness.

The entire human race forms an extended community of mutual feeling and intellection by virtue of the ability to communicate. This is why the Catholic Church is one as all humans are one. We are implicated in one another's existence. No sin or virtue is solitary for the simple reason that we need each other. We are born part of the collective body of all lives that have gone before us and are part of all lives that shall follow us. We are each knit into the fabric of history. Our reflection is incorporated into each person that we meet and that person is absorbed into us as well. Professor Moriarty in contrast has set up a universe that denies the most basic observation that he might make, that he is not alone in the universe. His is a metaphysic with the necessary prolegomenon that the world is not as various and multiple as it is. He has been too long alone with his own thoughts and the result is the philosophical disease of solipsism. Even his protestations of a desire to do justice are simply his own version of what justice might be. Justice without love is non-attainable because it does not consult the beneficiaries of our efforts. Even God cannot bestow salvation upon us without our consent. To actually exist alone would be to be deprived of even the language of thought, which we receive as a legacy and not as our own creation. We are already mortgaged to the rest of human effort at our birth, it is too late to claim a fee simple absolute over the universe as Moriarty is attempting to do. In the last analysis his entire position is that of a baby crying for food and angry at the delay of its desire. What does one do with a petulant infant? One comforts it; one feeds it.

July 8, 1893
Kings Pyland

On the following evening we ate an excellent dinner in the great dining room at Kings Pyland. Professor Moriarty played the gracious host, a role that it amuses me to see that he clearly enjoys. We did not refer to the subject of yesterday afternoon but rather confined our discussion to horses and hounds. The particular genius of the British is our sense for the good life of the country. An English gentleman is at his best when discussing his garden, his kennels, or his stables. If he is so unfortunate as to possess none of the above, he is at his best when he reads in his daily newspaper of the doings of the local hunt or the country-house party of such and such a duke or duchess. The common English people enjoy a vicarious sense of nobility and the existence of the peerage gives a sense of pride to the entire nation. We will be the last of nations to surrender our monarchy.

I could not but think of the long transition to the gracious life now being lived by Professor Moriarty, the last of his line. I was aware that his mother had perished in the great famine of Ireland and that his father had escaped to Liverpool in 1847 with the boy looking for employment. Both were mere skeletons on the roads of Yorkshire when my father hired the elder Moriarty as a groom. After leaving the slums of Liverpool they had spent the summer of 1846 walking across Yorkshire seeking day laboring jobs. Finding themselves as the autumn rains drew on near to the Holmes Estate at Sigerside they could clearly go no further. The boy had rickets and was almost dead. It was always my father's opinion that the elder Moriarty would have long since abandoned the boy but that the lad's appearance was so pitiful that it invited handouts that the father was then able to share, probably taking the larger share. The young Moriarty had fulfilled his usefulness in this way and if my father had not taken him into the main house and had him carefully nursed during a two-month convalescence he would surely have perished.

My brother Sherringford, who was always jealous of paternal attention, resented the presence of what he called at the time "that wretched Irish baggage," which did not please my father. It was perhaps natural for us to fear further illness in the house however, for my mother already suffered from consumption. Young boys in the fullness of their strength often scorn disability and feebleness. The young Moriarty manifested both and thus drew from my father an unaccustomed tenderness. The bond thus forged remained and accounted for my father's desire eventually to educate the son of his former groom left an orphan after his father's death.

While the elder Moriarty lived the brute came to hate the son who was treated better than the father and he thus took every opportunity to beat the boy in secret when he was returned to the stable yard to do light chores and to make himself useful in some manner. In this fashion was the character of the young Moriarty formed by death and by penury and by the later brutal treatment of his father. He was though one of the lucky few who survived Ireland's great period of trial when the Irish were forced to abandon their beloved land, when the land itself seemed to rebel and the potatoes year after dreadful year rotted in the fields. Only one who has ever known such hunger can appreciate the mere spectacle of a well-appointed table and the luxury of being able to offer hospitality to guests.

Professor Moriarty seemed to savor the spectacle of my enjoyment of every mouthful of lamb and my glass was never allowed to be empty. Perhaps it pleased him to make some return to my father through serving me, for I had noticed that he never spoke of my father without respect and deference. We did not tarry long over our port. Evidently, Moriarty felt that he had scored a quick victory with his first salvo of the campaign and was allowing me time to nurse my wounds before departure. He was surprised therefore when I proposed to extend my visit at Kings Pyland if that was quite agreeable to my host since I had found our conversations most stimulating and hoped that we might continue them.

He consented readily enough, for there is little that a dualist enjoys more than the clash of sabers. He was quiet though over our brandy in the library, for having had two runs at me already one at the university and one here, he was willing to play a defensive strategy now for a time. I had yet to state my own position. He must at the very least have been somewhat curious as to how I had got on with Colonel Moran during my travels. He was surprised when I told him that I rather enjoyed the Colonel's company and explained to him that though our views differed, the Colonel had proved to be an excellent companion at times and that I much appreciated the sacrifice entailed by lending me such a man to serve as guide and guardian, a man who had proven to be so useful to the Professor in the past and whose absence therefore must have been keenly felt.

"Well you were welcome to him. He is not a man to have about one if he is not occupied. He is as restless as a tiger. The man is a born assassin," opined the Professor. "Even the Tuggee Sect of India came to fear him. He thinks like a tiger; that is why he is the best big game hunter in the east. He thinks nothing of waiting by a water hole through a day and a night until his quarry appears. He is all rest one moment and all action the next. That feature of his personality is also why he is so good at cards. He is willing to lose several hands in order to set up one winning one. He will give ground only to turn on his foe, just as a tiger will. Never underestimate him, Holmes, remember that the tiger has no friends. Even I do not trust him, but I pay him well. Always remember that a tiger may turn at any moment. He will purr one moment and bite off your head the next before retiring to lick his paws. Still, I prefer a tiger to a hyena like that vulgar blackmailer, Charles Augustus Milverton."

"You have heard of him? Of course, he is rather in your line. You have spent much of your career preventing scandals. That is one thing about the upper-class; they will always pay to keep their family name clean and intact. It was a minor line of my own endeavors, blackmail. I only took it up because it paid well. Assassinations are all well and good, but they do not keep bread upon the table. I was even forced to plan some minor crimes of burglary and extortion at times to pay my people, while of course retaining some small portion for myself as carrying charges to eventually pay for my current gracious retirement. You have feasted tonight on the proceeds of my humble efforts. I hope that this reflection will not give you dyspepsia."

He laughed in his own sinister way and then continued, "This whole business of moral goodness amuses me. Except for your little indulgence in cocaine you seem to have lived a remarkably pure life, Holmes. No music-hall girls climbing the midnight stairs at Baker Street when Watson was away. No taking advantage of grateful governesses. No escapades with Arab youths along the way in your journey. Colonel Moran would have told me. You are quite the mystery to me, Mr. Sherlock Holmes. I often wonder if even the Pope finds you so. Oh yes, I have contacts with the Roman Church through a certain Cardinal Tosca."

"You see no one knows more about evil than the Catholic clergy. I hear that in confession one must often be quite specific about one's sins, because certain circumstances may heighten the degree of guilt. I have often wondered just how much detail the priests need to know to give valid absolution. I like to think of prelates savoring sin from a distance. Or do they beat their breasts and give thanks for the temptations they have been spared? I of course could spare them any anxiety. It is surely the greatest of vanities to think that one's sins really matter to God. Once having accepted that human life is a great cesspool, one is no longer shocked or appalled at the smell."

"My own weak body has spared me the various crevasses of carnal pleasures and since I have never loved, I feel no jealousy. Pride can hardly be present when one knows that one has shaken off illusions and I am not so dishonest as to profess a false humility. The result is that I feel comparatively sinless. But if I did sin, I would not pester God with my remorse. Is there anything more self-indulgent than a guilty sinner who wishes for absolution while knowing full-well that he will sin again? How can he not? Most people's sins are their only joy in life. What would a gossip-monger be without her gossip? What would a lustful man do without the coy smile of his mistress? Or the glutton without his groaning table of eatables? We choose our sins to match our character; lose our sins and we lose ourselves!"

"This is the idiocy of all moral discourses and sermons; that they make a man or a woman dissatisfied with life. Religion ruins the too brief joys of our brief existence. I am quite democratic in this regard: I grant every man his sins if he will not burden me with recounting them. I am shocked by nothing but virtue. I can never forgive one who, unwilling to be happy himself, must ruin the joys of others by pointing out their failures of character. There is a reason why the virtuous do not figure well in the dramatic theater, Holmes. It is because virtue is boring; only crime is of interest. Surely you must admit that or why are you a detective? Perhaps that is your sin: always being above the fray with your blasted answers to every problem."

"Who do you consult when you are lost? Who is your consulting detective? Do you then have recourse to God in prayer? How dull it must be to get no answer from him, although I for one am not displeased by the silence of God. I should hate to have the hum of the divine displeasure whispering in my ear all the time like a great buzzing insect. I would look about for something to swat and find only the great hum of the universe shouting at me, 'God, God, God!' I much prefer silence the better to hear my own voice. What is it to me if bushes burn on Sinai? Does God care that I am not upon my face at the appointed hours facing Mecca? I prefer if I must think of God at all that he be like an English gentleman of one of the better clubs, a good tipper who has little to say. But all the gods that I encounter in world literature seem to demand worship! One might as well take on a mistress as a god, for she also demands worship and only complains when she is neglected. Some trinket soon sets things right."

"What God would stoop to demand worship? Perhaps the Greek Pagans had it right after all. Their temples are filled with vain and jealous goddesses. It might be expected of a goddess that she would demand constant ministrations from her followers. It would be like her to burden man with the inscrutable oracle of Holy Scripture and to have generations slaughter each other over variant interpretations of sacred books. I prefer the gods of the east."

"Who can look at the world and not think that the most believable of the celestial pantheon is the Goddess Kali? Did you know that the men in charge of the relief sent to Ireland during the famine years thought that the famine was god's will to clear away the Irish barbarians and that the great hunger was heaven-sent? Tell me then, were men like Sir Robert Peel and Charles Trevelyan Christians or were they worshipers of Kali! Well I have learned to respect that same goddess with time, only this time I will choose the victims!"

"You see, Holmes, I do not deny the moral instinct in man. The problem is that man refuses to accept his own stature as the creator of the parameters of his own mind. Nature may have stumbled upon mankind by accident and now cannot stop us. Perhaps we will someday destroy the earth itself! And what if we do? Perhaps nature designed the human brain simply by the accidents imposed by the survival imperative that we see in all the rest of nature. Conscious reflective thought may be a bizarre aberration. Is not nature the mother of all the strange variants produced by evolution?"

"Nature is characterized by nothing if not by its excess. The great whales once lived on land, did you know that? The flukes of the whale are the result of a fusion of the limbs. Even we humans have vestigial tails and evidence in our necks of gill slits. We carry about with us the baggage of all of our ancestors. Man is not a destination but a way station. Evolution is a process and not an end. There is nothing so likely to go extinct as a species completely at one with its environment; change one thing and the well-adapted species dies. The best chances of survival lie with species that may go in many directions and adjust to change. Success in living depends upon the ability to adapt and to adapt quickly. The human species has a surfeit of capacity for just that end. We thrive on indeterminacy! Chance is our tutor! In the past humans used that surfeit of cranial capacity to produce language and the various technical arts such as the manufacture of clothing and shelter. With time though, the minds of individual men also allowed them to question the process of thought itself and to realize individuality and singularity. Current human thought is an aberration as seen from the perspective of evolution. It is not impossible that as with many hyper-evolved species we are one of nature's mistakes like the great size of whales or the huge but useless tusks of mammoths. The mind is the simian equivalent of the long tail of the peacock, one great superfluity!"

"The human thinking process has begun now to feed upon itself rather than directing its thought outward to the exigencies of survival. Even our skill in the arts of war, which seemed designed to aid survival, will finally destroy us. Man has become the greatest enemy to man! Each year creates new elaborations in the art of killing. And what is killing but the desire to monopolize resources that will be used for survival. In the past man's aggression and territoriality served a purpose. It resulted in the dispersion of the human race to every environment of the globe. It is scarcely possible to find an area so insalubrious that some tribe or other will not be found to live there. We are the only species with such a universal range."

"So much was cause for triumph, but now alas we have reached the extent and limit of our expansion as a species. What will happen now? Man will turn upon himself. Eternal war is the future of the human race. We will turn upon ourselves and gnaw at our own flesh. Man was born a cannibal you see, Holmes. The reason that the eating of human flesh is a taboo in most cultures is that the practice would soon be universal if it were not prohibited. You see that we are now escaping from the mists of illusion and are coming to realize our own perfidy. Incest is condemned for the very reason that humans who live in proximity soon begin to mate indiscriminately and to mate within the family group would soon cause jealousies that would rip apart that most basic structure of human society. Man's moral instinct is in the last analysis an adaptation to save us from extinction at our own hands and to preserve tribal identity. The origin of even the gods is a tribal affair, a point of origin for all subsequent stories of heroic exploits."

He paused to offer me more brandy before continuing. "Where was I? Ah yes, language serves the same function. Each language bears the history of its use over time. Words that serve no purpose are eliminated. Perhaps a time will come when the word 'god' will be forgotten because it will be found to serve no purpose. The age of the gods will be seen then as a time when men thought that they required some universal source for the multiple realities presented to the human mind and some general guarantor of the moral order. God's function is precisely analogous to that of a surety signature upon a loan. If humans fail to obey other humans then some god is trotted out to validate the transaction and to assure that all parties are paid in the end. The belief in gods is the function of living in an unstable age. Men are most likely to turn to religion when they are about to do something very foolish and need some guarantee that what they propose meets with divine approval and is thus safe to do."

"The perfect example is the Jewish conquest of Palestine in the Old Testament. Have you never thought, Holmes, that the real reason for leaving Egypt was simply that there was a problem of unemployment there or perhaps of jealousy, a corporate shake-up? Nothing so irritates a lazy upper class than a rising middle-class with greater sophistication and industry. Why else would the Jewish people follow Moses out into the desert? No it was a simple lack of work that drove the Jews out. After all, one can't keep building pyramids forever; too costly in men and materiel!"

"I have often thought that far from opposing the Jewish emigration across the Red Sea, the Egyptians were happy to be rid of such a fractious people. Perhaps, the reason that no Egyptian troops emerged out of the Red Sea was that they never entered it in the first place beyond a few scouts to report back that the rebellious former workers were really gone at last. But that sort of story is hardly heroic and makes for a poor audience in the re-telling. Grant me my presupposition though and let us continue. Let us continue the story from an objective point of view."

"The Hebrew tribes, after wandering about in Sinai for forty years finally realize that even the risk of dislodging the indigenous tribes of the north is preferable to their marginal existence in the desert. Moses has with great difficulty kept the tribes together for forty years, but he is getting old and they are naturally losing patience. The great danger is assimilation into the more successful people living on the margins of the land where they have been living as a nomadic people. Moses realizes that the Hebrews need a new infusion of that most seductive of all conceptions, the belief that they are special and favored by a god. Here Moses shows his genius as a leader, for he does not deny the existence of other gods (for I doubt that even the idol worshipers were so sunk in the abyss of fetishism that they really thought the image was their god). Moses comes down from the mountain with more than the text of the Ten Commandments; he comes down with the conception of a God of gods and proclaims that if the Hebrew people will enter into a covenant with this unnamed God whom he has privately encountered, then they will be given the lands of their enemies as a reward, for this new God is the God over all other gods, in fact over time He becomes the only God!"

"Thus are all the gods born among us Holmes, they are born out of our need! It is the purpose of religion to stay the fears of man and to create social order. Man creates gods because the mind of man has evolved too far. We are like the whales in this, only the whales suffer from excessive bulk of body while man is surfeited with too much mind! Our cranial capacity exceeds our needs. All this nonsense of seeking an ultimate purpose for our lives only detracts from simply living. Look about you, Holmes, and you will see what I mean. What do people do when their labors are done? Go to the East End of London and observe the ways that even the poorest citizens seek out food, drink, and an opportunity for coitus interspersed with music and laughter. What does the average man or woman care for transcendent values and ultimate purposes? They know that they will die and they are content to do so, for death will bring an end to their pain and degradation at the hands of their fellow men. They take what pleasures life offers to them and of necessity learn to rest content with their lot in life. They do not need the added burden of being told that they will be resurrected only to endure even worse sufferings because they dared to grasp a few passing joys along the way in their brief and bitter lives. And why are they put to the burdens of religion but to vindicate the tribal ambitions of the Jewish people who insisted on burdening the world with their national aspirations and their recriminations for failure to live up to a moral code that no culture has ever managed to fully embrace."

"But let us continue our story. The Hebrew people prove to be successful in their wars of acquisition and manage to carve out a small niche of land where they set up the twelve tribes of Israel; but now a new problem arises, the God that got them to the Promised Land has now served His function. Once made comfortable in Canaan the Jewish people (for they are now more than a set of allied tribes) needs to maintain its solidarity to repel other invaders. Once again their unique concept of a Supreme God comes to the rescue. They have by now elaborated a code that far exceeds any mere Ten Commandments. They have elaborated rituals that would be absolutely absurd if it is not born in mind that the function of these rituals and the associated prohibitions is to maintain group unity and solidarity and to keep this people from being dissolved back into the tribal mix of the deserts that surround them. Thus we have the contributions of the priestly class that ever and again reminds this people that they are unique. Every invasion or interruption of the comfortable way of life in Canaan is then interpreted as retribution exacted by an irate God due to infidelity to the Torah which has by now grown under priestly influence to truly gargantuan proportions."

"It is difficult to see how the Jews were being unfaithful of course, because the business of offering sacrifices was no doubt in full operation. But let us even assume that the Jews may have grown a bit careless over time in their religious observances. After all, what could be more natural? After all they were at peace in the land. But the need for social coherence remained, for social coherence is the *sine qua non* of survival. The Jewish people had by now confused the ebb and flow of history with their ability or inability to live by a covenant now in the distant past. The result was that in addition to the priests, a set of men evolved whose sole function was to nag and harass the people and to convince them that they had collectively been unfaithful to the covenant, the prophets of Israel."

"It is to these men that we owe the conception of a Messiah, which in turn led to Christianity. The concept of a Messiah is the true mark of the further genius of the Jewish people. The promised advent of a Messiah explained the indefinite delay in the fulfillment of God's part of the covenant, which was to eventually to extend Jewish rule beyond Canaan to all the other nations of the earth. Let us return to the terms of the original contract. Its terms were, if I recall correctly, that the God of Israel would be faithful to His promises and would make of Israel a great people with descendants as numerous as the sands of the sea. It was this very apocalyptic belief that resulted in the most highly elaborated ethical code that the world has ever witnessed; so much was good, but it was all predicated upon a final fulfillment of the covenant. Remember that, Holmes, I beg of you, for it is essential to my point."

"The years pass and still no Messiah arrived as promised by the prophets, although the tired old sacrificial business of the priests is at least still going on year after year. The memory of even the exile in Babylon becomes only a dim memory. Besides a few zealots like the Maccabeus sect and later the Pharisees, most of the people have adapted to Roman rule. The Jews are allowed their temple and their rituals by their Roman overseers. They are even allowed a Tetrarch or sort of powerless sovereign to maintain something of Jewish national pride; but the cauldron is beginning to simmer and the lid is about to blow off."

"Then out of Nazareth, in Galilee of all places, there arises a man who will forge the greatest religious synthesis of all time and he will do so by dying rather than living to a ripe old age like Socrates. His teaching will take a course that no prior religion would even dream of taking. He would deny the primary function of all the gods of all other religions, which function is to make life better and more certain for a select group, even at the cost of some initial inconvenience in keeping certain ritual observances. This man, Jesus, stands all that upon its head by claiming he is the long awaited Messiah!"

Moriarty paused at this crescendo of his argument before turning his thin and skeletal face towards me and whispering. "And then he manages to get himself crucified!"

The entire room suddenly seemed to grow colder all about us. Moriarty remained silent, his face grim and frozen in the shadows of the fire that had once again burned low in the grate. After a few minutes I wondered if he would continue his exposition or whether he had drifted off to sleep.

At last he continued, but so softly that I could barely hear him. "Rather than casting out the Romans as expected, he perished at their hands. No wonder the Jews rejected Him. They knew in their hearts that religion was supposed to enhance life here and now. Everything depends upon a short term pay-off at the gaming table; otherwise the great wheel of faith grinds to a halt. Men have short memories of past benefits bestowed by their gods. A god may give a people a fortune and the first words will then be, 'What have you done for us lately?' The purpose of the belief in a Messiah, as any well-fed priest could have told them, (but then he would have been out of a job) was not to have the promise fulfilled, let alone fulfilled in such a fashion insulting to their hopes, but to delay fulfillment of the Promise indefinitely. The very survival of the priestly class depended upon delay!"

"The High-Priest Caiaphas understood this perhaps better than many. He realized that if this man succeeds, the whole game of priestly sacrifice would be over. He must have said something like this to himself. The High-Priest was in the best position to know that Jesus had no chance of succeeding against he Romans with this pacifist talk of an immanent Kingdom of God, one not of this world. Besides, the rest of his claims were so outlandish as to prove that he could not be the Messiah, for he was even claiming some sort of unity with God himself, the ultimate blasphemy! The whole claim to superiority of the Jewish God was that He could not be defined, confined, or even named in the Hebrew language. Instead this Jewish God was defined by His absolutely unique unconditional and singular quality of existence, by His refusal of any need to justify Himself before mankind."

"Caiaphas realized that even if the message of this ungainly latter-day prophet was accepted by the people and there was a general uprising, it was doomed to fail; because this Jesus preached about loving your enemies! The God that had spoken to Moses on the other hand told the nascent Jewish people to kill all who opposed them and their children too! No doubt Caiaphas wished for more of what the American revivalists would term, 'that old time religion.' In any case Caiaphas determined to take the prudent course by saying that, 'It is better that one man should die to save the people.' He was probably unconscious of course of the irony of his statement, for that was precisely what Jesus intended to do (or at least that was the interpretation that his followers later placed upon the event)."

"The result of course was a foregone conclusion: Jesus was condemned and executed. All looked well and good and things bid fair to return to normal after a couple of hectic days of uncertainty. But then suddenly it was not well and good; and why; because under the pressure of events (and despite all precautions in the chaos of events at the Passover) no one could find the body of Jesus!"

"This might be characterized as a typical case of administrative oversight and as quite forgivable under the circumstances, but in this case it was critical, for this Jesus was not alone in his desire that the time of the Messiah should have finally come at last. There existed in Palestine a Jew named Saul. If the immediate followers of Jesus already realized that their new religion needed to make a great investment in the future by an act of faith in the resurrection of Jesus, a point that they insisted on if their new religion was to keep up with the competition with that of the Jews who still kept to the old formula of keeping the fulfillment of the promises of God always in the future, never in the present."

"Saul (or as he was later called, Paul) realized that the age of tribal deities had come and gone. Paul was the first religious genius of this caliber since Moses. He alone realized that what was called for now was a universal God, one who would rule over all peoples. Oh the Jews would still get some credit for making the introduction of their faith to the other investors who would now pool their general credit and place one huge bet on a single number in hope of the biggest payoff ever recorded in the great religious game of chance that is life. What is that game you ask? The game of survival beyond the confines of this life, the biggest game of all! It is the game played by evolution that produced the mind of man in the first place. It is the game of every duel to reproduce of the great rutting beasts. It is the game that causes the courting behavior of every species upon the planet to survive! Only now this survival was placed beyond even death itself and applied to the individual not just for the tribe or the species ... if, that is, this man Jesus was still alive as His follows claimed he was!"

The voice of the Professor now faded into silence so that the last sentence sounded more like a question than a statement. He found it necessary to take several drinks from his glass of before he could continue with his remarkable exposition.

"You see, this man Jesus claimed to be more than the Jewish concept of a Messiah. He claimed far more than even the outer perimeter of messianic hopes. He claimed to be, in his very person, God himself! Christianity with one great leap had just left all other religions behind with this claim. Even his closest associates, with the possible exception of Peter, could not grasp it and I suggest that it is only our familiarity with this claim that makes us easy in our customary affirmation when we recite the Creed."

Professor Moriarty said this last phrase almost reverentially; but perhaps I merely mistook his tone, for I could see that he had grown weary in the telling, as with one who has repeated a story many times, one often told before, if only to himself.

I could see that he was growing restless. At last he said, "The whole thing coalesced over a course of about forty years or two generations after the death of Jesus and we are all still living in the shadow of those marginally told events. Jerusalem fell after all and the Jewish nation was dispersed over all the earth. In spite of all that Caiaphas had tried to do, the people did in fact perish. Thereafter, they were scattered like seed to the winds among the diverse peoples of the earth while still retaining their identity and their hopes for a Messiah; but so were the Christians also, with these two groups living side-by-side through the course of history, both waiting for a Messiah: one to greet Him for the first time, the other to welcome Him back in glory."

The Professor, who had been looking into the fire, here tuned to face me directly. "That is where we stand today, Holmes, still waiting; and during all of that time no synthesis of these two faiths has ever been possible."

The Professor then succumbed to a sudden fit of coughing; but after taking another drink from his glass, he attempted to press on with his assessment of the underlying dynamics of religious belief. I could not see him clearly, but I had the impression that it was as though for all his earlier air of certitude something eluded him still, something that I could perhaps supply.

I stopped him though. "Pardon me Professor, but since I am certain that your views are not the subject of a momentary insight, but of much considered reflection, I wonder if you would be willing to postpone further elaboration upon this theme until tomorrow. I have had some alarming coughing spells myself in recent months and I promised Mycroft to keep to early hours."

The Professor nodded and rose from his seat in acquiescence to my wishes. He smiled at parting with an air of triumph before wishing me good night. Shortly after that I adjourned to my room to write up these notes while the words of his discourse were still fresh in my memory.

July 9, 1893
Kings Pyland

I slept late today and came down to breakfast to find myself again alone at table. I am still marveling at the range of ideas and strange interpretations that Professor Moriarty placed before me yesterday. I am surprised that the man is as familiar with the Holy Scriptures as he is. His effort to explain away any concept of divine revelation or any role of providence in the history of the Jewish people shows that he views scripture as mere sociological data for analysis and refutation. His relation to religion is as distant and objective as if he was simply running a chemical analysis of an unidentified white powder or a fractional distillation of coal tars in his laboratory.

His tone was mocking and irreverent in the extreme, but I cannot tell if he is using this tone simply to demoralize me or to test the strength of my own convictions. He may be simply baiting me so that I will go recklessly on the attack with my own string of abusive comments rather than taking him seriously and meeting him point for point. I am resolved to follow the method that I have applied thus far in my dealings with him and to allow him a great deal of latitude in his remarks without either objection or correction. It is more important that I discover the trend and motivations of his ideas than to oppose him and only have him go to ground and dare me to make my own case against him. I am only more convinced with each day that his strategy is to overwhelm me quickly by a frontal assault and thus be spared hearing me present my own long elaborated arguments that I have set down in this journal thus far. Can this be because his great intellect is already gnawing away at his own bland assumptions and easy conclusions? Ah well, we shall see.

I was surprised after dinner a few hours ago to observe the ease with which the Professor took up again the line of his argument of yesterday as though a night and the daylight hours had not intervened. He began his discourse as follows...

"I believe that we left off last night with the historical fact of the awkward co-existence side-by-side, of the Jews and the new sect of people that came eventually to be called Christians. The Jews have through the ages been like a burr riding along under the saddle of a dominant Christianity for nearly two thousand years and the Christians haven't liked it one bit with the result that Christian civilization has persecuted the Jews at all times and places while forgetting in so doing much of what Jesus ever said. Anyone observing this fact might conclude that Christianity suffers from a bad conscience with regard to the Jews who naturally resent what they view as the unnatural grafting of gentiles onto their ancient faith."

"Then for added confusion to the Abrahamic stew that is western religion we need only stir in the Arabs who think that after Mohammed they became the real chosen people above both the Jews and even the Christians. Building on the military genius of Mohammed, Islam had been engaged in building its own extensive world-wide civilization that may someday come to rival both of its competitors for domination over the conscience of the human race. And of course we must not forget the Hindus and the Buddhists whose upwelling from southern Asia may come to dominate the world."

"This whole vying for divine preference reminds me of children competing for their father's affection. There seems to be a contest of sorts to frame who shall be regarded definitively as the infidels. I hear that there is even an odd group in America who want to start writing the whole story of Christianity over again from scratch based upon a mythical anthropology in the Americas. These men claim it was God the Father who was the one with a body and not just Jesus. Mormonism does demonstrate however the genius of the Americans who cannot abide that any other nation might possess something that they did not invent themselves. Americans would like a patent upon all ideas, not merely in technology but in cultural pursuits as well. It is evidently their national ambition to be the greediest people upon the earth. By reducing the spiritual to a mere physical progression of gods and implying that each Mormon male may in his turn (particularly if he is allowed multiple wives) become a god siring innumerable spirit children, the Americans have turned their natural entrepreneurial instincts loose even in the religious arena."

"I of course have no quarrel with them because they have taken the very position that I have been arguing here without knowing it. At last a religion has evolved that is a pure motivating force without any real spiritual content. It has not forgotten the value to be obtained by leaving an authoritative text behind that can generate over time an extensive derivative literature and thereby ensure the employment prospects of otherwise idle or superfluous theologians. By harnessing sexuality instead of opposing its force as the Catholics have done by maintaining a separate caste of priests (a leftover from temple days) the Mormons have taken a great leap forward—wedding sensuality to religion. Of course the women in a polygamous marriage must suffer from neglect, but then at least they will have someone to engage in intelligent conversation of an evening when the shared chores are done and the husband, much harried by lust, is engaged elsewhere."

"Ah well, the Mormons may still win out in the religious sweepstakes and do you know why, Holmes, because they gratify the normal human desire to excel, to grow, and to leave as many offspring behind as possible. This polygamy of theirs was an ingenious idea. Give a woman one man and she will bedevil the poor wretch to death every time that he notices another woman, which he is biologically programmed to do. But put three or even a dozen women together and they will consort with each other in friendship and amity and leave the poor fellow who is married to them alone of an evening to read his newspaper after tilling the fields to a point of exhaustion to feed them all. You see sexuality ceases to be particularly stimulating when it becomes a duty rather than a transgression. This is why Catholics never cease coupling its exercise with the spicy prospect of eternal damnation."

Professor Moriarty laughed heartily at his own witticism, which brought on another alarming coughing fit. When he was quite himself again he continued.

"I beg your pardon. As you see my health is little better than your own. My lungs in turn are little better than the skeleton that supports their use, but still allows me to walk to the stables and to conduct my classes. Speaking however of women, have you ever noticed that it is always the women who keep religion alive? Walk into any Church in Christendom and what do you see but women praying for their children. It is the nature of women to hunger for relatedness just as it is the nature of men to pursue rank and power. The masculine western religions therefore promise power to the men and comfort and protection to the women. It is the only way to get men to take religion seriously and to distract the women from engaging in worldly affairs that only puzzle and perplex them. The Jews and the Mormons in particular make it their practice to initiate their young men early into adult responsibilities; this limits the natural destructiveness of male youth."

"The Moslems do even better than the Jews and Mormons by enlisting their youth into the practice of armed warfare by sanctifying violence and martyrdom in battle. The women lose interest in taking their normal religious roles in nations where Islam prevails because religion in these nations has been taken away from the female domain almost entirely. This is why the Moslems make virtual slaves of their women and wrap them up in various guises like a tarpaulin thrown over so much pillaged or stolen booty. There are no greater brutes than the Moslem men or any that are more cunning. Do you see why I say this? Very well; I will explain. The Moslem men do not confine their brutality to the treatment of their women, but to the young men as well. The problem with polygamy is that it leaves a superfluity of unattached young males who cannot find a mate. What does one do to keep them from raiding the harem? It is simple really, kill the young blighters off in war and tell them that they can get their share of virgins in another world! They get fifty or sixty, I forget the exact number, but that is immaterial; the point is that they don't get any here and now. Their elders are safe and the women, if not necessarily happy, are at least well provided for by the older and richer Moslem gentlemen. There must be something to the practice because Islam has managed to survive as a religion. A religion must always be evaluated for its material appeal."

"As for the Koran, it may be admirable as poetry if one has nothing better to read, but once translated into English it seems little more than a string of redundant assurances of a final day of judgment where the unbelievers will receive the punishment of unbelief. I should have thought that one reference would have been sufficient. But the initial audience was a bunch of battle-ravaged nomads, so maybe Mohammed needed to hammer the point home. I should not like to compose scripture myself. I prefer mathematics. One concise formula has about it more of truth and utility than long lists of Levitical prohibitions and liturgical duties, both evidently of interest to God. Well all that I can say is if that is so then God is easily amused."

Professor Moriarty looked up as if to assess my reaction. "You no doubt find it offensive for me to speak of God so slightingly and as if God was a person or a concept like any others. I assure you that I have not lost my metaphysical bearings by speaking so tangentially about the absolute being of God; but is that not what all theology does, to speak about what cannot be spoken of? Let is recall, as we so seldom do, that words are a human phenomenon; the universe does not speak to us in words but in events, in phenomena. This is why the only true phenomenology lies in pre-verbal perceptions. The mind of man grasps at reality before engaging in reflection; then reflection in turn produces words that formulate and memorialize the pre-verbal event. The old question of whether a tree falling in a forest makes a sound simply points out this fact: the tree falling would create a disturbance in the ambient air but it takes a perceiver to hear 'a sound.' I will go further still and suggest that the phrase, 'a tree has just fallen,' is memorializing an event by formalizing it into words. If those words in turn are actually spoken and to a listener who in turn can hear that phrase, then an act of communication has taken place. But even if the hearer witnesses the falling of the tree in solitude the habit of translating the event immediately into words is so built into the way that our mind operates that the words seem to jump forth simultaneously with the event that elicits them."

"Do you follow me thus far? Excellent! So now let us turn to this habit of speaking familiarly of God, a habit as familiar as it is erroneous. God is not an event like other events, rather God stands behind events and can only be known through them. Therefore, to speak of God is to leap beyond events to their cause without noticing the conceptual gap between them. God as God cannot be spoken of because the mind would then be probing across an indeterminate 'space' (note the metaphor) that separates *what God is from what God does*. This is why blasphemy to my way of thinking comes closer to God than orthodoxy because the blasphemer at least realizes that any human incivility when directed at God is a futile gesture. God is not accessible to our insults, at least not as God. God would have to become one of us and subject himself to our conceptions before He would be an object for our derision or of our praise. For this reason I find the worship of God to be as disrespectful as to abuse Him. Both imply that God would ever stoop to our level. I prefer mathematics, a language that merely formulates the laws of nature while saying nothing of the great mathematician who may have set those laws in place."

"We may be getting too far afield; but let me anticipate an immediate objection that you will raise. You will insist that the Bible is *the word of God*. Am I right? Ah, I see that I am; but what does that phrase actually mean? Is the Bible a collection of words that God speaks to himself (to take the tree falling in the woods analogy that we have just used)? Does the mind of God perceive events as words before or after the fact? Did God say 'I will now make a tree' and then proceed to make it? Is God subject to time and space? But if not then where shall we find Him? Does God premeditate His actions before engaging in them as we do? Would it not be absurd to imagine God needing to reflect upon alternative courses of conduct before acting, (and in the best manner possible) when it is God himself who defines that which actually is the best course to pursue by simply acting at all? Surely this is why the very idea of God ever contradicting himself is also absurd. If we are to understand the will of God all we need to do is to observe what is and by definition that must be the will of God. Even contingent events (if there are any such things) must be allowed by God. God would need to vacate a theater of existence (again note the metaphor) for us to act with free-will, although we will never be able to validate that position (the existence of free-will) as the British philosopher, David Hume pointed out."

"But if the Bible is not *the word of God,* then what is it? I suggest that the anthology of books collected to form the Bible is *the word of God for us*; in other words it is the word of God insofar as we can conceive of God having words at all. That fundamental insight is the basis from which any theology must begin. Hermeneutics must precede any effort in theology. We must acknowledge that our wishes and desire for God must play an equal if not even more salient role in the composition of the Bible than God. The Bible is a book written by us, to express what we conceive God to be, in order to live up to our idea of God. The Bible records the creation of God by man at least as much as it records the creation of man by God."

"Who can read the Bible and not remark the ever-present themes of blood and death of conquest and subjugation? Who can review the long record of Christian civilization and not observe the working out of those very themes under kings and popes and under the nobility of the feudal orders, the dukes and barons in alliance with the bishops and the priests who are their vassals. Who were the ones sacrificed in all of the wars, the crusades, the executions of heretics, the witches burned, with the laity left to die of hunger in the ruined fields and then told that the earth is blighted and God affronted by their sins and therefore they must suffer and die. Their pain is their fault and they would even now be languishing in paradise if they had not dared in the person of Adam and Eve to covet the knowledge between good and evil, a difference that their own rulers make daily manifest to anyone who cares to observe or to recall the course of history."

"How long shall the nations of the earth and civilizations every bit as venerable and ancient be subjected to the sentiments and narratives filtered down through the ages from the wrinkled parchments in Hebrew and in Greek, languages of dead kingdoms and empires artificially preserved by ritual and by indoctrination beneath the threat of blood and subjugation upon the innocent peoples that lived in unity and peace with the world and found it to be beautiful and good. These native peoples revered whatever forces stood behind and in intimate union with their daily lives before the arrival of the Europeans. By what right are their native myths displaced only to have grafted upon them by force and slavery the unnatural growth of a desert culture so different from their own fertility and plentitude? This is the course of empire, one greased and enabled by religious doctrines, and it is this course of action and subjugation that I oppose."

"If I can convince you in no other way that any authoritative text, one not derived from empirical evidence and subject to later review and correction, or made more credible by parallel validation from other sources, such as the Bible claims to be, should be approached in the utmost suspicion, let this argument suffice: the same institution that proclaims the Bible to be the Word of God derives its own authority from with the very text that it then proclaims to be true. One hand washes the other! In other words the Bible says that Jesus appointed twelve apostles as his definitive witnesses entrusted with His authority through their successors the bishops, but the existence and extent of that commission is dependent upon the very document upon which they must pronounce a judgment of validity. The circularity between text and institution is evident at first glance and everything that we know of human nature suggests that wherever power and control of the lives of others is concerned bias and a tendency towards self-interest must at least be suspected."

"You of course will answer, 'But these are holy men that we are speaking of!' to which objection I will answer, 'They are deemed by you to be holy because their doctrine proclaims them to be so, whereas I desire to subject that very doctrine to a critique!'"

"If you still persist in objecting and insist that I judge the doctrine by the results that it produces for the individual and for the social order, then you fall into my trap because I will then use empirical evidence to show you that Christianity produces little more than guilt, fear, and anxiety in the individual and social fragmentation in the countries where that unfortunate belief system has been introduced. Christianity has been the fomenter of wars for two millennia and the instigator of conquest of foreign lands among people that have managed quite well to govern their lives and to prosper without it. So now let us pause to summarize my position. You see how the habit of the classroom has infected my every utterance."

"I maintain that the gods serve functional purposes in a creature like man that has, quite honestly, evolved beyond its natural station. We were meant by nature to be happy fornicating monkeys. Like rats and mice we were meant to survive by a constant series of pregnancies. Young women bloom in a day and wilt before noon. The Arabs at least realize this and their society keeps women supported and pregnant by the men best able to ensure their safety and fecundity. The Mormons have copied them and polygamy is *de rigueur* in the American deserts of Utah. But to stick to my summation, religion has over time grown to fail in its survival function for the human species. You may ask 'How has religion failed?' My answer is by elaborating too many strictures and making the ultimate pay-off contingent upon keeping the endless commands and adhering to the elaborate codes of conduct and worship devised by priests and imams. This merely makes for a great number of unhappy fornicating monkeys, depressed as they contemplate the proximity and inevitability of hell for the majority of the human race."

"The exclusivity and refinement of the path to salvation will by definition leave vast swaths of humanity outside the door of paradise. Only men like John Calvin enjoy a religion where the majority of mankind no doubt must go to hell. Meanwhile, there is nothing as obnoxious as a disappointed monkey, especially if that disappointed monkey is of the priestly caste! Out of sheer envy he will make life universally miserable by condemning in others the very things that he would like to do himself. Such men see evil everywhere but in themselves!"

"There is then this entire question of choosing the correct religion among so many contenders. The sheer multitude of religious persuasions makes a rational choice of the correct one virtually impossible. The reasoning man today is beset everywhere by contending bidders for his soul, but to choose any one religion is to be condemned by all the others as an infidel. The man then who would really wish to save his soul will clutch them all to his breast, play a variety of hands, and hope that at least one will have a good supply of aces; or he will do as I have done, believe in none of them, adopt a functional analysis towards religion, and commit himself to survival and then live is life not by indirect means to obtain heaven, but by direct ones to make this earth a better place for the innocent to live."

"Such a man will look to the promises of the future that are made in the Messianic prophesies and do his best to make them actualize them by his own efforts. He will cease to condemn men for being men and women for being women and if he chooses to exercise the so-called higher virtues, he will do so expecting no thanks or reward in heaven but only his own approval of his own actions freely chosen. He will not waste his few short days and nights in regret or penance but rather get about the business of living!"

"We all must die you know, with religion or without it. We perish and none shall call us back. Others may take our place, but they will be others and not us, and it is they who will reap the harvests of historical progress or regression. I do not feel compelled to be virtuous or for that matter evil either. I think that both terms are mere tools for casting guilt upon those who are more successful then we may be. When I gaze at the young, oblivious in their beauty and with their whole lives ahead of them, I reflect that surely these young creatures are rich enough without adding to them my own privations to purchase more for them. Is it not enough that they will inherit the Pantheon, the Great Pyramids of Egypt, and the Palace of Versailles? Yet I do not covet life. I am weary, Holmes, wearier perhaps even than you with your recurrent bouts of lung fever. So I have elected to use my last years to live in comfort and to make a contribution to posterity by eliminating one of the chief causes of misery in Africa, India and China by destroying the British Empire. So if my words mean anything to you at all I must ask, 'Why must you oppose me?'"

Professor Moriarty paused to light a cigar with a coal from the fireplace before continuing, "The Buddhists recognize this great weariness that comes with age, the realization that life was not so beautiful after all, so that one would wish to indefinitely prolong it with the few chance pleasures that come our way. What is one more epic act of fornication or one more feeding at the trough after all? The good Buddhist shakes his head at the lecherous Mohammedan, dreaming of his garden filled with Houris. Buddhism counsels the believer to adopt celibacy and to despair early on in life. Desires beget nothing more than more desires. The Buddhist position on life and death is close to my own position, so I respect them. Buddhism counsels that one should forget and abandon any hope of futurity. I believe that there could be no greater vengeance that God could ever enact upon man or woman than to allow them to live forever. After a few billion years we would beg for extinction out of sheer boredom."

He smoked for awhile in silence.

"But then I have quite run away with myself again have I not? You now know my views. I wished today to hear more from you, to hear of your travels. I hear from Colonel Moran that you kept a journal and that you labored on it constantly while you were abroad. I hope you will not ask me to read it. Surely a summary will suffice. If the existence of God is self-evident, then a few simple equations may make your entire manuscript superfluous. As I grow older brevity has become my only passion and I have broken my own rule today merely out of a desire to be comprehensive. Garrulousness seems to be an inbred trait of old men. That is why their passing is seldom treated as a great tragedy. Pray try some of the tobacco from that humidor there on the table.

It is a mixture of American Burley and Turkish from Smyrna with just a touch of Latakia. I do not smoke as much myself as I would like to do. My constitution will not permit it, but I do enjoy the aroma of fine tobaccos."

I proceeded to do as the Professor indicated. I lit my clay pipe and as the smoke circled about above my head, I looked beyond the old man who sat before me and seemed to see again the vision of the starved lad that he once was when he came to us at Sigerside so many years ago, with his dull eyes so very near to death. The death that had eluded him then was now closer and I could sense somehow behind all of his confidence and braggadocio the terror that he felt at the coming extinction of that great brain in its crippled and aged body. I was surprised again at the diffuse and spontaneous nature of his discourse.

I had expected his approach to the questions that lie before us to be dry and systematic. I suppose that I expected him to draw a few equations on a blackboard and to explain that though they might exceed my comprehension, they proved definitively that there was no God. Instead he had overwhelmed me with a series of observations, the general import of which, was that religion may serve a function on a quite practical level and must therefore be a mere human construct.

But if the human mind may apprehend truths beyond itself, which it may in what I believe to be any valid epistemology, then it should be able to assert definitive propositions about the world and of God, even if those propositions are religious and exceed human sense perceptions. Certainly mathematical truths would seem to be indubitable and not a result of our own practical use of them to measure and to design. I believed that this might provide an opening for me, so I proceeded to appeal to mathematics when I began my answer to him.

July 12, 1893
Kings Pyland

I hope today to reconstruct the remnant of our most pregnant conversation the other day, one where I felt that we had finally come to grips with each other.

"Professor Moriarty, you have chosen to adopt a cynical and mocking tone as you have described the history and nature of the various faiths. I need hardly remind you of the logical fallacy of the *non sequitur*, which you have employed throughout your discourse, perhaps merely to intimidate me by force of rhetoric. Much of what you have set forth is idealized. Your critique of history ignores the fact that without the Bible as a moderating force the course of European history might have been even more horrific.

To begin then, it is not a valid argument against religion to show that God may have led His chosen people through quite prosaic events rather than to have depended upon the miraculous at every turning point of their history. That the Jewish people may have adopted a literary style that gave emphasis to the extraordinary in order to punctuate and even to accentuate the cardinal points of their particular history in their written accounts is a quite natural human tendency after all. What nation does not attempt to distinguish its history from that of its neighbor nations by elaborating its own mythology of great men and astonishing and heroic events?"

Professor Moriarty answered, "This is true Holmes, but not every nation has chosen to burden the other nations of the world with their private national God. I am quite certain that the Sioux and the Navaho have a belief in a deity of a sort but they do not expect the world to worship that deity. Here we speak of the case of the Jews, an obscure tribal people, one that by the mere chance of reducing their own vision to writing in the form of the texts that were later chosen to be assembled and preserved as the Bible, claim to record the definitive religion of the entire earth, tribe that has dared to make their moral vision normative for all times and places. Surely, this was a great presumption, particularly in view of the rather checkered history of the chosen people themselves."

"The main burden of the scriptures that they have recorded seems to be to recount one long series of violations of the supposed compact they claim to have concluded with God. Why should we take their word for anything other than the manifestation of a troubled national conscience? The Jews seem never to be happy. If I must worship any god, I should prefer one whose chosen people are optimists and who affirm life rather than one whose primary character seems to rest in a desire to issue an endless stream of commands that the issuing god should have known in advance would be certainly broken. If I were a god I would try one commandment at a time and wait a few hundred years until its practice became universal before adding another. I should not waste my time with mandated sacrifices of birds and other animals. I should not, among other things, consider victims of leprosy to be seen as morally unclean or worry about fringes to be placed on garments. You must admit that most of the commands of the Torah seem designed to give employment to the priests of the temple. Judaism is the apotheosis of the arbitrary. The whole thing seems to me to savor of mystification rather than of mystery."

"Or let us turn to the Koran that was supposedly written by God himself; if so, he is surely repetitious! The whole thing seems to consist of warnings that there will be a final day of judgment that the unbelievers will deny, thus meriting a severe chastisement. Very well, but must one then waste most of an entire sacred text haranguing those very unbelievers? They will be unlikely to read the text in any case. I should rather make room for those believers who would like to get on with some actual ethical teaching. The gospels at least do pose a rather impractical but definite program for believers. Still, I suppose that Mohammed did manage to weld a diverse people together into a single purpose and to get the Arabs past the stage of worship present in mere animistic beliefs, so at least some progress was made at the time."

"The result was that a great army was forged that spread

the Islamic message over half the earth. I will even admit that for sheer civilization, Islam was at various times in history well in advance of Christian culture, particularly in mathematics, but also in mercy shown to other belief systems. Christianity in contrast seems to be a religion with the primary criterion that one should not take-up the sword, but rather to pray for one's enemies. Unfortunately, this demand has, even today, yet to be attempted by any Christian nation of consequence. As an example, I have always thought that the absurd *'Battle Hymn of the Republic'* sung by the Americans that supported the Union cause, as they proceeded with a war that slaughtered their brothers of the southern states, represented in its sentiments the very nadir of Christianity in America. Most Christians seem to be never happier than when they are at war. Seek to deny this and you must ignore two thousand years of Christian history."

"The followers of Islam, on the other hand, always speak of war but prefer peace, while Christians speak of peace but prefer war. As for the Chinese, they simply wish to be the Middle Kingdom and to exact reasonable tribute from other national groups in exchange for contributing Chinese concepts of arts and civilization to the world. I personally much prefer the Chinese way! I suppose that if I must have a god, I would prefer that he be manifest in nature and any scripture longer than a poem from the Tang dynasty is probably repetitious and superfluous."

Here Professor Moriarty paused to await my answer and when one was not forthcoming he proceeded, "If God is simple and undivided and one, it would appear that there is little more to say of Him than what could be said in a short poem by Lao Tsu. I prefer an aloof god who lets men be men, one that is satisfied to let the rain fall on the crops and to allow the grass to grow. The religions of the world that seek a closer acquaintance with God seem really to distort the benevolent nature that we must assume such a supreme being would possess. The result is that a vast theology must be elaborated to explain why a generally benevolent God needs to vindicate His dignity by being offended when men and women sin, which by the way they would not do if so many things were not forbidden them in the first place!"

"Again we return to the superfluity of moral strictures. Add into this mix a need to actually ascertain whether one is saved or not and you have the aberrations of John Calvin who must have been a most sour individual, a haunted man who wished to be better than he was. It is the desire for moral perfection that makes most people become religious brutes. They wish to whip mankind into shape as it were, so that the kingdom of God may be realized here on earth, whereas I believe that Jesus Himself said that His Kingdom was not to be one found in this world. Christianity proclaims that God is merciful, but only until a man dies, after which mercy is withdrawn and judgment occurs. Therefore, when God's mercy is most needed, it is found to be absent. Most men die in their sins, unrepentant and imperfect, but nevertheless still manifesting some degree of virtue and of dignity. Do these go to hell or does God look back and credit them with the few good things they may have done in their life and credit them with at least some evidence of a lasting good-will? Is the time of judgment simply a matter of chance and the outcome dependent upon the availability of a priest at the time of death to absolve? If that is so, then every good Catholic such as yourself should pray for a long lingering death and hope that he is not struck down suddenly while in the arms of his mistress."

"But do go on with your own presentation. You must allow me an occasional observation though since it will shorten our discussion. No doubt you would wish me to simply read a catechism and then to check-off the mysteries as I go through them page by page until at the end you would suddenly find me to have become a believer. But is this the way men and women actually come to embrace faith? Or is it not rather that they first embrace the Catholic faith in the vaguest of outlines and only later realize how many dogmas they must accept later on in order to stay clear of apostasy. Catholicism has always seemed to me to be a trap—once one enters there is no graceful way to escape. One starts by a vague desire for community and ritual and ends up with the strictures of Canon Law! So perhaps you may not speak freely while remaining a Catholic. If that is so, then our dialogue is pointless. If I must steer clear of blasphemy all the way, then I must silence those questions that are precisely those that should be placed before any sincere catechist or catechumen for answers prior to conversion. How may one commit one's whole soul to what one does not even understand? Yet I venture to say that if one purged from the Church all of the Catholic faithful who have only a primary level of understanding of their faith, there would be few to attend Mass on Sunday and fill the passing basket of offerings. It is fortunate then that through most of Church history the faithful could by and large not even read."

"Perhaps stained-glass windows have saved more souls than the writings of even St. Thomas Aquinas! Even now, which persons fill the pews but old women and dried up old men? I have observed that one's devotion increases as the proximity of death approaches, but if youth is the time of sin and age the time of repentance, when does one finally get around to the task of demonstrating one's love for God? If most men and women are damned merely to provide a pleasing stench rising up from the abyss, does God truly love mankind or was Calvin right after all. Is the entire drama of creation and redemption merely staged for the proportionate equivalent of a parlor audience? Meanwhile the devil seems content with the *status quo* and lets each man be his own god in life if he wishes, knowing that most will come to the devil in due time."

This seemed like a good point to put in some of my own observations. "Your supposed tolerance, which you claim is shared by the devil, is the very problem with your argument," I interrupted drily. "In contrast if you will allow me the liberty I shall propose a new definition of hell. Hell is getting exactly what you want if what you want is not God."

My comment caused the Professor to pause. "What did you say?"

I repeated my formulation and then said, "Let me expand

the observation a bit. God does not appear to intervene directly for the most part in human affairs, although he does so more than most people ever suspect, and this is not for God's sake but for ours. Many men and women are quite satisfied with the results of their sin. It is a peculiarity of sin that it reduces man and woman to its own stature. Man and woman are deflated to the level of their own choices by what they do. We do in fact create our own natures. Freedom is more than mere moral choice, Professor. To act in any given instance is to define one's self by the choices that one makes."

"St. John states that we are god's children now by virtue of our adoption in Christ by the sacrament of Baptism, which makes grace available to us to accomplish what in our own nature is impossible to accomplish. God nourishes the soul by divine grace so that the soul may grow in God. The Catholic Church has not formally defined the contents or the parameters of hell. Rather it concentrates upon teaching the way to heaven. The Catholic Church never takes its eyes away from Christ who is the way, the truth, and the life. It will do no good for you to scour away at the dirty floors of the cathedral and to show me how many rags you may soil to show me how dirty the Church has often been. I would rather have you on your knees for another purpose."

"I will grant you that Christian history is often dark, but that is only so that Christ may show the brighter in what He offers to man and woman, a life with God. What that life is exceeds our present comprehension as it must; for if we could comprehend it, then truly it would be a human creation and not of God. If God communicates with humankind, that communication must meet us half-way as it were. If parts of revelation in the Bible appear to us to be absurd, one must remember that the message intended is still only conveyed to us in words and concepts that we are ill-prepared to receive. Even our most orthodox conceptions must fall far short of the reality of God. Perhaps the best way to conceive of dogma is not therefore to see it as definitive but as indicative. It is a direction and not a destination. The role of the Catholic Church is to chart the shortest and most definitive path to salvation; not to foreclose entry but to show the way for the ardent soul to attain to God."

"From this perspective for a person to be too preoccupied with hell may be the best way to end up dwelling there at last. The devil is never more offended than when his efforts are seen for precisely what they are, wholly silly and inadequate as solutions for our lives. We are made in the image and likeness of God and that image remains as a defining one for us, even in Original Sin. To get about the business of salvation is simply to become what one was always intended to be by the Creator. Why tarry along the way if the banquet is ready at hand?"

"I will grant you that the religions of the world all seem to be inadequate. If I had not found them so, I would not have sought a closer acquaintance with each of them by traveling to the sites of many of their origins or compared their various revelations to obtain a personal faith. It is true that I might have done as much by staying at home in Baker Street and opening a few books, but I needed to see actual men and women practicing their different faiths. I found nothing along the way to cause me to abandon my initial position as a Roman Catholic. Still, I must say that a man always begins by seeking God and always ends by realizing that God has been seeking him. God does the work Professor. That is the doctrine of prevenient grace."

"For that very reason it is not my object to convert you, nor is it within my own ability to do so. The responsibility for each man and woman is to their own soul. The fate of man and woman is our own choice, to live with God or not to do so. It was this choice made in Eden by Adam and Eve when they preferred as it were to strike out on their own. Men and women may indeed make their own natures. Great latitude is left to us in this regard. Some are beasts and content to remain so. Some are tyrants or termagants and would have it no other way. It is the broad way that leads to destruction. God's way in contrast is always the glimmering star of possibility, one dimly descried upon the horizon at evening. God draws near to us because we are often so far from Him and by our own choice. He even risks appearing foolish, as Jesus must have looked on the donkey entering Jerusalem. God will even be foolish if by doing so He may reach out to us. No pains are spared to find us, not even those of crucifixion! That my dear Professor Moriarty is what I have come to tell you, because that is what I have come to believe at last."

found that I had been quite carried away by my own enthusiasm of the moment. I found these words coming to me unbidden and unasked. The Professor had listened very closely and quietly to me. The air hung heavy in the room on this ripe summer evening and all outside the house was quiet, the same quiet that filled the room. My pipe had gone out and I lit it once again. After a pause of some ten minutes during which I smoked in silence the Professor stood up and turned to face me.

"I believe that we are finished for today. You are welcome to walk about the grounds and to do as you wish tomorrow. Ask my servants for anything that you may require. I believe that I will lie down for awhile. I will of course see you tomorrow at dinner."

With that he walked out of the room and closed the door behind him leaving me in the library with its shelves of books that contained much of the history of the world and many about God or such as we conceive Him to be.

July 13, 1893
Kings Pyland

fter our first encounters each of us now understands something of the other's position towards that ultimate question which must haunt all thinking men: Is there a final basis or substratum for the way that we think? Some have maintained, as does the Professor, that nature is adequate in itself to validate our thought and that the man of science is like a cephalopod reaching outwards with the tentacles of thought to embrace the part in order to know the whole. The man of religion on the contrary begins with the whole in order to understand the function of the part. The problem with science, as I see it, is that all of the facts of the world, no matter how accurately described, do not provide a reason, a purpose, or an end for existence as a whole. Science assumes that man wishes to know merely so that he can translate raw data into some adequate and accurate formulation, to make the world replicable in another form in the minds of other men. The moment that the mind of man turns beyond mere practicalities and utility achieved through technology focused on ever finer degrees of accuracy and begins to ask ultimate questions that have no immediate purpose beyond simply knowing the answer, religious aspirations become inevitable.

It might even be maintained that science is a type of religion in that it enthrones truth even at the cost of surrendering our prejudices and illusions. Science as a project must by its very nature exceed the lifetime of any one scientist or contemporary group or school of scientists. In this sense it is a species project rather than the artistic creation of an individual. There is altruism in the search for truth as such. Many a scientist has exhausted his personal resources to extend the reach of mankind as a whole. In this lies the tragedy of human life. Time does not spare the benefactors of the human race. The mind of the great scientist dies with him and all those who will someday receive the contents of that mind will likewise die and perhaps someday the entire human species will also perish.

If that happens, there will remain, as far as we now know, only the great mass of the universe, silent again in its incomprehension of itself, manifesting its various properties still to the indifferent brains of the other animals. The earth then will be crawled over by the non-questing species that remain on the earth, those happy beings that are not troubled like their human cousins with the need to formulate and to replicate knowledge, those not troubled with a need to justify their actions by comparing them to the standard set by religious conceptions of a final end and purpose for existence itself. The emotion of awe and the impulse to worship appear confined to human beings.

Mankind is obsessed by the teleological as well as the logical. It is our great undoing as a species. There may indeed be bestial humans, but humanity as a whole may never be reduced to the status of a mere beast. There will always be the few men and women, and perhaps more than we think there are, who will wake in the silent watches of the night and wonder if they are quite alone in the universe, whether it is not possible that a great and supreme mind broods over all things and intends something. Do such conscious beings as humans arise by chance out of a universe that lacks a mind corresponding to its own greatness? Does the rose bloom in such splendid color only to attract insects or to draw lovers as well on a summer's night to the gardens where they grow and to remind them with its thorns of the pains of love that must accompany all beauty? Are the senses of scent, touch, taste, and sight but the dull senses that allow for survival? Is music only an irritation of the auditory nerve or is it perhaps the best analogy to that celestial harmony that pervades all things?

It seems to me that to reduce mankind to mere transcription agents of scientific formulae is to deny so much of our experience that we may no longer claim that science is characterized by real objectivity at all. The scientist who does not honor the subjective must look at the world through a tiny aperture. He suffers from a sort of intellectual glaucoma which narrows his view to a pencil's width. The true scientist in contrast is like a great detective who must discard no clue, however obscure, but give all facts their proper weight as evidence. If he does so, he will find himself led to precisely those speculations that have haunted me all of my life. Such a man will perhaps find God at the end of his quest. At the very least he must, if he probes deeply enough into his own widest experience of life, come to entertain the necessity of the religious question.

I tried to point this out to the Professor during the subsequent conversations that we engaged in over the following days. These conversations have assumed a certain pattern. The Professor spends his mornings watching his horses as they go through their paces and I often join him at his training track. His obvious enjoyment of the grace and beauty of his horses has provided me with an opening to discuss what I feel is the path that most men and women must follow if they are to approach God.

I felt that it would be advisable to assert that position early in my stay at Kings Pyland. We had concluded our luncheon and had repaired to the library. It was clear that the Professor wished on this third day for me to take the initiative in the day's discussion, which I was happy to do after allowing him to take the initiative during the previous days, so I began at once as follows...

"You have had me at a disadvantage Professor Moriarty during the past days. You are a scientist, while I am in most respects an artist. If you insist that I produce from my travels a mere collection of raw data rather than a series of sketches and impressions you are holding me to a standard that I cannot possibly meet. My proofs for religion's efficacy and even necessity are not capable of being reduced to a mere objective formula. My manner of knowing is artistic after all, for I maintain that God is the great artificer of all that is and not a mere collection of forces without personality and without something of what we might even call emotion. A passionless God could hardly be said to have the attributes of mercy and of love. I must therefore beg you to allow me to proceed in my own fashion without subjecting my assertions to the distorting conditions of any previous idea of God that you may now possess. I do not wish to reinforce any long-standing prejudices that may have served to alienate you from God, but rather to draw you to Him, not merely to thwart your plans, but to enlist your aid in His service."

"Very well," answered the Professor. "You are entitled to proceed in your own manner, if you will allow me to proceed in mine. I promise nothing though beyond giving you a proper hearing. Do not presume though to use charm where reason is wanted if you hope to achieve your ends with me. You shall not twist me around your little finger as you do with your friend, Dr. Watson."

"Agreed Professor, I can after all not produce what is not in my own nature. My arguments, if they may be characterized as such rather than as merely a set of propositions, stem from my own peculiar talents as a detective. The so-called science of detection is actually more a matter of refined intuition rather than mere deduction. The detective without imagination and insight into the drama lying in back of the crime will usually fail by drowning in a mass of unrelated details. He may assemble any number of clues into a pattern of sorts, but find it impossible to assemble them into a coherent and actual picture of the whole. If I may say so, the scientist is in a similar quandary with regard to God. As the scientist knows more about the universe, he finds himself increasingly unable to assemble the parts into a whole and to see the Divine purpose in all of creation. Faith begins first of all then as a matter of intuition, of insight rather than deduction. The task of religion is, in the last analysis, derived from the need to personalize the universe. Then follows the second task, the believer must personalize himself in relation to that personalized universe. Let us consider these tasks in their proper order."

We will begin with the conception of a scientist as a collector of data to be later organized into various truth statements. Already we have some evidence of a proto-theory of religion, one generously provided by you of why religions exist and how they function; now we need the same proto-theory for science. We must ask the scientist on what basis he separates relevant from irrelevant data. More than this we must ask the scientist what motivates him to engage in his inquiry in the first place. Assuming that the supply of data in such a complex universe is virtually infinite how shall the scientist decide upon a criterion of what area to probe and which data are relevant to focus his search? He must even at the beginning of his quest have a basic standard of relevance. Where is he to find this if not in some intuition of the nature of the whole? But if he attempts prematurely to arrive at complete universality, he will simply reproduce the universe once again as a mere chaos of impressions rather than as distinct observations assembled around a central theory. I mention this because we must dispense at the outset with any idea that a truly objective account of the universe is possible without any consideration of the prior categories which the mind imposes upon experience."

"The second that a scientist observes anything, he has already encased some portion of reality into a discrete package. He has in other words been primordially selective. He has already made a decision as it were to include and to reject some part of what otherwise would be a mere continuum of impressions, of objects merging into other objects, of color without a limiting dimension. The human mind is condemned to select and to reject by the nature of our senses and our knowing apparatus. It was for this reason that Hume and Kant both despaired of ever attaining true human knowledge of the thing-in-itself. But if we despair at the very beginning of ever being able to arrive at some sort of knowledge, our enterprise is at an end and both you and I must abandon the field at the outset; our little game would be over."

"We must both therefore assume at the start that we will not lose confidence in human knowing and adopt a facile skepticism, even if that skeptical position has been advocated by such admittedly great minds as those of David Hume and Immanuel Kant. We must press them beyond their own strict standards of truth and falsehood by assuming that such knowledge as we may obtain is sufficient for our purpose today, which is to seek to prove or disprove God. Let me suggest here that if that is in fact the object that we both have in view we must agree upon a jointly formed methodology, one appropriate to the object of our inquiry. That methodology will become clearer as we follow the historical approaches already used to answer the question of what God is and if that knowledge has any basis other than faith."

"Let us proceed initially from a purely scholastic perspective and explore the position taken by St. Thomas Aquinas, who above all men believed that reason might prove the existence of God and illuminate the nature of God. One need not be a strict Thomist to grant him his points as they are stated. The mind of man seems to require a point of origin for existence as a whole. To assume that time, which is the source of our knowledge of cause and effect, extends backwards infinitely with linkage upon linkage of cause and effect in an infinite regression is to assume that the universe in all of its variety and forms is the product of mere cascading causes and effects with no first cause to set the whole process going."

"However, just because the human mind revolts at the prospect does not mean that the first-cause theory is correct. Suppose some natural latency in nothingness might suddenly burst forth without any outside influence at all. In that case time itself would emerge to accommodate the actualization of that spontaneous event. Similarly if time did not exist at all then by definition that latency would remain forever un-actualized, locked in mere potentiality. Therefore cause and effect relationships are dependent upon time and space in order to occur at all. This means that the focus of our inquiry and hence of our methodology, Professor, must be focused upon time and space as the ground of any being at all. Anything less would be to accept a mere assessment of local conditions after the process was already well underway; but if we are in pursuit of God we are forced above all else to focus on origins on being-as-such. Are we in agreement thus far?"

Professor Moriarty nodded his head in token of assent so I continued.

"I suggest that any valid metaphysics must focus on an admission that no method in science can hope to traverse the gap between origins and our present position in space/time, for I link the two concepts as the ground of any objectivity or event whatsoever. As to anything occurring outside of space/time we can say nothing at all. In fact the real problem in both science and in philosophy is that our language is inadequate to what we are trying first to formulate and then to convey. We will return again and again to the paradoxes of language as a vehicle of knowledge."

"For now let us simply pose for ourselves this question: if there was no point of origin or prior stability that needed to be set into motion by a first cause and even if we may imagine time as proceeding infinitely into the future from a causeless progression of events, what shall become of everything? Will events simply cease to occur at some point of time having lost whatever dynamism sustains them, thus bringing time to a screeching halt in some final state of space of maximum dispersal? Or does energy from some unknowable source continually stoke the fires of being so that entropy will never reach an end point of exhaustion. I suggest that we can know neither the beginning nor the end; we have come into the theater after the play has already begun and we must be content with taking up the thread of events as they unfold before us."

"The mind of the scientist is caught between two infinites on the narrow ledge of the point in time in which he makes observations and assigns data and must then assert that what is true today must have been true in countless yesterdays and will remain true when distributed over endless tomorrows. Unless a scientist can do this, his physics breaks down and becomes a mere recording of present conditions. The scientist then must begin with a certain faith in the timeless universality of his own language of present perception or he must simply cease to make any assertions that are not so hedged-in and qualified as to be practically meaningless."

"You see of course, Professor, how restricted scientific discourse must be. The means of attaining to all human knowledge, if we stop with science alone, will become so narrow and limited as to make the search for truth impossible of attainment. If we adopt universally such a strict standard of objectivity we hobble the full powers (limited as they are) of the human mind. We must then grant a certain degree of latitude to the powers of human knowing beyond science. This means that philosophy and perhaps even theology must be allowed as possible avenues to truth."

I paused here to make way for any objections that Professor Moriarty might care to make, but he remained silent, wary but attentive. I therefore continued my discourse.

hall we begin with your own subject of mathematics? It seems to me that here we have the perfect example of a reflexive language, one focused on fundamental internal relationships, a language that precedes any direct application in the empirical world of events. Theology in many cases mirrors this same reflexivity by implying that certain essential relationships would need to be true so that God would not appear to act in an arbitrary or contradictory fashion. Both mathematics and theology begin with set and invariable relations, the first dependent upon consistency of form and result, while the second is based upon the conviction that scriptural language can express Divine Revelations that are absolutely true and capable of being formulated as doctrine or dogma. Doubt in either of these realms is not permitted, because they deal in certainties."

"However, I suggest that any direct comparison between the two realms of knowledge is inappropriate, because I would agree with you that Biblical language is often dependent upon metaphor and analogy and upon myth and allegory, all of which can never hope to have the precision and immediate power to compel assent that mathematics possesses. We must assume that mathematical truths are more than mere poetry and that the relationships existing between mass and energy for instance are both mathematically expressible and empirically true. Yet, we must remember that by calling them mass and energy we are assigning names to things unknowable in themselves, but are knowable only in relation to each other. Man learns by assembling webs of definitions and applying them to the world surrounding us. By using these webs of relations, the scientist reaches the conclusion that his observations are not merely true today but have always been true as long as the same conditions prevail as those during which he has made his observations. He projects these conditions both backwards and forwards in time as far as his eye may see."

"Man's biggest problem as a seeker of truth is thus reducible to time. If time were to have an origin in one great creative event, then human knowledge could as it were tie one end of the string to that event and claim that God was the origin and cause of that event. Because time flows in only one direction, he could then simply adopt a wait-and-see attitude and see if the same God who set all things in motion is waiting at the end as well to observe the now exhausted course of events. The individual scientist would of course be dead, but some distant successors, if the human race survives, might someday metaphorically speaking find the other end of the string and tie it to whatever harbor-mooring they may then find.”

“The human race would then at last possess a comprehensive human knowledge of all experience, but at present we do not have this degree of comprehensive certainty at our disposal and even our projections into the string of tomorrows are without experiential proof until tomorrow arrives. This means that our conclusions remain mere theory until then. Science thus becomes, if we apply the strictest of standards, a mere daily description of events. Scientific truths are in that sense a mere set of intuitions supported by partial data. They are also not dispositive of the question of the existence or the non-existence of God, thus atheism in the strict sense becomes impossible. Much of your attack on Christianity in recent days then is reducible to personal distaste rather than absolute proof and I suggest that your attack has been little more than a glancing blow on the sociology of religion made under the assumption without adequate proof that Christianity is explainable on alternate grounds than the actual existence of God and of Divine Revelation.”

Professor Moriarty spoke up here, “I am willing to concede your points so far, although I ask you to note that you are ‘throwing a very wide loop’ as the American cowboys say; be careful that your cow does not escape when you try and haul him in.”

“Excellent, thank you, Professor, you are being most generous to your guest. Let us turn then to the position of the agnostic, one who claims that the question of God is not resolvable granted the state of present knowledge. His position is that of the religious skeptic, the one who demands complete objectivity in all things, but he is selective in saying that only God’s existence is unknowable while assuming that his knowledge in other spheres is valid and complete at least in principle. However we have just demonstrated that this is not the case. The knowledge of scientific truth that we possess is sufficiently limited in the face of the two infinities of time as to be a mere photograph of a single summer's day in our species' adolescence, when like most adolescents we claim to know much about everything."

"The problem of the agnostic then is not that he is agnostic about God, but that he is not agnostic enough about everything else! He doubts the existence of God, but never thinks to rein in his own presumption of knowledge in other areas. By a similar set of proofs I could soon cause him to doubt his own existence. Descartes claims that his own existence was demonstrable because he could not doubt that he was in fact thinking, which he could not do if he did not exist. But Descartes could never prove that it was not impossible that it was the thought that was thinking Descartes and not Descartes thinking the thought! Perhaps our self-consciousness is only a derivative phenomenon of a physical event. Which is cause and which effect? We only observe the process of thought, but upon which side of the equation we exist is not strictly demonstrable. We might even be an epiphenomenon of a larger process not confined within the contours of our separate bodies. No man knows until his death that he is not alone thinking the entire universe. How disappointing it would be to find out that one was God after all and through some unaccountable accident one was undergoing a spell of amnesia and only gradually re-awakening to the fact that one is God!"

"Solipsism is a theory that might be adopted if one wishes to be completely objective and the complete agnostic may find that he may have circled around to prove the existence of God by in fact finding that God exists because he himself is God after all and that he will remain alone when all else vanishes. Can we disprove this assertion of a divine pathology? So let us then leave atheists and agnostics behind us, shall we? Those who share either position must find at last that they only lead one to muddle about in the quagmire of one's own mind."

"In other words Descartes was wrong; the real first principle is better formulated as *'We think, therefore I am.'* Absent our collective languages and traditions the discussion we are now having would be impossible and even our own consciousness of self would be problematic. Humanity must seek God if they are to seek any knowledge at all. It is here that religion makes its contribution to human knowledge by providing a foundation for thought. It does so by offering a systematic and revealed account of God. Religions in varying degrees claim to be the effort of God to communicate with man, rather than the actions of man reaching through the acquisition of knowledge in order to find God. Religion then will be valuable to us, not insofar as it takes human objectivity as its norm, but rather insofar as it presumes a radical subjectivity in man to whom God makes His appeal. God reaches out to man in his totality as a man. God does not see man fragmented, but man as whole. Therefore if man is ever to find God it must be by first contemplating his own structure as man and by finding meaning in his own existence as such to open himself to Divine Grace. Man does this not by becoming 'objective' and paring himself down with the knife of thought until even his own existence as a thinker becomes a matter of doubt, but instead by first positing a God and then proceeding from that starting point to deduce all other things. Man must dare to live up to the exalted image of what he would be if there in fact is a God. It requires that God shall be God if man is ever to be man!"

I paused here to let my last sentence resonate before continuing. "All of which is to say that if man is to be man at all and not a mere worm, he must believe in God. Without the belief in God and the God-like in man's own nature, the human enterprise qua human is at an end. Show me an atheistic government and I will show you first tyranny, then decadence and finally extinction. But there we touch on politics and we must leave that discussion for another day. For the present, we merely need to see that if God and the belief in God is a necessity, how we may sift the various revelations in order to find the one that is most God-like according to our intuition. We may find that the religions of the world may each possess their own peculiar genius and that God may have intended that in due time each might learn something from the other."

"It was for this reason that I undertook my journey Professor, and left you to your racehorses. My journal records my findings and conclusions and even my trepidations at needing someday to return to you and to have this very discussion. I will be happy to provide a transcription of it in the years that lie between us until 1897, the year when as you have said your own plan for the destruction of the British Empire will be mature. I hope that I may sway you from your projected course by then. Today, I trust, I have made a beginning. If you have followed my presentation thus far, you will at least have reached what might be called that state of mind, that position of true objectivity that will at least allow you to consider the suggestions that each religion makes regarding the origin and destiny of man, while simultaneously revealing something of the mysterious nature of God."

I fell silent at last and after a respectful interval Professor Moriarty spoke up. "An excellent presentation, Holmes, but I still would question why this need for a comprehensive grasp of all things, which is clearly the distinguishing feature of the human mind, might not simply be doomed to frustration. You have perpetually returned to the idea of a pre-existing relationship with God, which might motivate God to give the human race a second chance after the supposed sin in Eden. But if our study of our origins shows that humans are in fact a late-stage development of more primitive forms of life as Mr. Darwin asserts, then what becomes of this story of Eden in the Book of Genesis? This is not even to mention the problems and improbabilities of the story and the chain of custody of what occurred with no written records to memorialize the event let alone to validate the accuracy of the quoted conversations. If continuous evolution is the rule of life, when was this supposed time and where did the man and the woman walk with God before needing to adapt overnight to a world of labor, of pain and death, with neither skills nor crafts to guide them and ensure their survival? Did the event even occur except as a literary formulation? What does it even mean to consort familiarly with the God of metaphysics? How did God appear to them? Or is Eden merely a romantic conception of our peaceful animal existence prior to being burdened with a human conscience?"

"Your theory seems to imply that humans were at one time both smarter and more virtuous than they are today and that during that period they committed some sin of presumption that was intended to make them equal to God. Where is the evidence that this exalted state of affairs ever existed? It seems more probable that the forbidden action did not take place in a momentary encounter involving forbidden fruit. The entire event as recounted is more likely to have been only a homely and simplistic summary of a general human tendency made manifest perhaps over many generations of human thought or actions and then dramatized into a single encounter with a serpent."

"If this more sensible assessment of the story is the better one, then the 'original sin' was committed, not by individuals, but rather by the human race as a whole and the realization that it had been committed becomes a late-stage realization of the writer or writers of Genesis who suddenly felt themselves to be alone in the universe and wondered how they ever became so. According to this reading and interpretation Genesis projects back into time a relationship that never existed that seemed editorially necessary to the author to describe the state of moral confusion observed in a complex society. The whole problem with the interpolation of this story in Genesis is misplaced genre, a case of attribution to history of what is only an allegory."

"I suggest to you that this theory of yours of the moral necessity of a God to vindicate man's existence if true is a latter-stage development of your own philosophical thought. To the more unsophisticated Hebrew mind no such necessity was implied. The gentle nurturing God of Christianity and the demanding God of the Old Testament become alike only in an evolving literary creation of the Jewish people, the same people whose nationalistic aspirations have now burdened all of mankind with this mythology."

Professor Moriarty paused to gage the effect of his words

upon me before continuing, "I will however grant you that intellection is certainly the greatest anomaly in a universe that does not seem to demand more from us than mere adaptation for physical survival, like the other animals. If mankind demands more of itself and seeks an explanation of origins and purpose, then perhaps that inexplicable tendency is our 'original sin.' The primal sin of man is in seeking an explanation rather than merely living and accepting death gracefully. For man to create the concept of a Perfect Being then is already to find his own human nature imperfect. To account for that imperfection he deems himself and his fellow human beings to be sinners. I suggest to you that man is innocent in the face of God, for God is a mere catch-all term for man's puzzlement before his own condition as man."

"Mankind creates its gods to help solve this puzzle and in no time at all the questing man is caught up in an even greater quandary. He must now explain to himself why God, being supreme, all-knowing and all-powerful, does not solve the problem of evil at once by divine fiat. If man is a sinner, why then the solution is a simple purgative process that should be well within the capacity of an all-perfect being: simply reach into the mind of man and purge it of its flaw! If God does not do so, then the fault is his, not ours. If I design a machine and it later develops flaws inherent in my initial design, either I discard it and begin again, or I correct the defective part. Surely nothing can be simpler. This elaborate account of yours that makes God need to adopt this circuitous route of what is called salvation history, reduces the very dignity that would be required for a God of all of creation, one who is able to design the laws of the universe. You must choose, Holmes, you may either have the Grand Creator God who creates planets and galaxies and the laws of evolution that finally resulted in man, or you may have your tribal Jewish God, who once walked about in Eden with our naked ancestors, the God later dwelling in tent or temple. But you will not convince me that they are the one same God who manifests such different characteristics. Once again I urge you to read the writings of the Jewish philosopher, Baruch Spinoza, who realized that God is the totality of all things and not an independent principle standing outside of the universe, drawing it forth from nothingness into being. There is no simple divine command that things shall come into being, no point of origin for time and space, and no dimensionless realm of the spiritual called heaven. God is implicit and co-extensive with the universe and the man who would wish to obey God must consult nature and not the sacred writings of any particular culture. I will in short grant you a God of sorts, but not a creator, and certainly not the God of the Jews, the Christians, and the Moslems."

"If that will satisfy you and if you will find in nature some reason to oppose my plans to destroy that most unnatural growth, the British Empire, then I will abandon those plans. If, on the other hand, you quote some supposed revelation to me and use it as a basis to condemn my actions, you will fail because no religious tradition anywhere in the world has so civilized the hearts of men that they have surrendered the use of violence to achieve their goals. Religious belief has always been spread by conquest and death to the unbelievers, as the Moslems know well."

"By the way, I have a certain fondness for the Moslem mind. It sees compassion in Allah, but shows none itself. There is no religion in extremes that is more brutal than Islam unless it is the Hindu worship of Kali or the ghastly sacrifices of the Aztec Indians of Mexico. Islam shows the implacable nature of the desert out of which it rose. It is a desert faith, just as Judaism is in its way."

I recall that I interrupted him at this point. "I must protest Professor. You have hardly given me a fair hearing today. I was attempting to simply show the philosophical necessity for a God and you have shifted the ground to a consideration of particular religious traditions. The two questions are severable. The first question is designed to open the mind. Yours was no sooner pried open before it snapped shut once again. I am perfectly willing to discuss the probability of any particular religious doctrine to be the most likely one to be true, but you seem to have rejected any possibility that revelation is a gradual temporal process that must be adapted to the relative sophistication and the readiness of the mind of any group of people in order to accept what is revealed. But since you have again taken the reins of our joint inquiry into your own hands, please proceed."

Professor Moriarty seemed to appreciate my spirited interruption, but he continued anyway. "Very well, I shall. If I were ever to adopt a faith of my own I think I would go to some lush tropical island and ask the inhabitants about their gods. I would consult a people of plenty eating sweet cocoanuts and bread-fruit or mangos about God and steer clear of the stingy and vengeful gods of the desert regions of the earth. These desert gods burden men and women with elaborate laws and demands before they may enjoy even the natural bounties of the earth. Such gods demand constant thankfulness like a burdensome parent chary of his gifts. Give me a god who is truly gracious and not some petulant being always taking offense at everything and hiding heaven behind the ghastly rigors of death! If my last sight of earth could be the green water breaking on a reef and of the mothers of my own plump and laughing brown-skinned children, gathered about me singing a song at my passing and pressing a last cool drink into my hands, what need would I have then of paradise? I would have had as much of it as any contingent being needs to have had in his life."

For a brief moment a remarkably serene smile reposed upon his face. Then he continued in a more aggressive tone, "Most religions are the creation of people who have never been happy. Happiness is reserved for a future state so that these people of religion may make life as miserable as it can be now with an endless supply of regulations. Religion was the advent of the bureaucratic mind. Long before capitalism enslaved man, religion had already done so. A priesthood or council of elders or an imam is always on the board of directors of the great corporate bodies of religion. That corporation promises to pay dividends from time to time in religious ecstasy and to repay the principal of one's investment after death in some version of paradise; but re-payment never occurs because the shareholder always dies before the maturity date on the celestial bond and the instrument of debt is cancelled."

"Show me a church or chapel without a collection plate! Look at Rome that is your own Mecca, Holmes; what is Rome but a city groaning under the weight of marble and corpses? I would rather the center of the Church had been Venice and not Rome. It would then be quietly sinking beneath the Adriatic Sea taking its glories with it, its two-thousand years of extortions from the faithful to feed the fat Cardinals in their red hats! Every religious leadership invalidates its own pretensions and message by its own conduct in creating the governing structures that ensure orthodoxy. Religion thus invalidates itself by simply being a religion. You see, I also seek the universal meaning, Holmes; if not I would not be the scientist that I am. I even seek morality and feel that I have found it at last, not in religion, but rather in revolution and in individual retribution imposed upon the great powers of this world!"

"Look at my hands, Holmes; they tremble at times, so that I may only with difficulty adjust the focus on my telescope. I gaze into the heavens and what do I find there but order and silence and the majesty of the stars. I seek nothing beyond them, but I would give to the earth something of their peace. When I destroy this monstrous England and its far-flung commerce, I will liberate the struggling masses of India, end the exportation of opium into China, and allow the natives of the Caribbean to drink the rum and savor the sugar that they export to the big landowners at home in England. Even Ireland will be free at last from British exploitation and if I live long enough I will turn to America and repay it for its slaughter of the Sioux and the Arapaho and the Cheyenne tribes of Indians. That is morality, Holmes, to kill the killers, to decimate the decimators, and to free the humble of the earth at last."

"If you oppose me, you only strengthen the hands of the masters of the world against those who labor to sustain the very structures of their unjust gain. Every generation should have at least one great purge of the malefactors so that equality may become again at least a remote goal and ideal for the vast majority of mankind. Our century has not yet had such a purge of the great powers, but it is coming. Mark my words, Holmes! The new century will witness a war of the great European empires for domination and they will all topple into ruin. When the war comes it will kill more men than I propose to do with my little scheme, so speak not to me of slaughter. Mine is a mere backfire to burn the undergrowth away, so that the final conflagration of England will be less intense. There is mercy in my madness, Holmes. If even God has his hell, then you must allow me to have mine."

There our conversation ended for the day. I did not attempt to give a rebuttal, for I needed time to assimilate the Professor's vision, which is so unlike my own and to attempt once again to find behind his words the roots of his own great bitterness. Some of his arguments were not without merit, but they seemed to me to show only the greater need for a Savior of all Mankind and to make necessary the advent of Christ. The coming of Jesus is the only good news that human beings have ever received from out of the mystery of life and death that we lead upon this troubled earth. If the evils of this world are so great that even the religions of the world have not been spared its presence in their conduct, it must have been necessary it seemed to me, that God must finally die upon a cross so that man might live. The great must become the small, the powerful must become the weak, and the Absolute God must assume the guise of the least of men as the Son of Man, which was what Jesus always called Himself.

Before I close this account of our spirited discussion today I recall that we began with the joint search for an answer to this question: where does one find God if not in subjective awareness? The bitterness of the attack that the Professor made upon the Middle Eastern religious traditions today and during our previous discussions make it necessary for me to attempt a summary of his position and to find a way to answer his objections, not by proof from outside, but from a proof derived and distilled from within the individual human soul, even the soul of Professor Moriarty.

He seems to be looking for a foundationless justification for his own actions by first undermining Christian thought by mounting an assault upon Christian praxis, whereas the basis of Christian belief is that sin is a reality and that God rescues us from all of our ills, not the least of which are derived from ourselves and trace their source to that very willfulness that Professor Moriarty insists on making the basis for his own actions, without facing the fact that he must then grant all other human beings that same scope and latitude of unquestioned action. He insists on morality but refuses to ground that morality in a source of certainty beyond his own convictions.

In contrast I am suggesting that Christianity rests upon a balance between the knowable and the unknowable, that axioms of thought are unavoidable, and that the axioms of Christianity for all of their poetic language are better grounded than the sterile data of the scientific imagination as it piles up formulae, but never condescends to deal with the most perplexing problems of the scientist's own existence. My own position is grounded in the most obvious sense of reality that we possess: our sense of joy and sorrow, of love and hatred, of hope and fear, of faith and abandonment. Professor Moriarty evidently wishes to ignore each and all of these questions because they do not fit into his prematurely closed universe where what any man or woman chooses to do must be accepted as singular and not subject to review by any higher authority than one's own perceptions and will. Tomorrow I will seek to dislodge that theory.

July 15, 1893
Kings Pyland

We met as usual in the evening surrounded by the Professor's extensive library with the leather-bound volumes serving as mute witnesses of the dead authors who had committed to paper and parchment their own assessment of the human condition over centuries of speculation and contested views. I began with a summary of what I believed to be the overarching philosophical basis for the views of Professor Moriarty.

"I must begin by taking issue with your reduction of Christian belief to a mere subset of European History and also with the individualistic tenor of your own position. The Catholic Church is by its very nature aspirational and directed to a supernatural end. As such it can never be summed up in the conclusions or actions of any historical period. Catholicism is also a communal activity that embraces individual human actions only insofar as they advance the Kingdom of God by transforming lives so that as St. Paul says so well that it is not he who lives, but Christ who lives in St. Paul. The goal of the Christian is to be so transparent that the life of God shines through him with only such tint or modification that grace is enhanced by the medium through which it passes."

"Your own position, as I understand it Professor, begins with the idea that each religion fills a cultural need within a given society and that to meet that need it adapts its doctrines so that what we end up with is not a true picture of God, but only a self-portrait of a people. My answer to that assertion is that assuming that God wished to communicate with us He would naturally do so in a manner that is most meaningful to us, true revelation must be one that best meets our needs. A revelation that does not meet the needs, not only of a society, but even of individuals precisely as each of us is with our own particular needs and concerns, would be unworthy of a loving God. Revelation must in other words be seen as valuable within a given cultural setting in order to be understood and preserved."

"Any religion that is incomprehensible to a being whose intellectual nature precludes the acceptance of any image of God that fails to live up to the cultural values of the group in which one finds oneself would be judged not as mysterious and impressive, but as foolish and of little worth. God can only speak to us individually and collectively as we are at a given point in our religious development and then gradually bend human nature through the action of Divine Grace and through the elaboration of religious doctrines that grow more clear and accurate as the experience of a people allows for a deeper knowledge of God."

"Your second point is that God is responsible as creator for every act of his creation and if creation should go awry, then either God is totally responsible and should accustom Himself to the flaws of his creation or should alternatively step in to interfere with our freedom. From this dilemma you conclude that there is no God. You conclude this because since God is perfect He could not create a flawed creation. But creation is flawed and therefore you conclude that there can be no God unless that God shares the same imperfection as His creation."

"God's very attribute of perfection should long since have demanded that He either obliterate our flawed and evil world or correct it by simply erasing any evil tendencies, even before they can work their ill intent. However, you then switch your ground and imply that God is imperfect after all, so that any worship of Him is to bow before tyranny and arbitrary actions on the part of God. If God takes offence at our sins, it must be because of a desire to protect His own Divinity and to secure His unjustifiable authority over supine creation. You believe that God is an all-powerful bully, rather like your own father was in his conduct toward you."

"I on the other hand would propose that our continued survival in spite of our manifold human wickedness is the best proof that we have for the mercy of God towards us, which is shown by His twin desire to redeem the wicked and to strengthen the virtuous. If man and woman are made in the image and likeness of God, they possess a dignity that we may only with difficulty comprehend. Part of that dignity is that God may not obliterate mankind any more than He may obliterate Himself, nor may he interfere with our freedom. Man and woman have an eternal nature and hence may never be comprehended from an entirely naturalistic point of view as mere animals. You may say that this is less an act of God than it is an act of the sheer presumption of an arrogant monkey whose entire history belies any sort god-likeness existing in human nature, but I in turn could show you instances of heroic virtue and self-sacrifice in human beings that makes the most ignoble actions of mankind appear to be as nothing in comparison. However, let us not debate the relative weight of individual cases of virtue and of vice in the balance of human history as bearing upon the stature to be afforded to human nature before God, but let us simply admit that both have been present and that the man who wishes to take a jaundiced or a romantic view of human nature will always have examples to cite ready at hand."

"Your third point is that a more sophisticated concept of God is provided by the pantheism of Spinoza to which a simple answer may be given that there is no evidence that the whole of creation is collectively conscious of itself. A God that is the mere totality of physical events can hardly be thought of as a conscious willing agent capable of creation or anything else. To assume that the universe creates itself is of course a mere tautology and we need not proceed in that direction. The only remaining choice would be to assume that the universe is a mere series of processes without a final cause or origin. One in effect finds a pot boiling upon the stove and presumes that it has always been boiling and that as the water evaporates it is constantly renewed. Is this any less absurd than to imagine that the energy of the universe has no source in God as absolute being in either a complete and sudden act of creation or by providing a continuous infusion into that creation in order to sustain it in operation?"

"There is simply no dodging the philosophical question that insists upon tracing time backwards to either a single point of origin from nothing or at the very least the search for an aperture or doorway leading to a preceding source of energy and matter from some adjoining universe the nature of which we cannot determine. If there is no act of creation then the science of physics is forced back upon a choice of one of three positions it seems to me: the first would be that the universe as a whole possesses an infinite supply of energy in which case it will simply boil on forever as it were, pointless and directionless in terms of any larger goal or purpose, all of which supposed purposes are as you have proposed merely the projections of human needs projected out upon an unconscious universe; such a universe being infinite, even if was conscious, could never comprehend itself because infinity implies a lack of closure. Such a universe would be infinitely generative and thus always beyond any final description."

"If this first alternative is the truth, then we might define the universe as essentially mindless, for all consciousness when faced with the infinite must of necessity fall infinitely short of its goal which would be to contain all of itself in a single act of comprehension. If it should be argued that an infinite consciousness could as it were run alongside and thus keep pace with the object of its thought there is still no end to the process and therefore no way to prove that an exception might not occur at any moment that might invalidate whatever knowledge has been assembled to date by this supreme (but constantly changing) consciousness. In any case the human mind balks at such a general solution of the problem of God. It may not in any case be verified from our own point of view, so our own intellectual quest for truth as potentially knowable fails *ab initio* if we adapt this view."

"Let us move on then to the second possibility which is that the energy of the universe is limited in nature qua the universe but that it receives a constant new supply of energy from an outside source. This of course opens the possibility of a creator as that source and we are back to God as creator or at least as sustainer. But let us consider a third option (which is the most orthodox one in Christianity), which is that the universe is limited in its energy yet requires no constant infusion from without to continue its operations."

"The universe is in that sense a discrete packet of possibilities determined by its initial supply of energy which is not to be renewed (at least absent a further act of creation on the part of God). Such a universe by its nature cannot be infinite, for it must eventually reach the limit of its resources and wind down just as a clock would if its mainspring is not rewound. Both the second and third alternatives leave room for a God you will note, but the latter assumes that God will keep his promise to renew creation, as Holy Scripture testifies, at some future date and to transform it into the Kingdom of Heaven. If we adopt instead the second alternative what we have is our pot boiling on the stove and constantly renewed so that it may boil on but no one will ever come home to dinner. The universe remains then a mere purposeless activity, existing for its own sake and unconscious that it is doing so, except for the dim intellectual light shown upon it by that presumptuous monkey, man."

"Now then Professor, which version would you choose as containing within itself the best chance of a final meaning for all things, at least as approached through the lens of physics? If the human mind seeks meaning, will it not choose that solution that allows the best opportunity for a successful result and the minimum of frustration of its own aspiration to complete knowledge, one final formula if you will that will explain all other formulae? I believe that the human mind will choose the third alternative and by so choosing leave open the possibility of a creator, which is God. But this does not alone get me to my goal, for the question still remains if such a creator God would endorse a particular moral scheme for mankind. But can we conceive of the alternative, that God intends man to be immoral, a mere survivor at any cost, a brutal as well as a presumptuous monkey? Can such a supposition be maintained?"

"Nietzsche in his bold attempt to re-value all values attempts precisely this task. He holds compassion in contempt and would re-create human nature in the image of the beast of prey, the conqueror. I understand that in recent years the poor fellow has gone quite mad and it is not surprising that he has gone mad because one may not stand human nature upon its head. The virtues and the vices of man have been evaluated as such by the greatest minds throughout the ages. The general conclusion is that are not mere historical accidents but a legacy of the image of God within man that defines morality objectively according to universal social ends that create harmony, justice, and happiness in living. Some of these dictates may have been premature, as we discover daily new facts about human nature, but the basics must remain true and may not be arbitrarily re-defined by a mere act of human will as Mr. Nietzsche suggests."

"But we are every day beset with similar fallacies of thought are we not? Marx would change the human desire for property by denying the legitimacy of the private realm and placing the means of production in collective ownership. The experience of the human race that only genius takes the risks to develop new technological methods while the collective mass of mankind are always in search of someone to direct them. The program of communal ownership must finally fail because it denies what we know of human nature. Nietzsche wishes to endow a race of super-men, only to find that he has created that nightmare vision of Thomas Hobbes, that state of being that exists before the social contract is formed, that state where constant conflict becomes the norm, where every man's hand is raised against the other as each man attempts to become a super-man creating his own morality."

"I suggest that beyond mere physics the realms of governance and of economics demand guidance that only a belief in God can provide. Show me a bad philosopher and I will show you dead bodies, Professor. Stupid ideas create terrible results when put into practice by ardent but foolish people. For this reason, God reveals objective morality to man to spare man from himself. Holy Scripture states that, 'God does not desire the death of the sinner but rather that the sinner should be converted and live.' The mission of the Catholic Church is to restore to man the image of God in man by nurturing the souls of men and women with sacramental grace. God has restored human dignity through the life and death of His Son, through God's intimate union with all people collectively within the Church, and individually through Baptism."

"This is the mission of the Catholic Church, to endow the universe with meaning and with truth. If that mission has at time exceeded the realized dimensions of the Church's activity it is an indictment of man and not of God. The pool of grace is never exhausted and the Church when it fails must simply resume its course and try to do better in future. It is here that one finds infinity Professor, not in vast and distant nebulae seen through a telescope, but in a microscope trained upon the hearts of men and women. Our task is not to understand the cosmos, but to understand ourselves! This can only be done by gazing into our own subjective awareness. The heart of man must realize its own emptiness if it will seek for and find an answer. It will find this answer in faith, which is a shorter path to truth than endless ratiocination. Life is too short to speculate forever. A man exhausts himself with equations and minute observations. Always the whole eludes him. The grand synthesis is left to madmen like Nietzsche and it always leaves the heart of man alone in a dead universe. Abandon religion and the quest for faith and the mind of man itself becomes only a dim ember, glowing in a vast black universe, always about to flicker out into nothingness, taking with it its own independent moral estimation of good and evil."

"I for one cannot admit this intolerable solution to human thought nor is it any comfort to me to make some expansive gesture of will in order to sum up my life. I suggest that such an act of will is inadequate also for you, Professor Moriarty, and whatever good you presume to accomplish by destroying England will not make up for the loss of your immortal soul! I tell you that to do as you propose is evil. It is not the work of God, but only the work of a bitter and disappointed man who fears death above all things."

"You spoke earlier of Christianity as a religion of death and blood as though human history has ever manifested anything other than death and blood and when these were not available to resort instead to privation and disease in order to destroy our enemies. To this ghastly record of sorrow and despair Christianity, when on occasion it emerges purified of those elements of the world that are constantly seeking to penetrate into and dilute its uncompromising message of love, offers faith, hope, and charity to build a better world. The paradox of Christianity is that it offers a vision of God that takes the world as He finds it and enters into history as an active and personified force in the person of Jesus of Nazareth. How else can we speak of a savior without admitting that this world as it is needs to be saved? Christianity is not surprised to encounter evil. The existence of evil is why Christianity exists and we should not be surprised that evil appears at times even within the very vehicle of salvation, the Catholic Church itself!"

"If the Catholic Church presumes to speak to all cultures and in all times it is because God embraces all cultures and all times. This is what it means to be apostolic, to be sent. Catholicism is not a religion of the intellect and there are questions to which the Catholic Church has no answers. It is quite enough if those who profess the One, Holy, Catholic, and Apostolic faith can reach into the hearts of men and women and restore what has been lost, heal what has been wounded, restore what has been laid waste, and left behind by these actions of love the hope that in these various acts and the acceptance of these teachings an answer to the riddle of human existence may be found. This message is meant to reach each individual in whatever condition of mind or body it finds them. The Catholic Church is not addressed to the individual seekers after truth. The Philosophers and the Scientists may be among the last to find God because they have sought Him everywhere but where He is to be found. God is with us and among us and if we are to find Him at all we must look to each individual as they present themselves to us—to be imitators of Christ as one body and rely on being a conduit to what we ourselves do not possess, the power to unilaterally design a better world all by yourself, as you, Professor James Moriarty have sought to do."

I ended my discourse with more feeling than I had intended to display and immediately feared that I had only pushed the Professor deeper into his folly. I was therefore about to berate myself for this when the Professor stood up and surprised me by uttering a single word, "Admirable!" before standing up and leaving the room without further comment. I have not seen him since for further discussion on our primary topic but only at meals where we speak of other matters and at the morning training sessions where we have spoken only of matters regarding horsemanship and breeding. During the afternoons I walk about the estate quite alone, while the Professor takes his afternoon nap. We have refrained from further discourse at the request of the Professor as communicated by a shake of the head when he sees me about to propose further discussion.

This has left my evenings free as well and I spend them walking in the gardens as perplexed as I am uncertain of where we stand. I do not know how to interpret his silence or his last comment to me. Dare I hope that I have made my case with him to some degree? Or have we reached a position of stalemate? In the absence of further evidence, I can only assume that his great mind is considering the assertions that I have made and that it is perhaps seeking an exit from the enclosure of the arms of the Church and of God that always reach out to him as they do to all men and women.

July 18, 1893
Kings Pyland

At last today the silence between us has ended and our discussions have resumed. Professor Moriarty seemed rested and in the best of humor this morning. After lunch he finally spoke up. "You must forgive my abstention from our most interesting discussions, Holmes, but I have after-all an estate to manage here and my own health often makes importunate demands upon me. Also it is no easy thing to disrupt the patterns of thought and conviction of a lifetime and I was startled to find myself agreeing with far too many of your points the other day. I must admit that you have more cranial capacity and deeper resources than I had supposed. I needed consequently to retreat for a time in order to assess any damage you may have done and to marshal my forces for a renewed attack. Today I feel more up to the mark, so we may begin again."

We retired again to the library as before and the Professor opened a new bottle of Amontiado before addressing me.

"As a minor point, since I do not wish to get caught up into the minutiae of Christian observances, I would like to point out that liturgy would appear to precede dogmatics. In other words ideas only emerge out of practices. The function of an idea is to explain to oneself what one is in fact already doing. Most people tend to assume that the reverse is true. They presume that practices like liturgical celebrations are the acting-out of preexisting theological notions. I prefer a more empirical approach, one based upon motion and dynamics. For instance as a scientist I cannot theorize about the dynamics of an asteroid until I observe it. The asteroid is already behaving; it is already in motion."

"So now let us look at theology: if dogmatics precedes practice, then I suggest that we have forgotten somewhere along the line to observe. We thereby reduce the phenomenon to a formula of our own devising. If God is more complex than the universe that He has created, then should we not first observe God in operation before we draw conclusions as to His nature and what if anything He desires from us? If we pursue an opposite approach, then we first assume some sort of perfect doctrinal synthesis, some sort of revelation, and then deduce everything from that set of axioms. But what if instead we adopt an inductive approach and assume as I do that we know nothing of God and then gradually build up our conceptions of what God would be by empirical observation? I suggest that this order of procedure would not only be more accurate, but one less subject to sectarian disagreement with all its deleterious consequences for mankind."

"By starting with some affirmation based upon an authoritative text or series of texts the prospective believer is set adrift in a theological marketplace a sort of traveling carnival with various touts shouting at one to come over and play whatever game they are promoting; and what is that game? It is the same game that the Aztec Indians played in their human sacrifices. It is the game of most religions, the game of life in contemplation of death. It is the same game played in the Roman Arena where the gladiators fought to the death, thus giving the observers the illusion of victory bought at the cost of the dead body of the vanquished below them."

"Religion is nothing without the prospect of an afterlife; take that away and what remains but ethical demands without reward or punishment. Everything would then be equal. Religion thrives upon being the one who remains alive. It really has very little to do with God at all. God is in fact precisely what the idolaters saw as the function of all the gods, a means to an end. I will however give you this concession; the God of the Jews is not one easily used to meet our demands. Yahweh has the good taste to be about his own business and Jesus demanded the same right to proceed with His mission without interference, even from His own family, let alone the High Priesthood of the Temple. One always pays a price in religion for taking the question of God seriously. That was the very point that the Danish philosopher Soren Kierkegaard understood only too well. Of course he wrote in a style that nobody could understand who was not already well-versed in the writings of Georg Hegel. Like most Germans Hegel wanted to reduce everything, even God, to a system; particularly if the system makes better sense in German than in any other language. Kierkegaard in contrast never stopped insisting that Christianity should never be comfortable, or even coherent for that matter. Such statements are not likely to win friends among the clergy."

"The liturgical movements that I observe in Catholicism seem to me to be instances that only obliquely honor God. Instead they are much more dedicated to the need for pageantry of the celebrants and the dignity of the clergy. I think that any God worth his salt would be either amused or disgusted by the embroidery that surpasses the simplicity of the God that these ceremonies hope to manipulate and to appease. The Protestants of course are no better. Devoid of any elaborate liturgy they are reduced to pure dogmatics or to an ethical haranguing of the congregation interspersed with a set of quivering hymns and the passing of the plate for an offering."

"So there you have it. If we remove the question of life or death and concentrate upon God alone without reference to human existence we arrive at the position of Spinoza: that God cannot be approached by any theology and must instead be studied by observation. This sort of study is the one in which I have been engaged whenever the leisure has been afforded me to pursue it. Crime for me was merely a hobby. No even that is to give it too much dignity. My crimes were instances where I was tempted to make direct changes in the social order without resort to politics. The key virtue of politics is to speak much and to accomplish nothing. Political actions of course are merely other instances of liturgy run wild. No democratic government has ever created a democracy; it is after all not designed to do so! Democracies are designed to bleed off the energies that would otherwise result in revolution if they were not contained; just as dogmatics give the self-appointed chosen ones a sense of being holy people without really making any real or sustained progress in that direction."

"If any actual saints emerge by accident in history, they are usually ridiculed in life and only venerated after death, when they can do no harm by demonstrating that holiness is actually possible. Not that atheism is a virtue either. The atheist is merely proud that he is too enlightened to accept any duty greater than the trumpeting of his own set of substitute doctrines. The atheist is dogmatic about being non-dogmatic! Beyond this he has nothing to offer. But let us not be led too far afield by debating liturgical differences. These are only window dressing to our deeper inquiry."

"Today I wish to question you particularly regarding the single aspect that I believe most telling against this matter of faith in any religious doctrines. Even assuming that a case might be made for a creator God in order to answer the questions of physics and of a moral God to enforce and give substance to the moral aspirations of a society, both serve an excellent set of utilitarian ends but there still remains the question of the role of the individual in any divine plan. To imagine that any supreme being has a particular interest in the individual seems to me the height of absurdity. Even societies see the individual as completely negligible. Capitalism sees only a collection of workers and socialism sees only the class struggle and eventual common ownership by the proletarian class and not the individual workers. Even kings and emperors are only segments of the rule of a line of ancestral descent. In few ideologies does the individual assume any importance or standing; the Chinese for instance see the family as the primary unit of society. Buddhism sees all differentiation of individuals or groups as merely an aspect of Maya, illusion. It would seem then that the individual is quite free of religious obligations to any supreme being that must of necessity ignore the individual."

"As you know, astronomy is my avocation. I spend considerable time in contemplation of the heavens. Perhaps you are unaware of the fact but there are billions of galaxies out there and the fact that they are observable at all is merely a function of our location in the wider cosmos so that the light can even reach us. In fact what we observe is not a contemporaneous phenomenon. The light that we observe was emitted long before this planet had begun to cool, let alone for life to begin here. Oh, I know that various absurd people prefer to ignore this fact, but I assure you that the evidence of the speed of light is quite indubitable. The time involved is a function of the distance of the stars from us."

"Now I ask you, is it likely that a God of such breadth and majesty would care about the fate of the individual or even of our entire planet, let alone to become one of us and die on a cross in an obscure province of the Roman Empire for our sakes? What is even the Roman Empire now but a smattering of ruins in a now impoverished nation? What is the Catholic Church but a ruined ideology guided by a so-called Sovereign Pontiff, a "prisoner of the Vatican," as Pope Pius IX, embittered and alone, proclaimed he was when he found himself bereft of the former Papal States due to the Italian struggle for independence? We are nothing, Holmes, and our discussion today is as meaningless as the sand dropping from an hour-glass, simply one more micro-micro-micro event on a planet that will someday be swallowed by a dying sun."

"In order to make my point clear, let me give you an example from your own experience. Let us take the imaginary position that you are now God. Imagine that you are walking by the sea and that you bend over and take-up a handful of sand. Already, that handful is but a small part of the whole expanse of sand upon the seacoast. That is the focus of your attention for a moment, but it distracts you from your greater vision of the sea, the waves green and white crashing down upon the shore with the dune-grasses waving in the wind. But as God you are of course at liberty to take pleasure in the sand streams coursing through your fingers, but for how long before in sheer boredom you take up again your normal occupation of creating universes. Handfuls of sand, Holmes, such must be the course of history to God. The lives and deaths of countless people are like the course of sand rushing into oblivion."

"But now let us imagine that God focuses for a moment upon a single grain of sand, one tiny black or white speck that still adheres to His hand, and turning his attention from land and sea and all of the other grains of sand upon the shore, scrutinizes this grain of sand, notes its shape, color, and minute features from every angle, and then rather than simply brushing it off, wishes to retain it and to gaze upon it now and then, so He places it carefully within a glass bottle and takes it home. What would we think of a man who behaved in this fashion? Would we not think him quite mad? Yet your faith, Sherlock Holmes, asks you to believe that the God of the whole of creation with stars and galaxies swinging like trinkets from his wrist is concerned about my individual sins, which offend him. It is beyond ridiculous! Do you not see the disproportion?"

"I am nothing to God, but all things to myself. I owe nothing to a being which is probably unaware of my very existence, but even then if He was aware, only as part of a larger whole. If I fail God, then God is not diminished; but if I fail myself, why then I have lost everything! Your arguments upset me Holmes; I frankly admit it, because they threaten the thought processes of a life-time. I have constructed a system of proportionality that serves me as your religion does you. I have accepted my own individual fate, which is to die after a life spent in illness and deformity and then to become nothing at all. Each passing second brings me closer to being no more aware than is that grain of sand in my homely analogy. All of my thoughts will perish with the consciousness that once entertained them. Nothingness like a great tidal wave will arch over my head. All of this I have long since accepted and now you, Sherlock Holmes, would abstract me from those mighty waters of oblivion that were my only comfort and plunge me into eternity where even time and space as we know them will be no more!"

Professor Moriarty paused for a moment due to another spell of coughing before continuing in a hoarse whisper.

"You do this by telling me that I will escape at last and end up upon some quiet shore or lie floating upon the sea with the great sun of eternity shining upon my resurrected body! Furthermore you ask that I follow the particular dictates of your Church! I tell you there is not enough time left in my life to entertain such possibilities if I am to complete the goals that I have set for myself. There is no time for such idle speculations and such remote possibilities. Each day I am brought closer to extinction. If I am to have any effect upon the world it must be in time, not in eternity. If I would attain my ends it must be now and by my own efforts. Even then history will soon fill the small crater left by my destruction. I know that all events are soon part of a greater pattern and that even revolutions give way to new tyrannies with time."

He shook his head sadly before whispering in a voice so low that I could barely hear him, "Why then do I act at all? Why not withdraw and seek a quiet retirement of horses and Amontiado and read the essays of Montaigne and find some degree of comfort in life before the end? This manner of life is precisely what I intended; and it is the way of life that I am already pursuing. You must imagine that I spend hours each day in my plotting; I do not. The destruction of the British Empire is for me only one final but essential obligation to myself after which I will wash my hands of the whole matter and be at peace having fulfilled a promise made long-ago when I left my mother in Ireland never to see her again. Even a man without any religion may honor a promise and I intend to do so, for the sake of one who is no more, who exists only here within this withered breast. You will never convince me that god cares for the individual, Holmes. Such a thing would be too, too ... disproportionate. I would lose all respect for a god who could love me. I do not wish a god to stoop down to my own level. It would degrade me to be the creature of such a god. I quite prefer to exercise unhampered this tiny bit of freedom that I possess and to pass judgment upon myself. I am my own religion in the last analysis and so must any man be who would be a man and not a worm, writhing about and asking a god to save him at last. When I die it will be with a raised fist, raised against the universe that mocks me by giving life only to take it away again. Why should I have been allowed to be only again not to be?"

"There is the true religious question! Religion is but an anodyne for absurdity! Once one has accepted the fact that the universe cares nothing for the individual, while the individual cares everything for himself, you have a basis for the great cosmic injustice. What sort of God asks everything from us because He has already determined that we must die as the price of daring to be like Him, a being knowing the difference between good and evil. Perhaps God of knows the difference between good and evil because He struggles with it Himself; otherwise why would He allow serpents into Eden to tempt us in the first place? Why did God toy with Job to test his loyalty? Why does God incinerate cities in Judea for doing what in Greek philosophy is a virtue?"

"No doubt you will think that I am selfish for saying that the philosopher, the self-conscious individual, would gladly obliterate the universe in order to preserve his own existence. This is the hypocrisy of a religion that claims to love God, but only on condition that God will restore our dried bones and decomposed flesh to what we once were when time meant nothing to us, because unfilled decades stretched out before us. Shall we simply admit that each of us would be as gods if we could thereby be immune from fatality? Is that not so? Who can ever be satisfied that the best years of our lives passed away while we were too young and foolish to appreciate the gift that was even then imperceptibly withering in our hands, the temporary illusion of immortality? At that pinnacle before the decline begins we were too short-sighted to know our good fortune. Perhaps the universe, realizing this impertinence in some obscure manner, puts the individual in his place by destroying him. But no, the universe is as unconscious of itself as it is of us. No God stands guard over that obscure and forgotten corner of time and space where for an instant we flicker into life and then flicker out again."

"I have proceeded on the assumption, the subjective stance that I share with Descartes that the only thing that I can be certain of is my own perceptions and conclusions. Unless I hear from God directly I am willing to match my wits with what is to me only a desperate hypothesis that God exists, until then I must take that place. In point of fact I do not agree with Spinoza, the universe in total is not God; but then what is this God that keeps haunting civilization after civilization so that we had to wait for Voltaire to finally liberate the mind of man from itself? Religion is the disease and only action is the cure."

Here I interrupted him. "Your confession of the aspiration to assume divinity, an aspiration that you believe is latent in each man: to be his own God is the best proof of Original Sin. And thus we end our discussion where we began. The Bible begins the story that you yourself have just expressed based on your own experience; so perhaps the Bible contains the ending of that story as well."

Professor Moriarty paused with a startled expression. It was an expression that I have never seen before upon his face. It was as though he had glimpsed some new thing that placed every prior conclusion he had drawn in a new light. He shook his head once and then staggered to his feet before collapsing backwards into his chair. He reached out and took a drink from his wineglass and then leaned back again in his chair. I waited for him to recover.

Several minutes passed before I said, "If man wishes to be like God then God, if he loves us, has no choice but to become man in order to save each of us precisely as an individual, but an individual in community because we do not exist alone. There is your requested proportionality, Professor Moriarty. You have asked why God values the individual; it is because God has become an individual in the person of Jesus Christ. From now on salvation is unique and particular. God relates to each soul as though that soul were alone in the universe. God dies for each soul as though that soul alone had sinned. God creates a place for that soul as though that soul alone was the reason for earth and for heaven.

That is what the love of the Trinity is: with such an intensity of love, even the Three Persons may be One God."

"When the Kingdom of God arrives the unity of God with creation will be as one. Yet our distinction as individuals will be maintained, just as within the Trinity the Divine Persons are unique. This is the mystery of the Christian faith, that what was lost is restored and that what is doomed to die will live. The Catholic Church is not a mass institution, a mere collectivity, but a living body unified and incorporated into a single Body of Christ. That Mystical Body concentrates its entire effort towards the needs of each individual soul so that what is distributed is not divided and diminished but retains its wholeness, just as in the case of the five barley loaves and two fishes that once fed the multitude gathered on the hillside in Judea."

"The teachings of the prophets speak of the abundance of God. Grace requires graciousness and graciousness is shown by its free-handed distribution. To ask is to receive, and to receive more than one dared to request. It is not God but man who creates scarcity. It is man who demands a strict accounting and puts even God to the test, to prove that God is God. Faith on the contrary demands nothing of God, but trusts God to supply both the substance and the measure."

"If this idea of life which promises that our highest aspirations may be met and exceeded seems too good to be true so that one would rather assume that our desire for the infinite is the delusion of a presumptuous animal, then let me ask you this question Professor: is a certainty of disappointment worth more than the slimmest possibility that the promises of Christ are in fact true? Since in the first case the only reward is a bitter and stoic certainty that gives no more joy than may be wrung from a dry rag, while the latter promises that our deepest aspirations for futurity and fulfillment are not in vain after all; which then is the more logical choice to make?"

Again I waited for a response, but still the Professor was silent; and so he remained when I got up quietly and left the room of mute and dusty volumes mysterious in the light of a dying fire.

Had he heard me or was his silence testimony to the futility of arguing from any fixed position to another equally anchored in a world-view incompatible with one's own; I did not turn back to see if he was asleep, but just as the door closed shut behind me and the great bolt slid into place, I heard a faint cry as from a wounded bird.

July 20, 1893
Kings Pyland

Thinking of our conversation two nights ago some thoughts occurred to me. This whole question of the closeness of God to creation, the interpenetration of the divine into the most prosaic elements of our existence is what the Catholic Church means when it speaks of sacramental reality and the divine grace that is both transmitted and made manifest through the seven sacraments. Unfortunately by segmenting the sacraments as distinct ceremonial celebrations and further anatomizing them into a union of form and matter in imitation of Aristotle western Christianity managed to distort and diminish the mystery of both God and the action of God in an effort to make them more comprehensible. Worse still by emphasizing the role of the priest as celebrant Catholicism inserted an all-too-human juridical touch that polices the abounding mercy of God and even on occasion makes of the sacraments weapons in an arsenal to be waged against an inadequate or deficient element of faith or fidelity of perseverance in the recipient of the sacrament.

This official position is quite similar to idolatry because it implies that God can be objectified and controlled by ritualistic observances. All too often the Catholic Church has used the sacraments in the same way that a timid commander uses his armaments, always keeping something in reserve. How many Catholics have felt that the very purpose of the Church has been to remind the sinner how disgusting and loathsome he or she is in the eyes of God? How many souls find the outer darkness more congruent and safe to their low estimate of themselves, a place of solitude where they even their pain becomes more congenial because it is their constant companion?

How many people leave the fellowship and healing ministry of the Catholic Church never to return with just such sentiments gnawing at their soul as they seek solace everywhere but where it could potentially be most easily obtained? It is not God that sends them forth, but people like themselves, sinners who fancy that God will show no more mercy than they consider appropriate. It may truly be said that religion is a vastly underused resource and this not by the will of God, but by the pride and folly of man. The boast of all too many Christians before God is, "Look how well I guarded your majesty and dignity from those souls most unworthy of your love. I stood guard over your sanctuary and kept the altar-light to serve as a lighthouse—stay far away lest you dash yourself to pieces on the rocky shores of the wrath of God!"

Or is it really the devil that most wishes to diminish the efficacy of sacraments as the means of salvation by ensuring that as few people as possible will avail themselves of the most potent aids that God has designed, aids prepared and ready for rough usage in a rugged world by the most ordinary and unprepared of men and women? The habits of alienation are not easily broken. Was this the meaning of the stifled exclamation that I heard behind me; or did my own ardor to reach the Professor betray and delude my hearing. In any case this morning Professor Moriarty did not join me for breakfast, but left instead a note for me expressing his regrets and that he would be absent all day seeing to matters on the estate. In pertinent part the note contained this passage as well...

"I do not feel that I need to keep you any longer from your other obligations. Our meetings are at an end for the present. I believe that each of us has made his own position clear. If you wish to send me any part of your journal in transcription that may advance your own cause, I will of course read it and append comments.

You have the right to know that you have yet to change my mind and to deter me from my objective, but you have done what I would have sworn no man alive could do. You have made me question some of my primary postulates; I will not say axioms. Until I have leisure to consider the implications of our discussions, further talk would be pointless. We have years ahead of us before my plans will be in a state to be ready for execution. This should allow each of us time to refine our relative positions. Events are moving swiftly for the world. Our two minds and all of our efforts may soon be rendered irrelevant by those actors, men of power, who thinking less deeply than we simply pursue the blind tides of circumstance. Men like us are perhaps already anachronisms, Mr. Sherlock Holmes. The world is not guided by principle but by opportunism and by chance. Great ideas never appear in the mediocrity of events. They are doomed to be diluted before their execution. We understand each other better than they can ever understand us. Adieu."

The note was signed simply, Professor James Moriarty. I have been dismissed from the presence. Did I press my points too strenuously? I hardly think so. Honesty was demanded. One does not merely tap upon a leaded door if one seeks entry. I had hoped to follow up before I left on the clue provided by the Professor when he said that his scheme was pursued as part of a promise made years ago. To whom did he make this promise? Was it only to himself? If I believe in the final point that I made yesterday, that subjectivity is the final criterion of our conversion, that religion must be relevant to each man's personal quest as well as an explanation for all things, I must seek a personal answer in the unique life that Professor Moriarty has lived.

If I am to open for him a path to conversion of heart, objective morality is a dry letter unless interpreted through the lens of each man or woman's moral struggle to embody the perennial norms in his or her particular and limited circumstances. I am not a Platonist who sees the virtues as eternal essences and looks for perfection in this life. Until a given virtue is reduced to actual action, is embodied to some degree in one's constant character, it remains in the mere realm of possibility and speculation. We are what we do, not what we think. To think rightly is a prerequisite of wise actions, but without the stamina of execution there is nothing finally to attribute to the soul that must perform those wise actions, which are the virtues in operation. Kant believes that duties emerge in all their glory as a categorical imperative; I suggest that duties emerge from the mélange of circumstances in which they are embedded.

After finishing my breakfast, I packed my clothes and my books and had my dog-cart brought round. In this manner I took my leave from the estate of Kings Pyland and from Professor Moriarty for a time. I stopped later on the way home at Baskerville Hall and discovered that no alarming events had occurred during my absence, but that nevertheless Lady Beryl still apparently lived on in a desperate state of fear. Sir Henry is troubled as things cannot go on indefinitely in this manner or her health will surely suffer. I must attempt to flush our tiger out of hiding then and to that end I will write to the one man who may be able to help me do so. I must write to Colonel Sebastian Moran for advice.

Book Fifteen

Sherlock Holmes in Ireland

Dr. Watson's Narrative Continues

It was only at this point that I realized the complex and yet personal focus of the discussions that took place between Sherlock Holmes and Professor Moriarty years before that autumn meeting in Devonshire recounted in the first volume of this immense narrative and taking place in the year of 1897. It was only then that I first learned that Professor Moriarty had not perished as I had supposed at the Falls of Reichenbach. I learned then that Holmes had emerged the victor in that long drawn out battle of wits and I let the journal speak for itself of the events leading up to that confrontational process. It was a battle the dimensions of which reached far beyond these two great intellects. Many of the questions raised were the questions of the age in which they lived. The debates spanned continents and the lives of millions were affected by the issues that they discussed.

Just what part does religion play in war and peace? How can speculation regarding the supernatural and an afterlife also play a role in how each of us lives in the present? Can public policy be governed by the same rules that govern private moral conduct? For that matter what has morality to do with a universe that is seemingly unaware that human beings even exist? Is religion only a subset of folklore and literature, the inspiration of artists and musicians, the basis for cathedrals and temples, but of little practical use in the current of world affairs?

Still, religious questions emerge at moments of crisis with all the power that they once possessed when both science and history were subservient to the great religious narratives that even now barely fill a single bookshelf while the interpretive literature fills whole libraries. How are we to explain the disproportion between the trunk and the immense foliage that it supports? Wars of religion have dominated entire eras while dynasties have passed in more rapid succession. Religion prevails while swords rust in the fields. Even the laws and jurisprudence, the secular equivalent of religion, for all of their endurance are as nothing compared to the alternative versions of divine revelation.

Whatever private comfort religion can supply, an entirely different dynamic is set up when entire populations are mobilized under religious enthusiasm. A sort of herd instinct develops and coalesces and afterwards men and women stand in the ruins and wonder how the aspirations of an elderly man like Abraham who was promised that his descendents would be as numerous as the sands of the sea could have managed to be the basis of three religions that three millennia later cannot prevent their adherents from killing each other.

I continued with my reading of Holmes' journal during our trip together through the states of that region of America that is still called New England. Religion played a central role in the foundation of the thoughts that created a base for the English settlement of a new continent. Holmes' journal had become for me, since I had first opened it over a year ago, a sort of ongoing catechism of life. I was in no hurry to finish it, but had instead opted to read it slowly over time, just as it had been composed. We are living in an age that values the summary so that it was a luxury to me to appreciate the open-ended and gradual exposition of his points of view.

I had long appreciated the great literature of the 17th century authors whose prose demanded that sufficient time be expended in the reading, time to explore a topical reference or a primal human experience in all of its ramifications, to follow a trail of thought or exposition into every crevasse and to seek the source of every river of insight springing from a new flash of intuition.

When time became a mere commodity rather than the background of life itself in the busy 19th century, much of this sense of leisure so essential to civilization was lost to us. When the cost of the reproduction of words falls, so often does the value placed upon them diminish as well; I often wonder whether one day we shall have a bargain press where foreshortened compositions, mere creatures of hour no longer bound in lasting leather, will be unworthy to be preserved beyond that period redolent of a passing taste or the shallow fancy of the year when they were written? Will the leaves of books become then like the leaves of autumn, no sooner green than brown and only worthy to be swept into the gutter to make room for the leaves of tomorrow in the crowding years? What then will be the value of writing at all? Perhaps the coming generations will believe that they may dispense with the written word altogether and rely only upon the bare sensorium of life's flashing images. Nothing then will have sufficient value so that one may bid it stay, to linger, so that one may meditate upon it and find therein the permanent wellsprings of our being. Sustained thought requires exposition and exposition requires a language steeped in tradition and a wealth of associations. Cheap times leave as a residue, monuments to their own vacuity. To overly streamline thought is to retard the progress of the human race, to reduce expression to a slogan or a phrase without qualification or nuance. It is to cripple the mind and starve the soul. Give me the richness of Herman Melville and of Nathaniel Hawthorne, whose homes I visited at that time. May the memory of Milton, Browne, Johnson, Defoe, and Donne yet live!

In this slow and thoughtful way I read the journal of Sherlock Holmes because I hungered to know the great thoughts of my friend and the nature of the mind that was their source. I saw as I read on that his own early claims to know nothing of philosophy and of literature were only his way of seeking to exasperate me and to gage the effect of his subtle mockery of my earnestness as he probed my convictions and sensitivities. He was always the detective, honing his skills by reading other people and where better to practice than upon his unwary fellow lodger. He would often take a position simply to see its effect upon me. His protean nature was a series of essays upon life, brief expeditionary raids into the foreign territory of another soul. As for his insights into himself, he was not beyond change; indeed I often saw in him something of a chameleon nature. He began, at the time when I first knew him, as one of the most free-thinking of men and might have become a cynical Voltaire as he aged if it were not for the fact that he wished to discover and explain the deeper well-springs of the moral instincts of mankind and thereby to find some explanation for the sorrows that beset us all. It was this inner need that drove him onwards to undertake his great journey to the east during his Great Hiatus and that explained his present expedition to America.

I recall that I had reached the point in his tale, when the joust with Professor Moriarty was at its height, when I interrupted my reading at that point because I wished to enjoy the beauty of the landscape that surrounded us and not to be distracted by the heavy guns of that intellectual battle between them, the echoes of which seemed to reach me even from the closed pages of the journal that I had packed away for a time in my baggage.

Instead, I turned to the living Sherlock Holmes who stood at my side each day as we toured the lovely autumn countryside of Massachusetts, New Hampshire, and Vermont and the western regions of New York State. Many of those memories are as clear to me today as if they only happened yesterday. We stood amidst the colored leaves on the shore of Walden Pond and I seemed to see the long thin form of Henry David Thoreau walking about collecting specimens of the local flora to catalogue later in his journal. Who can read the pellucid thoughts of that most independent of men and not feel within the dignity of being an individual? Which of us creates his own zone of sovereignty around our own Walden Pond?

We stood upon the shores of Lake Winnipesaukee in New Hampshire where we ate freshly caught trout and catfish and drank from a well by our cabin tinged bitter with an iron taste distilled from the surrounding granite hills. The bucket at the well was covered with ice each morning and the smell of cooking bacon filled the morning air as I walked back to our cabin. From New Hampshire we crossed into Vermont and lingered by the broad shores of Lake Champlain and gazed across it into the wilds of Canada. From thence we went to Buffalo and visited the great falls at Niagara. I could not but reflect that we had once visited a similar falls in Switzerland where our adventures had begun. No Professor Moriarty menaced us now, but he had been succeeded by other adversaries. There is no end to the struggle with evil in this world of ours and also of course of that same struggle within our own nature.

To gaze at the cascading waters of Niagara was to feel the majesty of the westward-tending continent and to understand something of the drive that would not cease to inhabit the pioneers until even the oceans had been reached and spanned. This was no justification for the depredations visited upon the indigenous inhabitants, but at least it was an explanation for what had occurred in America during the past century. Were not the floods of immigrants as unstoppable as the falls at Niagara? The pent up hunger of generations in Europe had burst forth like an all-embracing wave. The hunger for democratic freedom may never be contained, not even when those who seek it must cross oceans to find it. It will burst forth even as the great cataracts that fell before us in a ceaseless flow over the knife-sharp ledge of granite into the boiling abyss below. The spray seemed to echo with the cries of Indian braves who had fallen before that great onslaught of humanity from all nations. I have often wondered if these masses of men and women had stayed at home in Europe if the long deferred revolution that will end forever the monopoly over the world's goods kept in the control of the few would have ended at last. When the globe is finally encircled by a common commerce and there are no longer frontiers to annex, perhaps then the heart of man may turn to justice and to plenty, not just for the few, but for all to whom this earth is entrusted by the benevolent deity who loves all of His children in the single embrace of the sphere that is our common home.

After a stay of two days at Niagara Falls we boarded our train and headed across the lush farmlands of upper New York State on our way to the states of Pennsylvania and West Virginia. It was Holmes' intention to see the impact of industrial development by visiting the coal mines and oil fields of Southern Pennsylvania, the great steel mills of Pittsburg, and finally the coal mining regions of West Virginia on the borders of Kentucky before proceeding through Virginia to Washington D.C. It was in the nation's capitol that we hoped to use the good offices of the Speaker of the House of Representatives, Thomas Brackett Reed, in order to arrange a meeting with President McKinley. We had delayed this critical meeting until the war with Spain might be brought to a proper conclusion. Until an armistice was reached the President would not have the time or wherewithal to consider the proposition that Holmes wished to suggest to him. That proposition was none other than for America to build a canal across Central America before the Dutch company now owned almost entirely by Baron Maupertuis could extend its interests into that region. Already the Baron had purchased the railroad that had been built during the time of the dictatorship of the man who had adopted the exalted title of Don Juan Murillo, more familiarly known by those who had suffered beneath his tyrannical rule as "The Tiger of San Pedro." San Pedro was the tiny village where he had been born. His advance had been as rapid as it had been brutal. His ties to the army and his willingness to supply the generals with whatever they demanded had sped his advance through the various ministries of his fair and illustrious predecessor, the man whom he had later had arrested and killed lest he be restored to power by the people.

Mycroft had informed us from London that British sources in Central America had reason to believe that the Baron was already pursuing discussions with authorities in various countries in the region about purchasing a canal zone that would cross that country. If the Baron should begin operations in earnest it might preclude a similar effort by the United States to control a passageway that would be essential to the future development of trade with Japan and China. The recent American annexation of Hawaii gave every indication that America had already determined to stake an ever-expanding claim over the Pacific region. But the ultimate fate of the new acquisitions of Guam and the Philippines had yet to be decided.

Would America grant the native patriots their freedom or would it seek to retain them and itself become a colonial power? Holmes hoped to dissuade the President from the latter imperial course, while still ensuring that the Baron's schemes would be defeated in Central America. The task was one requiring the greatest delicacy. For that reason, Mycroft had taken the step of making his brother an unofficial ambassador, but one who could sound out American intentions in complete confidentiality. England and America had reached over the last hundred years a relationship of friendship and mutual accommodation of each other's ambitions. The British government had no wish to see these friendly relations spoiled by a new struggle for domination of the trade with China. In any case England feared the threats posed by the Germans and the Russians even more than the traditional mistrust of French designs. Mycroft had said as much to Holmes before we even left England. It was Mycroft's view that the new century would require England to gaze eastward with the Netherlands and Germany as the primary threats to British domination of the trade with East Asia. Both nations were substantial maritime powers at the turn of the century. The Dutch had an interest in the far eastern trade through their control of the Dutch East Indies. Germany in turn knew that it must build up its defensive naval forces in case of war or any embargo involving the passage to its ports on the Baltic Sea, primarily Hamburg and Danzig along its northern coast. These could be effectively blockaded by superior British naval power in case of war. The German colonies in Africa would be rendered insecure possessions if they could not trade in rubber and other essential raw materials with the fatherland.

The fragmented German-speaking nations had always felt themselves to be second-rate powers with the exception of the Austro-Hungarian Empire, but the victory over the French in 1870-1871 by a United Germany had made Germany under Prussian rule the key power in central Europe, even over the ancient Austrian Empire. Germany intended to keep that power secure by maintaining itself as the preeminent land power, but it felt that it must also break out into the seas in order to market the output of its great industrial factories. German ingenuity in science and engineering at the time excelled even that of Great Britain. A growing potential for international conflict seemed to be emerging in Mycroft's view of world-events. It was for this reason that he desired that England should secure a friendship and informal but secure understanding with America. The best way to accomplish this was to assure America that Her Majesty's government was behind and would support any effort by the Americans to outpace the Dutch in the building of a Central American canal before any continental power or combination of financial interests such as that represented by Baron Maupertuis could do so.

This was the delicate task that lay before Sherlock Holmes in that fateful autumn of 1898. Holmes had handled delicate cases before, many with international implications, but none had ever possessed the possibility of having so great an impact upon world history as the task that now lay before us. It was a great irony that at the very time when Holmes desired to wind up his career that he would be called upon to undertake perhaps the greatest case of his professional life, no longer as a mere solver of problems for private clients, but rather as one whose actions might alter the lives of millions, all of this at a time when his health was at its most precarious, as I knew only too well.

It was also a time, if he were allowed to follow his own inclinations, that he could have remained safely at home in Devonshire discussing the latest finds of his friend Dr. Mortimer and writing his monographs upon early English charters or perhaps a paper for an archeological journal about the possible presence of Phoenician tin-traders upon the shores of Cornwall before the coming of the Romans, or even a philological study of the ancient Cornish language looking for the presence in its lexicon of possible Chaldean roots. All of these private interests, he had been forced to set aside and to assume instead an active role in world history.

He explained all of this to me at the time as he outlined one day his views on the sacrifice that he was being called to make as a loyal son of England, yet one not so blind that he would forget the demands posed by his own conscience as a Catholic gentleman.

"History," he told me as we stood above the falls at Niagara, "Is a puzzle with which I have no desire to meddle. Blessed is the man who is forgotten within a generation of his death. He will have less to answer to before God. Show me a man who has influenced history who has not been forced even while still living to pay the price of that exercise of power. In most cases blood is upon his hands, even if he is personally a man of peace. Even that admirable man, Abraham Lincoln, who wished to bind up the wounds of a nation, had first to create them if he was to save the union. Gordon of Khartoum, though a Christian, was also a soldier and his vindication will someday bring a scourge upon the Sudan by Her Majesty's forces. The conflict will be bloody in proportion to the issues of honor involved. One army will be defending an Empress and the other the Prophet of Islam. Wars begin with ideas and end in slaughter. Principles soon devolve into a will to inflict as many casualties as possible while still preserving one's own life. This is why it is essential to every army to provide a sense of transcendence and of identification with larger units that may taste victory even if the individual soldier perishes."

"Personally, I have no wish to be a hero, Watson, but to someday maintain my soul in peace. Surely it is enough to have addressed the potential threat once posed by Moriarty; that alone was all that I wished for in order to complete my own career. Ah well, perhaps some good may come of it after all, this meddling of ours in history. I am not the only man of insight and good will and there will be many intervening factors that may cancel any errors that I may make. We must act as best we can. Yet who can control the parameters of events once they are set in motion? We act within a circle of firelight, while outside in the darkness moan the winds of change that may deflect all of our good intentions and turn our most moral actions towards evil effects. But then, perhaps good may come even out of evil. Perhaps all events cancel out in the end and what happens is the will of God under the inscrutable dictates of providence."

The ongoing action of God and of His providence in human history is one of such importance and significance to my whole design that I feel it appropriate to pause and address it immediately and in depth, so if I may be allowed at this point in my story a brief digression, I will attempt to correct certain false conclusions that have been drawn regarding my relations with Sherlock Holmes during and after our mission to America. I will seek here to explain my reluctance to pursue my story beyond the course of events that took place during the last years of the 19th century.

Already a great transformation was taking place. World affairs grew increasingly to demand that Holmes would assume a public role in the great events of the times in which we both lived. I often blame myself for my excessive candor in my accounts of our adventures, but it has always been my aim to tell the truth in every detail whenever possible and I shall continue to do so in this present account sparing only such circumstances as I must to maintain promises made to Mycroft Holmes at the conclusion of these remarkable events after we had both returned to London from America.

It was during this final active period of our long friendship that I grew to better understand my good friend, Sherlock Holmes, with a greater clarity than at any previous time of our acquaintance. It was not merely having the privilege to read his own inner thoughts as recorded in his journal, but in observing him during those tumultuous years between 1897 through 1899 that I realized that his entire life might have been spent as a contemplative rather than as an active man of affairs. There was something profoundly reminiscent of the Cistercian Monks in the man. I had never understood with greater clarity why Holmes was always content to live his quiet life at 221B Baker Street when he might have left our old rooms behind as his practice grew and his income increased.

Perhaps the primary reason was that our life there in our youth had been pleasant for us both. Even now I look back upon those years as most precious ones. After Holmes retired in 1903 I saw little of him until the outbreak of the Great War that began in1914, a war that still rages as I write these words. On the other hand his address soon had the same notoriety as the fame that followed the man. I flatter myself that even Number 10 Downing Street is not better known to Englishmen than the address of Sherlock Holmes. Even now it is something of a pilgrimage point of persons visiting London. Holmes maintains our old rooms still for occasional visits, but resides elsewhere.

It was following his retirement that he was able to use his last years, as all men must, to complete the many unfinished tasks that remain, even to one who has led a full and busy life. Since the war began he has been called into government service, much as his brother Mycroft had once been, although the roles have not been identical. But of that I may not speak freely yet, even here. The hidden years between 1903 and 1914 must also await a separate volume of reminiscences should I live long enough to complete it.

For the present, the purpose of this brief digression is merely to illuminate the forces in play during the early years of our partnership. I do this not to celebrate myself; because I realize that to the reader my sole function has always been to act as a mere placeholder for the reader as the facts of the case are laid out before him or her. With this apology for my extended role in this saga I feel it not inappropriate to clarify certain mysteries that may have troubled my readers by providing a few clues to my own character.

When I first met Sherlock Holmes I had just returned from Afghanistan, but as a broken man. I had seen there the slaughter of

British troops at the battle of Maiwand. I had lain for days among the barren hills before my parched body was found by local women who hid me in a crevasse and tended to my needs with food and water until I was strong enough to limp back to the tattered British lines. When I chose my unlikely fellow-lodger I had no idea that this strange man would play so great a role in my life. His entire manner of living was one immense contradiction. He would alternate spells of the most violent exertion with days when he would lie about in a dressing gown, playing lugubrious airs of his own composition and smoking his infernal pipe while reading unsavory literature such as Lautreamont's *"Song of Maldoror."* There were times then when I thought him to be quite mad. But, ever and again he would surprise me with some new display of his unique gifts and genius and soon I could not imagine leaving him. He was, if nothing else, a distraction from my own melancholy.

Who could see his comrades slaughtered in war and not at times regret his own survival? At last I grew to love the man for his virtues and to respect the struggle involved in maintaining the precarious interior balance of his life. His own early follies had turned to wisdom. I succeeded in weaning him from the artificial paradise of his drug use and he showed his gratefulness to me by allowing me alone to witness the inner workings of his noble soul. He was not the man to be demonstrative or even to express his affection for me. Indeed most of his comments in my regard were deprecatory, in tone at least. I was forced to exact my own revenge by developing what he called "a vein of pawky humor" at his expense. I would allow myself to appear even more dull than he assumed that I was, merely to take him by surprise when he least expected it.

Besides, it was a pleasure for me to elicit his remarkable demonstrations, which he would lay before me like a geometrical proof that I could later record in the versions of his cases that he allowed me to lay before the public. I came over time to consider myself a conduit to a reading public, both in England and America, and soon throughout the world that was hungry for his exploits. My small medical practice gave me a meager living, but my writing soon became the mainstay of my existence.

Such has always been my function, one that I have undertaken here again in writing this present account of our joint adventures together on the involved series of cases that I am only now assembling for the public eye. I cannot say of course when the public will ever see this account, because it has not been uncommon for Holmes to give me permission to write up an account, only later to withhold his consent for its publication. This in turn has forced me to alter dates in order to try and harmonize the particulars of his cases as published with the actual facts of his career. I wish to say here that I do not cultivate inconsistency for its own sake and to say that it would be unfair to reproach me for circumstances in the composition of my writings that were often beyond my own control; but I have had to take my subject as I found him and to give him belated credit for results that he alone was able to obtain when Scotland Yard often preferred to take the credit.

There were often reasons of most signal import for the reticence of my friend and hence for mine. Holmes always deplored my tendency to make of him a romantic figure, but it must be recalled that many of my readers are women (many of them unmarried) and some of these no doubt would have long since laid siege to Holmes in Baker Street if I had not made him appear most obnoxious in his personal household habits and insisted on his disposition to remain the confirmed bachelor that in fact he was. At the same time I tried to convey to my readers the courage and valor of the man. This effort to place Holmes in a heroic light, in spite of his irregular habits, meant that many young ladies still called from time to time at Baker Street and in consequence Holmes often needed to distinguish between real problems requiring a solution and those mysteries that were created for the occasion by desperate and flighty damsels, simply to obtain an interview with the great detective.

I hope that I do not unfairly disparage the wiser and more balanced members of the fair sex when I take note of the determination and pertinacity of a young woman who abounds in the life-force spoken of by Schopenhauer in his philosophy. Those were days when much speculation was conducted on the idea that genius is transmissible through heredity and many a foolish young lady of obvious animal vigor imagined that the union of the seed of genius like Sherlock Holmes with that of a body abounding in pulchritude and vitality must of its nature produce the man of the future celebrated in the works of the dramatist, George Bernard Shaw.

Throughout the course of his career it was not uncommon for Mrs. Hudson to be forced to turn away governesses who imagined that all manner of nefarious doings were occurring at the manor house where they taught their young charges. Mrs. Hudson used to keep copies of *Northanger Abbey* by Jane Austen, which she would give away to the more persistent cases hoping that they might gain some insight into their febrile condition.

Mrs. Hudson, and I when I lived with him, always acted as a sort of outer guard for the great detective. Yet he needed at the same time to be available to the public if he was to be consulted in cases where his efforts were truly required. It was above all essential that he should be secure enough in his person that he might live that contemplative life that was most attuned to his own desires. His fame upon his return in 1894 was so great and so numerous were his clients that it finally led to his collapse at the end of 1896. It was then that he joined me in Cornwall or Devonshire for an occasional rest. Still his lung condition had worsened and by early 1897 he had been forced to return to his cottage in Devonshire on a more permanent basis. There he had just begun to recover before the events that this longest of my many tales seeks to memorialize began.

Thereafter I found myself to a degree hitherto undreamt of pried out of my own perhaps premature retirement and launched upon our longest adventure yet by being drawn into the complex orbit of Holmes' theological speculations and Professor Moriarty's search for an explanation without axioms for the universe and his search for a seemingly unmotivated private vengeance against the British Empire and all that it stood for. Worse still I had been entrusted with a mission to the Vatican that Holmes had been too ill to undertake in the course of which I had succumbed to the lure of Catholicism and become a Catholic myself at perhaps the most perilous historical period of the existence of that perennial and venerable institution the foundation for all other varieties of Christian belief.

The facility with which various mutations of the Christian faith have emerged, despite the strenuous and even brutal efforts of the Mother Church to invite or to compel heretics to return to the one true faith, can be traced back to the tenuous character of the origins of Christianity. This is not to gainsay the efficacy or reality of the event of the Pentecost to which the Catholic Church traces its origins, or to imply that Jesus was not resurrected from the dead and thereafter ascended into heaven. But it is a fact that the earliest testimony to the life of Jesus comes to us as already embodied in conclusive documents that manifest a fairly advanced theology and an ecclesiastical apologetics that can provide the skeptic with grounds to wonder whether the function of the New Testament is itself tendentious rather than an unbiased and objective unity as one might hope considering that it must act as the basis for all that follows.

An alternative reading might conclude that the life of Jesus Christ as presented in the gospels was edited if not invented so as to support the convictions of the early Church rather than the other way round. Without adequate parallel citations to unbiased testimony of a contemporaneous nature certain gaps remain to trouble the mind and perplex the heart. The constant refrain of the necessity of faith then becomes a case of special pleading to cover the lacunae in the evidence that Christianity can bring forth in support of its own legitimacy as the successor to Judaism. Once launched Christianity tended to follow its own path of evolution with an ever-growing certainty and provenance as the centuries passed.

It is far beyond my capacities and capabilities to resolve what two-thousand years of Christianity has not managed to accomplish, but I must admit that my faith is not perfect and depends as much upon my acceptance of the mere fact of existing ecclesiastical authority as it does on personal satisfaction of all the questions that I have not the time or energy to resolve before I die.

I am sure that my readers will feel some sympathy for my position and wonder why I was so willing to inconvenience myself at a moment's notice whenever Sherlock Holmes crooked his little finger at me. If I could answer that question, as with most of the inscrutable questions of life, the course of my own history would have been far different than what it turned out to be. I might even have become an atheist. For instance it had long ago occurred to me that just as the Americans had a Constitution designed to ensure the survival of the American Republic, the writings of the New Testament, particularly the Gospels might best be read as a tale told to justify the institutional survival of Christianity that at the time was in deadly conflict with the Judaism of its day.

The exportation if the natal faith beyond the confines of the Jerusalem Church presided over by the ever-practical St. James and its later appropriation, first by the fragmenting Roman Empire and then by Western Civilization as a whole may have been entirely fortuitous. Who was this Jesus anyway and why had culture after culture succumbed to His personal appeal, particularly considering the fate that followed his naïve system of ethics when applied to the deadly earnestness of the times in which he lived? Even now I am troubled by these thoughts and suppositions, questions that I of all men cannot answer. Instead I have embraced a faith that I cannot understand and made an effort to profess a way of life that troubles me to this very day.

I realize that I am not alone in this situation. The same historical conditions that once made Christianity the general ambiance in which every man and woman existed has now been supplanted by conditions where religion, except in conditions of near-death or at funerals, seems largely irrelevant to daily life. Religion has largely become the care and province of clerics and of professed individuals in various orders and congregations of nuns and priests. Now and again a popular mystic may arise who claims some direct contact with the supernatural, but these individuals are the exception not the rule. Then there are the modern spiritualists and followers of various occult practices who engage in necromancy hoping to reach across the iron reinforced gateway to eternity. My dear friend Sir Arthur Conan Doyle is one of these. He has been most useful to me in an editorial capacity and as a go-between, but certainly not as regards access to the other world where God is said to reign supreme. For religion I rely upon my own humble parish church. I say my prayers and receive the sacraments and try insofar as I am able to forget many of the deeper issues that I have had to recall for purposes of writing this book.

Everyone approaches the ultimate mystery of existence in his or her own way. My approach has been largely dictated by the occasional heroic figures that appear in human history. Holmes, a more saturnine individual, was accustomed to upbraid me for my supposed romantic outlook on life. This outlook was most evident in my assessment of women and my attachment to the married state, a proclivity much resented by Holmes who had grown through the years to depend upon my own dullness to sharpen his wit.

Actually there is a darker side to my nature; it is precisely those of a romantic temperament who are more downcast by the never-ending train-wreck aspect of human history. For this reason I have an affinity to the writings of Sophocles, Seneca, Aeschylus, Gibbon, and the more tragic plays of Shakespeare. Holmes in contrast, perhaps because he expects less of human nature is more likely to forgive and to tolerate what I am more likely to condemn and disparage. Holmes enjoys maintaining a balance at all times and his choice of reading material supports this view. He enjoys music both for its passion and emotion as in Beethoven, Dvorak, and Wagner and for its serenity as in the music of Debussy and Grieg. A review of his reading shelf would find volumes by Fielding, Sterne, Balzac, Thackeray, and Voltaire as well as Zola, Dickens, De Quincey, Chekov, Gogol, and Dostoyevsky. This extensive collection would be further enhanced by the spice provided by the decadent writers like Huysmans, Dowson, and

Wilde. Finally these were given sinew and strength by selections from the great philosophers and even the scientists of his day.

Our contrasting temperaments no doubt account for our long association and the depth of our mutual affection and respect; my sanguine hopes for mankind were again and again counterbalanced by Holmes' seasoned realism. It seems to me that faith, the ground on which I saw Sherlock Holmes and Professor Moriarty contending, intersects with the limits of human knowledge and understanding. Even to formulate the articles of faith requires the use of language and there is no way to describe the ineffable without resorting to metaphor. Even the most sacred concepts of the creed are confined to human understanding and expression.

When one adds to this the unavoidable cultural overleaf that must confuse even as it clarifies the etching underneath of absolute truth we arrive at an object that can never hope to contain within its confines the immensity of God. Then from the human side the act of faith is conditioned by all the impediments of improper motivation and incomplete consent when the prayerful supplicant says to God, "I believe all that the Roman Catholic Church proposes for my belief." Then there is the further difficulty of the requisite moral adherence to the truths believed and the commandments that are derived from them so as to transform the sinful soul into one ready to dwell with God and His saints for eternity, all of this in the face of a world that daily calls into question all these matters in the headlong rush to procure the means of survival in a competitive society. It seems to me that what remains is neither comedy nor tragedy but only improbability coated with layer upon layer of opposition and contradiction. Faced with all of this, is it any wonder that only simplicity and solitude could provide my only refuge. A point is bound to come when both the world and its conflicting prospects are too much to be endured and remain sane.

This I began to realize after the death of Queen Victoria. By being a living witness to history I realized that in my very being I had outlived my allotted lifespan; it was time that I like all the living was catalogued and consigned to rest among the dead. But first in the twilight years of age I desired to gain some perspective on all that I had lived through, even as I saw Marcel Proust doing in the first volumes of his great work, *"A La Recherché du Temps Perdu."* The search for one's own past for that quintessential root out of which all else has grown is the primary task of that period of life when maturity ebbs away and options diminish in proportion to the remaining time to actualize our designs.

The thought that history stands still and can rotate around a single nation let alone a singular iconic figure, even one of the stature of Napoleon or Queen Victoria reveals how deep the need is for each human being to surrender that most arduous of all tasks, to stand alone and to affirm one's values and beliefs. It is this drive to surrender to larger historical forces that makes a succession of tyrannies inevitable and also explains the need for religious belief, the projection of the good and evil of our own hearts outwards into hypothecated beings. We create our gods and devils in our own image and likeness so that in turn God can create us in His own image and likeness, a task never really completed.

The idea that man and woman have an essence either for good or for evil seems to me to be a case of the misreading of a wisdom text as a historical text. The Book of Genesis is less of book of history than it is an early work of anthropology, an explication of human nature in an idealized set of figures and circumstances. The reason that there is no mention of how Cain and Abel found spouses to populate the earth is that they are figures of design and not individuals at all. Woman played only a marginal role in order to make the author's point as memorialized by her derivation not as a separate creation as even the animals could claim, but as a skillfully modeled appendage taken out of man.

Revelation is not dictation. If the Bible is a superior account of religion than the Hindu Vedas, it is because God inspired the intuition of the Jews to create a more accurate rendition of God, one more adaptable as a universal creed, based upon their own history and intuition. The Jewish God is a function of the kind of God that Jewish history and culture needed their

God to be. Our gods are derived from the tasks that are demanded of them.

Here I speak of intuition rather than revelation because the latter term is a judgment of the Church upon some theological content that the human mind operating on its own would be incapable of producing, an infusion of knowledge of matters that are held to be infallibly true, but knowledge that could not have been arrived at by the customary modes of human experience without the direct action of God.

This intuition of course remains a human act, but one proceeding under an impetus that exceeds human solitary capacities. The truths affirmed by revelation therefore cannot be arrived at by either inductive or deductive methods; therefore I am referring to them as intuitions, insights that emerge from a prayerful contact with an outside force the nature of which remains undefined prior to the intuition through which its nature emerges with sufficient clarity and conviction that it can later be embodied in a text as an affirmation. This is what we mean when we look at Holy Scripture and proclaim that it is "the word of God."

But returning to the topic of the hypothesized subjective awareness of Jesus of His role as the Messiah: pushed to its ultimate extreme the theological position I have outlined would propose that Jesus died on the cross because the Hebrew literature had set conditions that only a dying God could ever embody and redeem. In other words Jesus was condemned to death by the very nature of the preexisting texts that defined His mission as the Messiah. One might speculate that if the prophets of the past had been more lenient in their demands and promises, a Messiah in the form that Jesus assumed would have been superfluous. The structure of historical vindication as set forth in these prior texts demanded the exaltation of Israel, an event so unlikely to ever be accomplished that it needed to be transformed instead into an ultimate defeat, not of Israel as a nation but by Jesus as the King of the Jews. This failure of expectation is the very corrective by which Jewish prophesies were fulfilled!

Whether Jesus comprehended His role with the foresight

and accuracy attributed to Him in the gospels would require an interrogation after the fact. Instead we are simply presented with the conviction of the Catholic Church, based on the gospels, that Jesus knew what He was doing and fully consented to play His role in redemption. The point is that if Jesus was actually resurrected and then ascended into heaven that these speculations are rather pointless. The degree of abdication of divine knowledge as part of the incarnation cannot be resolved.

The question is whether the proclamation of Jesus as Lord was demanded by Jesus or whether it was a later product of the earliest members of the Church reflecting on all that had happened while seeking an overall and composite meaning in the light of prior scriptural passages now applied to Jesus as both their source and fulfillment. This is what I mean by intuition leading to revelation as a divine process of the interaction of God with the human mind. Or perhaps the drama of the life of Jesus was simply the greatest coincidence of all time; Jesus thought he was the Messiah and lo and behold God accommodated Him!

Of course such daring and perhaps inadvisable speculations are peripheral and may even endanger a less reflective analysis of the mystery of revelation; they deny the easy solution of a primary and surface-level reading the Biblical text, a reading that sees God taking a primary authorial stance in each word and phrase of the Bible, so that everything therein happens as God wills it to happen and just as recorded.

The problem with this simplistic if venerable and traditional approach to interpretation, no matter how orthodox it may be, is that it involves the strange presupposition that God is a victim of His own need to never reverse Himself in order to react to contingent events. The Bible's own text however has instances where God appears to change his mind and follow a different course than He originally intended to pursue. It is only the Church that assumes that with the salvation mystery completed God is the victim of some sort of promissory estoppel (a legal doctrine) and cannot at a later date add a codicil or amendment to the celestial contract or covenant to admit other parties to the benefits conferred through the redemption wrought by Jesus Christ. I say this in reference to the doctrine of *ex ecclesia nulla salus* that has often been set forth as a radical limitation on those persons to be admitted to heaven. I cite these speculations on a proper hermeneutical approach to be applied to Sacred Scripture as an example of my sometimes daring and arcane suppositions or hesitations where my faith is concerned.

I continue to experience much the same confusion and doubts when I think back on my time with Sherlock Holmes. By 1903 I needed time apart for an intellectual sabbatical in order to reflect on all that I had learned at the side and under the influence of my friend. Holmes in contrast was still determined to apply His faith to the great events that cascaded down on Europe as the old rulers tottered upon their thrones and in consequence took the world to war over their imperial possessions with nationalistic fervor.

Meanwhile Catholicism under Pope Pius X had proven itself to be completely ineffective in preventing the war; instead it waged an internal dispute over theological differences that went by the name of "modernism." Catholicism had become so adapted to and entangled with the various royal houses that democracy could only be seen as a repeat of the excesses of the French Revolution of 1789 and the years that followed under Napoleon.

As the years have drifted by since my conversion in Rome when I first embraced the Catholic faith I have become more aware with each passing year that the religions of the world have less and less to do with God talking to men and more and more to do with men talking about God. If the entire world was a court of law and testimony was being heard, most of it would be disqualified as hearsay. Witness after witness claims to speak for God, but to each the objection can be made that they are speaking for an absent witness. God is not subject to a subpoena to appear directly and to testify in His own behalf to a changing world. The result is an abiding conflict waged between what I call "incommensurable discourses," arguments that meet on different planes that therefore cannot be resolved; they can only be repeated and occasionally backed up with force.

This is why secular governments such as that of the Americans exist; to prevent the fragmentation produced by different religious sects at war over what God says and how those sayings are to be actuated. There seems to me to be an inherent danger in religion, particularly when it is allied with power to compel belief, let alone to dictate public policy. It is not the function of the state to improve the moral fabric of the nation. The nation rules through laws, while God rules through revelation and providence. Both are largely inaccessible to the ordinary citizen. Petition and protest are to the first what prayer is to the second. Laws affect us directly and are immediately perceivable, whereas the action of God and whether that action is accomplished or facilitated by direct and immediate action or are merely delegated to an angelic host of representatives is not for us to ascertain.

Ritual plays a large role in both human and divine governance. The function of ritual is to impress the recipient with the dignity of the source of a power greater and of another order entirely than is evident in ordinary social discourse. This solemnity and even incomprehensibility ensures acceptance and compliance with commands and standards of behavior. Both are prerequisites for social order and without them discord and alienation would undoubtedly emerge over the course of time. Anarchy is an ideal unlikely to ever be achieved except in a society of self-effacing saints and even there variations of interpretation and emphasis would no doubt create divisions that would over time lead to open conflict. The history of Christianity proves my point. Even the effort to evolve a sensible and workable legal system can never be commensurate with morality and for this reason appeals to transcendental concepts in legal opinions must be seen as mere rhetorical devices. The law works best when it involves process and consent to be bound by a neutral and disinterested arbiter rather than by a judge; the more Godlike the proceedings the greater the chance of injustice.

Theology is not different in this regard. The habit of theologizing is one easily acquired and one abandoned only with difficulty. There is no person so sure of his knowledge as the one who presumes to speak definitively about God. For this reason I am convinced that religion like the love between spouses should be a strictly private and consensual affair engaged in behind closed doors. The minute that religion spills out into the public square violence is bound to occur. History is the proof of this assertion. I of course remain faithful to the Catholic Church as far as my conscience allows me to be, but I expect little from the Church other than the sacraments. Its own internal resources seem more inadequate every day to the historical tasks demanded of it. In the last analysis the sacraments are its only stock in trade and when these falter little remains but the elegant architecture and elaborate ceremonies that impress the senses but have a museum-like quality in the modern world.

Protestantism of course is no better. Its vague concept of a covenant and the bland congregationalism of the meeting-house are as aesthetically vapid as they are theologically deficient. As a doctor I learned to accept when a patient was beyond my ministrations; the religious leaders of our day have yet to adopt this attitude of resignation. History pursues its own course and appeals to religion for guidance will for the most part only make matters worse.

Both rest upon the New Testament, a text that contains within itself its own problem of tendentiousness. The New Testament considered as a unified anthology betrays the early struggle of Christianity to emerge from a parallel structure of intact Jewish belief that continues to this day. The Jewish remnants of Israel after the destruction of the temple and the resulting mass suicide at Masada followed by the Diaspora persist to this very day, as a people in exile. The legend of the Wandering Jew is only an individuation of the history of the Jewish people; although there have emerged elements that seek to restore a Jewish state, an opinion shared by the Prime Minister David Lloyd George.

I am dubious of the possible consequences. It is always a mistake for human beings to seek to achieve directly and unilaterally what God manages to accomplish in His own mysterious ways. For all of the discomfort involved the genius of Jewish literature its character is always beset by tragedy. The difference of this tragic portrayal of human life from that of the Greeks is that the Greeks learned over time to accept tragedy as the nature of human life, and one shared by all races of human beings, whereas the Hebrew literature is one long effort at protest at the human condition. The Western religions: Judaism, Christianity, and Islam are convinced that the course of life should be better than it reveals itself to be and as a result each has found a way to memorialize that conviction in authoritative texts that embody that conviction in whatever miraculous happenings they can use to prove that their communications, those projected outwards into the world that surrounds them are not in vain because they are received by God. More than this, each religion believes that the primary communication originates with God as the sender with humankind as the recipient. God cares about us, is aware of our existence, and has plans for us, a destiny beyond our present imaginings.

I find this hard to believe; but to believe the contrary—that our consciousness is the sole instance of perception and reflection of a somnolent (and worse than somnolent) an utterly insentient universe is impossible. Even forgetting the argument of those who would prove the existence of God by an argument from design I feel that the best argument for the existence of God is that *we demand that God exists*. We need God in order to validate the phenomenon of our own consciousness! Why are we alone capable of finding meaning and order and purpose in a universe that in itself has no meaning, order, or purpose beyond that which we create in the brief dream (or nightmare) before we return to become mere objects among objects whirled downstream in the chaotic river of time?

Perhaps the most astonishing aspect of human life is that roughly one third of our existence is spent in sleep where we float about in the same state of quiescence that we presumably occupied in the womb. So great is the attraction of sleep that even in a state of wakefulness the claims of slumber can now and again so overcome us that our awareness sinks involuntarily beneath the horizon of perception into the twilight or even the darkness of unconsciousness.

Even when we are conscious our efforts to find concepts that allow us to discourse about God leaves us with a ladder that falls short of our goal. Some philosophers when faced with this fact say that the word, "God," really only serves as a placeholder, a blank space without contents. Every attribute that God is supposed to possess is only an excess of some admirable quality carried to infinite dimensions, some trait that we find to be rare or admirable that coalesces into God. To say that God is great for instance actually says nothing because it will always exceed whatever point along a scale when we choose to stop and assess the qualities present at that very moment for praise and worship. In other words superlatives are only directional and can never be distilled into a stable substance—every "best," becomes a mere "better than," whenever something higher shows up.

God in other words in order to just be God must always be conceived as better than our precious conception of what God is. This is where theological language, let alone the concepts that it creates, fall short of what is necessary to give any substantive insight into God. The mystics in contrast to philosophers and theologians concentrate not on what God is, but rather upon what God is not. We come closest to encountering God when we fall silent and let God come to us.

Speculations that try and locate God in time and space are even more futile. God does not appear, at least in the Judeo-Christian concept of God, until He enters a relationship that allows God to appear as God-for-Us. Every appellation of God thereafter becomes descriptive of what God has done, is doing, or will do for His chosen people.

We enter into and are transformed when we encounter this God—we are taken out of ourselves and the limits of our own consciousness to encounter the substrate of any being at all.

Without God's grace everything loses direction and freezes into immobility. With God, the center of all things moves and changes so that Jesus assures us that God desires to dwell among us. God even desires to dwell within us! This indwelling breaks the usual borders of the self so that we can expand to embrace all things in the natural order as constituted by God.

Human consciousness is never solitary; it is in constant dialogue with a speaking universe. The proof of God, whatever we conceive that proof to be, corresponds with our sole and communal history. Each person, thing, and event becomes a part of us, both those of the past and those of the present. The American poet, Walt Whitman, was correct when he claimed to contain multiplicities. Each of us contains a fragment of the entire history of every life-form that needed to exist in order for us to exist at this very moment. We in turn are preserved in the corporate consciousness of the universe that has for a brief period contained us. Whether we shall return as we were an infinite number of times, as the philosopher Nietzsche asserted, whether we shall ever emerge from Plato's cave to see things as they really are, or whether we will be both elevated and transformed after death in the Kingdom of God as Christianity asserts, shall be revealed and emerge in God's own time.

I only knew that I needed time alone to reach my own conclusions on life and death; so it was that the looming separation (but I must again stress not antipathy) that has existed between Sherlock Holmes and myself ever since 1903 was not instigated by mistrust or saturation with his demands (for I love the man still); it was simply motivated by the busy existence and extraordinary efforts later to be expended by Sherlock Holmes (a man who is after all only slightly younger than myself) so that I could not find the strength or the will to follow him deeply into the new century. This lamentable fact combined with my own need to spend the years since 1903 in the process of finally discovering who Dr. John H. Watson was without his all-embracing influence must be born constantly in mind, lest my readers suppose that we quarreled and thus chose to part ways after 1903. I shall now return to my story of our time of union on the railroad journey in the early autumn of 1898.

Our trip through the state of Pennsylvania allowed us to witness firsthand the many contradictions of America. There were first of all the lovely green farmlands. I have seldom seen a more fertile and prosperous land than that of upper New York state and Pennsylvania. The harvest time was in full swing. The barns were filled with the year's produce and the early winter festivities would soon begin. The cider presses were at work, pumpkins sat atop fence posts, hay was baled, and the smokehouses were fragrant with the curing bacon. Everywhere there was cheerfulness and more that rarest of things, human satisfaction.

But as we proceeded southwards we met the stench of the coal-smoke boiling up from the city of Pittsburg that lies in the great bowl of a river valley. Even the countryside as we approached the city grew scabrous with pit mines and oil rigs. There were wooden shacks upon the hillsides and ill-clothed children picked through slag heaps for the refuse coal allotted to the miners by the mine-owners. There were lines of despair etched into the faces of the women as our train passed the mining camps. Many of the women though still comely in figure and clearly in their young womanhood, were already missing teeth, a fact that they bravely attempted to hide whenever they would smile shyly as our train passed.

The men in contrast were lean and enduring as old leather. I saw none older that forty or fifty. Though ill-fed and poorly housed these men put in twelve hour shifts in the mines, only returning to be fed corn grits or beans and salt pork coupled with whatever nameless greens grew around the miner's huts, there to catch a few hours of sleep interrupted by fits of coughing. While we were in this blighted region Holmes and I heard tales of the last great effort to unionize the miners, a struggle that was brutally opposed by the mine owners association and the thugs they were able to hire. This powerful organization brought in foreign labor to break the strike, most of them the newly landed Italians. The Irish and Scottish miners were then evicted from company housing and many perished in the winter snows of West Virginia, not a few of whom had been soldiers in the war between the American states.

It was some years since the Scowrers of Vermissa Valley had brought to the mining families some hope of resistance and vengeance. These members of that secret society, whom I had always believed were mere assassins, were revered in the mining regions as early martyrs to a just cause. We were actually able to visit the Vermissa Valley only to find that the name of Birdy Edwards and his brother Pinkertons were still universally loathed as strikebreakers and thugs. All of this had come as a surprise to me and something of an embarrassment. I could only think back with regret at the manuscript that I had written during the years when I believed that Sherlock Holmes was dead and before I had any evidence that Professor Moriarty still lived as well.

The book was entitled, *"The Valley of Fear"*. In that book I allowed myself some editorial discretion in Part Two to imagine the events that had once occurred in Vermissa Valley from a dramatic perspective. I had done so using the same writer's prerogative that I also exercised in the writing of my first book about Sherlock Holmes entitled, *"A Study in Scarlet."* I must confess here that I could never quite resolve the question of whether I was a creative artist or a sober chronicler of my friend's career. The temptation to mix vocations sometimes led me further afield than Holmes would have preferred. His constant deprecation of my efforts only made me at times more determined to seize the bit between my teeth and run a bit. I could now see that my portrait of the Scowrers as cads and villains may have been one-sided and based upon my own personal loathing for murderous tactics and rebellion. I have never quite been able to accept the fact that the most nefarious actions are often committed by people whom society deems respectable and that behind every great fortune is often a great crime. I have preferred to think that the established social order was the correct one and that social change must come slowly and not by revolutionary means. To take liberties with the law was to my way of thinking me to risk chaos.

As I have grown older though I have developed sympathy

with desperation which can no longer tolerate sustained injustices. Social change often comes too late to aid the victims of oppression. They cannot be told to wait while the very substance of their lives is bled away. Perhaps this was true of the Scowrers of Vermissa Valley. If I were to write the tale over again today, I would not hold that secret criminal organization up to derision but would paint more vividly the circumstances that they faced in such a way that they might be viewed in a more favorable light. Holmes in contrast was always the first to place himself in the position of the one whose acts although technically criminal might still exhibit certain extenuating circumstances. The rigor of the law seldom considers the unique circumstances of the criminal. For this reason Holmes placed his conscience above the law on more than one occasion. We had on occasion argued about this propensity of his and I had expressed my view that if everyone acted similarly, social order would fail. To this objection Holmes had answered that the social order was little more than an illusion. Beneath what we term social order is always a great underlying magma of injustice. Social order is the bare crust that keeps the chaos of fear and madness in check. To assume that any order of affairs is anything other than a brief compromise of opposing interests is to assume too much.

It was this attitude that made Holmes so dismissive of titles and honors offered to him. He was likewise impatient with the class of the nobility. The esteem of the great was as unlikely to impress him as was its occasional contempt shown towards the amateur detective practicing out of his humble lodgings in Baker Street to intimidate him. That the world finally had beaten a path to his door showed me that Holmes was correct all along and that a man who possesses his own soul in peace and dignity need not fear the contempt of the ignorant. His dignity rested always in his assumption of the full measure of the dignity of man and the right of the individual to determine his own destiny even before God.

God does not bludgeon us with commands but rather offers a way of life that in fact is the only true life that accords with our true human nature. To choose God then is not to yield up one's substance but rather to find it. The most perfect contrition is not made manifest in servile cringing, but in the restoring love of God and its impact upon us, so that if God were to foreswear punishment prior to contrition one would still know sorrow at having spurned His love. If God preferred punishment to absolution would He have sent Christ to us? When all of the world might be reduced to cinders at a breath, why does God forebear to remedy blasphemies and atrocities? Has God grown impotent since the days of the cities of the plain? Or is it rather that as the world progresses, God demands more of us; that of the full stature as sons and daughters of God and scorns to exercise the full measure of His wrath as incompatible with our dignity?

I often ask myself whether God might even prefer the honest heretic more than the complacent follower of orthodox belief. To unify the many manifestations of God in the Bible is no easy task and certainly beyond my poor abilities. Does not God have the right to be capricious? Great danger lies in seeing God as personal rather than as a mere predictable force as Spinoza did. That danger is the risk of any relationship—a personal God may act with choice and preference; but to go too far along this line one may end up as a Calvinist saying that God chooses those whom He wishes to choose and denies those whom He wishes to deny.

This theological habit of mind characteristic of fideism is the mother of invidious introspections. The individual soul becomes preoccupied with knowing the mind of God. What bug scurrying for cover to escape the light when a great stone is upturned would be more frantic than a soul seeking to escape the eyes of God if God proposes to dangle the soul over an abyss of fire as Jonathan Edwards once said that He did? This is the source of the terror of Adam and Eve who hid from God in their nakedness, the fear that God would see how really helpless they were and of how really helpless we their children would remain if God should choose to take offence at us. If God had not become man in Jesus Christ that servile fear would of necessity remain as our destiny. But if the witness of Christ teaches us anything at all, it must be that God has forsworn violence to vindicate His honor. Even in the days spoken of in the Book of the Revelation to St. John with its lake of fire we witness the last sputtering out of the older conception of God in the apocalyptic literature of the age in which it was written. Holy Scripture seems to vacillate at times between conflicting images of God.

Was St. John in his island retreat of Patmos mad and grown bitter that Jesus Christ had yet to return; or was he not rather the eternal optimist who wrote his great book, the final book in the Bible, to encourage the churches in a time of discouragement and despair? Had not Jesus told St. Peter that the beloved disciple might remain until the second coming? Did St. John daily rush to the shore in anticipation of that great reunion only to see the glaring light of the Mediterranean sun and the mocking blue sky, clear of the clouds of glory that he had anticipated?

Where now were the twelve Apostles that had sat around that paschal table with Jesus so long ago? What more bitter fate than to die alone on Patmos rather than in Jerusalem or Rome or even India like St. Thomas, the one who had doubted but endured? In the Book of Revelation a final exhortation is given to the universal Church to endure the same exile that St. John was feeling and out of hopelessness to somehow find hope. Christ leaves us to endure our own share of his passion and death with only the same Holy Spirit to comfort us, the same Holy Spirit that rested upon Him at the Jordan River when He was baptized when a voice was heard from heaven. "This is my Beloved Son in whom I am well-pleased."

Truly we are baptized into the death of Jesus. If we are truly to become Christians we must learn to accept exile and bitter tears as our lot in life. Our only comfort comes from being no greater than a servant should expect to be. To expect more comfort than Christ knew in his final hours might be our prayer, but that is not our condition as human beings. The Christ Event poses the one great but dual question to humanity—"Who do men say that I am? / Who do you say that I am?"

How strange that God allows us say what God shall be! He no longer says to us, *I am that I am.* That great but circular definition in essence says, "It is not for you to name me; it is enough that you know that I exist." Such a coy but accurate definition is appropriate upon initial acquaintance. How different it was to be, after the coming of Jesus!

Now God places Himself at our mercy and in effect says to each of us, "I will be what you wish me to be. I will give you what you ask, if you ask it. You may be as you wished to be in Eden and determine for yourselves what is good and what is evil and you may bend the Godhead to your wishes and approach the Tree of Life /// or you may accept my Cross and become my children by showing mercy to Me by believing in Jesus, the One that I have sent, (Jesus of Nazareth now called the Christ). I come to you empty and helpless—will you (man and woman) condemn Me or approach Me in the only way that I can ever be approached ... in love?"

There was this dignity accorded to man and to woman to be found in the miners' huts that I saw in the coal fields? What priority of a nation could mandate that the primal green and fertile forests must be tainted by the smoke and refuse of the mines? As Holmes and I wandered about the towns of the Vermissa Valley I could think only of the region as one vast burial ground for the hopes of mankind. No African slavery could be more degrading than employment in the great coal fields that fed the industrial might of America. Lungs meant to breathe the pure air of democracy here choked upon the fumes and sediment of coal dust and rock slag.

The very trees were heavy with dust. A sullen autumn rain ran down the train's windows and washed the black dust into the mountain streams that ran parallel to the track polluting them just as the souls of the heartless mine-owners were polluted with greed. We left behind the green fields of summer. As we passed beyond that bitter region of mines and mills it seemed to me that this was the perfect time to go down at last to Washington and see if anywhere some remnant of the old dream of democracy could be found in America.

A few days later we arrived at last in the nation's seat of government. An armistice had recently been declared and negotiations for a peace treaty were underway in Paris that would end the war with Spain. Events had proceeded too fast for Holmes and I to dissuade the Americans from pursuing the path of empire. America had chosen in this momentous year of 1898 to follow the path dictated by the abundance of its manufactured products, to seek greater access to world markets to absorb the surplus of mechanized production rather than to take the alternate course of letting domestic prices fall so that the many poorer Americans could afford them.

Oversupply and deflation are the bane of excess productive capacity due to abundant cheap labor and technological improvements. Rather than passing these cost benefits on to the workers the profits are funneled upwards and outwards to stockholders and in competition with other countries through enhanced export trade. The imperial desire for markets and for raw materials are the drivers of colonialism; the rush of nations to spread their influence abroad works against the democratic pretence of social equality and self-rule at home with the result that aspirations take the form of rhetoric over reality. Politics thus becomes an exercise of hypocrisy and manipulation of the ever-gullible public. Patriotism is the measure of the distance between promise and fulfillment like an ever-fading mirage. If religion is added into the mix, then the promise of future national glory becomes interwoven with the promise of the eventual realization of the Kingdom of God to the detriment of both. The measure of disillusionment is the degree of social unrest and criminal violence that a nation can endure without resorting to a revolution or a *coup d'état*. Labor unrest causes a reduction of production and employer resistance causes the closing of factories that would be necessary to get prices to reach their former levels of equilibrium once again. The imperatives of capital and mass production now dictate policy at the national level rather than the good of the citizens.

This was the process that Holmes and I observed when we

visited America at the turn of the century. It appeared that the government henceforth would be less a government of the people, by the people, and for the people and would be a government led by the need to avoid economic panics by seeking ever larger markets through the political subjugation and dominance of foreign lands. There is logic in events as Holmes had pointed out to me. Ideas when they are embodied in institutional arrangements have unpredictable consequences. America was now a land governed by a new aristocracy: the great railroad land-barons like Gould, the mighty lords of the steel industry like Carnegie, and the great shipping magnates like Vanderbilt cast their gargantuan shadows over the land.

The promises made to craftsmen and to independent farmers of equality and self-rule were now as empty and desolate as the land of the great trusts and corporations governed by the desire to reduce the costs of production by reducing wages in order to compete in world markets. Everywhere In America the dignity of laboring-men and the sanctity of women were being violated to meet the demands of the new god of mass commerce. We had seen the results of these policies in Pennsylvania and in the thronging slums of New York on the first day after we arrived in America. Washington in contrast appeared to be built in a style of Olympian splendor. It was a city but newly arisen from the tidal marshlands, but it was already a place existing in an atmosphere of wealth and privilege. It was meant to embody an ideal, but that ideal had already been betrayed in practice. It was the ideal of the sovereign rights of man and the ability to seek and moreover to find a measure of equality and happiness upon the earth. Alas, America was now divided by more than the fruits of a bitter civil war. It was divided by that most invidious of distinctions the one bred from unequal distribution of capital and of the nation's vast resources. It was divided by that greatest of all gaps, the gap between professed ideal and sordid practice. This was the disease that infected Washington in 1898 so that a man like Thomas Brackett Reed was planning to soon leave Congress never to return. Even a man who loathed war as much as President McKinley was in that decisive year of 1898 destined to lead his nation to embrace the fatal road to empire by its chosen war with Spain.

one of this fatal new destiny was visible though as we walked through the streets of the city, many of them only now being paved as the city grew. The nation was busy congratulating itself upon its recent victory. The costs of the war seemed negligible in the face of the newly acquired territories that now spanned the great Pacific Ocean to the gateway to China and its lucrative trade possibilities. The names of Admiral Dewey and of Theodore Roosevelt were on everyone's lips. The contempt once felt for the hesitating McKinley was but a dim memory and he was cheered wherever he went. His substantial bulk seemed to promise the nation a new security as a world power and the path ahead seemed to be paved by the gold standard that had been the hallmark of his campaign for the Presidency of the republic. Holmes and I had come to Washington to convince the Americans to build a canal across the narrows of Central America, not because we favored it, but because we opposed Baron Maupertuis who intended to do so in the name of the continental powers. These powers would inevitably threaten English supremacy over the seaways of the world. England had in the person of Mycroft chosen the lesser danger of entrusting America as its former colony with policing such a useful passage that would end forever the difficult journey to the east around Cape Horn even though that passage was guarded by British control over the Falkland Islands.

The great nations of Europe were looking outward in 1898 to China and Japan. To choose the American venture was to frustrate the Dutch and the Germans and the French effort to build a canal had already failed and been abandoned. Holmes had reluctantly consented to carry his brother's message to President McKinley and to urge the Americans to undertake the building of a canal before Baron Maupertuis should move on from the railroad that he had acquired in Costa Rica to the project of building a canal through the northern isthmus of Columbia, the region known as Panama or perhaps through the longer route of Nicaragua. What better time to urge such a course but now when America felt in the first flush of victory that all things were possible! Still, I could tell that Holmes did not relish this assignment. To choose between the powers of the world that nation least likely to exercise tyranny when it achieves victory was beyond his powers as a detective. He had told me as much on many occasions over the course of the summer. At the height of his career Holmes seemed more than anything to crave obscurity. His fame since his return from his Great Hiatus had spread throughout Europe and the international calls made upon his abilities might prove to be his undoing. I even doubted at the time if he could ever take up his former load of private cases whenever we returned to England. There still remained with him though a sense of the obligations that must come with the possession of any extraordinary gifts. To think first of himself and of his health was anathema to him, so that I as His friend and physician had taken it upon myself to demand for Holmes the space and time that would prevent him from ending too soon his valuable life.

He had grown from the dreamy and self-indulgent young man that he had been at the commencement of our acquaintance to become an English institution, the court of final resort for the insoluble no matter what the nature of the problem brought to him might be. Yet in spite of his great abilities, he had only grown more humble with the years, so that he was content to kneel at daily mass with the char-women and old men of his parish and to receive the comforting presence of Christ in the Holy Eucharist and to find in that action and the daily labors that followed through the course of his day the only real and necessary tasks for a human life.

Access to power seemed to Holmes to only raise the risk of human temptation and error. Power was the one thing that man and woman had craved in Eden and it has brought us no end of misery since. To exercise power over events is to be caught in the most treacherous of the webs of circumstance, so that even the man who intends the good usually finds that his best intentions are thwarted, and evils subtle and unknown soon invade his initially beneficent designs. One need only think of the example of Abraham Lincoln whose hope to preserve the union was only achieved at the cost of so many lives, including in the end his own, to realize the truth of Holmes' opinion of the costs of the use of power. As Holmes and I walked through the crowds of Washington in the days that followed we observed the workings of democracy as America became adjusted to the fruits of victory. We both wondered if America had not already left its best days behind when the nation had been content to determine only the fates of the thirteen colonies and not the destinies of people across the ocean. As we had toured through the coal and industrial region of Pennsylvania we had been able to meet several of the men with the Pinkerton Detective Agency. They had heard of course of England's great detective and were only too glad to explain their own methods of dealing with labor unrest. I recall one conversation in particular with the head of the district. He was a self-important little man and his explanation of his duties I shall reconstruct from memory...

We are private agents of course, Mr. Holmes. We owe our loyalty to the mine-owners association as our client and we do our best to prevent any trouble. Mostly it's a lot of outside rabble coming in trying to stir things up. We make the district to hot to hold them; you may be sure. The trouble is they breed discontent and usually leave a group behind that tries to form a union. The profit margin of the mines doesn't allow for such excesses. We are at the mercy of the railroads that haul our coal and they keep us on a tight leash I can tell you. In '93 many of the mines folded-up and that's a fact. The county is too poor to maintain a proper police force to guard lives and property. If we weren't here it would be back to the old pioneer days damn quick. The Scowrers of Vermissa Valley once bid fair to control this whole valley and the hollows beyond. We tracked down the leaders and hung them up like so many fox-skins to dry. The mine-owners learned a valuable lesson. It's cheaper to pay us than to raise the wage rate paid to the miners. We keep the coal coming up out of the ground. By doing this we serve the nation. I like to think of our work as the work of patriots."

The man sat back in his chair before stating with an air of assurance, "We don't use your methods of scientific investigation of course. Our problems are not involved with solving complicated questions. We know the miners want us out. It's us or them as I see it. When trouble surfaces we find the leaders and we make examples of them. Better to hang a few then to see the mines go bust. Then nobody gets paid. Where would these people be without the mines anyway? Mountain trash, what else are they good for than to mine coal or scratch out a living as sharecroppers with a few acres of tobacco? Whatever they earn they drink up anyway; cheap corn-squeezed whisky! Most of these folks will be dead by the age of forty of the drink and black-lung anyway. As miners they perform a useful function for the nation as a whole. This nation needs coal and plenty of it if it is to thrive and prosper. The western farmers need it to get their grain to market. The navy needs it for the new steamships. We Pinkerton men are an essential link in the chain. We do our part and we sleep well nights knowing that we did it. Labor is an essential of production and with the Italians and the Poles coming in droves there are always men willing to work for whatever wages the owners care to offer. No sir, we don't need unions, not in Vermissa Valley; you may sure of that and we don't need any anarchists or socialists here either. In fact we don't need ideas of any sort. Men here need to know how to swing a pick and a lift a shovel; that's enough for them. An outside group of Quakers was down here last year; tried to open a school. It was all a lot of nonsense. The people hear from the bible come Sunday and that's enough. God wills a man to accept his lot. That's my view in a nutshell. Some is born to labor and others to have it easy. Far be it from me to question the ways of God."

I noticed that Holmes did not try to change this man's opinions and after we left I asked him if he had agreed with the sentiments expressed.

"Of course not Watson, but I know that if that man did not believe his brand of nonsense he would forfeit the tiny ledge on which he balances. Most of American society is made up of men just like him. It is no small part of the secret of amassing great wealth to keep each man in fear of the man below him who just might take his job. Each laboring man lives in fear that he may fall back one notch in the scale of existence. The presence of so many impoverished men and women keep the rest struggling to hang on to the few freedoms that they are allowed to possess. There is nothing that an American fears more than going backwards. America is a nation of fugitives from the old world. Each immigrant came here with great ideas of building a new society and behold they have built only a more brutal version of what they left behind. Americans have stampeded across this continent leaving destruction behind them. They are like a plague of locusts ravaging the land. Now they have even taken the bold step of reaching out across the seas. How will it all end I wonder? What force will stop such a frantic people, a nation that uses fear and intimidation simply to procure the means of gaining a livelihood? I fear that Americans will always be in search of some enemy, never knowing that it is they who are the threat to the nations that they will despoil in their headlong rush of acquisition."

He went on as follows, "There is a species of ant in South America that sweeps over the land during certain seasons or years leaving nothing standing behind the track of its sweeping hoards. I never think of that species of ant without thinking of the Americans. They come thinking that they may remain individuals, but they learn soon enough that they are only part of a mass movement. The growth of a civilization requires stability and time and Americans have neither, not as a nation and not as a people. In order to create a national identity much less a culture there must be sufficient leisure to develop the arts. Culture is a matter of selection and exclusion. Without the occasional inventor or author to define a national ethos what remains? Americans behave for the most part like blind herd animals. America is attempting to weld into one nation a multitude of languages and cultures and in addition to unite the separate states into a single entity. Only a great central tyranny with its arms, the great corporations and trusts, can stabilize such a great heterogeneous mix. Freedom might have found some support within the original conception of semi-sovereign states, but now? Well you have only to look about you when we arrive in Washington. That city will soon unite the power of purchased representation with military power into one vast oligarchy living within a few miles of each other."

"Still we must not judge America too harshly; if the nations of Europe have never known peace, then why should we assume that the mere transplantation of European people to a new land will change their unique characteristics? America might seal its borders today and it might still take a century for Americans to devise a culture that will be applicable to all of its citizens. As it is Americans are defined not by what they are, but by what they aspire to obtain, which simply means, in the absence of a common culture, more material property. The pursuit of material gain by individuals is none other than that struggle for survival that Thomas Hobbes states must precede the institution of any civilized government. In other words, Watson, the Americans have chosen to make struggle and economic gain the very definition of themselves as a people. It is to this that they owe their remarkable progress in this century since the founding of their republic."

"But can a nation, the very identity of which involves a passion for acquisition and a desire to enlarge its national borders be anything other than a plague upon the other nations of the world? If Americans always resort to arms in order to forge a specious unity among their own citizens, will they ever foreswear violence as a means to obtain international ends? I fear that Americans will always be a people that will resort first of all to the gun or the sword, not only among themselves, but as directed towards those who oppose their national aspirations. The present war with Spain is but an instance of what will no doubt become the preferred national policy, just as it was national policy to destroy the former inhabitants of this continent. America seeks more than just colonies. It seeks whatever it may obtain by force of arms and it will sooner or later devote most of its resources to support its military ambitions. I fear that madman, Roosevelt, who we met in

Newport this last summer, will someday be President. How can he not be? The views that he expressed in Newport are precisely those of the nation he would govern. McKinley on the contrary, from what I have heard of him, is at least a man of caution and reflection. But he is no less an American for all of that and he has now taken his nation to war, but only because of a felt necessity welling up from below. Roosevelt on the other hand has contempt for peace. Peace for that man represents weakness in the body politic. He believes that war purges the body just as 18th century physicians believed in bleeding the patient to rid him of the predominant excess humors in the blood. Americans will do anything but reflect upon their own actions. The enemy is always without, never within. America craves enemies and relishes attacks because they invite reprisals."

"Would the war against Mexico in 1849 have succeeded without the prior instigation of a few border skirmishes? One need only think of the massacre of the indigenous people at Wounded Knee. Was the threat of a mere Indian religious ritual so great that it demanded the deaths of unarmed women and children? Or was what the soldiers really feared that the Indians, even defeated and unarmed as they were, still refused to become white Americans? To desire peace or freedom on their own terms was to threaten the idea of America to its core. When after all was Abraham Lincoln killed? Was it during the war? No, but at the advent of peace! Any man who advocates peace here is a threat to this nation, one that will never be sated in its lust for blood. America will always find enemies to fight because it craves them. I foresee that there is no foreign border that will be respected by the Americans as the years pass and its power as a nation grows. There will always be a national interest in growth, in expanded markets, in new opportunities. Even the nation's laws do not contain or record anything but the American desire to test the limits of every concept. The result is not a legacy of precedent but of contradiction. There will never be an American version of Blackstone's Commentaries, although I hear that Justice Story is attempting a synthesis of American jurisprudence."

"To prove my point one need only consider the trial that was given to the defendants after the Haymarket Riots in Chicago. Those men were sacrifices to the Moloch God of the Americans. It was not an execution for a crime, but only vengeance and fear combined to make of those men an example to others who believed as they did. No Watson, I have no illusions about what we will find in Washington, which is the very belly of the beast. It is there that the many private interests come to seek patronage. We will be but one of many petitioners before the throne, but we come, not to seek our own ends, but to set one devil upon another. That man Maupertuis is the worst of the Old World and if we are to stop him we must use an instrument proportional to his own malice. America must be that instrument."

I recall that the vehemence of Holmes' opinions surprised me at the time and I believe that I said as much to him, because he then explained further why he spoke as he did.

"You are hearing my frustration that we cannot follow our initial design and use the papers of Murillo to show the Americans the vipers who once sustained that man in power in Costa Rica. It might be a timely lesson to them. Instead our own loyalty as British citizens demands that we urge the Americans to continue on their present path. We have come to conjure forth a demon Watson in the name of the British Empire; may that demon not turn finally upon us! Mycroft knows that England may not for all of its naval might stand alone against the continental powers if a general war should break-out. Even the conflict in South Africa has severely tried our national treasury. What then would be the result of a general European conflict upon the destiny of England? England sees its enemies close at hand and would now use the power of all of its former American colonies to come to the aid of the mother country. But I fear that it will be at the cost of all that makes us Englishmen in the end. Mycroft was always a practical man, not a man of principle; but as he has so often said, 'When it comes to the struggle of nations, there is no morality; there is only relative power.' It is a creed that I believe these men in Washington would heartily endorse."

hortly after our arrival in the nation's capital Holmes and I called upon Thomas Brackett Reed, Speaker of the House of Representatives. We found him in his office in the great domed House of Congress. For me it was the most impressive building in Washington. The House of Representatives, the members of which with their short term of two years, was clearly the chamber of Congress where the voice of the people could best be heard. The drafters of the Constitution clearly intended that a representative could be swiftly replaced should he fail to represent the common will, since he must answer to the people every two years. The House of Representatives was the gage of the popular sentiments that would determine the national policy and character. Legislation would originate there for later approval by the Senate. The great office of Speaker of the House required a man who could tame this often fractious body and produce legislation that would keep the nation to a steady course. No more imposing man had perhaps ever held that great office than Thomas Brackett Reed. Few men would care to risk his ire or to run the risk of the censure of his wit and eloquence. Yet, when we met with him upon this occasion, we beheld a man who had known the most singular defeat in his long career. His words soon explained the reasons for his gloom.

"Gentlemen you see before you an anachronism," he stated after greeting us and seeing us comfortably seated. "My counsel has been spurned by my own party. This country has decided to join the folly of other nations and has opted for an expansion beyond its natural borders. America might have depended upon its own domestic markets to absorb its manufactured goods. Instead it covets foreign markets. Foreign trade brings about foreign entanglements. My friend, William McKinley, as good a man as I have ever known, once knew this and shared my sentiments. The McKinley Tariff promised to keep cheap foreign products from our shores so that our working-men might be fully employed and our domestic markets made secure. Now it is contended that so great is our manufacturing capacity that we must seek out foreign markets or see an overproduction of goods and falling prices. I have a simple solution to this problem, which is to pay higher wages to the workers so that they will be able to afford to buy what they produce. If too much of any given class of goods is made, then re-tool the factory and make what the people actually need until all primary needs are satisfied at a reasonable price. All of this talk of national growth and expansion is nonsense! This nation has yet to catch its breath after a century of expansion. Must we now annex islands in the Pacific that are located thousands of miles from our own shores? Surely our already straining and extensive borders are such that we might find a sufficiency of abundance of nature's gifts close at hand in what we already possess. Our appetite for foreign conquest only grows as we seek to surfeit it."

"We are clearly in advance of ourselves! Let us now take time to contemplate and give thanks for our good fortune. Let us pause for a bit and seek a sabbatical in attaining justice for all Americans. Let us stem the tides of humanity that flood our shores and let them seek justice in their homelands by emulating us. Let Europe shake off its decrepit aristocracies by an exercise of the popular will. Instead, America is busy emulating Europe the ills of which caused us to flee to these far off shores. What is Newport but a testimony to the greed and frenzy of this gilded age? One need only look at the great houses along Fifth Avenue in New York City. Beneath all their pomp and pride is a sordid affair of sticks and wire all strung together and hollow at the core. It takes time for a nation to reflect upon itself and to know what it is. We have not had the time yet to do so and we will not have it until America turns away from its premature desire that its own beliefs shall be dispositive for all mankind. If our form of government is meant to be emulated, let us show that we are first worthy of being a model of something beyond mere greed and acquisition achieved by force of arms. If not, there will come a point where the nation is starved to garrison the ring of martial encampments upon foreign soil. We have already made a beginning with this affair of the Philippines."

"What does our prospective annexation of the Philippines have to do with our original desire to see a just settlement in Cuba?

Must we defeat Spain in those far eastern regions in order to liberate an island that is located only a few hundred miles from our shores? Or was Cuban freedom not our intention after all? The entire affair reeks with duplicity! I thought I knew Bill McKinley well. He seems to feel that he is acting as some sort of great liberator and not as a new tyrant over a subject people."

"Meanwhile the press is shouting, the people are cheering, and the costly arms of the nation are growing. Where will it all end at last? I at least have seen the horizon of my usefulness. My own party has deserted me. I have arrived at that hour when a man wishes to retire knowing that he has left his nation in good order and in peace to a new generation. Instead I leave a nation in a state of chaos with a resentful working class below and a frivolous and depraved aristocracy above rather than a united nation based upon equality."

"Surely the days of Madison, Jefferson, and Washington are but a dim memory now. They will be honored in name, but few will ever think to read their writings or adhere to their example. They have been reduced to mute idols of a vanished age. The law itself is the minion to this urge for endless international expansion. It will grow as the country grows until the very texts of the law will descend into irrelevance. Laws will be weighed not for their reasonableness but for sheer volume and weight like so much wheat in a scale. At last the law will become irrelevant and there will only be the search for power. That is my vision of the future for this country gentlemen and it is time that I retire from a stage where I can be of no further use to the nation I have loved but can no longer respect."

It was a sad thing to see the disappointment of a man who was as noble and generous at heart as the man who sat before us that day. I could see the sympathy in Holmes' eyes as he looked across at the great man. I could think of nothing to say to him, but Holmes at last spoke up.

"Sir, you find yourself in good company; I in my own person agree that our respective nations have taken the wrong course, yet I am here as an emissary of that very expansionism that you so rightly deplore. England is also a nation like yours that has long depended upon its seas to defend it. We have grown in naval might simply so that we might exist at all and not have been annexed long ago by France. We are now a martial nation and must be martial still because the naval power of Germany is rising daily. Germany will soon be the greatest power in central Europe. It is a peculiarity of any nation that occupies a central location surrounded by rivals that it has no fixed borders and will often be threatened by the peripheral nations that surround it. Her Majesty's government has even made peace with its old adversary, France, in order to contain the resulting German ambitions. I do not know if you are familiar with the name of my brother, Mycroft Holmes, but his opinions are often sought out by our government. His advice has been dispositive of national policy on more than one occasion. I have been entrusted with a delicate mission here, not as an official ambassador, but as a private citizen. My credentials are confined to my own reputation as an effective private inquiry agent. I am here only to make a suggestion. That suggestion is that America should soon begin work upon a vast project of construction, one unparalleled in the history of the world, by building a canal through Central America to unite the oceans and to enhance world trade. Now that the war with Spain seems concluded and peace is at hand such a policy becomes even more imperative if America will be able to administer its new acquisitions in Hawaii, Guam, and the Philippines. I am therefore here to request from you an introduction to the President so that I may lay this suggestion before him and thus complete the mission assigned to me by my country. After that my mission is fulfilled, distasteful as it is to me personally, my promise to my brother will have been discharged."

Holmes paused to gage the effect of his words before proceeding as follows, "It is not a mission that I have relished. But I am an Englishman and the threat of a combination of powers upon the continent against England is a real one. You may have knowledge through official but unnamed channels of a man in the Netherlands named Baron Maupertuis who is already dedicated to controlling trade through the isthmus region of Central America by his control of a railroad in Costa Rica. I fear that if America does not act first a canal will eventually be built by a Dutch or a German company. If this should happen, American interests will be subject to control by European powers in any commerce that America wishes to maintain with China and Japan. England would rather be dependent upon the fairness and equity of America than to acquiesce to the prospect that any continental power should be able to stifle commerce and deny equitable access to the east by the control of such a canal. I will be quite frank with you sir. England sees the growth of American power as the lesser of two evils. I wonder if that will continue to be so in the future. If in the course of a single Presidential administration so much change has been possible in our concept of England's role in the world, what might America become once international power is no longer an aspiration but an accomplished fact? Can any nation resist the desire for world domination when that prospect lies before it with some likelihood of success?"

"Conquest directed toward world hegemony and empire always begins in the same way, by speaking of the necessity for rational self-defense of its own territory or essential economic interests or to uphold previous alliances that must be honored. Then that momentum will broaden the legitimacy of any claim to include an expanded version of the nation's vital interests to a spreading and prosperous democracy. Finally, the nation's leaders will speak of the necessity to defend its destiny and its presumed right to expand its borders or sphere of national interest or control to the fullest extent of its abilities."

"No nation assumes limits voluntarily. It assumes its rightful station under duress and resistance, because the community of nations soon presses in upon it to thwart its heroic ambitions. This is what political realism reveals: that in the face of a multiplicity of nations there is both advantage and also a threat of immanent war whenever an opportunity to grow in relative power is perceived to exist."

"America will only be secure to the degree that it adapts to its new role in the proper containment of the international system by balancing the power of Europe in this hemisphere. Mutual fear must be balanced with mutual cooperation. The one flows from the other. Concessions extracted with impunity and without opposition do not need to be subject to trade; instead they become tributes to superior power. This is the force that drives nations to assume colonial possessions and to aspire to the status of empire. Every empire in turn invites revolution along the periphery. Empires expand until the center, long since abandoned and bled to support their armies upon the frontier, falls into decay. Gibbon does a splendid job of recording the process as it once took place in the Roman Empire in the course of its decline and fall.”

Thomas Brackett Reed paused to consider his words carefully before agreeing too readily and acceding to Holmes’ request for an introduction to the President. “I believe that you are a man of honor, Mr. Holmes. I hope that I deserve an equal assessment in your eyes. I would not serve my country well by enabling it to pursue a path that I regard as a betrayal of our national character. On the other hand your proposal may just manage to recall Bill McKinley to his senses. The cost of a canal would be a tremendous drain upon the national treasury. Perhaps if he realizes the cost of building a fleet to service these new acquisitions in the Pacific Ocean and the cost of building a canal through a jungle so that these ships may obtain ready access to China, he will realize that any trade advantage that he has hoped to gain by this war will be rapidly exhausted by the new costs which must be paid for by domestic taxes. No political party cares to ask Americans to bear the burden of a national income tax! It would require an amendment to the American Constitution. Bill has always preferred tariffs to direct taxes, to let American any ambition to trade in foreign goods pay for itself and to shift the burden of lowering their domestic tariffs to other nations if they wish to obtain access to American markets. International Trade by its very nature seeks a balance of payments between nations. One does not trade for what may be produced just as well at home.

America is a land rich in resources. We do not need to import raw materials from colonial possessions let alone finished manufactured items from abroad. We are a land rich in inventions and the organization of labor. We need not import manufactured items from foreign shores to supplant what we can just as well make for ourselves. We are quite capable of existing upon the base of a domestic market. If there is any overproduction, let us use the surplus to enrich the lives of the working men of America. Let us use the surplus to reduce prices or to raise wages for the good of all."

"Why should other nations benefit from the cost advantage of our efficiency? Why allow their citizens to benefit from the ready availability of cheap American goods while our own people exist in penury? Imbalances in sharing the fruits of industry have allowed the owners of private capital to grow exceedingly rich by harvesting the produce of labor to the detriment and disadvantage of most Americans. The function of capital lies in providing investment in plant and equipment; but why should private railroads enjoy public lands by the grant of extensive right-of- way concessions to undertake what they were willing to do in any case? The public land is the rightful common-wealth of all of the nation's citizens. Were the people of America ever paid a gratuity for these gifts to the railroad millionaires? Would the railroads have failed to be built had these subsidies been denied them? I think not!"

"Profligate overstimulation engaged in at the public expense was responsible for that very overbuilding of railroads that caused the panic of 1893 from which we are only now recovering. Or let us discuss this whole question of free-silver, which was the basis of the Democratic platform in the last election. William Jennings Bryan is a good man, but he was foolish in his supposition that increasing a nation's money-supply would automatically advance the interest of the entire populace, particularly the western farmers. A rising demand for silver would have only inflated the currency and would have disproportionately enriched the great mining companies that are owned by a few men in California, Nevada, and Colorado. The nation would have been forced to purchase silver from them for coinage and what is the nation finally but only its people? It would have been a reverse tax paid by the nation in favor of the silver producers. The people would have had to pay to enrich the few. If this ever occurred where would it ever stop? Would not a point come where the banks would demand from the government the right to issue paper-script as notes with government approval? Believe it or not Mr. Holmes, members of Congress have already been approached by certain bankers who wish to form a private cartel of centralized national reserve banks of which all of the other local private banks would be put in the position to be consumers. Such an extensive institution, in return for acting as an insurer of bank deposits, would be granted a private monopoly to issue paper money, which power should only be reserved to the people's own national treasury, not a private cartel."

"In order to feed this great beast of a cartel, the treasury would raise money by printing interest-bearing bonds for sale that would then be purchased with this pretended money. Thus the government would become a debtor and the banks the ultimate creditor and who would pay the interest on those bonds but the people in the form of taxes, the poor benighted people of America who little understand such machinations!"

He paused to catch his breath and to see if we could see as he did how inverted the relations of government and the wealthy private sector of the country was becoming.

"It would not stop there, Mr. Holmes. The next step would be for these private banks to inflate the currency by printing ever more money. The result would be a general rising of the price of essential goods with which wages cannot hope to keep up. Interest rates will then climb to keep up the pretence of trying to stem this inflation, now portrayed as an excess of demand over supply. The banks will then make more money while the people will be selectively impoverished by the twin devices of inflation and high interest to be paid on their loans. Like any magician the banks will point to wages and say that the inflation is being driven by excess demand fueled by wages that are too high. Wages will then be cut or layoffs will occur in factories until a sufficient balance is achieved once again."

"At least once in every generation the bankers will schedule one of these inflation periods until the people grow to expect them as a normal part of the business cycle. This was not the intent of our Constitution when it gave the government the power to coin money, not to delegate this function to monetary wizards! Governments are instituted among men to guard them from the predation of their fellow men. When government is controlled by the very men who pose a threat to the common good, it becomes a force for private exploitation. That as why we had the revolution in 1776 in the first place. Will we now become a colony maintained by a few men who are our own citizens? That is the course that we have followed since the end of our civil war. I trust that all of those gallant men did not die merely to produce out of the restored union a sordid empire bent upon conquest abroad and private predation at home!"

Thomas Brackett Reed fell silent then and the room contained a sense of futility that emanated from the one man who of all the silent and absent people who were his fellow citizens could only lament what the rest had to endure in the newly constituted Republic of America.

Sherlock Holmes at last spoke up, "I begin to see what is really at stake at this present time; these are indeed very deep waters. But surely there must exist in any republic a safeguard against these developments that you have foreseen."

Mr. Reed laughed bitterly, "Well, there is the institution of the nation's laws. The common law is a legacy bequeathed to us by your own country. It is a marvelous instrument based upon the common experience of England over centuries but it is not proof to amendment by legislatures. Our legal tribunals grind exceedingly fine and someone must bear the cost. As the laws multiply a point is reached where one will only invoke the law at one's peril because the law itself will devour one in legal costs. Where is an efficacious remedy when it only matches the cost of obtaining it? No my dear sir, the laws will soon only grease the wheels of the coming juggernaut of the acquisition of private power at public expense. Now you know why I have opposed this war so vehemently. This war with Spain was just a distraction so that our countrymen could feel collectively a sense of triumph to mask their individual defeats as they are being ground down beneath the juggernaut of the corporate domination of world trade."

"In any case why would we ever wish to take the place of Spain? Only recall its history as an imperial power! Banks do not generate production; they can only serve it. How much steel is produced by a room full of accountants? How many crops are produced by farms that have been foreclosed upon by banks? The Spain of the conquistadores was a vulture feeding at the dead body of the indigenous empires of the Aztecs, the Mayas, and the Incas. Spain was awash in gold and silver for a century, rich in palaces, monasteries, and cathedrals and poor in every class of the populace, a poverty that finally left Spain so weak that America could conquer it in a single year. Let us rather read in its defeat a prophecy of the fate of those who embark upon the path of domination and greed!"

Again he paused to consider his course of action before standing up and walking over to shake hands with Sherlock Holmes.

"Very well Mr. Holmes, I will try to bring you together with President McKinley. But I will come along also to attend that meeting. If I cannot make Congress see these essential points of our drifting national policy, perhaps I can appeal to the President even at this late hour. If I fail there also ... well then it is time for me to retire to my retreat in Maine and resume the private practice of law. I have always thought that the best of men pursue public life only as the shortest path to a return to the freedom and joy of a private life. If one remains too long in politics one forgets what it is to be a man pursuing life, liberty, and the pursuit of happiness. Such things require time, leisure, and reflection upon the ills of this world the better to prepare for the next."

Holmes bowed deeply and said, "Thank you sir. We are both embarked upon missions that we wish were unnecessary. If we discharge our functions according to our conscience, then we must leave events to follow the course that they always do. There is a quality of blindness to the course followed by what we term the collective will. It never becomes conscious of itself. History is the result of the unpredictable combination of forces which sometimes reach consciousness in a few men who are close enough to events to perceive what is happening. They alone influence it by being first converted to the uses of history. However, as past experience shows men do not so much make history as they embody it. Individual men are mere reference points from which we look into the maelstrom of events. Even a President does not make war if that war is not to the taste of the people; nor may a single man of peace impose reason if folly is the order of the day. We must discharge our respective duties, Mr. Speaker; we may do no more than that. We will await your summons that a meeting has been arranged." With that we departed. As we walked to our carriage Holmes remarked, "We were given an extraordinary privilege today, Watson; we have been in the presence of a great and honest man."

After informing Mr. Reed's secretary of our address at the Washington hotel where we were staying we withdrew. On the way back to our lodgings Holmes turned to me and said. "It is a privilege in this life to have met some of the great men of the age. We were in the presence of one such man today. I must tell you Watson, that if I did not fear the Baron as much as I do, I could wish that my mission here would fail. It would be better for America to know an early defeat, the better to return to its proper place among the nations of the world, than to succeed now but lose its soul at last."

We had left the great marble halls of the Capitol building and were met outside by Inspector Stanley Hopkins. He had not been part of our private meeting with the Speaker of the House, but he was always at our side so as to provide an escort and guard for us. The Inspector was always well-armed and his eyes scanned the multitudes of people in the streets for any sign that we were being followed. Our movements by train over the last month had presumably shaken off any pursuit, even if we had been tracked to Newport by agents of the Baron, but it was still advisable to use caution.

We did not however forego visiting the many places of enlightenment and interest that we found in the nation's capital. On the following days we visited the great Smithsonian Museum, the Supreme Court, and other public monuments. In the evenings we went to the theater. Irene Adler's theatrical company had by then arrived in the city. The play in which she had the lead was filling the theater nightly and promised to have a long run. We met her after her performance on one of the first few days after our arrival and entertained her at a late dinner at our hotel. She seemed delighted to see us again and I noted, not for the first time, the easy familiarity that existed between her and my companion. It was impossible to define the nature of their relationship. It seemed to me a compound of trust and esteem. I still could not say that a romantic interest was involved; it seemed rather as though each of them had managed to do that rarest of things, to get beyond the normal divisions and mistrust imposed upon the sexes and to achieve an abiding respect for each other's talents and character. Too often what is termed a romance is but an effort by each party to remedy their personal deficiencies by basking in the glory of another's gaze.

I did not feel that this was true of them. Instead, each seemed to relish the triumphs of the other and to require little in return. Each might exist independently in his or her own realm, but they chose to enjoy the other's company to enhance what was already complete and adequate within their own natures. It was the sort of love, if love it might be termed, that is only possible with the coming of age and maturity. It was no less delightful for being calm and its gentle ironies bore no hint of the hidden cruelty of lovers who are often engaged in testing the degree of each other's affection by equivocal actions and comments.

As the days in Washington passed we fell into a routine, which if not as enjoyable as our time spent along the coastline of

Rhode Island over the summer with America's new aristocracy, was at least as informative. We were able to observe at close range the workings of the political institutions of the nation. Speaker of the House Reed introduced us to several Congressmen and Senators and we were soon receiving invitations to dinners and to the various other winter entertainments and soirees of the nation's capital. The often stifling heat of the eastern summer had given way to the mildness of a southern winter. I was still concerned though about Holmes' health and I made every effort to see that we kept to a schedule of early evenings and that he retired early to bed after we returned to our hotel. It was during those long evenings after Holmes had retired for the night that I was left free to pursue my own interests and could find the time at last to read with great interest the sections of his journal after his time spent at Kings Pyland.

These pages recorded the events of the last months of 1893, beginning after he had returned to his home on Dartmoor after leaving Professor Moriarty. They also recorded his trip to Ireland and his time spent living in a monastery there. As I read these sections of his journal I was to learn more of his labors on behalf of Sir Henry, of his continued efforts to solve the problem of Professor Moriarty, and of his final return to London where I was soon to meet him when he appeared under the assumed disguise of an old bookseller and to discover that my great friend had not in fact perished as I had long believed at the Falls of Reichenbach, but was still alive! His meetings with Professor Moriarty had proven to be inconclusive at the point where I had stopped in my previous reading, but I could see that Holmes had at least managed to cause a breech to be made in the Professor's adamantine defenses.

It remained to be revealed how Holmes had managed to widen that initial gap over the years succeeding 1893 to the point that Moriarty had finally agreed to abandon his plan and to aid Holmes in his efforts to prevent the harm that the Professor had once intended to inflict upon the lives of so many innocent people in England. Was it a question of religious conversion or a mere capitulation to superior rational force that explained this action on his part? I was to discover that the answer to this question was not a simple one; Holmes gave me no hints on the matter, preferring that I discover the answer in due time by reading the journal entries in their proper sequence.

He did however mention one day that some ground was gained by a discussion that the two of them had regarding an early treatise of Professor Moriarty upon the binomial theorem. It had led to a question of why regularities should be present in mathematics and why certain mathematical constants should even exist. Were the observed regularities and various symmetries such as those that result in crystal formation purely fortuitous and a matter of accident? Was an asymmetrical and arbitrary universe even conceivable; or was it merely that our own mental processes demand closure and consistency so as to set our own thoughts at rest.

If this hunger for regularity and consistency applied to physics and chemistry was it possible that the same could be said to exist in the moral and in the aesthetic realms as well? Finally, what part did human freedom play in the constitution of the universe? Could it be that our very act of observation and measurement determined the character of what was observed? Was the position of the observer in any way relevant so that the universe at all levels might be in some way aware and reactive to being observed and thus able to frustrate his designs by keeping one step ahead? To my puzzled expression Holmes gave no answer but merely pointed to the journal with the unspoken demand that I read on.

From the Journal of Sherlock Holmes

July 24, 1893
Grimpen

I return home without any clear understanding of precisely where Professor Moriarty and I are positioned in regard to the wager reached between us. Perhaps my assumption that any question of significance can be approached as a mere set of binaries on a linear scale was misconceived. A quick review of our ordinary thought process will demonstrate what I mean: time/space, left/right, up/down, positive/negative, good/evil; what have these to teach us other than to focus us on the awareness that these polarities merely define a field on which any particular event must be plotted. But suppose we add a dimension of depth to that planar surface; where are we then? Is there a position that hovers above and looks down upon the entire field of human endeavor so as to put all things in their proper perspective? Is that what Professor Moriarty means by a philosophy without axioms, to escape from the easy binaries that capture thought? But is that ever possible? Even the human brain is bifurcated into twin hemispheres only weakly linked by the *corpus callosum!* What would then become of the magisterium of the Catholic Church, the source of all dogma and doctrine without the ability to infallibly define and thereafter to pronounce a verdict of condemnation on those who dare to maintain an opposing position by saying, "Let them be anathema?" Can such definitive statements ever be simultaneously a question or even a petition to God to grant us greater insight into our human situation, one that generates such binary perceptions in the first place? In any case I cannot unilaterally resolve this point. The past days since my return have been very busy ones. I returned to find a letter awaiting me from Isadora Persano. It contained a strange and almost meditative rendition of the character of Roger Baskerville. If I ever needed proof that Mr. Persano is not only a sane but a remarkable man, I will only need to refer back to this letter. Mr. Persano has left me well-armed to pursue and to confront my old foe and I will share what I have learned with Colonel Moran when he arrives. This communication from Persano has come in due season. Colonel Moran writes me that he has at last grown bored with Monte Carlo and wishes to enjoy the winter season of this year in the card-clubs of London. He also plans on meeting with Professor Moriarty for the first time since the destruction of their criminal organization and the events in Switzerland that followed and to receive any instructions that the latter may have for him.

Am I foolish to bring together these two men who were formerly (and perhaps still are) among my most fearsome enemies? I think not, for these past years have wrought a subtle change in our relations. I cannot forget that I have owed the preservation of my life on more than one occasion during my travels to the swift instincts of the Colonel. I must also bear in mind that Professor Moriarty, far from being the unprincipled "Napoleon of Crime" that I once thought him to be, has shown me that in his own mind at least, he is a man of honor if not of virtue. He believes that he is correct in answering to the moral imperative of his own nature, one that demands that he assume what is the sole prerogative of God of knowing and thus determining the nature of good and evil. He is proud of his depredations and unrepentant of his crimes. His particular type of evil has this about it: it is predictable and consistent and for that very reason perhaps not completely depraved.

Real evil on the other hand, the evil that I associate with Roger Baskerville and with men like him, is usually arbitrary and capricious. It often has about it the stench of a depraved innocence and is reckless of its own true best interests, even while spreading its harm to others. In this it is chaotic and even mindless. Which of the two types of evil: principled or unprincipled is the worst, I cannot say; but the first seems to be at least approachable through rational discourse, while the latter must be simply constrained and defeated because it is surely a form of madness. I will transcribe here Mr. Isadora Persano's letter in its entirety...

My Dear Mr. Holmes:

I must begin by thanking you for your efforts in procuring for me the security of my present retreat. I believe that when you hear, as you shall in this my exposition of the character of the man who threatens us both, you will understand my reluctance to remain at large where I might at any time be a target for his peculiar malice. There are men who are never more dangerous than when they appear to be your greatest friend. Baskerville is one of these. His nature does not have the honesty to declare open animosity, but rather insinuates himself like a serpent into one's private heart, the better to achieve his evil ends.

The devil never makes a point of displaying his horns. I have never known a man who was better in the art of appearing to be a man of virtue and of what I might even term an enlightened vision. He is always engaged in some scheme of human betterment and it always ends up in causing some great harm to those whom he professes to wish to aid. His plans have only this one consistency: they are always grand and far-reaching. He has a love for great canvasses and thick pigments. He is subtle only in his means but never in his ends. He promises great results without sacrifice or cost. For this reason he is often taken up by the many and even the few who should know better find their normal skepticism quite overcome by his enthusiasm and charm. He has above all else a sense of novelty about him and appears to be perennially young. He must surely be of later middle-age by this time, but though I have not seen him, I know that he will appear to be a decade or two younger than his real age.

He is particularly deadly where women are concerned. Women appear most often to love men whom they imagine that they may improve or mellow with time. No woman appears to want perfection at first hand. She cherishes even flaws as long as they appear to her to be challenging but harmless. This gives her room to tailor her husband over time to meet whatever particular idea of manhood approaches that perfect lover the image of which every woman maintains within her secret heart. To such women Roger Baskerville has all the charm of a basilisk! But he is no less appealing to men of principle. He promises such men that with his help they may fulfill whatever particular mission they may entertain. Each man is a Napoleon in his own eyes and each has the equivalent of the steppes of Russia before him to entice him to overshoot his mark and bring ruin upon his own head.

Roger Baskerville is of course nothing in himself, but he has the capacity to seduce others, which is the primary characteristic of all those who have led humanity to ruin; I have no doubt that he will rise again and seek to find his place among the powerful. His present eclipse is an unnatural condition for him to occupy. It may breed an attitude of desperation within him and cause him to throw his usual cunning designs to the winds. It is that which I fear most, for a cornered beast is the most vicious one. You may wonder why I who am one of the foremost duelists in Europe should have such great fear of this one man. I ask you not to think of me as a coward, for I am not. What I am is a man of system and order and hence vulnerable to a man whose very being manifests a chaotic soul.

The duel is one of the most formal exercises of mankind. The number of paces is set, the pace of walking is slow, and the result predictable, if one only thinks for a moment of one's technique as one turns to fire. All preliminary matters must be settled in one's own mind before the fatal morning. Killing a man is a dreadful thing of course and no matter how prepared a man may believe himself to be, when he turns and fires there comes a brief micro-second of hesitation before the act. A bullet travels over the distance of ten paces faster than the quickest of thoughts and when a man has once been hit his opportunity to return the shot accurately is considerably reduced if not eliminated. The man therefore who fires accurately and first is the one who will survive the encounter. I have systematically trained myself to do my thinking beforehand and to fire calmly, accurately, and always to the heart of my opponent. I find human suffering to be appalling and to misplace a shot through my own negligence inexcusable. In any case thought, reflection, and prior practice give me the slight margin of advantage which in a duel to the death is always decisive. My preparation eliminates both fear and hesitation and gives me the steady hand of accuracy.

I do not covet duels, but I do not turn from them. The duel is the final test of honor and sincerity and as such it has value among gentlemen. I never kill a man whom I hold in contempt. It would be foolish to risk one's life to conquer a knave. Rodger Baskerville is a knave; I know that now. The man who shoots him down will rid the world of a beast and not a man. But this beast is rather like the cunning leopard that only attacks from secrecy and from hiding. Ambush is in the very character of the beast and of the man. Against such a man reason fails and no advantage is to be gained by practice and preparation. The odds are always in his favor for he acts out of impulse and instinct at the critical moment. His form of genius, if he has one, is to create that critical moment.

For this reason I fear him above all other men. His habits are impulsive, whereas mine are ordered and formal. He will risk all for even a trivial goal, while I risk little even when the goal is a matter of importance, and even then only under force of necessity and with an opponent worthy of my skill. I cannot fathom his motives, for they are as inscrutable to me as those of the devil himself who would leave heaven to become a mere seducer of the naked residents of Eden. In short, I fear this man because he is evil and I, though you may consider me ruthless after hearing this confession, am still withal a man of honor. I do not cheat in the duel. My opponent is as welcome to take the duel as seriously as I and to prepare accordingly; that he does not do so, practice and prepare, is not my fault.

No doubt my opponents believed that they proved their bravery by scorning danger. They forgot that the purpose of the duel is not to prove one's bravery but to survive the encounter. One has already proved one's bravery by simply arriving at the scene of the duel. I never confuse the action with its motivations. The act of bravery is in risking the possibility of the duel, not in its actual execution. A man who initiates or accepts a duel is brave in doing so, but after that his test of bravery has been accomplished. All has been proven, for a coward will avoid a duel at all costs. Once the duel is set, retreat or escape with honor becomes impossible. It is then that deliberation must come into play to ensure one's survival. The reasons for the duel become irrelevant to my mind until my victory has been achieved. My mind focuses all its faculties upon that single shot upon the success of which everything depends.

In the act of fighting a duel a man places his entire life within his own hands. How often is this power over oneself realized among us in the ordinary course of life? Most of a man's life is spent waiting for an ignominious death that may ambush him at any time by the bite of a mere mosquito or a drop of tainted water. Man fears death for the same reason that I fear Roger Baskerville, because death is usually a factor of mere chance and not of will. The duelist is I believe the only free man, for he places his very life at voluntary risk before the specter of some spontaneous and chance but trivial extinction can claim him. He runs a risk not to be found in nature. He courts death, but only to spurn its embrace at the final moment by the triumph of will and execution that allows him to retain his life and to walk proudly away from the field of honor.

Only the matador among others who face voluntary danger knows such a feeling of freedom or attains such happiness at the supreme moment. When a man realizes that he is free of his peril and may assume again the vesture of his life, that life which he receives back seems to be an eternity. A mere moment ago might have been his last, but now the riches of the years ahead descend upon him as though they were a legacy beyond his wildest dreams. I tell you sir that I have never lived more intensely than at those moments. But soon alas, the pall of boredom returns again and one must risk everything again to express extreme opinions and by doing so to risk again the danger of giving mortal offense to some man who is willing even to die to demonstrate the sincerity and rightness of his own convictions. You will say that a moment's elation is not worth the sacrifice of so gallant a gentleman, but you forget that even to die has its own joy for such a man. To be remembered for one's gallantry may be the only source of immortality that he will ever know.

As my opponent lies before me, bleeding upon the ground before he leaves forever behind him the fair prospect of life and of youth; I who am the victor salute him. I who live do not scorn the dying man as the mere carrion his body will shortly become; but as a brother, nay I will even say a beloved brother, I salute him. I have never admired any living man as much as I have admired a vanquished foe. So dear to me is such a man that I would people the world with such men and eliminate the others as so much dross. If I might only achieve this supreme act of purification, I would be content to abide forever in this world of waste and mediocrity and would perhaps hold it too dear to ever risk my own death again in a dual.

In short sir, I entered upon the practice of dueling to prove to myself that human life is of value. If I had not done so, I fear that I would long ago have placed a pistol to my own head and fired so great is my distaste for the majority of the human race. Most people seem content to live in a world where men are mere beasts lapping up the sweetmeats of life and begrudging death as their enemy. They would extend their bland existence into an infinite futurity in a kingdom of heaven with an insipid god in a pale pastel paradise. I seek out no such god, no god whose image is thought up by pale spinsters knitting in the back of evangelical chapels or by artists commissioned by robe-wearing eunuchs that fancy that they are successors to the apostles.

My god, if there is one, is a god who looks on at the deaths of millions with equanimity as when Mount Etna or Mount Vesuvius erupt. I cherish the god of the Lisbon earthquake that even awoke in Voltaire a feeling of appalled awe. I cherish the god who never interferes with the course of human slaughter or the thousand plagues of earth. Such a god is indifferent to death, unless it is of one who has courted extinction in the full-knowledge that his loss is forever and without any hope of resurrection. Such a sanguinary god may then do for me what I do for my dying opponents. He may then interrupt his usual pursuits to salute me as I disappear forever beyond even the capacity of that indifferent god to recall me again to life.

Of course I know I will someday die. I will die forever. It is my final desire though that neither woman nor God will weep over my grave. My ideal god will think and speak only thus of human life...

"I created the world and all that men see as a contemptuous afterthought, an idle amusement of a boring eternity and ever since I have watched the ants of humanity crawling about on their anthill fetching in money and pleasure and begging me to extend the term of their miniscule lives and even to make them eternally happy. These foolish beings forget that if I wished them to be happy I would have long since done so. Am I not God? But I have created them merely to exalt my knowledge of my own greatness in contemplation of their preposterous arrogance in attempting to worship me and to witness them squirming about in their vanity and squalor. Their worship only cheapens them in my eyes! If all the fleas of a dog were to stop feeding upon his blood and worship him, he would remain a dog for all that. If I am to be a god I do not need worship from what are mere fleas to me, but rather I await the one who would prove the worthiness of even being a flea in my creation by defying me and by doing so without hope and risking in doing so my infinite displeasure; this would please me most. Only such a man could I ever love! The man who dares to scorn

even his god is alone a man worthy of the trouble of creation and I have not known such men and women since Adam and Eve. May I be spared all obedient slaves! Give me one free man who dares to sin and to scorn me to my face. Only such a man can be said to have been created in the image and likeness of God!"

That Mr. Sherlock Holmes is my religion and I endure this life only so that I might practice my unique faith for a few more years. Am I mad? What is madness after all? Every man's religion is madness to those who do not adhere to it. Surely the tenets of my faith in their simplicity cover the facts of the case as well as that of the Christian God of love, whose only sign of love was to include His Son among the tortured denizens of this earth.

Of what use is a sacrifice in atonement for sin when sin has not abated? The men of religion grow fat on what they pretend to despise. The evils of the world make their own existence necessary. I despise their rituals and I scorn their proxy power of forgiveness. Who are they to forgive me when I do not forgive them? It is they who murder god each day by turning him into some censorious prude affrighted by the desires that have been placed within us not merely to populate but to express the life within us while ignoring the violence that their own religion unleashes upon the earth. If I who scorn both tenderness and mercy feel pity for a man that my own hand has killed even while honoring him, where is a correlative pity from a god that witnesses all evils and does nothing to prevent them? Until this question is answered my own religion must suffice. I will not close this letter with the usual polite appendage of claiming to be your obedient servant; I sign it with my name alone, for that is all that I have and all that I will ever possess,

Isadora Persano

I put down this letter with horror in my heart. What depth of inner terror must this man know to need so vehemently to despise all humility by demonstrating a pointless and futile courage in this manner? I can only hope that his present fear awakens him again to his humanity and to that of others as well!

As I reflected upon the sentiments of his letter I saw that this man had just articulated better than I could ever do the inner philosophy of Professor Moriarty as well. Here once again was a man attempting to fill the great gap that is left if one has no faith in God. Such a man must seek within himself for some code of conduct and some explanation of his origin and destiny. Worse still, he must concoct some scheme for society that will help mankind as a collectivity to thrive and to achieve happiness without God.

Such a man's obsession is to be a legislator not merely of his own particular existence, but he must prescribe also some sort of normative conduct for all other men as well, unless he is to turn to some alternative secular faith which ignores the metaphysical question entirely. Such individualistic belief-systems take a single aspect or characteristic of human nature or experience as we find it and universalize it to cover the whole of man's experience. Thus we have economists who see men simply as mere agents of production, or aesthetes like my friend, Mr. Oscar Wilde, who insists on seeing man as simply an artistic creation and a cincture of various excessive and colorfully shaded emotions, or political men like Karl Marx who reduce everything to the role of class struggle for historical dominance.

Only the great western religions, particularly my own faith of Roman Catholicism, take man as a being whole and entire in all of his innate capacities; and not merely in his present state of being, but by believing that man is not an end in himself but is made for the glory of God, these godlike faculties imply a transcendent purpose for human existence. If man must seek only within himself for his own meaning that meaning no longer remains objective and universal but becomes only a subjective projection of each man's fallible individual being. The part would then determine the whole which is logical nonsense. Man is man not because he is great in himself but because made in the image and likeness of God, he participates in a Being which as source and origin feeds and sustains all that is not its own Trinitarian Being.

The great insight of the early metaphysicians was that all

being that is not God could not be self-sustaining. Energy that is not renewed is necessarily diminished over time. Only God is in His very nature self-sustaining and immortal and he may preserve in being whatever he wishes. Severed from God man becomes what he once was ... nothingness. Worse than nothingness he may even like Isadora Persano raise a fist in rebellion against that which alone sustains him. To make of one's life such a gesture of defiance is not merely ungrateful; it is petulant and absurd. Yet so many Godless men and women think that they have done something wonderful by acting in this manner. All such people manifesting existential pride in the last analysis loathe themselves. Here in Isadora Persano I beheld a man who needed even a rationalization that would allow him to kill others simply to support his own attitude of despair by his desperate attempt to save his own self-respect at all costs. It is just such men who most need to ponder the words of Jesus Christ: "Take my yoke upon you for yoke is easy and my burden light and you will find rest for your souls."

I folded up Isadora Persano's letter and put it away carefully. It may be useful at some later date. His insight into Roger Baskerville at least seemed to me to be both accurate and telling. I seem to be gathering about me an assembly of many of those who have been maimed by evil each in his own way. By using these instances as case studies I am able to devise a mode of opposition. Each of these men is proud and contemptuous of those who do not share his own dispositions, but each seems instinctively to know one another's vices and weaknesses as though some dark ligature connects them. Perhaps in hell each lost soul mocks the sins of his neighbor. Hell might be defined as a society of mutual distaste for each other, just as heaven is defined by love for one another. Each creature in hell is nauseated by all that they find unlovable in their neighbor while remaining blind to their own imperfections which in hell are now all that they possess. Each soul in hell cannot imagine why he is not in heaven after all. Such a soul's vision of heaven would be shared with no one else of course but contain himself alone, particularly when his own sins are so minor (as such a soul views it) when compared to that of his fellow inhabitants of hell.

The saints on the contrary always consider themselves to be among the worst of sinners so conscious are they of their own failings to respond to Divine Grace. The eyes of the saint are fixed always upon Christ, not upon themselves. Their virtues seem to them to be entirely derivative as in fact they are! The saint is aware of the directional nature of grace which is always downward and gratuitous. Just as the organs of the body are nothing in themselves without the blood that sustains them (cut off the blood from even the heart and that organ dies) so in this very manner the soul dies without the constant sustenance that is provided to it by Divine Grace. Even in his sin man is not deprived of the impulses of grace entirely, for without them even repentance would be impossible.

It was this primary insight that made Luther attribute salvation to grace alone and seen from the standpoint of ultimate causality, he was correct. Luther's only error was in forgetting that grace does not coerce the soul, it only enables it. Martin Luther's need to feel definitively saved by grace alone was simply a residuum of his fear of his own nature and his lack of trust in God. God cannot ever forget man whom He loves, but man is quite capable in his own darkness and pride of attempting to forget God. The task of the saint is to impose no obstacle to grace but to be as the clearest of glass to admit the light without presenting any resistance. The source of the light always remains outside the glass yet when fully illuminated, the glass shines with light.

July 26, 1893—Grimpen

As I mentioned in my entry of yesterday, I wrote to Colonel Sebastian Moran who agreed at my urging to come to England. He will, no doubt, spend considerable time with Professor Moriarty at Kings Pyland as well as taking up his usual lodgings in London. The Professor is quite capable of issuing commands in furtherance of his great plan to Colonel Moran and through him to any other associates who remain loyal to them. But his mere physical presence here on Dartmoor is no greater threat to England than it would be in any other location, because whatever threat that

Professor Moriarty is contemplating must be extraordinary and complicated in nature and international in its scope. Besides, I have been assured by the Professor that his plans will only mature in the year of Victoria's Diamond Jubilee of June 20, 1897. I have plenty of time then still at my disposal to discover and thwart his plans. I have done all that I can at present to seed the ground for his ultimate concession and I must now be patient. The attainment of faith is not the work of a day for most men, still less will it come swiftly to one who has always used all of his powers to avoid it as the Professor has done.

I may therefore concentrate all of my efforts for the present upon this problem posed by the re-emergence of Roger Baskerville. The problem of course is that I have no idea where he is at present. He may not even be in England. Perhaps his strange appeal to Isadora Persano has already been abandoned, but I must not presume this. The safer course is to assume that his menace remains and that sooner or later he will attempt some manner of assault upon Sir Henry and Lady Beryl. He has a tidy mind. He seems to be able to segregate portions of his life for immediate attention just as the collector mounts one exhibit at a time. I doubt that he has forgotten as significant an item as Lady Beryl once represented in his collection. If he has heard of the marriage of Lady Beryl to Sir Henry Baskerville, his cousin and the man that he must hate above all others, it can only be a matter of time before he returns to exact his revenge. My task then is to keep his plans for Devonshire an afterthought for him by providing more attractive options for him in distant places. The immediate problem of course is that I do not know where he is to be found so any direct communication with him is impossible. Even if it were possible, direct communication with him would clearly elicit the demand for a bribe that he keep away from Devonshire, and as is invariably the case with bribes and blackmail they do but strengthen the hand of one's opponent. Once such a one knows the scope of his power, he is sure to only increase his demands over time. The trick then is to lure him away without letting him know that we are aware that he is even still alive. If he has kept that fact a secret for so long, he must have good reasons for doing so. I may only hope that those same reasons still prevail with him to some degree.

If his immediate need is for money, as Mr. Persano has indicated, then money will be the best bait to draw him away from Devonshire. I know his skills and may guess at his *curriculum vitae*. Why not then place an advertisement in the local papers for a man possessing just his qualifications to be posted overseas. He will suspect a private advertisement as being precisely what it is, a private bribe to exit Devonshire. The source of the advertisement must therefore be as formal, broad, and general as possible. I think back upon the technique used by the prospective bank robbers in the Case of the Red-headed League. The target in that case was only a single individual, but to avoid suspicion a net was cast that appeared broad enough to bring in hundreds of red-headed men as applicants though only one was to receive an appointment to the billet. The device was a stroke of genius by Jonathan Small and I must use the hint that it has provided to me now.

I shall therefore appeal to Mycroft to issue an advertisement for a government posting to Central America, let us say British Honduras, for I do not wish to be too obvious by mentioning Costa Rica. Besides, Rodger Baskerville is too well-known in that country. Time and his own considerable knowledge of disguises though would be sufficient factors to make him risk a posting to Honduras. The problem will be making a visible identification of our man when he presents himself to be interviewed for the position in London no doubt under a fictitious name. I must see if Lady Beryl possesses a photograph of her former husband. If so, I can send it along to London. I believe that Inspector Stanley Hopkins would be the perfect man to act as the interviewer. Hopkins is intelligent and an expert at penetrating disguises. Mycroft can of course use his influence to provide a posting to British Honduras.

Yes, I think that this ruse will work. I have of course considered the possibility of simply clapping the man in irons at once and having him tried in court for the murder of Sir Charles and the attempted murder of Sir Henry several years ago, but what would be my case before a court of law at this late date? The first murder was a case of a heart attack induced by running from the hound. It would be a matter of remote causality and a mere civil tort at worst, but not a crime. Similarly, the attack on Sir Henry could hardly be prosecuted now based upon our remembered testimony about a now non-existent boot that was meant to place the hound upon the scent of Sir Henry. Even a barrister of average skill in advocacy would get the man acquitted. In any case the crime was only one of attempted murder since the plan was not successfully executed and the sentence would only purchase a few years of freedom for Sir Henry until his cousin emerged from prison to exact his revenge.

I shall put all of these considerations to Sir Henry of course before deciding on a definitive course of action, but the wiser course seems to lure our man away to Honduras and hope that he never returns. If his present need for revenge was greater than his need for money an attempt on Sir Henry's life would have already been attempted in all probability. No unusual occurrences have been reported to me by Sir Henry. This may mean that the man has already departed England and given up any pursuit of aid from Isadora Persano. If so our problem is already solved, for he is busy seeking greener pastures elsewhere. Still, I would like to know where our man is to be found in the future. If he is in Honduras in a government position, I may always be sure of his whereabouts. What can be better for now than to place an ocean between Roger Baskerville and his cousin? I will assume that he is still present in either London or perhaps even in some retreat in Cornwall or Devonshire and advertise accordingly in various news dailies.

If this plan should fail, then I must rely upon the direct action of Colonel Sebastian Moran, the old tiger hunter. He may be willing to accept a private commission and to use his own considerable skills to take our quarry down. Colonel Sebastian Moran is precisely the tiger to set upon Roger Baskerville. There is a certain justice is using the means thought up by Roger Baskerville himself during the time that he was calling himself

Stapleton in order to defeat him now. I do not wish him to be killed outright, although Colonel Moran could do this successfully as his past history as an assassin proves. Still, he is a dangerous man and if matters go too far...well then he has brought his own fate upon his head and this may be the only way that Sir Henry and Lady Beryl may ever be delivered from the danger that still exists all about them as long as this formidable man remains alive. He is an imminent danger as deadly as the family curse of the Hound of the Baskervilles. The question of a preemptive action to avoid a proximate and probable evil before it occurs will always trouble moralists. Statesmen are under no similar doubt regarding the right path to pursue. The rule of sovereignty will always remain the rule of superior force. The margin between threat and execution is thin indeed and that is why wars are not only conceivable but inevitable when the right conditions for their execution prevail.

July 27, 1893
Baskerville Hall

Today I have come to Baskerville Hall to share my plans with Sir Henry and to see about the possible existence of a photograph of our man. Sir Henry listened carefully to my plan before getting up and pacing the room nervously. "I have half-a-mind to track down the man down myself, Holmes. I have money. I could hire detectives. Say the word and I will..." he expostulated.

"I believe that you already have a detective ready at hand Sir Henry," I interposed with a smile.

Sir Henry looked up at me and chuckled. "You are quite right Holmes, and I am not using his skills and judgment in preferring to use my own resources, am I? But you see I hate to see this man getting off as easily as he will by being provided with an attractive and secure billet overseas in Honduras."

"Oh, I don't think you need concern yourself upon that score, Sir Henry. A government posting to Honduras has its own trials and tribulations. Ask anyone who has been posted to a colonial office if the boredom, the wretched climate, and the risk of coming down with tropical fevers are not quite as bad as any punishment that might be imposed by a sentence to prison or transportation to Van Diemen's Land. If he were not desperate, I doubt that he would accept the post. But he will be on familiar ground there at least in Central America and the prospect of intrigue in Honduras using his old and former methods will no doubt appeal to him. Let him weave his webs there rather than here and purify this English soil by his absence. I really think it is the best course available for us to pursue. But we must first find a way to identify our man, since he will doubtless appear for his interview for the post under an assumed name. Does Lady Beryl perhaps have a photograph of your cousin, Roger Baskerville her former husband?"

"If so, Holmes, I can hardly think that she would have retained it," objected Sir Henry with some irritation.

"Still, we may as well inquire. I am sorry to broach so delicate a subject, but the success of our plan may depend upon it."

With that we got up and proceeded to Lady Beryl's morning room. She was engaged when we entered in answering some correspondence. Her life has been a busy one of late. As the Lady of the Estates of Baskerville she is engaged in many charitable endeavors. She looked up as we entered the room and cast a questioning glance at her husband. She must have sensed at once that something was amiss from the expression upon Sir Henry's face. He has already strengthened the guard that he keeps about the perimeter of his estate and Lady Beryl never leaves the grounds unless she is accompanied on her visits to the moorland tenants by one of the servants, but her haggard expression as we entered showed us that she had never known a moment of peace in recent weeks perhaps due to a premonition of what was to come.

Sir Henry had expressed a fear that the strain would be excessive upon her nerves if we confirmed to her that Roger Baskerville was indeed still alive. But now there was no more room for choice remaining in the matter and we had decided that she must be told the truth. Sir Henry did so quietly and she took the news with a demeanor that showed her bravery, a courage that I have always associated with her character. We both realized at once that our prior efforts to shield her from any confirmation of her fears had been unnecessary. It appeared that she had never doubted that her former husband was indeed alive from the moment that she had first heard about the tale of Isadora Persano and the extraordinary moth larva that he had found in a matchbox. She in turn had been endeavoring to protect Sir Henry by her silence upon the subject, because she feared some rash action on his part. Now we were all together in our acknowledgment of the danger that surrounded us all. When I brought up the matter of a picture of her former husband as delicately as I could, she was silent for a time. At last she looked up and with tears in her eyes confessed to the existence of a cameo photograph of him that was taken in Yorkshire many years ago. It was still in her possession.

"I beg you to understand, Henry," said she, "A woman possesses very few things in life besides her own past. If that past contained foolish choices, it is still all that she has of her own. Does not a man keep track of his travels and investments and some at least of his conquests of the heart? How shall I ever appreciate the full measure my own present good fortune in finding your love, if I have no means by which to see again the eyes of the man who formerly claimed to love me, but did not? Even now I cannot believe that I could have been so misled by him until I look upon those vacant eyes. In the past his every failing only made me more determined to nurture all that remained of his affection with a still greater love on my part. I could not admit failure in a choice as important to a woman as the man I was to marry. Even now, knowing what I know of him, now that I also know that he is alive, I am aware that in the eyes of the Church, that evil though he is he is my husband still unless an annulment is granted! If his vows to me were perjury, mine to him were not! I promised him all that I was and am and that promise shall be kept until he dies or until an annulment of the Church leaves me free to honor my wiser and truer promises to you, my dear Henry. What else can I do and remain an honest woman? What else will allow me to be what you love? You, who are finally worthy of all that I dreamed a marriage of true hearts might bring, deserve no less. If circumstances have been cruel to each of us, then this is the price that love exacts! How foolish is the man or woman who enters upon the path of love to obtain comfort and happiness! Love is a daring risk of all that one possesses and believes, not so that he may be happy, but so that he may be worthy to be called a child of God. If God himself risks even his dignity and honor to foolishly love those who betray Him, can we do any less towards Him? Even if I am wrong and do not understand these things, I at least know my own soul and the demands of my conscience. Do not ask that I be less than you believe me to be!"

After saying these bitter words she put her head down in her hands covering her face and wept. Sir Henry rose and went over to her and pulled her to him and down upon his lap where he held her while she cried. I stood up then and quietly left them there together.

July 28, 1893
Grimpen

𝔍 left Baskerville Hall this morning and have returned to my cottage with the cameo photograph of Roger Baskerville in my possession. Sir Henry gave it to me this morning in the name of Lady Beryl. The photograph will not be used to prosecute Roger Baskerville but to speed him on his way out of the country. There are artists at Scotland Yard who can reproduce the photograph and make it larger and more detailed while true to the original so that it may be used for purposes of identification. If Rodger Baskerville accepts the government position that we will offer him, well and good; if not, then Colonel Moran will be furnished with a copy of his portrait. I have learned not to underestimate a deadly foe twice.

I owe Sir Henry the duty that I have assumed to protect him as well as I can manage. Colonel Moran is not my first choice, but he alone is proportionate to the threat posed. Colonel Moran may return quite openly to London now. He like the Professor is now immune from prosecution. Even my best efforts in the past proved insufficient to gather sufficient evidence to win a case against him before an English jury. There were two other men as well who were highly placed in the Moriarty organization. These men were a threat to me in 1891. One of these, deprived of the great organizing brain of Moriarty, tried to replicate the organization abroad but failed. He was later killed in Odessa by Russian police. The other went into British politics and is currently serving in the House of Commons. He has taken up the strange hobby of training cormorants in his spare time when he returns to his district on the west coast of Scotland. He is a cunning fellow and who can say how far he will rise in the government.

As I approach the month of August 1893, I find that I am no longer pursued by my old foes. Indeed, my existence is virtually assured until 1897 at least as far as Professor Moriarty is concerned. He wishes me to be alive and well to witness his triumph in that year of the Diamond Jubilee of Queen Victoria. If he persists in his plans, I must of course do all that I can in order to defeat him, but it is my hope that he will come to see matters differently and abandon his present course. In any case I have made my arguments to him as best I can. Our next interview must be at the invitation of the Professor. I do not wish to press him just now. I seem to have at least opened his mind a bit at the conclusion of our last encounter

I will meet with Colonel Moran in London in a few days. He has promised to wire me when he is settled into London lodgings. I have received no further word from Isadora Persano, which is just as well. Perhaps our bird has already flown to parts unknown. It may be that Roger Baskerville has other resources and has left the country already. In any case, I have been in communication with Mycroft about securing a government posting for Roger Baskerville to Honduras. When all is in order advertisements will be placed in several quarters. We shall then see if our careful baiting of the waters shall bring in our shark.

As to other matters, my mind has turned of late to my

future. Once I have concluded this matter with Sir Henry and Lady Beryl, I shall be quite free to return to London and to resume my practice as a consulting detective. My lodgings in Baker Street have been retained and kept just as they were when I left for Europe. The costs have been paid for by Brother Mycroft using my own funds from my trust account, which is reinforced periodically with my share of the rental income from Sigerside. Those old rooms are awaiting my return. But I am I ready to resume the dull routine of my consulting practice? There is first of all the question of my health to be considered; the fresh air of the moors combined with the comparatively warm climate of South-west England has been good for my lung ailment.

I hesitate to face again the late summer months spent upon the stifling pavements of the great city of London only to be followed by the fogs and coal smoke of an autumn and winter, but Watson is scheduled to return by Christmas from Louisiana. I have had Inspector Hopkins make some discrete inquiries for me about his plans to return from America. Watson will no doubt return to his Kensington practice. I believe I should therefore return as well to my own work as a consulting detective, if nothing else to demonstrate that my silence and absence were by necessity and not by choice.

I wonder if the old fellow will consent to again sharing rooms with me as he once did so many years ago prior to his marriage. His presence with me is always valuable. In fact, I cannot face resuming my practice without my Boswell at my side. My work is rather like that of a performing artist in many ways. What is the play without an audience? Always in the back of my mind in my most successful cases, there stood the great standing question, "How will I explain it all to Watson?" The requirement to assemble all into a coherent narrative to Watson was my guarantee that I would leave no loose ends in my proofs. He is the proctor of my tests and I find that until he renders his grade to my performance I am like a school-boy gnawing at his nails. Will he say, "Excellent, Holmes?" or will he rather say, "Hmm, my dear chap, not quite up to the mark on this one." I find that in many ways it is he rather than I, who is the senior member of our little partnership. I present my work and he grades and records it for posterity. Would my fame be such as it is without his remarkable skill as the writer of his little romances? He has even managed to make my poor lodgings in Baker Street into a virtual Mecca. I have noticed men pointing out to the lady standing at their side my rooms on the second floor as though they are some sort of tourist attraction like the Nelson Column! If I return now will I be so overwhelmed with visitors and well-wishers that I cannot hope to carry on my trade in privacy and peace? Well, at least I have now my retreat in Devonshire to which I may return if it all becomes too much for me.

Perhaps at first I will request that Watson lay down a false trail by informing the public that I am busy keeping bees off somewhere in Sussex. I wonder how I shall manage to introduce myself again to the dear fellow after in a sense rising from the grave. It is really too good an opportunity to waste. Perhaps if I manage it well enough, Watson will forget to be angry with me in the mere joy of seeing me once again. Better to shock the system and purge all the noxious elements of recrimination that I so richly deserve; perhaps an old book seller saying, "Ere now Govner, I as a few volumes as might just be of interest to an old squire like yourself." Then I'll shove a few obscure volumes up at him and into his hands before popping off my disguise, splashing a bit of peroxide and a bandage afterwards on the wound of his discontent, and then bind it all up securely in the cotton-wool of forgetfulness; ah that's the very thing!

A deeper healing will no doubt take time. But that must await his homecoming from America and the reunion that I both dread and anticipate with joy. For the present, my time is soon about to be my own again. Autumn will come all too soon upon the moors and with it the drifting rains of winter. Perhaps I will return to the continent and see if Irene Adler has taken my advice and returned to the stage. Perhaps a visit to some German spa may be advisable to seal my present recovery. Perhaps I will seek again the cold airs of an early autumn in Switzerland and rid myself at once and forever of this ghastly consumption. Perhaps I should even return to Meiringen and stand by the Falls of Reichenbach and look again into that dreadful chasm where perhaps the ghosts of Sherlock Holmes and of Professor Moriarty will always reside locked in a proverbial deathly embrace. I wonder if the old me perished there after all. Am I today that same cocksure fellow who entered so rashly upon a wager with the Napoleon of Crime and set out to find My God? Is anyone ever truly himself before his death? That is the great question the answer to which lies not in our hands but in that of the recording angel of God. Can our personal hope of immortality exceed that of the religion that is its base and origin?

I have been reading the great Roman stoic philosopher Seneca on the topic of the shortness of human life. He points out that the course of human experience is such that it is only at the end of life that we have acquired sufficient wisdom and self-possession that we are at last ready to live. Might we say the same thing regarding the great religions of the world? What we term ancient is really only yesterday when placed in a proper perspective. The 19th century might be considered the century when geology as a science finally came into its own. Hitherto the Bible provided a solid foundation beneath the believer so that history formed a continuum anchored at both ends between creation and a final day of judgment when a new world beyond our imagining would supplant the earth beneath us and the stars above us would fall from the heavens. Geology by extending the age of all things beneath us and in partnership with astronomy to study the stars and galaxies above us caused history to collapse into a tiny particle of recorded time etched into an immense silence.

The consequence of this realization was that any religion that depended upon a narrative of historical events for its foundation was reduced to a brief annotation, whereas before it had appeared to be a weighty volume. The role of the human being was proportionately reduced from a starring role to a short walk-on part in a negligible drama hardly worth the effort of a review. Religious faith no longer seemed an immediate and obvious conclusion deduced from evidence gathered and carefully recorded and preserved by reliable witnesses. Instead it now appeared to be a reckless extrapolation from the known facts. Suddenly the grim admission of the stoics seemed more rational than the extravagant hopes of the Hebrew tribes whose own kingdom reached its summit with a ruined temple and the hope maintained by a minority that a kindly prophet was in truth the Son of God.

Christianity and the bond between the two testaments needed transplantation to Rome if it was ever to thrive, to take on synthetic form, and to move beyond the Roman Empire into the savage regions of Europe and Asia by making new converts. Everything since is the record of that historical process of theological diffusion and the need to defend it. Each successive age has assumed that it had reached the summit of belief. Every generation has assumed that its enemies would be damned while a remnant no matter how narrow and confined would be exalted into the realms of glory to which they alone were entitled.

Theology is the never-ending refinement of definitions resting upon a foundation that is sufficiently dubious or unknown (and hence unacknowledged) by the majority of the members of the human race. Even the most tender-hearted clerics, whatever their missionary zeal might be, have not been able to escape the stern conviction that outside the church there was no salvation. Even the most virtuous of their neighbors, let alone the wise stoics like Seneca, would be damned along with men like Nero and Caligula if they died outside the Church. This fact was no reflection on the goodness of God or the efficacy of the life and death of Jesus Christ; it was simply deemed true because any text in order to be definitive and believable at all must leave nothing unsaid, let alone to imply that any phrase might have been extended beyond the original intent and situational applicability in any written document. Is it too daring then to imagine that the true era of Christianity is only just beginning and that the apocalyptic end so eagerly anticipated by the righteous is derived from the need for vindication rather than from the will of God?

August 1, 1893
London

oday I traveled up to London and had dinner with Colonel Sebastian Moran at Simpsons after which we took a long walk along the Thames embankment smoking cigars and finally ending the evening outside the door of his club. He listened carefully as I explained the matter of the recent and surprising resurrection of Roger Baskerville who had been so long presumed to be dead by his wife and by Sir Henry and even by me. Colonel Moran chose to treat the matter in a humorous manner in order to chafe me a bit.

"So you have come around at last to my own way of thinking Holmes, which is that certain men must simply be pruned out of life if this world is to function properly. That has always been the view that the Professor and I have taken. Certain men and even some women pose a threat to the human race by, to take an example, an excessive accumulation of capital that they fail to disperse among the masses by paying a just wage to their workers. These become a threat to the social order and must simply be removed. Since this class usually owns the government, they are usually joined in their extortions from the body politic by the government itself. This fatal combination is wedded into a common force to despoil mankind. The extensive union of capital and the laws that protect it leave out of consideration the fate of the varied and numerous concourse of humanity that must manage without such extensive holdings. This mass of mankind must sooner or later shake off their bondage. They dare not wait for the governing classes to come to their aid voluntarily. Whether it is though disproportionate and regressive taxes or worthless and intrusive regulations or expensive overseas expeditions of the military, no relief is yet at hand to educate and improve the lot of the struggling masses. It requires a determined and resourceful private agency to set matters right again. That was the business of Moriarty and Company. We took of course a small fee for our services, as was only right and proper, particularly since we had a monopoly upon our unique trade and always produced results. Until that is, one presumptuous detective stepped in and forced us into receivership. Now that very detective wishes to hire us to eliminate a man whom his own shoddy services failed to dispose of some five years ago. If you cannot find him yourself, we will be only too glad to accept the commission."

I tried to ignore his rather boorish comments. I explained to him that my plan was to lure Roger Baskerville out of the country not to kill him. Only if that plan was to fail would the services of Colonel Moran be necessary, and even then only to pursue and capture Roger Baskerville not to assassinate him.

"Ah, that is clearer. I thought for a moment that you were about to surrender your most excellent principles! Well then, that is another matter. How am I to find my man? Do you have a photograph of him? Excellent! Still there is the matter of where he may be. You can hardly expect me to dash about all over England peering into faces. I do not intend to waste my precious time in England by hanging about the pubs in Devon on the odd chance that he may surface. Really, my dear Holmes, you overestimate my powers. I prefer a sitting target when I can get it. Unless you can tell me where my man is, I am afraid that I cannot help you."

He had a point of course. I had indeed no idea where Roger Baskerville might be located although I have had many reproductions made already of his photograph and have put the men of Scotland Yard upon the case. My only chance seems to be that he will see my advertisements and be drawn into my trap. I explained further to Colonel Moran how I had hoped that I might use his unique talents.

"I have brought you in to deal with any contingencies that may emerge where the official police may be unable to act," I stated stiffly. "You are a man of resource and imagination and just such a man will be required to face as dangerous a threat as the one that I believe is posed by Roger Baskerville. I have learned through my own past failings with him not to underestimate him. He may strike from any direction and he is a man who will stop at nothing when once his course has been decided."

"You must pardon me, Holmes. I will of course look into the matter. You flatter me by your confidence in me who am after all a mere blackguard with higher social ambitions. I ask you though to understand that I have in a manner of speaking retired from the hunt. I will though, since you wish it, enter into service again in this one instance, but I am afraid that I must raise the delicate matter of payment for my services."

"I believe that Sir Henry's credit will prove adequate," I informed him in a cool and distant manner.

"You seem offended my dear fellow, but you must excuse me if I regard business as business; it is always wise to settle monetary matters beforehand is it not? I occasionally accumulate losses at the gaming tables and my manner of living when away from home is not cheap. If I am instrumental in bringing matters to a successful conclusion by tracking him beyond the limits of London my compensation or bounty should be on the order of 500 pounds should it not? Oh well, in light of our previous association and our delightful rambles about Asia, I am willing to reduce my usual fee. Two hundred pounds, there it is clear and square and as honest as the best tradesman of London. Do you have the authority to accept my terms? Excellent! There will also be the matter of any small travel expenses and my cost of lodgings. I will keep complete records of course. You agree? Splendid! Well then, our business having been concluded I think we may continue with our delightful stroll."

After a bit he said, "I trust that you are doing well, Holmes, not coughing up blood and such? I am afraid that camel-riding over deserts did not agree with you. You really did use yourself up a touch too freely and if it is any comfort to you, you quite exhausted me at the time also. I have grown rather fat recently on the excellent cuisine of the French Riviera and the Principality of Monaco as you no doubt have noticed. Now I am proposing to add to my girth by spending a winter in London where there is nothing to do but eat, play cards, and visit music halls. Ah well, such is life. How did you get on with the Professor? I really must pay him a visit after I am well settled here. Did he lap up your sermons and mend his ways? Ah, I thought not. I am afraid it will take more than one ministration of the healing balm of your religious views to turn him from his own sternly held faith in himself. Professor Moriarty is his own religion you know. His mind seems to him quite adequate to explain all things; and where that great mind came from, whether from chance or from some distant deity is a matter that he feels no need to resolve. He is getting older, Holmes, as are we all. He wants one more great triumph and I doubt that even you will manage to get him to surrender that desire. Still, you may try if you wish."

After a time he turned to me again after leaning against the railing overlooking the Thames. "London has its own peculiar charm. Look how the moonlight is reflected off of the water and the silhouette of the Houses of Parliament dark against the sky. You see, I am not without an appreciation of the aesthetic values in life. Perhaps I am not quite the brute you have always taken me to be. I have my own refined enjoyment of the pleasures that life offers. What I sacrifice in the quest for ultimate meanings is well compensated by present pleasures. If you do not mind my saying so, your philosophy has too much of the lean paintings of El Greco and the writings of Cervantes. You demand that a coherent account be given of the whole of life, while I, humble as I am, seek only to comprehend my own small role in this earthly drama and to leave my mistress happy with a new dress when I leave her of an evening. Also I am not ungenerous in other matters as well. I always tip my coachmen and servants well. My conscience, such as it is, is at peace and I always sleep well after a good dinner. I do not trouble the midnight hours by waking God with the singing of Matins in some cold monastery, nor will I burden him with some hypocritical death-bed confession regretting sins that at the moment that I committed them were sweet. These very sins will no doubt appear even sweeter in memory when I lie gasping out my last breaths upon this earth."

"Ah I can read your disapprobation on your face. Why if I feel the need to copulate do I not take a wife and raise a great bustling family, sons and daughters of the church? It may surprise you to hear that I pay the cost of my miscalculations and that I leave no woman in distress and penury raising children I am not temperamentally prepared to nurture and to educate in the delicate ways of the world. They in turn are spared from resenting me and casting greedy eyes on a patrimony that I am as likely to lose as to preserve."

He paused to see if I was listening before continuing, "I have no real quarrel with God you know. I seek in my own way to share His indifference to the sins of men. I like the vast acquiescence of his silence as history unfolds. He even shows good taste in not answering our prayers. I should despise a god that always came running over like a fat nanny to fulfill our every request or even to comfort us when we fall. I like a god with a long beard preoccupied in the study of devising his own vast plans for the cosmos. I think my dear Holmes that you would get further with the Professor if you proposed a god more worthy of the Professor's steel. Abandon your compassionate Christian God when you speak to the Professor! Why? Well I would have you know that the Professor told me once, in an unguarded moment, that he last prayed to that very God for the life of his dear mother when she was dying. She died anyway of course. She died in the Irish potato famine of 1845-1849. She gave her last crust of bread to the Professor so that he could at least survive on the boat passage to join his father in England. Her brute of a husband then took the boy away and left her dying of typhus on the streets of Cork and sailed for Liverpool without her. Professor Moriarty has never forgiven either his father or himself for abandoning her. Nor has he forgiven God for not dispensing a last-minute cure upon that good woman. I am afraid that was the end of his faith forever. What was true for the lad is but more true for the man. You must find some other ground than faith to use then if you would work his conversion at this late date. You will keep what I have just told you in confidence of course."

We walked on then in silence but my brain was spinning. Had Colonel Moran just given me the lost key to the darkest chamber of the heart of Professor Moriarty? At last he said, "Well then, shall we proceed to my club? I can offer you a nightcap there of some excellent brandy. I will study carefully the portrait of this man Baskerville or Stapleton and await your call should your own stratagems fail to produce the results that you hope."

We left the Thames embankment then and walked on through the crowded Strand to the entrance to his club. I remained deep in thought over our brandy in the comfortable club bar while Colonel Moran continued with his jaunty train of discourse and explained to me his theory of winning at whist.

August 2, 1893
London

Mycroft hosted me at luncheon today at the Diogenes Club. He was in his usual somber mood. Every day he is the recipient of countless reports from all sections of the government that need to be read and evaluated. He also pays daily calls to Parliament and to Whitehall. Today he offered some comments upon the political process when we had withdrawn to one of the three private parlors maintained by the Diogenes Club where actual speaking is permitted.

"Personalities, Sherlock, personalities are the great problem in governing mankind. If government could be reduced to law and to operational policy, all would be well; but it is not. Government requires governors and legislators and administrators. Each office must be filled with men and each has some prejudice or pre-conceived idea or set of ideas according to which he evaluates the facts and assigns values and significance to them. Everything as a result requires compromise and discussion, all of which takes time. The final product is usually some horrid composite monster of a policy with five arms, three legs, and a body bloated with waste and expenditure."

"You need only look about you to see the results. Ireland seethes with resentment and desires home rule, the working classes remain dull and ignorant and unemployed, vice and promiscuity are rampant everywhere In London, and the wealthy country squires of England for the most part waste their time chasing little foxes about with baying hounds and horses. There are times when I believe that the English are the most frivolous and absurd people upon the face of the earth and the poorest cooks as well. The whole country subsists on overdone beef, stale crumpets, and fish and chips. Thank God we have a French Chef at the Diogenes Club. By the way, how did you like your lunch? Brittany Oysters and Salmon is one of Pierre's specialties. Well, how did you get on with that bounder Moriarty?"

I informed Mycroft that I had made a beginning but that only time would tell if any of my presentation points had made an impression upon him.

"So the fellow expects us to simply await his pleasure and ignore his threats! Bah, I have half-a-mind to simply have the fellow abducted and transported to some distant station in west Australia with the aborigines. Let him plot there if he wishes. But there are matters of legality to be considered I suppose and he keeps a staff to guard his person. His sudden disappearance would be noted and a swarm of barristers would soon be at the door of Whitehall demanding his release. Well, you must continue then in your own way and Scotland Yard will do its best to discover and trace any efforts he may make to advance his preposterous scheme whatever it may entail. "

"Now then, I have some good news for you. We had a fellow in here yesterday applying for that position in Honduras. He appears by your description of him to be this man Stapleton or Baskerville. He will be back today for a second interview and you may observe him in secret and give us your own opinion. I believe that you met the fellow in Devonshire some years ago; of course he may have changed since. It is imperative of course that he should not see you or the game is up. You must be carefully secreted but close enough to observe his mannerisms. We could of course clap him in irons and take him off to some dungeon as was once standard practice in England. There are times that I long for the old days of the Tower of London and the Bastille. Our forbears knew how to deal with troublemakers. But again, we are hampered by the laws."

"I wish we could be like the Americans. You may recall that riot in Chicago of some years ago, the Haymarket Riot I believe it was called. Well the whole thing was caused by the police but they managed to stack the jury and to hang the anarchists present at the time who were only trying to rally the masses. No direct causality could be proved of course and the judge was biased when he wasn't asleep during the trial. The whole thing was a travesty of justice but some dangerous men were no doubt eliminated. The Americans have at least advanced to the point where they can conduct a proper play-act version of the law where money is concerned. Someday they may master the actual substance of the law. I should say that the guiding principle of the Americans is that they do precisely what they wish and find a way to give it legal form afterwards. As Englishmen though, we are burdened with the need to stick to form and substance and to honor the actual rule and spirit of the laws as well as its procedural formalities. I am afraid therefore that we will have to let this fellow assume his post in Honduras after all. He shall be watched however, make no doubt about that, he shall be watched."

When I left Mycroft at the Diogenes to return to Baker Street I found myself to be still mulling over the problem of taking direct action to remedy evil. I was delighted, as may be imagined, to hear from Mycroft that our ruse might already be proving to be successful. I had also felt a temptation to simply settle with the fellow at once. If I were to do so however I would be adapting precisely those means and that guiding philosophy that was the basis for the actions of Moriarty and Moran. The great question in dealing with evil still seems to me to be why God does not simply directly thwart evil designs. If God can design a paradise after our death, at least for the righteous ones who will end up in heaven, then why not do something to improve matters now?

It is the old conundrum that tries to account for God being all-good and all-powerful yet tolerating evil in which case he would seem to be either not all-good or not-all powerful. The answer of course appears to be that God is also all-knowing. The mystery of evil is that it serves the ultimate goodness of all things in some fashion. There appears to be a dimension to good and evil that is not apparent to us from this side of the grave. Perhaps both good and evil have further dimensions in eternity that require the present order.

We are inevitably biased in asking this fundamental question by the shortness of our point of view. We operate under the assumption based on ordinary experience that the earth is flat and ultimately find that it is round. To proceed in one direction is to find oneself returning from behind and tapping oneself upon the shoulder. Perhaps it is the same with all dimensions, even moral ones. Good and evil are part of a spherical moral realm. To proceed in any straight line is for the one to become the other by incipient degrees. Too much virtue becomes a vice and vices if taken to extremes soon point out their own absurdity and one finds oneself becoming virtuous. This phenomenon would account for the subtle cruelty of some of the saints and the strange appeal and charm exuded by confidence men and villains. Jesus, while he was still on earth often hesitated to condemn obvious sins traceable to the flesh, perhaps seeing them as less malicious than the pride and presumption of the Pharisees who after all were merely trying to do good as they understood it.

Even Pontius Pilate as governor of the Roman Province of Palestine was trying to keep the peace that dreadful day by condemning Jesus. Wouldn't most administrators similarly situated have done the same? It always seemed to me that Pilate's greatest failing was his lack of imagination. Like most literalists and police he followed established protocol. There is nothing so obvious in complex events that a man who with no insight or imagination will fail to notice it. Such men might as well be stones. Evidence does appear however that Pilate attempted to avoid the full measure of the law when considering this strange case placed before him. Apparently he even received a warning from his wife not to meddle in the affair.

A private colloquy of sorts took place where in an informal setting Pilate asked Jesus directly for any grounds that Jesus could supply that would give Pilate an acceptable excuse to release Him. The brief defense put forward by Jesus in the gospel account seems as directed to the reader of the gospel as to Pilate. Once again Jesus turns the question around to ask Pilate to come to a position regarding who and what Jesus is. Of course, from Pilate's point of view, this question is irrelevant. To Pilate the key point is that Pilate has the power to put Jesus to death and the burden is upon Jesus to explain why that power should not be exercised. Jesus answers by placing the power of Pilate in the larger context of what God as the Father of Jesus allows; in other words all power is derivative and must be exercised in constant reference to the will of God. Of course from Pilate's point of view all power is derived from the Emperor in Rome and any appeal to a Jewish God is simply nonsense. Pilate's final response to Jesus at the end of their colloquy is to ask, "What is truth?"

Jesus gives no further answer because Jesus has already consented to the purely *de facto* nature of the Roman power, not just over Jesus, but over the Jewish people as well. It is this lack of resistance that sets up a vector of circumstances that then unfold with a grim inevitability. The question posed by the narrative then is whether Jesus is a victim or whether in a sense He is the source and reason for all that occurs. This seems the only possible conclusion based upon the evidence that Jesus had told his disciples that he would die in Jerusalem. The death of Jesus paradoxically reveals the truth of Jesus! The Christian answer regarding truth has already been given in another context; in fact it is the entire purpose of the gospel accounts to announce Jesus Christ not merely as the Messiah, but as God Himself!

Jesus says unequivocally: *I am the way the truth and the life. No one comes to the Father except through me."* Such an affirmation would make no sense to Pilate whatsoever. He is a man who prefers a trouble-free existence. Judea is a stepping stone to greater things. No governor enjoys dividing authority with the king of a subject people, in this case King Herod as Tetrarch of Judea. Pilate on that fatal day was being pushed into precisely the situation that he most wished to avoid—having to enter into a religious squabble that could upset the delicate arrangements that allowed a fractious people always on the edge of insurrection into open tumult to live in relative peace with Rome. Now he had to deal with some idealistic youth talking about a Father in heaven and posing the unanswerable question: *What is truth?"*

This question haunts the entire narrative of the crucifixion and death of Jesus. It is a replication of the question put to His disciples by Jesus: *Who do men say that I am?* This same question is placed in another form immediately after receiving the ambiguous answer that essentially means that there is a difference of opinions on the matter. Jesus then asks his disciples: *But you, who do you, say that I am?"* Peter answers, *"You are the Christ, the Son of the Living God."* That is the affirmation of the Roman Catholic Church to this very day.

But a similar question might be imaginatively entertained in regard to Jesus himself. Jesus must have known that He was walking into Jerusalem and about to kick over a hornet's nest. Until then Jesus had made every effort *not to me made a king!* Now Jesus enters Jerusalem and is proclaimed (and proclaims Himself before Pilate eventually) as a king, but one whose kingdom is not of this world. This title is ironically later placed in a notice upon the cross of Jesus as partial vindication of the claims made in their private conversation but more than that as an insult to the Jewish authorities who had demanded the execution order that Pilate was so reluctant to give.

A critical question remains however: *Did everything that happened need to happen in just this way or is the salvific meaning assigned to the crucifixion and death of Jesus a later reconstruction of the events by the Christian Community as the forerunner of the Roman Catholic Church?*

Might Jesus, just as well, have spent a quiet Passover at home in Galilee as in Jerusalem; not every year is a good year to be in Jerusalem! Perhaps a few more miracles or a few more feedings of the multitude would have put Jesus over the top with the Jewish people and their leaders so that His mission as Messiah would have been a success. True revolutions always begin in the provinces and only later spread to the capital. Jesus might even have started His mission with the gentiles or the Samaritans and left the people of Judea to sign on later. Perhaps what worked so well later for St. Paul with the gentiles might have worked for Jesus as well.

Or to carry this hypothetical speculation farther afield Jesus might have done better to first seek out a secular victory among the philosophers in Athens or as a statesman with the Senate in Rome. Maybe the human race had advanced since the death of Socrates in Athens. Why go first to the very people who were from all contemporary assessments least likely to accept Him? One could hardly expect to dethrone the Torah in so short a time or convince the most literal people on earth to abandon the only thing that had ever made them special, the Covenant made with Moses and the people. The whole point of the Covenant was that it had grown to be seen as a real estate transaction: obey the Torah and God will reward you with land! In this case the suffering and death of Jesus was unnecessary; the whole thing was a most unfortunate miscalculation of the mood of the masses by a young man who read himself into the ancient Jewish writings by taking the whole thing personally ...

Unless that was precisely what Jesus (and His Father) had in mind from the beginning: *to show the dark side of goodness by being crucified and counted among those who are condemned by this world as the ultimate proof of the love of God!*

If good and evil are in fact so close that at times they are indistinguishable to mankind it is only God who (acting as a sort of moral prism) can separate each moral color so that all may be clear at last in the final judgment at the end of time. It seems to me that the advent of Jesus Christ is precisely that event that would be necessary to make it clear to man and to woman why they may not become as gods. God alone determines the essence of what is good and what is evil. Even when God aids man and woman with revelations and even with the Christian message of the gospels as testimony some evil still remains in our goodness and perhaps God in His own way brings greater goodness out of that residual evil.

Still humankind is born to struggle with moral questions, but God does not condemn the sincere heart even when that heart is in theological error. Too great an insistence upon orthodox belief then may bring about the very illness that could only be remedied by the death of the Son of God.

Fractured Christianity has yet to see the full dimension of the significance of Jesus as the Son of Man: the one who emerges out of human experience and the one who provides the definitive answer to every question that arises out of human experience. This is the way that Christianity truly emerges as Catholic (all-embracing and universal): the meta-answer and the micro-answer, the communal answer and the individual answer. We are parts of each other.

The religious zealots crucify the savior; the horrors of the Spanish Inquisition are an example of such theological overreach. But to ignore the moral law and to be a crass voluptuary like King Herod also brings about the crucifixion of Christ. We do indeed as St. Paul once wrote, *see in a glass darkly;* and so shall we always see until the Son of Man is finally revealed in His glory complete in His extended body of all of humankind at the end of time. Two thousand years of Christian history seems to show that our prayer must be not so much to be saved from the unbelievers as from our fellow Christians!

This is my central thesis, the one that I hoped to convey to Professor Moriarty. It requires a Shakespeare to explain the vagueness of the human heart. How much more difficult is it to speak of God? Perhaps Watson will someday see this journal and wonder at the folly of Sherlock Holmes the detective who helps one foe to a new life in Honduras and the other to a stable in Devonshire. Maybe these reflections may help dear old Watson to understand the motivations of his old friend at last!

August 3, 1893
London

Today I saw Roger Baskerville standing there as bold as brass in a great room at Whitehall. I was cleverly concealed behind a heavy wooden cabinet and against some heavy drapes before his arrival; the light from a tall window shown full upon his face as he stood before the desk of the Prime Minister who was speaking to him and I was able to hear their conversation clearly.

"England requires a man in British Honduras who knows and can appreciate the nuances of our position there and who speaks the language well. The next few years may be decisive for the future of our interests in the region. We do not intend to allow the Americans to possess a free-hand in Central America or in the Caribbean. Fortunately, the American navy is still quite small. Nor have we much to fear from their land forces. The army has taken an inordinate amount of time just putting down the ill-armed Indians of the plains. If our interests in the northern regions of the continent are to be made safe we cannot allow American arrogance to proceed too far. I understand that you once held a diplomatic post under the former government of Costa Rica? Ah, you know the area well then. I do not need to tell you that it is a beastly hell-hole full of mosquitoes and disease. Yet you wish to return there now; may I ask you why?"

Rodger Baskerville answered clearly and amiably, "I am fond of the people, sir. I have had some experience as an educator and I am a scientist. I like to study things. The entire region is one vast laboratory for a curious man."

The Prime Minister answered gruffly, "That is all very well, but the duties of a diplomat are not research, although naturally we will rely upon you for periodic assessments of the situation down there. You must have a clear idea of what is involved and that the duties of a diplomat include a significant amount of routine paperwork. It can all be rather dull. It will not be your function to make policy. We are not concerned with adventurers. I should not wish you to enter the area with too many romantic notions in your head. The man we choose must agree to a long posting. The contacts that you form and any trust that you may cultivate may be useful to this nation and we do not wish to begin again constantly and have to regain the confidence of the men in power all over again. Can you promise us that once posted you will make Honduras your permanent home?"

"I should not have applied Sir, if I was not quite serious in my commitment to the task at hand. I believe that I may achieve in Honduras some of the same results that I managed to do in Costa Rica, but without as you say becoming an adventurer. I know the temper of the inhabitants of the region, their peculiar sense of honor, and I know how to make them see that it is in their best interests to cooperate with British rule."

The Prime Minister smiled, "Excellent, a firm hand in a soft glove is always the best approach when dealing with these people! Well, I believe that we may offer the posting to you, although your references are somewhat dated. We are trusting largely to your own assessment of your abilities and your confident manner. We require a man with energy and dispatch. There will not be a great deal of time to spare since the post is vacant and we need someone capable of taking the helm without delay. Your outward accommodations will not be luxurious. We have a supply ship leaving in two days. If you can manage to conclude your affairs here on such short notice, your passage has been paid for and a stateroom reserved. Should you need any personal items I have here a draft for fifty pounds as an advance on your salary. If you would read over these papers and sign them, I believe that we may conclude this interview. Baskerville, Baskerville, hmmm, are you by chance any relation of the Baronet in Devonshire?"

"No sir, though it is kind of you to suppose it. My father mined silver in Bolivia. I took a belated grand tour of the continent as my father wished me to do. Beyond that I have spent very little time in England. The cold and damp here are not congenial to one who was raised as I was in the mountains. I shall be glad to get underway at once before winter sets in. Here are the required papers with my signature appended." He placed the requisite papers before the Prime Minister, who rose to shake his hand before his departure.

"Congratulations and good luck, young man. I have met quite a few candidates for this position during these last several days, but none in whom I felt that I could place more confidence than you. I hope to hear good things of you in the future. Remember, the firm hand in the soft glove. We are after all British are we not? There's the good fellow."

The Prime Minister led him to the door and closed it behind him before walking over to my place of concealment. Had another man than Roger Baskerville presented himself, I was to have interrupted the proceedings. So when I failed to do so, the Prime Minister knew that we had indeed found our man at last. I have arranged for Colonel Moran to follow him to his lodgings and to keep him under guard as it were until his departure. It is not that I do not trust Scotland Yard, but there is something about the official police that a man like Baskerville would soon scent and we should take no chances of his getting the wind up and disappearing. At the same time, we cannot afford to take a chance that he is merely testing us before pocketing the fifty pounds and disappearing. Colonel Moran has the patience of an old shikari. Baskerville will not escape when once the Colonel is on his trail. Still, I will not rest easy until the ship departs with our man safely on board en route to his assignment.

He did indeed appear today to be still a young man. There is something of Oscar Wilde's character, Dorian Gray, about him in that his evil nature does not show upon the freshness and ingenuousness of his face. He is as likeable a man at first sight as any I have ever seen. Indeed, if I knew nothing of his dark and checkered history, I might conclude him to be just what he appeared to be, an earnest and honest young fellow looking to serve his country well. I can see now how Lady Beryl had been deceived by him, particularly since her temperament though muted now by suffering is of the hot-blooded Latin races who do not surrender their hearts lightly and for whom a great passion once begun is not easily extinguished.

I returned to Mycroft's lodgings after giving Roger Baskerville time to exit the building and after a brief conversation in parting with the Prime Minister. He was kind enough to refer to my efforts on behalf of the government when I had crossed through the region of the Sudan during my travels. He did not of course know of my reservations when it comes to any engagement of British troops in taking Sudan.

"Her Majesty's government is quite pleased with your efforts last year taking stock of the situation in the Sudan, Mr. Holmes. We read your appraisal of the situation there and found it to be most informative although we have reached a different conclusion than you might expect. Your position was that diplomacy might reach some sort of agreement with the current ruler of that benighted region. You failed to consider though that there are a great number of Mohammedan fanatics who desire to create another Arabic Empire there. As it is, we have the Turkish Ottomans to contend with already and we do not intend to see a spread of this jihad nonsense to other regions. Best to put it down now, pull the weeds up by the roots so to speak. We have made Egypt secure to protect the Suez Canal and now we must subdue Sudan to protect Egypt. In Africa, it is the interior that matters."

"As for northern Africa we are quite content to let the French keep the Sahara regions as long as we control Gibraltar. As for Spain, well Spain is on its way to becoming a third-rate power. Spain may have whatever they can hold on to south of Gibraltar. The real riches are in the south and in the Congo. Unfortunately that bloody bastard, King Leopold, controls the Congo. When we have secured Sudan though, we will see about the Congo. At present the Belgians are under French protection and we cannot risk a war with France at this time. Our task is to keep the French and the Germans focused on the threat that each poses to the other. Russia of course is focused on the Balkans and nothing of any good can come out of the Balkans. It is too late for the

Russians to do anything in Africa. Russia is already a third-rate power."

"Still they managed to defeat Napoleon," I remarked smiling.

"Well so they did, so they did," the Prime Minister admitted laughing, "But that was some time ago wasn't it. Now they can't even beat those kimono-wearing Japanese! Portugal could have done better; at least they have a presence in Africa."

"What about America," I inquired. "Are you concerned about the spread of American power?"

The Prime Minister chuckled, "Oh, I don't think we need fear anything from that quarter. The Americans have a tiny fleet, somewhere around tenth in the world. Besides, they have been too busy killing red Indians to think about Africa. Their absurd Monroe Doctrine is a delusion that we allow them to maintain to salve their national pride. They have nibbled away a bit at Mexico but we have Guiana and Honduras; we control the Caribbean region and we have the Falklands so that we may police ships going around Cape Horn. As for the west coast of South America, the Spanish dug out all the silver and hold centuries ago; besides the region is too remote. Our concern now is not with America but with the Sudan. Suez is our path to India and we will not have it threatened by any wogs with outside alliances."

"In any case that was not what brought you here today; so that was the chap eh? I must say he looked quite a decent fellow if a touch idealistic, but you did not speak up while he was here so you must be quite sure of his identity. Very well then; off he goes to Honduras. I will alert the governor there on your word that he is not to be trusted. We'll keep him buried in routine paperwork, no influence in that, but we'll pay him enough to keep him at the job. Will that do? Good, we are happy to make some return to your brother and to you too for all that Mycroft Holmes does for England. Do you know that his salary has not increased in the many years during which he has held his position? I have never known a man so easily satisfied. He appears only to exist within the gambit of his own mind and of course that beastly club of his.

The whole place is a sort of mausoleum if you ask me, but I have heard that the food served there is excellent. I insist on dining where there are people about and a bit of excitement. Still, if your brother was not as he is, I doubt that he would be able to keep track of the many facts that he keeps in that damned memory of his. He is the great reference library of the Empire and you, my dear sir, are a source of pride to the nation as well. I hear you have been living down in Devon lately. When will you return to London?"

I answered that I contemplated resuming my practice sometime in the next six months although my health was still delicate after the strain of my travels abroad. He nodded sagely. "You are quite right to guard your health, that's all we have you know. I myself have a touch of gout and rheumatism that often makes my life miserable. But let us not go into that. I am happy to have been able to help you today. Please convey my greetings to Sir Henry and his good wife and tell him how happy we are to have been able to help to restore him to peace of mind and to rid him of a nuisance. He can now return to the good work that we hear he is doing among the simple folk of Dartmoor. Beastly area though; that's why we chose it for a prison!"

I took a local's pride in repartee, "Remoteness has its charm. Perhaps you are not aware that I purchased a property near to Sir Henry. I am something of an antiquarian and archeologist and I find the place fascinating."

"Sorry, I meant no offense. I've only been through the area once or twice. I found it all a bit eerie, all those stone tors and remnants of alien religions. Too astrological by far for my tastes; who can say what mischief those ancient people's were up to before the Romans arrived and before the Irish brought Christianity over to England. It was the last civilized thing the Irish ever did. Now they want Home Rule and I have done my best to give it to them. The Bill has passed in the House of Commons, but I'm afraid it may come a cropper in the House of Lords. I'm too old a man for this sort of thing. Politics is the very devil; and Irish politics is Satan himself!"

I stood up then and we shook hands. He walked me to the door and I was soon again in the busy London Streets. I took a hansom cab to back to Baker Street where I ate a quiet dinner alone. I reflected that with the departure of Roger Baskerville, I would again be at liberty. Autumn will soon be upon us. Before I am again put into the traces of professional life, I desire one last gallop in the pasture. Shall I return to Italy for the winter? Shall I go to Switzerland for a mountain cure? Perhaps a jaunt down to San Sebastian or Biarritz would be the thing. Ah well, there are plenty of days ahead for me to decide. For the present though, I think it only fair to write to Isadora Persano and to tell him that he may leave his retreat if he wishes to do so, and that so long as he stays clear of British Honduras, he should be quite safe from any threat posed by Roger Baskerville.

August 4, 1893—London

I received a most unusual letter today from Professor Moriarty. It is sufficiently odd that I can make nothing of it, so I will only record its contents here and place it for later reference on my book shelf where I keep what I call my "commonplace books," collections of interesting and entirely uncoordinated data listed in alphabetical order for later reference. I have found them useful in my professional thinking process by providing a beginning on almost any topic. The beginning of any inquiry whatsoever requires some degree of mental traction in order to move forward. My "commonplace books" although not functioning in any sense as a source of doctrine or dogma give me sufficient traction to proceed with any inquiry whatsoever.

Dear Sherlock Holmes,

I was sitting over my crumpets and marmalade at breakfast today and lamenting that I dismissed you so abruptly, because I would have enjoyed your immediate reaction to a sudden hypothesis that jumped into my head this morning. As you know the physicist is placed in the awkward position of taking the universe as it is and reasoning backwards in order to find a point of origin where all of the physical forces operative in the universe can be described by a single equation. Even if you were not aware of this "job description" of the physicist, you know it now.

The problem is that through a process of diffusion all manner of events have followed from this presumed "great simplicity." The scientist is stuck poking about in a great junkyard attempting to reconstruct the condition of each item that he finds. The task is well-nigh insurmountable and that is why so few people pursue it. The salvation of the world lies in the intellectual lethargy of the majority of the human population; but since you and I share the curse of a hunger for explanations I thought that I would just throw this your way:

It suddenly occurred to me that most problems are contextual; we keep playing the game according to rules of thought that appear to be determined by what we see rather than what we do not see, in fact cannot see, because we refer all of our observations to space and time, the only dimensions of which we can be aware. But what if space and time, indeed all of what we term physical reality is only an illusion, an evanescent projection of a thinking being in a temporarily fevered state of mind, what you might theologically speaking call "the original sin." If this hypothesis could be proven (which of course it can't unless we should recover from our "fallen condition" the result might help us to understand our ontological dilemmas the foremost of which is the existence of God and the problem of good/evil—our limited human existence. What if everything that we observe round about us is one great simultaneous event? In other words what if from a point that we might have shared with God (granting for a moment your religious hypothesis derived from the Bible) past/ present/future are all self-contained within a higher dimension where all problems cancel themselves out? Would that not be a good working idea for what eternity would be?

Theology continues to speak of eternity as though it is infinitely extended time; and when considering space theology speaks of the heavens as though they are located somewhere. I suggest that this manner of speaking is inherently fallacious and that any concept of God must in consequence of that fundamental error be either self-contradictory or absurd. No human language can speak of God except in the most domestic and culturally-linked terminology. A metaphorical gap must therefore exist in all theological language, even the most sacred. If that is so then even the Bible is nothing other than a picture-book for children because they have yet to learn how to read. (Lest you think that I am being irreverent let me point out that the books of science are equally deficient). Thought processes, being immaterial can leap over these problems of space and time by using a language not bound by time/space limitations. Instead mathematics grasps and describes relationships sub specie aeternitatis, *from the perspective of the eternal, and by doing so escape from the problem of God and the problem of good/evil. Transcendental topics require a transcendental language in order to be accurately described and not to fall prey to mythological or other inadequate linguistic or cultural overlays. Perhaps we should pursue our future discussions along the lines suggested by these thoughts.*

Respectfully,
Professor Moriarty

August 8, 1893
London

Roger Baskerville has left England. If he knew how many men from Scotland Yard were dispersed among the crowd along the docks to apprehend him should he have any last minute change of heart; and how closely his movements were watched during his last days here by Colonel Sebastian Moran, his pride and self-importance would have been gratified. As it is, he walked up the gangplank languidly smoking a cigar while carrying only several newspapers and a small portmanteau just like any other of the many passengers aboard the ship that was to carry him to British Honduras. The ship is one of some speed and its first and only stop will be Honduras before proceeding on to

Kingston, Jamaica. We will hear directly by telegraph when once he has reported for duty at the foreign office. His departure marks the first time in months that I have been able to displace from my mind an abiding sense of danger. I may now consider my own position.

What have I accomplished during this long absence from Baker Street? I feel at times that I am a stranger in my own country. I have used up those physical reserves that formerly allowed me to neglect my health and to always feel as though I might draw upon some infinite reserve of will in times of crisis. This illusion from which I suffer is that the whole world might be put right quickly if only I might discover some overarching key that would harmonize all things; it is this paradoxical illusion of omnipotence that still obsesses me. I am impatient with the labor that one must accept, the resistance imposed by life to every endeavor.

I realize now that simply to continue to live requires that a great harmony should reign within the human body. To assume always the presence of good health and vigor is surely an exercise in temerity and presumption. In my youth I always imagined that there would be plenty of time for any number and manner of new endeavors so that I might re-create myself a hundred times and explore every facet of the gem of our human existence. Even now I keep a list of monographs in my head that I intend to write upon various subjects. But year by year they remain unwritten and the "Encyclopedia Sherlockiana" consists only of this journal of mine. I wonder if I will ever keep another journal in my later years. If my conclusions about life are not complete by now, then of what use will be another twenty years to diverse speculations?

Each year I fall farther behind in my grand quest for the comprehensive synthesis that I imagined I could create by filtering all prior thought processes through my brain just as the baleen whales filter plankton. New books are published faster than I can read even those prior classics containing the mere rudiments of essential knowledge. I blush to consider the many classic authors that I have yet to read. My grand synthesis is thus more of an essay, a skeletal fragment, than an encyclopedia. If each man contains a universe within himself, then complete knowledge of the outer world is an *ignis fatuus*, a will-of-the-wisp, flitting over the marshes of human thought. How many drown in the bog holes of false sentiment and error. How I long for the 18th century certitudes, of even Byron's pride that in his extended poem, "Don Juan," he had managed to say all things and to reveal the folly of human life once and for all. All is finally as Shelley once said, "Life is a dome of many colored glass, staining the white radiance of eternity, until death tramples it to fragments."

I believe that each man has within him one great utterance, one vast symphonic performance and he is fortunate indeed if his days and nights last long enough to enable him to take at least one great leap into the darkness where the fruits of his creativity dwell. What must it have been like for the deaf Beethoven to look at the notes of his Ninth Symphony, one that he would never hear played, or could his great mind synthesize those notes from the inorganic page where they were written so that his cranium echoed with music that had transcended the usual ministry of the auditory nerves? Do we ever really see the world or hear it in all of its fullness? If all of consciousness is but the activity of the intricate language of the nerves and if our brain made of soft tissues dwells floating in the fluid medium of the skull, then whence and wherefore does the world exist but in the human mind? It would not surprise me if all of life was a dream. Perhaps it is God's dream after all and woe betides us should God ever wake and shake free of the delusions wrought in slumber. The man who thinks too much must of necessity be melancholy. Such a man must realize finally how small is that fragment of experience that he has been allowed to accumulate in his one life. All of the treasures of his memory must therefore seem accidental and as such wholly inadequate. Each man or woman is simply dropped into life and must begin to swim immediately or drown! What are the cries of the newly born infant but a recognition that its long exile has begun with those first labored breaths. The infinity and security, the all-sufficiency of the womb is replaced by light, sound, cold, demands for food; all needs reaching out from within the unique and particular self, now severed and incomplete, a being so lately at one with the harmony of all things and now in exile.

As each man ages he tries to recreate that bliss by his own efforts. Are the concepts of the Garden of Eden, the Moslem paradise, or the Buddhist concept of nirvana only variations on a dream of what we once experiences when cradled in the ocean of the womb? Is the great cosmos in which the earth drifts only the amniotic fluid of time and space? When shall those birth pangs arrive that will usher in a new universe? Is God in labor even now to create it? Was the first creation just a pre-conception and not a birth and does God delay to remedy evils now because to give birth too soon would discharge only a miscarried creation with features not yet knit into that degree of health and vigor that would allow it to survive on its own and someday to know God? We exist at the portals of the mansion of eternity; the door has not yet swung open to show us what lies within that ultimate domain. All that we know is only a prelude to the life that truly is. Perhaps this alone explains why the dead do not speak to us, for how could they hope to convey the knowledge of our futurity in their former native tongue, a language now fallen into desuetude and abandoned because the vocabulary of Eternity is incommensurable.

It must therefore be reduced to the humble language and promises of Christ to us and to the unique and individual action of the sacraments upon each human soul. No two communions with God are alike. God adjusts Himself to the receptivity of each soul to whom He speaks. God is the universal solvent of the soul to heal all its wounds, to grant to that one soul a place in the kingdom; and yet for all of that individuality, to assemble all souls into God's oneness and to create an integral yet various heaven for his Bride the Catholic Church at last.

Only the Catholic Church as a whole is adequate to answer the deepest theological questions; for this reason any individual theological synthesis is temerarious and impossible of attainment. Similarly faith is not mere belief because faith involves commitment and a change of heart. The object of faith is more than a mere belief let alone an admission of some trivial degree of credibility, mere good manners shown towards an interlocutor.

Faith must match the magnitude and significance of what is to be believed. Faith must therefore destabilize all prior convictions or models whatsoever. Anything less than this is not faith but sheer open-mindedness or worse; it is indifference. This is why religious tolerance is a contradiction in terms. To be religious is to be committed irrevocably to a set of beliefs that provides the horizon for all other data whatsoever. This is why secularity can never be a faith but only a pragmatic adjustment to life as we find it. An uncommitted assessment of religious claims must then be reduced to an exercise of pure imagination. It is impossible in the same sense as to as to describe in detail the sights and sounds on a road that one has yet to travel. Nevertheless I have been proceeding here as though the contents of Christianity can be cataloged from outside or even from taking an oppositional stance to faith by applying some exterior standard or methodology. What has been going on between Professor Moriarty and me is no more than a prolegomenon to a synthesis that neither of us can supply.

The question arises then why both of us are not rather kneeling at the altar in the Catholic Church to do what Jesus in the gospels asks us to do rather than engaging in fruitless debate: to receive our God in the most simple and visceral manner possible:

Take and eat for this is my body. Take and drink for this is my blood, the blood of the new and everlasting covenant, the mystery of faith.

Yet still I persist. I do so because the message of Christianity must perforce encounter a world of unbelief. The presence of God dislodges and relocates every other consideration whatsoever. It questions our origins, it implicates the reliability of texts, and it supplies an economy of salvation to a world with far different economic structures; but above and beyond all of these Christianity calls into question the space/time matrix in which all events are said to occur. We look for God when according to the Word of God we have already found Him, (just not in the manner that we supposed).

The religions of the world claim to be definitive and final pronouncements and not mere cultural artifacts. Every effort to escape the consequences of the beliefs of others is unattainable, therefore we must talk of what we cannot hope to comprehend; we must debate the non-debatable. We must do what Professor Moriarty and I are doing and as a result I must continue this journal embodying my side of the great equation while not losing sight of my specific tasks in the struggle for existence.

The struggle for existence is ultimately the quest of every philosopher. From the time of the pre-Socratic philosophers like Parmenides later philosophers have been struggling to understand what everything is by explaining what everything is not. The drawing of distinctions, the elaboration of various definitions, the positing of axioms; what are all of these but efforts to get something down and to preserve it prior to their dissolution into nothingness?

It is as though being itself were a temporary condition constantly being threatened by the nothingness from which things emerge. The physicists proclaim, in the Law of the Conservation of Energy, that energy can neither be created nor destroyed, but only transformed or perhaps defused, and finally dissipated into some irrecoverable state of unavailability. Unless some sustaining outside agency winds-up the clock of the universe it will eventually run down. Order turns through a process of transition into disorder and decay. The energy may still exist but the form is forever lost.

The marble of a broken statue remains, but where has gone the temporary form the marble had assumed under the artist's hand? And what are we, our identity, but an ongoing process of self-aware transition both identical with and different from the person that we were at some prior stage of our life? If the form is not identical to the substance that temporarily encodes it, and moreover if that code has for any length of time been irrevocably etched into the time and space that once contained it, then it should to that extent at least be considered permanent, and if permanent recoverable by whatever agency set being up in the first place.

If events should cease, would time as a dimension cease as well? Can space persist without time? But the time/space continuum, the field upon which all events occurred would theoretically remain but in a state of suspense, a waiting for something to happen. But waiting implies time' after all even waiting is an event of sorts. This means that a non-event existing in space/time or time/space might, if time were to stop leave only space, three-frozen dimensions in which nothing occurs. But even this nothing is still the something of space; but if space no longer moves forward in time, its existence would be pure potency, not a state of waiting or even of expectation for there would be no-thing to wait or to expect. Yet everything that had ever occurred would, from a theoretical outside perspective, still exist as history and be subject to recall as once having been.

Is the past replicable or transferable? Even if no groove or path might retrace again an identical series of events if the whole drama of existence was played again; at least from an outside perspective having once been is to exist forever from the perspective of God, just as we recall people who have died who still exist within us as they were. We can close our eyes and in memory walk again though a house where we once lived, a house that no longer exists. Does God see us in precisely this manner and if He wishes to take us from one set of conditions like a familiar toy and place us again in another setting, one where time and space are alien concepts, can we resist that transference? The new language of eternity must be learned. The curve of human existence extends beyond the horizon of death. The narrative of our story must traverse—a gap.

I met Colonel Moran today at his club for dinner and in the sitting room over brandy we pursued our conversation regarding Professor Moriarty. He was quite pleased with the fifty pounds that I gave him for his efforts in London keeping his eye on Roger Baskerville until his departure. I then turned the conversation to Professor Moriarty.

"I am intrigued," said I, "By your revelation that Professor Moriarty was devoted to his mother. It raises certain possibilities. Could it be that the Professor's desire to bring down the British Empire has its roots in that dreadful catastrophe, the Irish Potato Famine? But forty years have passed since then. Surely the England of today is not the England of forty years ago."

"Are you so sure of that Holmes? If anything England has grown worse. Ireland was the first British Colony. Did you know that Ireland was engaged in exporting food even during the worst years of the famine? The problem was not a complete lack of all food but only a lack of money to purchase anything but potatoes which were all that the Irish peasants could afford because they raised them themselves. A great majority of the peasants were evicted after the potato failed and even many resident landlords were destitute as well with no rents coming in from their tenant farmers."

"The English were reticent about providing direct aid. Ireland was supposed to be self-supporting by taxing the resident British overlords. When what was then called the poor-rates were not paid by the local landlords, even the workhouses, which had been providing some measure of relief by distributing Indian corn were closed. That beast Trevelyan who was in charge of relief operations even went so far as to claim that the weeding out of the Irish by hunger and disease was a providential action of God to decrease a tumultuous and fractious people who worshiped the false God of Rome. The British therefore used the famine to purge Ireland of superfluous slaves, for that is what the tenant Irish really were, slaves in their own land. As to a changed present, why even now Ireland has not been given Home Rule by the English; so you see that the Professor's plan is not merely a gratuitous act of private revenge but will be an act that will liberate subject peoples throughout the British Empire. He intends to strike at the roots of that great tree of world domination."

"I do not believe it is possible for one man to make good on such a boast," I replied.

"Then even you have failed to realize how great is the reach and resources of Professor Moriarty. He intends to set world history upon a different course. When Britain falls, all the other industrialized nations will adjust to the huge vacuum that will be presented by England's fall. Undoubtedly another empire will arise soon enough to take England's place, but it will be one against which the Professor holds no private grievance. If there is no providence to guide events towards justice, then the globe is spun about only by the great men of history who in daring to act without moral constraint, bend the world to their will. Most human beings are mere accidents of history whose story will never be told. They are like schools of fish that disappear into the mouth of the shark or plankton when a great baleen whale scoops them up."

"Is insignificance such a dreadful thing?" I objected. "My own faith contains this advice from Jesus Christ, *'Learn from me for I am meek and humble of heart.'* I have a story to tell you. My friend Doctor Watson told it to me and I have never forgotten it. It was during the Punjab campaign during the time of the Indian Mutiny. Watson was a mere medical orderly attached to an advance column and a very young man. He went out to India intending to spread the light of English civilization to a subject people. The atrocities committed on the resident English troops and their wives at the outbreak of the rebellion were appalling, but the reprisals exacted in return were worse. He told me of one case where a father whose wife had just presented him with twin girls was killed along with the babies who were a mere three months old. The father had left his young wife to procure food for the family and when he returned a short time later the house had been reduced to rubble by British artillery shells and his family was buried beneath the stones. Even with the bad feelings that Watson and so many others had entertained the sight of this man's desperation moved Watson to the depths of his soul. It was as if a great sponge had suddenly erased everything that the bereft man held dear and his mind simply could not conceive of such a loss. Every effort to comfort or restrain him was in vain. He was in a perfect paroxysm of grief. Life had suddenly lost all meaning and dimension so great had this man's love been for his family. Their loss was as inconceivable as if the sun itself had tilted and plunged into the earth; any difference or separation that Watson felt disappeared at once and he spent days tending the man who was now alone in the world to the neglect of his other duties."

The Colonel inquired, "And what became of the man?"

"He simply disappeared," I answered. "Whether he recovered from his loss will never be known. But if he made another man feel the same pain by turning from the victim to the aggressor his pain would be doubled for he would need to see again the same dreadful pain written upon another countenance and know that he was the cause. How many such cases would Professor Moriarty create in order to fulfill his plan?"

The Colonel was silent for several minutes. At last he spoke up, "There are no individual cases where war is concerned; those in the vicinity are swept up in the same manner as if a great storm had swept them away. Expectations for happiness are illusions in certain historical epochs. That man had no business having children or even a wife at such a time and if he already had them, he should have considered them and himself as well as already dead."

"And what if you were that man," I asked in a shocked tone of voice.

Colonel Sebastian Moran was again silent for some moments before answering simply, "But I am not."

later we discussed the disasters of world history and the many promises of historical renewal, each with untold costs in human lives. I brought up the promises that the philosopher and economist Karl Marx brought forth in his revolutionary works on communism.

Colonel Moran addressed the topic in these words, "It is pointless to speak of the glories of communism. What is a dictatorship of such non-entities as constitute the working class? If a common ownership were ever established among men, there would still need to be a core of administrators to prevent individual hoarding and the reinstitution of private property. These in turn would become the new masters. The mass of men demand that they be herded like sheep to benefit the few. It takes a man like the Professor to strike at the head of the beast, those few who think that the present order will maintain their own comfortable role as rulers. The mass of the people always fear individual sovereignty because it ushers in the inevitable jealousy of inferior men for their superiors. They keep their fear in check however, because they are cowards at heart. The Proletariat will never rule without a strong man to symbolize the collective will. Even the Americans were no sooner free than they instituted a Republic with limited suffrage to govern them so that the landed gentry would rule. How soon was it before America boasted an even more rich and vulgar aristocracy than the French were able to maintain until the French Revolution and its absurd promises of liberty, equality, and fraternity. Most men are incapable of tolerating actual freedom. Instead, they settle for symbols and minor concessions to their immediate wants and appetites. They await a leader to tell them what to do and what to believe."

"And which class of men do you belong to, Colonel Moran?" I asked him with some insolence on my part.

"Oh I am in no way different than most men," he replied smiling good naturedly. "Give me my club and a good brandy and I sleep well at night. I leave it to the Professor, these dreams of change and revolution. He is welcome to any joy that it gives him to contemplate general ruin. I am content to live in my own age of history and to make the best of things as they are."

"Yet you aid him," I objected.

"Yes Holmes, but for a fee, I am always well paid for my services. Well, I believe that is all that I may safely divulge upon the topic of the Professor's natal feelings. You may use that knowledge as you think best if it may do you any good at all."

August 10, 1893—Grimpen

I thought during the course of my train journey home to Devon about the unique insight that Colonel Sebastian Moran had given me into the character and motivations of Professor Moriarty. I was relieved to know that Professor Moriarty was not devoid of that essential human sympathy within us which is the beginning of all moral and religious aspirations, the love of at least one other human being. To know any love at all is to perceive that human beings are not mere units of the social calculus, but that each of us exists as utterly unique, both in ourselves and in our relations with God. It is perhaps the greatest realization and concession that we can make towards the omnipotence of God that His concern for the whole of humanity in no way distracts or detracts from His attention reserved for the individual.

This is made clear in the parable of the lost sheep. For this reason, it is not too much to say that God relates to each man or woman as though they alone existed in the universe. God is not divided and segmented. His love is whole and entire in each manifestation of His grace, so that to know God is to be affirmed in our entire being as beloved of God. It is sometimes assumed that God loves us only insofar as we are part of Christ within the Church and that thus we partake of only a derivative affection. This is not true. We are loved already, loved even while still in our sin. God would not have sent Jesus Christ at all for the redemption of the world if love did not remain in God for us collectively and individually, even while we were still in a fallen state. This clearly indicates that the intention of God is the universal salvation of all souls. The concept of special election dear to so many Christians is, in contrast, one of exclusion. It seems to me the height of impiety to believe that God's universal will towards salvation is as easily set aside by sin as many Christians believe it is. The narrow path to salvation is often made narrower still by the persons who as self-appointed gatekeepers are anxious to exclude the very people that Jesus came to save. No one should shout, "REPENT!" unless he is looking at his face in a mirror. It is the sorrow inherent in sin that leads to repentance combined with the still and yet insistent voice of conscience.

The true concept of election is the comfort in knowing that God has not abandoned us and that every motion of the soul towards God will have its reward. The concept of election then is meant to comfort the man or woman living in grace and to encourage them to persevere. It has not always been understood in this way unfortunately; discouragement and despair only aid the devil. Election is not meant to strengthen the effects of the temptation of the devil who likes nothing more than to encourage despair in the unconverted by getting such a one to believe that he is not among the elect and simultaneously to encourage pride and presumption in those who have already responded in some manner to the instigations and influence of Divine Grace. The Christian should be encouraged to adhere to God lest he lose what he already possesses, while the unconverted sinner should be encouraged to augment his hope for salvation even when he is prey to discouragement.

The belief in the possibility of sanctity reserved for each individual human being and his or her unique worth gives the lie to any human calculus that would treat men and women as mere social units. All wars and revolutions as well as atheistic communism see the individual as a mere means to an end, valuable only en mass. Yet God sees each individual as worth all of creation. Our ability to deny our own humanity and our own dignity at times and to fail to remember that we are made in the image and likeness of God is the source of most social evil. Each man or woman is a cathedral in which God may be worshiped. Each contains the full measure of the divine intention that once brooded over Eden. So it is that to love one other human being is to know how to love all of humankind. It is to see the world from the perspective of God.

When I discovered that Professor Moriarty had loved his mother and that for him "the original sin" of his life had been his abandonment of her in her hour of greatest need, although she had willed that he do so in order that he might survive, I knew that I possessed the key at last to his dark soul. It was his hatred of himself and of his father that had wrought the great distortion from which he still suffers. His entire life had been spent in one great act of vengeance, to kill anyone who reminded him of his own sin. Every murder of an oppressive land-owner or industrial magnate, each assassination of a member of the House of Lords, was but a step forward in his own effort to redeem his soul through his own efforts and to satisfy his own demands of strict and implacable justice.

His current plan to destroy the British Empire was the natural culmination of his prior life's work. Yet, to do so was pointless. Another unjust system would no doubt take its place; they always do. The world has never known an end of Empires. Christ did not conquer Rome by destroying it, but by allowing it to collapse through its own vanity and excesses. Rome was already doomed before the birth of Jesus. Already, the Senate had become captive to the ambition of the Caesars. Soon it became a virtual death sentence to be elected to wear the laurel crown of the Caesars. The legions of the empire became the determinants of who should rule as Emperor.

Power always invites its own dethronement. Honors only lead us to the grave. Blessed is the man then who lives in obscurity, for he is limited in the harm that he may do, and he is spared the envy of others who would rejoice at his downfall. It is the mercy of God that counsels one to adopt the virtue of humility and warns us that we will be judged more strictly according to the measure of our gifts. This insight was behind the hunger for the desert of the early cenobites and the hermits who sought above all else, not to be known among men, so that they might find their names more firmly inscribed in the Book of Life.

Power deceives even the man who would do great good by

using power for charitable purposes. Such a man usually exceeds his measure of grace and attempts to decide the course that history should pursue instead of leaving this to God. The truly astonishing thing is that God is never defeated by history. He draws his saints forth even during the most brutal of ages. Even the Church is never more in danger than in its hours of triumph and domination. It is then that even the spotless Bride of Christ forgets Christ, as the Bridegroom and begins to worship her own image in the glass of time rather than in eternity. God allows even the Catholic Church to know dark hours so that it will turn again to Christ who is always its strength, its source, and its end. The Church never ceases to need renewal, which usually means to return again to its beginnings and to do well again what it has done well before.

General repentance means to turn back by ceasing to advance along a path that will only lead one to ruin. It is time to suspect that one is on the wrong road when one looks about from the dais of honor and esteem and finds that one is quite alone there. It is then that the veil of the temple is ripped from top to bottom. The temple which contains only our own certainty of our virtues is one where God no longer dwells among us. It is then that we should fall upon our knees and beg Him to return to us, for only by so doing can we return to Him.

August 11, 1893
Grimpen

If the idea that God is concerned for us as individuals seems to be disproportionate to His majesty, further reflection may explain that to accept anything less would be to sever God from His creation. The gospel is clear that every hair on our heads is numbered. Though our world is indeed in a fallen state since Eden and although the gospel speaks of the devil as "the prince of this world," God's ultimate sovereignty remains intact. The final outcome of all things has been long decided (but not predetermined so as to exclude human freedom).

God's providence works in such a way that it is always

superior to every contingency, using even evil in a most mysterious fashion to advance the good of all things. One need only turn to the Old Testament to realize that whereas all other religions entertain some vague idea of a deity or deities, only the Hebrew Scriptures describe a God whose primary characteristic is His Holiness. God is not a mere force, not merely a tribal God to be controlled or placated, but rather a God who must be by His very nature nameless. He is a God who approaches man, though in Himself He is unapproachable. God is not found as though He were a mere object. Rather, it is God who does the seeking, the choosing, and the comforting of His people. The initiative always remains with God. Jacob might wrestle with an angel, but God manifests Himself directly only when He wills to do so and for our benefit. The great genius of the Jewish faith and the *raison d 'etre* for the law of the Torah with its intricate demands was that it reminded the Jewish people of the purity and perfections of their God, so that to serve Him required the greatest care, even of one's own kosher purity.

Idolatry was severely condemned because all idolatry has a reductive tendency. One cannot imagine the purely transcendent if one may see it clearly delineated in an image. Idols have borders, shape, and size; but God who as the Holy One transcends not only image but also concept and conception has no such limits. Of course the human mind cannot properly conceive the Holy, because by its very nature Holiness in its purist form is only predicated of God. Holiness exceeds all of the other transcendental concepts such as beauty, unity, and harmony. So great is Holiness that even the Seraphim and Cherubim are said to veil their faces from the presence of God!

I often think that the most beautiful words of the Holy Mass are the very first ones, "*Introibo ad altare Dei*, I will go unto the altar of God." I have often thought of the temerity of those words. Only an adopted son of God would ever dare to do so. What is man that he, in his own mere essence and without specific invitation, would dare to approach the altar of God? If man stands at the foot of the mountains of the Himalayas and looks at the distant peaks swept with bitter snow and cloud, if he stands before the ocean knowing that he would drown before he had barely left the shore if he sought to cross it unaided by a boat, if he stands before the great African desert but would be hard-pressed to count the grains of sand within his mere palm, then how, how, may man approach the altar of his God?

It has always seemed to me that one should climb a great many stair steps to every church or chapel simply to remind one of the great and indeed incommensurable distance that man must traverse before he might even dare to cast his eyes up at the mere portals of heaven. If God did not condescend to come to us, in the person of Jesus Christ, there would be no hope of us even daring to worship God as God deserves to be worshiped, in spirit and in truth. This is what our derivative holiness means! We worship in order to gain access to what God wishes to communicate to us of His very being.

It is not that God is best conceived of as mighty or powerful or the first cause or "the unmoved mover," although He is these things metaphysically speaking as well, but that God is above all Holy, and alone Holy in all possible universes, and it is this that makes God to be God, the one God, the only God. So remote is such Holiness that it eludes any definition made in terms other than its own; only the Holy Trinity participates in the fullness of Being; although we, according to the promises of Christ, may share that life in heaven, if we die in possession of the grace of God.

What will it mean to share this Divine Life in all its fullness? That has yet to be revealed. The genius of Christianity and the proof of its truth may be seen in its refusal to go too far and to offer us a coherent image of beatitude. Similarly, hell is not explained beyond the concepts of bondage and anguish. To refuse the transcendent is to opt for limitation. I have spent time in opium dens where the drug which promises freedom from pain only betrays its users to suffer greater pain. I have seen the besotted dreamers who are lost in a maze of their own minds and only imagine themselves to be happy. I have seen in those contorted bodies in the smoke-filled and heavy air as clear a vision of hell as any man requires. To be left infinitely to one's own devices is another definition of hell.

The existence of man or woman without God is inconceivable; even the atheist who opposes belief in the vain hope that the human is explicable on its own terms must admit a residue of doubt regarding the reality of God as the horizon of all perception. But, human thought processes, values, and desires so exceed those of the animal kingdom that to conceive of the human without a Divine origin is to imply an effect completely in excess of its cause. To do so is as though a random series of sounds might combine by sheer chance to produce a beautiful symphony. Nor is it a valid argument that human existence is its own explanation that however unlikely it might be the forces of evolution might have produced the human being, it has nevertheless done so.

Human intellection has the capacity to precede experience and to imagine what does not yet exist. This creative aptitude shows that the human being possesses a trans-temporal awareness, an ability to reach beyond the normal borders of space and time and to intuit at least what an eternal realm might look like. But this intuition must always be a vulgar and incomplete approximation of the reality of eternity. Even the austere language of mathematics is inadequate to account of the source of being-as-such. Any conception of God so far removed from the individual and concrete that such concepts and methodologies must represent a type of pure reason, of relationships that may build non-empirically on other theological relationships, cannot reach across the gap that separates our conceptions from the reality of God; this why petition and praise in prayer are the only means to approach God.

The all-encompassing ground of being cannot be approached as though it were an object in a field of its own creating. Meanwhile the human need for concrete verification by applying equations to the behavior of concrete objects in motion becomes in the end a mere condescension made from time to time for demonstrative purposes, of what can be known of contingent-being. If a final solution to the most intractable problems of physics is ever achieved, that solution is likely to be so beyond experimental verification that its truth must rest only upon its own symmetry and elegance, in other words it would be a poem! The human mind would then acquiesce to its truth, not because it may be translated or reproduced in a laboratory, but because the human mind has the capacity to escape at times out of the waters in which it swims and like a great fish to enter the pure air of Eternal Truth. If all truths could be reduced to mere sense impressions or their derivatives, such intuitions would be impossible.

Divine Revelation provides to mankind those truths essential to the full realization of human destiny as originally intended by God. Revelation does not exhaust all truth of course. It is in the nature of a primer, a prelude, an overture. It has the function of drawing the audience from the lobby back to their seats like an *entr'acte* or interlude before the next act in an opera begins. God has yet to show us what he has prepared for us. The proper human response to revelation is simply one of assent to a work that God performs within us. Just as man cannot be like God knowing good and evil, so man cannot weigh the content of revelation in all its dimensions. Insofar as it is revelation and not metaphor, revelation exceeds all human ability to verify or to refute. Our relation to it is therefore one of will and of act, not of intellection. The formulas of faith do not become meaningless or arbitrary to us though, for some dim outline appears for us when we contemplate them. The focus however is necessarily blurred by our own inability to pierce the veil of Eternity.

Faith is not an abandonment then of the intellect but an honest acceptance of the limits of the human mind. This is easiest to achieve by those "little ones" spoken of by Jesus who have never relied excessively upon the complex and sophisticated outer limits of human performance imagining that they can understand all things. For the great mass of humanity faith is not so difficult because they have not tested or traversed even the ordained limits of human thought; so they feel no frustration when forced to accept the human mind's inevitable limits that bar complete comprehension when directed at God as an object of thought. They are not tempted to ascribe to human intellection abilities that this faculty does not possess.

Those most in danger of intellectual pride are precisely those who believe that they are keeping pace with eternity. Alas, they are like the tortoise that imagines that it may run with the gazelles. This is not to degrade mankind, but to awaken us to a sense of astonishment that God takes notice of us at all. If God were not love itself, He would not do so. The Catholic Church celebrates the revelation that God loves men and women and has come to remain among us through the mystery of the Incarnation of Christ in His Church. All of which is to say that we only begin to become fully a child of God when we accept the invitation of Christ and approach the altar of God to receive God's gift of our very self in sacramental form, as conveyed by the Holy Eucharist—where we meet our God directly.

August 13, 1893
Grimpen

After several days I am still deeply engaged in reflecting upon and refining this whole question of the importance of the individual soul in relation to God. It may seem to be fanciful to state that each and every person is precious to a god who is capable of creating a universe with vast galaxies of stars and the sheer infiniteness of space and time (at least as these vast distances must appear to our eyes peering out upon them through the lenses of a telescope). Why should such an immense and powerful God squint as it were through whatever incomprehensible visual apparatus He must possess and focus in upon the human race as a whole, let alone certain obnoxious individuals whom even their fellow men hold in contempt?

A short walk through East London will immediately reveal to the strolling observer certain men and women who are sufficiently noxious, gin-soaked, and belligerent that one readily flees from their mere malodorous proximity, let alone thinking that one has just met the god-like in human form and a fellow heir of eternal life. Does not my entire thread of theological reasoning break down in the presence of such individuals who would even dishonor the beasts let alone seem to share a common humanity with the more illustrious members of our species?

Yet these are precisely the anvil upon which I have hammered out my position against Professor Moriarty with all of his immense knowledge and acumen. It is precisely because these marginalized people manifest the results of human limitation and even of evil that the greatness of God manifests itself in relation to them. If God behaved like a stuffy society matron and turned (just as these so often do) away from them, would Divine Love be divine at all?

Christianity astonishes us by proclaiming that these last and least shall be first in the Kingdom of God! If this appears unjust we need only reflect that God does not require them to augment his goodness and thus His generosity is shown by the degree of its utter gratuitousness. At the very moment that we look down upon such as these we should recall that from the point of view of God the small gradations of human virtue must be equivalent to ants quarreling about the relative height of their anthills. We are closer to the greatest of sinners than we are to even the lowest of the angelic orders. Yet we are also said to have been made in the very image and likeness of God! How can this be if that image is so easily tarnished and obscured by our actual behavior? Let us go further still and ask how Jesus could be, as St. Paul said that he was, made to be sin for us? How can perfect innocence become not merely as a sinner but become sin itself?

Again we are faced with the vastness of the disproportion that seems always to characterize every act of God in our regard. Truly God's ways are not our ways! God alone can make something out of nothing. Perhaps then the elevation of the souls of such as these is the moral equivalent of making something out of nothing. God does this by so interpenetrating our nature with His grace that all that diminishes us or defeats us cannot affect God's essence when transmitted to us. All too many Catholics presume that such

Sanctifying Grace is easily lost.

How then was it ever possible that Jesus, who was without sin, could become sin for us and by doing so redeem us? God alone it appears can even merge such contradictories. If this is so, then what greater dialectician is there than God? For Jesus "to become sin" and even to die was to extinguish both sin and death forever. God alone can cancel both the burden of sin and its result of eternal death for the soul.

What better way to manifest the complete Sovereignty of God and to actualize it in space and time than to allow Jesus, the Beloved Son of God, to be put to death as a sacrificial offering by wicked men who did so in the belief that that by crucifying Jesus they were actually adhering to the highest ethical norms that they had received from God Himself? God is pure action and what He does is the most real of all real things.

The sacrifice of Jesus Christ was not a mere metaphor but a historical happening with actual flesh and blood and all of the attendant degradation that such a death would entail. Actuality shatters the most pregnant of human poetic metaphors. No crucifix can capture the bruised and broken Christ in His appalling and shattered flesh and bone. Divine malice towards sin is thus translated through the prism of Christ into the salvific rainbow of God's love for the sinner. Compare this recognition of the power of salvation with the common and all-too-easy assumption that the majority of the human race will end up in hell. The most abject sinner cannot see himself until he sees his own reflection in the light of the love of God for him. In our unloving world that vision will of necessity be deferred until the hour of our death when God meets the soul now stripped of all the accoutrements of our present life. Perhaps only in the moment of death each soul will see itself in relation to this love as manifest in Jesus Christ and its full meaning will then burst upon it. Many saints have spent years in contemplation of this mystery and still found themselves as stunned and dismayed as the first observers must have been when the body Of Jesus was taken down from the cross and immediately buried just as it was, bloody and broken in a tomb of stone.

August 14, 1893
Baskerville Hall

I immediately wired Sir Henry from London that I had seen for myself that Roger Baskerville in fact still lived and I wired him again when the ship containing his cousin sailed for British Honduras. I felt that Sir Henry and Lady Beryl would need several days to absorb this confirmation of their fears. I hoped that hearing that the ocean now separated him from them would bring some comfort and relief to the couple, but I was not unaware that the survival of Roger Baskerville could not but change the nature of their former marital relations. It meant of course that Lady Beryl was still married to Roger Baskerville and hence that Lady Beryl was no longer the wife of Sir Henry in the eyes of the Church. Lady Beryl had shut herself away from him and Sir Henry had been forced to entrust her care to her friend and secretary, a woman who was at least from her own country and in every way familiar with the temperament of her mistress. I finally called at Baskerville Hall today and found Sir Henry in his library. I met a man who appeared distracted, pale, and desperate.

"This whole matter is intolerable to me, Holmes. I have half a mind to set off for Central America and challenge the fellow to a duel," he cried while wringing his hands in his vexation. "Does she still love him? Can it be that this beast still has a hold upon her heart? I thought that I had given her everything and finally made her happy, yet she draws into herself now and mourns alone."

I did not know well how to address him. I have never married so I can only imagine that deepest of unions between two souls; but I have at least loved a woman, the woman Irene Adler. The congress of two souls in marriage is a mystery no less majestic in its way than the truths of religion. It is for this reason that marriage is viewed as a sacrament. I thought I might point out to Sir Henry that his love would survive until it might enter again into that fullness that he had known formerly with Lady Beryl and that to force the issue in any way, let alone by a duel, would blight all further trust between them. He might best prove his love to her now by guarding and providing for Beryl until she might again assume her title and her place by his side in the fullness of their married life by seeking an annulment of the prior marriage.

"But Holmes, I wish to create an heir for the estate of the Baskervilles. What if that vile man should produce an heir of his own in Central America who will return to England after my death and claim the estate?"

"You forget that he is still married to his wife Beryl, Sir Henry. Absent a divorce he cannot produce a legitimate heir through a new marriage while she lives. He has clearly abandoned her though. By the laws of England she might seek a divorce from him; but she is still bound to him under Canon Law as a Catholic and will not produce an heir for you until her former marriage is annulled. If she refuses to divorce him you can block him from taking possession of the estate as long as you survive."

"But what if I die, Holmes? Rodger Baskerville is next in line of succession," Sir Henry pointed out in distress.

"You can of course delay the passage of the estate of the Baskervilles by granting Beryl a life-estate. The title of baronet in any case is personal and will pass with you. The house and grounds are another matter. I am sure that no power on earth would compel Beryl to resume marital relations with the man. In any case I assure you that with Mycroft's help should he ever return we will make England too hot to hold him. As to the fine points of succession to landed estates I have at my disposal copies of several early English charters that may bear upon the matter that I would be willing to review with a barrister if you wish to accompany me."

"Thank you, Holmes, but you misunderstand my concern at this present hour. I trust that I shall live a long life now that he is removed from England and I have already consulted a solicitor about my legal options and how I may manage the estate so as to deny any heir of his a legacy. But that is nothing. It is Beryl's present mental state that concerns me. I fear she may go mad over all of this. Why should she be allowed to suffer so? I would risk everything to finally rid the world of the evil of this man."

The line he was taking troubled me; I feared that his own

brave and impetuous nature might cause him to take matters into his own hands. "Then indeed you would risk all, Sir Henry; I tell you that you will best defeat this man and save the love of your dear lady by bearing this situation in patience and to leave the rest to God. You cannot rid the world of evils by a series of assassinations and of duels. If you think so, I would be happy to introduce you to Isadora Persano who currently resides in a madhouse or to Professor Moriarty who has something similar in mind with regard to all of England. Evil must be tolerated in this world yet quietly opposed, but it will never be eliminated. Even nature itself is thronged with evils. What are plagues, famines, and fire, what are flood and pestilence if not a sign of that deformation of all matter that came with a fallen creation? All of creation has been distorted and warped by the refusal of man and woman to be as God intended them. Evil and good are so interwoven that they are inextricable in this life. It is fortunate for us that this is so for do we not all dread the Final Judgment above all other things? Then God will indeed rip asunder and sever forever the good from the wicked. But wicked as we are, is it not a blessing that God tolerates evil for a time? If he did not, where should we then be? What is the Passover with its blood upon the lintel or later in salvation history the water from the side of Christ that is the water of Baptism or the Blood of Christ in the Holy Mass but a sign of the mercy of God? These are not mere symbols but actual water and actual blood by which God chooses to save the world? What is the wrath of God but His final showing forth that as God He indeed knows the difference between good and evil and that that knowledge will finally sever the two forever and render to evil what is its due?"

I paused, but my words seemed to be restoring him to a measure of resignation and calm determination. I therefore continued as before. "I assure you, Sir Henry, that just as we are taught to pray daily that we shall not be led into temptation and that we shall be delivered at last from any final evil at the Day of Judgment, the petitions of this prayer must sustain you now. You must rely upon a power not your own. We may not deliver ourselves from evil and for this very reason let us not be in advance of God in rendering to wickedness what is its due, but rather let us bear up in good grace and have patience in our present state of struggle against the powers of darkness."

My words seemed to calm Sir Henry. He collapsed into his chair by the fire and placed his head in his hands. At last he spoke in a voice that was choked with emotion. "Very well, Holmes; I will do as you suggest."

As I walked home to my own simple lodgings I could not but reflect that the ills of the human condition strike each of us whatever our outward circumstances may be. I have never consented to believe that the whole purpose of our present sufferings is to test our patience or to develop our character. I do not wish to be like the friends of Job when confronting trials that I could not myself bear with equanimity. There must be more involved than some grim calculus that allocates trials to the virtuous while sparing the scoundrel. Yet I do not believe that mere chance is involved in that seemingly unjust distribution of ills. Many people abandon their faith in adversity, the very time when faith is most essential to the troubled soul.

Let me suggest a possible solution to this enigma by drawing a parallel. If evil as the philosophers maintain is derivative and parasitic upon a preexisting good, then its ontological status must lie in negation. The question of the ontological status of nothingness has troubled philosophers for years. It has been maintained by some that the vacuum of space that separates the planets is the physical analogue to ontological nothingness. Others maintain that the vacuum of space is not nothingness at all but rather a measurable distance between astral bodies. Space allows for the transition of light, a form of energy that only appears when it encounters an obstacle that reflects or refracts it. The speed of light is such that it requires a constant source to be perceived; otherwise it would leave the perceiver behind if not constantly renewed in a steadily renewed stream that travels unimpeded until it collides with some unyielding substance that absorbs some of its energy while altering the direction of entry and re-transmitting whatever energy remains.

Now the relevant questions are: does space come into being to accommodate the transit of light, or does space always exist and have a constant value and a theoretically ascertainable position no matter what passes through it at whatever speed as registered in units of time? In other words are space and time a rigid net that contains pulses of energy so that if those pulses ceased space and time could be assigned a net value of zero? Can space stretch as it were to accommodate different usages?

For instance can smallness reach into the same infinity as immensity? Is there some point of reduction in size that would constitute absolute zero, a point so small that it would be nothing at all? Or would that last entry always allow for a division that could be extended into infinity? The dimension of space would need to stretch to accommodate such simple division. Perhaps time is no different; it must accommodate itself to what passes through it at different rates of speed.

Then by analogy, if such relativity can exist in physics, then should we be surprised if God allows some latitude of expansion and contraction of the moral dimension to accommodate human actions? Perhaps God takes on any burden and inconvenience engendered by that variability? The search for moral certitude seems to be a denial of the necessity of the Lord's Prayer: that we petition God to help us deal with temptations and to deliver us from evils that surpass our ability to bear on our own.

August 15, 1893
Grimpen

I am still puzzling over the question of how to approach Professor Moriarty, not with a general morality but one that is specific, one that calls forth from him some one specific duty, to abandon his project and to assume a different course in his life. The task of the religious life is to bring together the most general with the most specific. As long as God remains for us only an impersonal force or a generic question, there can be no question of a real relationship with God. One is then a believer by mere default, simply because it is customary or convenient to be so. One has not yet risked one's entire life by seeing God as the only chance for a coherent and meaningful existence in this world, which of course He is. But is this fundamental act of maintaining belief such a great risk after all? Can it be any sort of risk to embrace God who alone promises all things to a being that possesses nothing in itself? Why do so many souls frisk about upon the pastures of this world like children who ignore the danger posed to them by the horns of a bull that has already plowed up the ground with its iron hoofs? The horns of this bull already drip with the blood of generations? How well-seasoned are all of the vices of this world and how comparatively untried are the virtues that lead us to heaven. Mankind always attempts first what it must later undo with great labor after much regret and repentance. The history of the world is a legacy of wasted opportunities; these have been lost somewhere along the course of history as though the gospels and the personal witness of the saints had not been quite clear about where ultimate happiness resides.

To locate the Holy is to discover that it exists in a specific place and is met at a specific hour. God does not need generalities but actualities from us. God is not like a scientist engaged in only discovering truth but rather is the source and origin of all Truth. God is not impressed then with elaborate justifications and explanations. The pure soul is always the simple soul who does what is just and right as naturally as breathing even though he or she may not know the furthest and most remote significance for what he or she has done. The Beatitudes after all need no elaboration; they are either self-evident or no explanation would ever suffice to make them attractive. As the human mind grows in subtlety it usually also grows in resistance.

Men tend to keep the search for God for the end of life, associating God with death and not with the fullness of life. The result is that the days of our youth are wasted in profligacy and one comes to God at last only with a sort of moral rheumatism. The

Communion of Saints is taxed excessively by its many petitioners. Similarly peace is sought between nations only after their resources have been exhausted by wars. The rising prosperity of nations is evident first in the money allocated to armaments. The implements of war grow in efficiency to claim more lives before an armistice is declared. In the future wars will only become more costly to opposing nations as the implements of war become increasingly efficient until at last perhaps nations will wonder why they must go to war at all if it demands so much sacrifice to attain such small rewards. New methods will be devised for the resolution of their differences. The natural logic of war then is to reach a point where no advantage is to be gained by going to war for either side, since even the victor must rebuild what he has destroyed if the conquered land is to be of any further use to the conqueror. So it is with any opposition to the manifest will of God; what is gained by sin but only to walk a long way from the right road while knowing all along that we must sooner or later retrace our steps to where we started with still no progress made in the acquisition of virtue.

The plight of the aged sinner is pitiful indeed. We should thank God for Purgatory as must the many souls who arrive there with the certain hope of attaining heaven at last. These no longer begrudge God's commands, but are grateful at last for one last chance to make even an inadequate return for all that God has given to them. The ills of this world, many as they are, show that all of life is purgatorial. We exist beneath the Sign of the Cross. What Christ was not spared, we shall not escape; yet for all of that this life shows forth more of mercy than of misery. Most of our ills are made worse by ourselves and not by nature or by fate. Holiness lies at our very door each morning and waits in the evening by our gates. To find it early is to enjoy its company in the heat of the day and to know peace at last in life's time of Vespers and of Compline.

Another year is advancing towards it close as so many have done in my life. The harvest already lies rich upon the fields of England. In Devon and in Ireland the Lughnasadh Fires burned at first harvest upon the hills; all about me I feel the teeming bounty of the year. Yet I am weary. I seem to feel already the coming frosts of autumn, not of this year's winter alone, but of a greater winter that is even now coming down upon the earth. Will I wither in turn before the equinox comes to winnow the land? How long may things go on as they have? Surely a dark time is before us. I do not know how long it shall be before a visitation of wrath or some great misfortune occurs, but the world seems about to undergo one of its great periodic purges. I feel it in my bones and my mind only confirms what the great rush of events portends. History has its storms and gales as the ocean does and there are those who feel the storm coming long before others. I fear that I am one of those who feel already the tremor of the leaf before the wind rises and feels the heaviness of the air before the first drop of rain falls.

Great events are not swift in the making but arise from conditions that have been long established, so that nations and peoples seem to adjust to them and compensate for whatever unequal pressures cause the storm to gather on the horizon. The rising tension seems contained within the rock strata of history. Anger and discontent burrow into the heart; fear lies latent along the nerves. Each day proceeds along its accustomed course. Yet, the event gathers momentum even in this immobility. The air fills with vapors like petrol only awaiting a mere spark to set everything into a raging conflagration.

August 16, 1893
Grimpen

I feel that I must escape for a time. I think often of Ireland and the great failure of Europe in its feeble attempts to provide a remedy for a famine happening on its very doorstep. Were the 1840's so different from the present age? If the British Empire was unable to meet the desperate needs of the Irish, then what nation will ever achieve a balance between needs and wants in the social order? Of what use is trade if such primary deficits are allowed to exist without a remedy? Yet Ireland is a rich and lovely land, but one not suited to industry. How odd it is that the rural economies often know starvation. One need only think of the Great Irish Famine for an example of this anomaly. The great privation was preceded by the years of subdivision of lands, the absent landlords unaware of local conditions, the dependence upon a single crop to sustain all of Ireland, the lack of reserves of grain, the poorly developed fishing industry, but above all else the grinding poverty of a conquered people held in fear and in hatred by the English for professing their Catholic Faith. Conquered races are always held in contempt by the conqueror.

England has had a bad conscience ever since England left the rest of the Catholic world behind deciding to serve its monarch rather than its God. The ruins of the old Catholic monasteries are like an accusing skeletal finger reminding England of its past, just as are the Irish people who have adhered to the old faith with a stubbornness perhaps only equaled by the Jewish people. The Irish are a living accusation addressed to their oppressors. What regions have known more suffering than Ireland or Palestine? Each is a land of compressed history and of long memories. Every acre of soil has been fought for, bled for, and carries the bones of those who have risked everything to obtain and to possess the land unhindered. This is why the Old Testament has as its background wars and rumors of wars. When Jesus said that these would be among the signs of the coming of the last days before He returned in glory, He was really saying that everything on earth would be similar to the way that the world had always been! Perhaps therefore all lands are like this; even snow-swept Russia for all its great size, the taiga forests of Siberia, which together seem more like an ocean than a land-mass, have known suffering as great as any. The Russian serf, theoretically free since emancipation on March 3, 1861, does not even possess his own soul let alone his own land. The land still owns the people who are seen as mere adjuncts to the soil and condemned to toil. Land is still the ultimate basis of wealth and our ultimate estate. There is a deep honesty in this statement. Man and woman be joined at last with the earth beneath their feet; the grave is the only leasehold that endures.

Ownership of any less enduring estate is an illusion; the earth never ceases to draw what is its own back into itself. The land cannot be permanently converted to personal use anymore than one may ever own the sea? Men even attempt to own each other and to accomplish this create penury out of the complaisance of injustice. Everywhere there is this same problem of unequal distribution of resources. Trade is usually unequal and adhesion contracts are enforced to draw resources from the poor to surfeit the wealthy. Colonies are stripped of their resources and labor. Foreign manufactured goods that they can ill-afford to purchase are provided in exchange.

History is the legacy of vampires! How strange it is that we use titles and peerages to dignify our rapacity. Should we not rather admit that our rulers and great factory owners are pirates and slavers; it is time to call them such names as will best describe what they in fact have done to purchase their eminence among us. I often find lately that I am more in sympathy with Professor Moriarty than I once dared to admit. My only difference from him is my choice of the means that I look to for deliverance. Moriarty would do so directly while I prefer to join my voice to the lamentations of the Holy Scriptures and to exercise charity. The prayer of chosen people has always been for deliverance from the oppression of evil-doers.

The essence of biblical prophecy is accusation. Yet the rich never tremble at their good fortune. The selective blindness exercised towards every passage of scripture that refers to them is the marvel of Christian practice by those whose great country estates contain chapels and oratories. Many of the great landowners will fully prosecute according to the laws of England as a poacher a hungry man if he captures so much as a superfluous hare upon the estate.

If the truth be told England loathes Ireland for what it has itself made of Ireland; it scorns the Irish and treats them as rebels when they only seek to possess again what was once their own country. Ireland is caught like a fishbone in England's throat. Even Scotland and Wales have never rested easy under English domination. What then can be said for India, what rights have the British to be there? But I have been to India and have yet to visit Ireland. I think lately of seeing the land from which Moriarty came as a boy but to which shores he has never returned. I could take a boat from Cardiff to Cork and from there I could tour the west and north of Ireland by rail before winter sets in. I have always wished to see the Aran Islands and to explore the coast of Donegal. The impact of the famine was worse they say in the north and west of Ireland. These are bleak and barren lands of rock and rugged seacoast. If my desire is to strip down human existence to the very bone in my pursuit of truth, I can think of no better place to do so than Ireland.

I must admit here though that I would much prefer to visit a green and well-endowed French Benedictine Monastery or perhaps to visit the Grande Chartreuse of the Carthusian Order and to watch the mists descending from the mountainsides, to feel the august presence of God in the grandeur of the French Alps and to hear His voice in the thundering waters of chasm and ravine. But then again I am a Christian not a pantheist like the poet Shelley.

Ireland has always seemed to me to be a holy land because the visitor is in the presence of ocean and sea where he may glimpse the might of God while at the same time he may witness in the bare and grim lives of the Irish, subject like the Jewish people to the reigning empire of its day. These are the poor of Jesus Christ. The Irish are close to God because their English masters have deprived them of all else but God. The vision of Ireland in its bareness and austerity requires no external rule of voluntary poverty to detach the soul and turn the thoughts of one to God.

Italy and France are too rich in the obvious bounties of nature to nourish the stern discipline of divine love. Ireland is a land to which monastic detachment comes easy, for it is the common lot there. Charity is often most found where the means to exercise it are most limited. The Irish having little have learned to share what they have. This has made them among the most hospitable of people. It may be time for me to sample some of

that grand welcome reserved by the Irish for the wayward
stranger.

August 17, 1893
Grimpen

So I am no sooner home than I am to be off again. Has this
habit of incessant travel so grown upon me with the years
that I will never be able to sit still again? What has
become of the old recluse of Baker Street? But then what I always
used to speak of as my craving for a new problem to present itself
to me for a solution was perhaps a physical restlessness after all.
To travel is to experience time itself in a different way. To see a
variety of landscapes in distant countries is to have a foretaste of
the ever new nature of eternity. Yet there is an equally great joy in
allowing eternity to reveal itself in those local variations that come
from my own neighborhood at home. A new shop opens on Oxford
Street; a new haberdasher has a woolen coat for sale with an
Inverness cape; a native of northern India has a sign-board that
one reads in passing and the rich smells of curried lamb twine
about one beckoning one to enter and enjoy the sweet taste of
mangos, curry, and coconut.

I often think back with a deep affection of the nights spent
before my own fire in Baker Street while Watson sat across from
me in his old cane-backed chair. Would Inspector Lestrade arrive
in a cab and come bustling up the stairs and knock in his peculiar
official fashion? After many offhand comments he would confess
that he was then in possession of "a little problem that just might
be in your own line because it presents certain features that are
quite unique?" All of this I miss. I miss the sight of Watson reading
one of his old adventure tales of the sea by Clark Russell. I miss the
smell of boiled beef and onions coming up from Mrs. Hudson's
kitchen below our rooms. I miss the way that the wind would come
booming down Baker Street from the Oxford Street end on a
winter's night.

Where now are the Wagner concerts I used to love to

attend at the Albert Hall? Where the long walks along the serpentine or along Pall Mall in the spring? Ah well, these can be mine again at any time, but how long shall I have the freedom to set sail again at a whim and go off to Ireland? In any case I must search for some remnant of Moriarty that may still be present in that ancient land. Very well, I am decided; I will go.

August 21, 1893
Cardiff, England

It has taken me some days to close up my little cottage outside Grimpen. Sir Henry has offered to stable my little cart-horse during my absence and see that my wolfhound is well-cared for. I took the train north to Cardiff where I booked passage in a steamer to Cork. My boat leaves in two days. Until then I shall tarry in Cardiff and enjoy its Welsh charm. Cardiff is a lovely port town that is protected from most storms. It provides ready access to London and the British heartland and avoids the often present fogs of the English Channel with the ever present danger of collision there from other ships and the sometimes contrary currents that make navigation there so difficult. It has all of the charm of a Welsh Village with the size and prosperity of a larger city. I have taken a room with an excellent view of the harbor with its stately masts from around the world. I have made a round of the various book shops and obtained some excellent Ordinance Survey Maps of Ireland.

From Cork I plan to go on by rail to Killarney in County Kerry to see its excellent seacoast. From there I will travel north through Limerick to Galway and see the famous Cliffs of Moher before exploring Connemara, Sligo, and Donegal. From Donegal I will get a boat out to the remote Aran Islands where I hope to spend the last of the days of September. I will then cross the great Irish plains and Lake Country to Dublin from which I will book passage back home to England before the winter gales arise and make the passage across the Irish Sea difficult. It will then be time that I think about returning to practice as a consulting detective.

An initial problem has presented itself in that regard; Mycroft is in possession of an account of my adventure in Switzerland in 1891, written by Watson and entitled "The Final Problem." Watson apparently wrote this account soon after his return alone from the Falls of Reichenbach after my supposed demise. He left the date of its publication to Mycroft's discretion, thank heaven. I am glad that the dear fellow did not rush too soon into print upon his return for had he done so I would be forced to explain to the public the awkward fact of my sudden resurrection. Its publication might have also caused no end of complications for Professor James Moriarty in his new teaching position, who might well consider that he has been libeled in it, for I trust that Watson does not flatter the Professor in any account that would record my death at his hands.

Mycroft at the time prevailed upon the good doctor to keep my old rooms just as they were and to give out the story that I had gone abroad for my health, thus delaying Watson's valediction until a more appropriate time. By taking this course he spared the public no end of grief, at least that portion of the reading public that enjoys Watson's colorful little tales. I don't know why he had to write up our Swiss experiences at all; no doubt he wished to enshrine my memory as he publicized my other accomplishments. Although I have always appreciated his good intentions, I have never been comfortable with the notoriety that followed. Nothing makes the job of a detective more difficult than to be noticed on the street and to have various and sundry individuals, complete strangers to me, running up to me with eager expressions and an autograph book. In addition few of my clients felt comfortable approaching my door with their delicate problems after a time as I grew more famous when they knew that they would have to fight their way through a throng of gawkers and idle folk gathered on the sidewalk just waiting to see who needed the help of "that detective feller."

I can just imagine the talk of some of these loungers and gadabouts. "Oh, you be after consulting Mr. Holmes, I wager. An excellent choice! Why you're the first this morning. His windows are the first over there on the left, top of the stairs. I'll shout up to him if you like. Oh you have an appointment? Well all is quite alright then. You would be that surprised though if I told you how many just drops by and rushes up the stairs without so much as a by-your-leave. Here stand back the rest of you! Can't you see this 'ere gentleman needs to get through?"

A horrifying image is it not? But if I gave Watson a free hand in these matters that is just what these infernal tales of his would soon have brought upon me. Soon any practice of mine such as it is would have been terminated; even as it was I have never felt the need to advertise my services. Those whose problems are such that my particular approach may produce results usually find their own way to my door. I have requested that only a small selection of my cases should ever be written up at all and these few have usually been such as might amuse by their novelty if failing to instruct in a truly scientific manner.

Prior to my supposed demise, I always requested that Watson would only publish the majority of his tales after my retirement. He might write them up at any time of course as long as their publication was delayed. I thank my own foresight in imposing these restrictions upon him because it is to these very restrictions that I now owe the fact that I may hope to resume my practice at will without the necessity for awkward and obtrusive public explanations.

This will not avoid however the one great explanation that I must make to Watson himself when he returns from Louisiana. I am afraid the poor fellow has never realized that though my name is only beginning to be known to the public, I am quite well known among the criminal classes of London. There are men here and abroad whose own self-conceit would have them believe that I have been consulted in their regard when I have not been consulted at all and actually have no idea what criminal activities they may have committed; that I am a court of last resort does not mean that I have universal jurisdiction over all criminal activity or that I am in any way omniscient. But some of these more narcissistic criminals have assumed that I am. It is these unstable types who may imagine that they have a grudge against me. They pose a continual threat to my safety and would have posed one to Watson as well if I had not taken my extended leave of absence. One of the hazards of criminal activity is that such activity courts an early death and many scoundrels have no doubt perished during my time spent traveling to the east.

I am afraid that Watson does not realize the dangers that each of us was exposed to in 1891 due to his prior publications and quite apart from Moriarty. By convincing Watson that I had perished in Switzerland I may have spared the poor fellow an injury. In any case I have spared him the divided loyalties that once took him from his proper place by his own fireside and his necessary services to Mrs. Watson during her last years before her fatal illness. If Watson has one great fault it is in his undaunted loyalty and admiration for me. Could I therefore imagine that he would acquiesce without constant worry about me when I was about to depart for those very parts of Asia that had once almost brought about his own premature death during his military service?

I am not without affection for him and could well imagine the daily burden that anxiety for me would have added to his cares. If instead he was allowed to assume that I had met my death by ridding the world of my arch-enemy, Professor Moriarty, he could then, after a suitable period of mourning, return to life as it might have been for him if he had never met me and been drawn into that circle of danger that I have made my own. It was the least that I could do for such a friend and I pray that when I confess my motives to him that he will see that I was right after all and will eventually forgive me.

August 22, 1893
Cardiff

Prior to my leaving Grimpen I received an extraordinary letter from Professor Moriarty. It has haunted my mind for some days. Indeed, my need to see Ireland owes its motivation largely to the content of his letter, which only confirms my sense that I am on the right track in my solution to the question of the nature of his mysterious soul. I will transcribe the letter here for easy reference later:

Dear Sherlock Holmes,

I have always been aware that you believe that I dare not meet you upon even ground but that I must always pursue my ends by clandestine means. I am determined to prove to you that your assessment of my character has always been wrong. I actually entertain an amused sort of affection for you, which combined with a sense of obligation to your late father, has motivated me to set puzzles for you that would keep you entertained and away from those vices that prey upon artistic and sensitive natures such as yours.

You possessed in your youth, if you will forgive my saying so, a certain tendency to embrace the decadent. You seemed to revel in the society of patrons of low opium-dens and bordellos or to savor the company of the gin-soaked denizens of Whitechapel. You have too much sympathy for human frailty to be quite Christian. Perhaps it goes with your Catholicism. Catholics have always had a sense of sympathy with the great unwashed multitudes. Perhaps the good Catholic wishes to be entertained by the squalor of sins that he dare not commit. What is the Mass after all but a great spectacle of redemption? If I was a Christian I would prefer the strict and imageless definitions, the non-sensual and rigid religion of the Scotch Calvinists; this might be the only area where Sherringford and I have ever seen eye to eye from reports that I have had of him. He was away at school you will recall when I was brought by my father as a boy to serve in the horse-stables at Sigerside.

A true Christian, it seems to me, should never smile. He should know that God hates mankind and in fact all of His creation. How else can one explain His fondness for setting moral traps for us? Who was it that placed the Serpent in the garden? Who but God created credulous Eve in order that she would deceive her somewhat dull-witted mate, Adam? I have always thought that Eve was the perfect example of the social-climbing woman who keeps prodding her husband to undertake business ventures for which he is neither temperamentally suited nor competent to perform.

What sort of god created Adam, a man so dull of wit and inclined to indulge his senses that the mere appearance of delightful fruit might tempt him to risk death and exile from Eden? Eve at least had a true spirit of inquiry and a desire for power, while Adam had not even the wit to debate nor the temper to correct his errant spouse. What all-knowing god would fail to have the foresight to guard His Garden in the manner that this god did? The angel with the flaming sword arrived to avenge and too late to forestall the very calamity that should have been foreseen and prevented. The untested couple was clearly not up to the task assigned to them. Or was the point of the tale to describe a later event in human history? It has always been my belief that such an oversight is incompatible with God's omniscience. God must have known all along what would happen between the serpent and Eve because he intended it to happen! Why should this have been so you may ask? It was because all fathers hate their sons in every mythology. Saturn was the only honest paternal deity.

My own father was no exception to this universal rule as you well know. He saw me as a misshapen insult to his own need to replicate an exact copy of himself, which alone he could love. Every man assesses himself as secretly a hero if not a god. He tolerates a woman for the sensations she may produce within him, yet he secretly loathes his need of her and the knowledge that he may never escape the bondage of the gate through which he first entered the world. The contempt and violence shown towards women and the subjugation of the fair sex, particularly by religion, is a testimony to the fear not just of death but of life itself.

It is woman who conceives life, nurtures life, and finally endures to witness life's termination. It is always and only *woman who keeps the vain cycle of life going with all of its mockery for the godlike within us. To her alone is entrusted the future of the race. It was God's little secret imparted to her alone. She was never designed to be a helpmeet but was designed by God to be the first betrayer of all of mankind as her daughters have been after her. She it was who carried to Adam the forbidden fruit. What was this savory fruit but the desire for her caresses that dethrones every man? What is even her love but a condemnation to walk the same walk of all the fathers whose own weakness is mocked by their sons who will in turn be mocked when their sons mature and their own time for death comes upon them.*

Each father desires, not successors, but only witnesses of his particular and personal glory. What father wishes competition derived from his own loins in the youthful person of a son? What are daughters to a man but the measure of the decline of his aging spouse? Time mocks the father as he ages, with new possibilities reserved for his offspring, while his own star suffers eclipse. His days only grow shorter as they become more precious. This does not trouble woman because woman is designed as a conduit of life. Her function is to keep sexual duty to her husband by night and to labor by day. I should not need to tell you who have only recently travelled in the regions where Islam prevails that this is true.

But even in Christian nations womanhood is scorned. The successors of Adam do not share his mildness towards his spouse. They rage against women and the burdens of the production of progeny that intercourse with her entails. Each man would gladly be a terminus of life in his own being and at the height of his powers. Each new generation knows that it is therefore born indebted and fears the wrath of the fathers.

This universal fear of the father's wrath is attributed likewise to the very god who secretly relishes sin so that he may punish it in due season. Which culture or religion does not fear the return of the dead who are really the ancient ones? What is ancestor worship but a desire to placate the fathers? Where are the mothers who dare defy their husbands when they seek to take back the life that they themselves have engendered?

The Chinese offer food to the dead lest they be devoured by dishonor which is only the condemnation of the living by the dead? All nations fear that their own is an age of decadence and therefore long for a mythical golden age of the past when times were not as they now are. What is the myth of a golden age but the doubt of the sons of the present age that they are worthy of life and the fear of the paternal curse? What Slavic peasant does not fear beyond all else the return of the living corpse who resentful of the living is said to become a Vampire that will prey upon them while they sleep? Even you, Mr. Sherlock Holmes, have been wounded by your past. You suffer still from the weak lungs bequeathed to you by a consumptive mother, whereas my own wound, my mother's sole legacy to me was her last remnant of bread given to me and the sight of her expiring in the loathsome stench of the typhus that killed her.

I shall never return to Ireland, that cursed and sorrow-sodden land where each turn of the plow may bring up a skull. Yet will I impose sentence upon the English for the crimes committed against Ireland. If vengeance is not justified in her case, it shall never be! You will say that I am an anarchist, a revolutionary, but I am not; I have no faith in mankind that would justify a proposed change in the present order. Tyranny and injustice will always be with us. My actions have this in common with God; they are pointless and will soon vanish in the stream of similar tragedies. My own actions in contrast to those of God are not capricious. I have a motive and I have here confessed it to you. You see? I hide nothing from you but the means of my vengeance and that vengeance shall be accomplished according to the laws of nature.

My hand raised in revenge is no more unjust than that of your God. I join Him in His hatred for life, which He still allows to be created anew in age after age so that He may be offended once again by the sins of man and woman that no reparation or redemption may ever extinguish, not even the death of His supposed son. You will accuse me here of blasphemy. Hah! Blasphemy is the one sin on earth that is never avenged, because the God to whom it is directed perished long ago. I am no blasphemer you see, but rather I am God's faithful ally in his perennial displeasure with the human race. The accusing finger from the skies will always exist and the prelates of the church have no greater function than to condemn what they can never defeat ... the sinful nature of man! How fond God is of sin we may only conceive by the magnitude of His wrath that like a great sea He allows to gather in age after age until it shall descend upon all creation at last and incinerate all of creation before him. The great and abiding mystery of course is why God manifests His wrathful judgments on supine humanity. Surely it must be a great effort to Him to revisit over eons our sorry earth! Yet the happiness of God is seemingly never greater than when He may measure his Greatness against our own insignificance by punishing us as the proximate cause of evil (while I suggest that He remains the final cause of all that occurs). Was the real original sin actually one of overly sanguine expectations for material creation on the part of God?

If so then as the great machine began to operate and the gears began to grind and the smoke to rise, first in the angelic orders, and then in all elements of nature; that was the time to allow the whole thing to groan and creak and come at last to a stuttering halt. Instead, like some inveterate gambler who keeps doubling-down his bets long after his tablemates have either gone to bed or sought the terrace of the casino to smoke a cigar, your deity continues to be faithful to His failing dream.

Worse still religion has a defense already prepared and your god is allowed to escape His own condemnation by blaming what should never have been summoned forth in the first place, the human race, for all its ills. Does your God punish us merely to spare Himself? Are we the victims of some divine duplicity, a failure to own up? These and many other questions can be avoided of course if we simply assume that there is no God. I am perfectly willing to propose a truce with you, Holmes, even at this late hour: to agree to say that all gods and demons are the projected fantasies of the human mind reflecting upon its own inscrutable nature.

Under that supposition the insensate pulsing of the stars knows no such trouble as the mind of man; they pursue their mindless courses in infinite peace. The tracery of the galaxies becomes only a vast painting upon an infinite canvas that requires neither gallery to display nor exposition before a critic like me to question and condemn. The true dignity of the heavens resides in the immeasurable distance between the stars that even when exploding produce no sound in the space that intervenes between them. Even the light of their extinction is soon swallowed up by the infinite darkness that surrounds them. All of visible space is a remnant of past events. Mankind exists in a mere backwater of whatever primal event we have long called divine creation. The distant planets of other solar systems that resemble our own earth may have harbored civilizations long since extinct with whatever gods they once worshiped.

If God ever existed at all, He may long since have forgotten all about us and moved on to greater matters just as a child does who no sooner lights one pyrotechnic device before he moves on to another and another still. Is it not the height of temerity to assume that God will ever thread His way through the dusty stacks of the old issues of his many creations to find the single back entry with yellow paper and dog-eared corners that is our universe, let alone that He would go on to peruse it and seek the single line or word that refers to you and me?

You now possess my two versions of God and you may take your choice between them: You may choose a God who does care for humanity because He shares some of our features and so may relate to us in which case the evils of the world would appear to be His own doing; or alternatively God does not care for humanity and shows his omnipotence by scorning to punish or reward what does not even deserve his notice and all of creation assumes its proper significance as a mere transient bubble, an idle ripple or eddy in the ongoing stream of the life of God.

I myself prefer the second choice, for it leaves me free to maneuver and to order the world in my own manner and to seek my own ends without fear of contradiction by any meddlesome deity. It also gives me some degree of opportunity to respect that indifferent God for the one attribute that I find admirable in Him if he exists at all, that He has the good taste not to linger over the compost heap of human history with any redemptive or condemnatory purpose. In any case, where is your God of love in this exposition of the ways of God?

I tell you that the religions of mankind have everything to say about man and nothing to say about God. Religion is the result of a flaw in the operation of the human mind. Man is a disease unto himself. He desires a purchase upon a happiness and immortality to which he will always be impertinent and a stranger. If we may not be happy though, we may at least know the satisfaction of escaping our illusions. It will bring me much satisfaction to bring down that great idol of self-conceit that is the British Empire. If you dare to oppose me, you may perhaps share its fate. I would however be sorry if that becomes necessary.

Professor James Moriarty

I was at first shocked by the reductive and blasphemous character of this letter; but upon further reflection I have come to see it as a cry of desperation on the part of the Professor. For all his grandiose talk of stars and galaxies I feel Moriarty is wavering. His blustering attitude betrays its weakness by the fact that I did not solicit this communication. Why is the Professor so anxious to bring matters to a swift close when he agreed before I left Kings Pyland that plenty of time remained for me to mount a defense to his plans? The result of receiving this letter is that I am even more determined to be off now to Ireland, that land of bogs and rain and sorrow.

All that Professor Moriarty and I have been discussing, even subjects that are most metaphysical in my opinion, may be traced to our personal impressions and condition at the dawn of our life-course. If my theory is correct then it is only in Ireland that

I may ever find the source of the "original sin" of the Moriarty Family that still lives on in the person of Professor James Moriarty. It interests me that the course of our discussions, its directionality, has swung round like a weathervane. This I had not anticipated. I had assumed that my angle of approach with the Professor should be to meet him on his own ground by speaking as a scientist and instead the focus of our discussion has not been upon where to locate God in physical reality but rather on how the will of God might be located in the ethical realm of historical injustices, in this particular case the Irish Potato Famine and the policy of colonial expansion embraced by the British Empire.

Evidently, Professor Moriarty sees me as capitulating to that exploitive policy out of loyalty to my brother, Mycroft. Professor Moriarty views himself as the ethical actor and sees me as "the evil one" who must be converted! I in turn hitherto presumed that Professor Moriarty is a godless atheist and international criminal who must be converted to a religious point of view: first by persuading him that the universe and all of its characteristics make it physically necessary to posit a god as the originator and cause of the order that we perceive all around us, and second to persuade him that the Catholic Church provides the best possible access to that god. Have I been seeing everything reversed as in a mirror?

This hunch or realization raises a significant question that I will set down here at once lest I lose sight of it. The biblical book of Genesis would trace the origin of all things by retreating back in time to the beginning of history. Its narrative presumes that the entire physical universe was set up in one single motion that bestowed order upon a preexisting realm of chaos caught in the poetic phrase that "darkness brooded upon the face of the deep." This sort of language evokes a sense of "ontological nothingness" whereas light, the first element of creation, evokes clarity and order. Reality becomes perceptible and intelligible.

Ever since this early period of Hebraic speculation regarding the source of all things the general and most basic pursuit of philosophy and finally the sciences of physics in combination with astronomy has been attempting to trace the origin of that first fundamental action of God, the creation of light, by tracing its footsteps as it were backward in time to a single point of origin.

This cosmic detective work assumes that the forces in play in the universe are instigated by an explosive first force of some kind: a sort of "big push" if you will. Everything radiating outwards as time and space unfold before it. But what if the contrary is true? What if what we call creation was instead a response to a call rather than to something brought into being by fiat? What if what we insist on calling "creation" is like the cry of a newborn infant reaching out in order to search for what it requires? What if "nothingness" aspires to being unbeknownst to it's chaotic and unformed self?

If this is true, then theology has been mistaken in trying to get "back to God" by returning to a point in the past, presuming that God is to be located someplace behind or above creation. What if instead the universe was not created at all but was simply placed in order by God; what in other words if the world that we inhabit is a semi-conscious response to a "big pull" rather than to a "big push?" What if a true theology is not a process of catechesis (of the installation or indoctrination of faith under threat of damnation), but instead a call from God to which we respond? What if the sheer variety of life in all its forms shows that same response in sheer biological diversity? What if God is not solely concerned with the salvation of souls but rather with the salvation of everything that exists? What if "the Kingdom of God" is being actuated each day by being pulled into the future where we will someday encounter God in all His fullness, but not in a disembodied spiritual realm, but as something so interpenetrated by God that our usual distinctions will simply vanish, space and time will merge into eternity, energy and mass will reveal their fundamental identity?

At this point physics and theology would merge and become one great multiplicity of insights, one so harmonized that differences in degree or tonality would only manifest with greater clarity the synchronicity, the integration and wholeness and the symphonic character of the Kingdom of God? Theology has been hitherto burdened and convulsed in a mass of inconsistent metaphors and analogical thoughts and expressions filtered through divergent human cultures and genres of expression. If theology is really the study of the process of life, even while enclosed within that very process, then it may at last be possible to gain some glimpse of the inscrutable reality of God.

If the direction of life is towards ever increasing beauty and diversity and if the impetus for being is not from behind in the abyss of the past, but rather a drawing forth into a future of ever increasing variety and dispersal, yet at the same time manifesting a path directed towards a focal point towards which all being tends, then the words from the Book of Revelation, words otherwise so mysterious and elusive make sense at last:

"I am the alpha and the omega, the beginning and the end."

Perhaps everything that has ever been will forever be, conserved and preserved in the mind of God. Consciousness, that most immaterial of all existing things will flare up again like a flame, identical and undiminished, whenever the proper conditions allow it to spring forth again. Perhaps time is not linear at all, as we have hitherto supposed it to be. Perhaps all of creation is periodically renewed, or if allowed to reach a state of maximum disorder, gathered again just as child with a spinning top can always wrap a string about it when it comes to rest and set it spinning once again. Perhaps the problem facing each soul is not death at all, but rather that being made in the image and likeness of God we are immortal beings, unprepared in our sinful state to accept the burdens and responsibilities of immortality. The Holy Trinity is showing us the only way that immortality can ever be made supportable ... by spending it in love. The central theological problem as I see it is that love is a phenomenal reality rather than a mathematical reality as in physics. Love can only be experienced and judged after the fact when we encounter love. Love is not subject to some exact measurement or even of any real definition except in terms of itself. By phenomenal reality I mean that it implies a relationship, so for instance the phrase that "God is love and those who abide in love abide in God and God in them" is essentially descriptive of a relationship as well as a definition of an entity called God. However, the adequacy of language itself breaks down when it is assigned this level of communication.

The phrase implies the following:

1. That the entity that Christians recognize as God through faith is not merely characterized by the quality of possessing love, but is constituted by that quality;

2. That the action of love-as-relationship implies that the "three persons in one God" doctrine of the Holy Trinity means that it is impossible to conceive of a member of the Holy Trinity as a separate entity because God is essentially relational by definition;

3. That as contingent beings our natural state is one of fundamental dependence upon God unless we presume that we could be able to stand against God by existing outside of the field of love that sustains us in being;

4. That nevertheless the test of our authentic existence is to abide (to remain) within the field of love provided by God's grace, which is nothing other than love;

5. That we achieve this state of being by abiding in love;

6. By doing so we become in turn definitively incorporated into God in spite of our being contingent rather than necessary beings;

7. That paradoxically that relationship of mutual abiding becomes reciprocal and that God in turn enters into us as well.

If approached in our usual fashion of thinking of everything as "substance" rather than as activity this use of language appears to be either entirely metaphorical or alternatively as just so much contradictory nonsense. But if we use our imagination and see love not as substance, but as relationship, the phrase although still bathed in mystery conveys a deeper meaning. The existence of the force called gravity puzzled Sir Isaac Newton because it implied action at a distance just as is the case with electro-magnetism. The problem is most salient in the case of a vacuum where no intervening matter can account for the transmission of the causal agent. It is the same problem that is raised by whether the soul can survive and be transmitted without the body to which it has hitherto depended as a foundation for consciousness to occur. Is human consciousness merely a record of a physical process? But if so who or what is the recording agent of that process and why does it conceive of itself as the agent of its actions? But if we return to my sense of the universe as "actions occurring in fields" much of this difficulty disappears. As an example if time is a dimension then we might better explain the momentum of time by saying that "we fall into the future just as an object falls under the force of gravity." it does so because of the principle of self-subsistence: matter may be conceived as bending time and space in order to stay as it was! What we call mass must distort the medium that contains it as a fundamental law of physics and of logic; as in the proposition A=A.

The attractive quality that we call gravity then is really not motion at all from this point of view but rather is the need to maintain its relative position to other objects in a shifting field. A moving body in turn by virtue of the energy implied in motion will similarly alter the space and time fields through which it moves in order for its energy to remain constant. I must remember to ask Professor Moriarty if his own thought processes confirm this strange insight.

August 23, 1893
On the Irish Sea En Route to Cork

I left Cardiff shortly after dawn today and after steaming into the open Atlantic the ship is making excellent progress in spite of being buffeted by a strong westerly swell. The Irish Sea crossing is often not a pleasant one and I am happy to be making this trip in the declining summer days and not in the autumn or winter. Professor Moriarty has granted me a time of respite if not leisure by delaying the execution of his great plan until 1897, the year of the Diamond Jubilee of Queen Victoria. It is no small part of his vanity that he intends his great crime to mature gradually and to break upon England with the force of a historical inevitability at a time of national celebration and triumph. He clearly intends that his name will join that grim pantheon of historical figures such as Napoleon who believe that they are the chosen agents of destiny to remake the world.

Perhaps, I have erred in attempting to reach Moriarty through appeals to ethics and to the very structure of human life as it is revealed by religious doctrine. Perhaps, I should have used history and pointed out that no agent of change has ever altered the sad conditions of human life and that every empire has eventually fallen and that every revolution has only made oppression more secure as the revolutionary government enters on an orgy of reprisals towards the previous regime and its representatives. We are currently living in a period of romantic twilight. Religion as a social force no longer plays the central role in domestic government or in international affairs that it once did, at least in the so-called Christian nations of Europe.

The days of the so-called Enlightenment that began with the idea of the inevitable progress of human equality and secular reason as outlined by Rousseau and Diderot never materialized. Instead the science of economics and industrial productivity, not reason and philosophy, came to decide the fate of nations and the prosperity of the rising middle class. The rising power of the British Empire was obtained at the cost of the laboring masses at home and the exploitation and virtual fleecing of the resources from other lands held as colonial possessions.

Instead of inevitable progress as the years have passed since the days of the social writers that were associated with the period known as The Enlightenment history has witnessed the greatest concentration of wealth and power in a ruling class that the world has ever known. So great are the disparities now in the economics of the human condition that we may as well speak of different economic conditions of human life and the classes associated with them as though they pertained to different species and not to one common human race. The majority of humankind lives in a condition of penury and squalor that is so far deficient in allowing time to develop literacy and time for moral reflection as practiced in the more advanced nations that the denizens of the impoverished regions may hardly be said to approach the stature of the human being. One need not of course travel to tribal New Guinea to encounter the aboriginal condition of humankind. Poverty and illiteracy abound even in the Victorian England of the 1890's.

For this reason I am often tempted to agree with those writers who, having despaired of the spiritual nature of man, see culture alone as a force of light that is capable of elevating the distinctively human qualities out of the beast that sleeps within us. To such modern reformers and writers as Zola and Balzac the delineation of the human is a goal that lies within the capacity of literature alone to bestow. Religion teaches as accomplished what sociology only promises as a distant goal. Humanity is then a continuous labor for the select few to attain, not an essential characteristic granted to us at birth. Perhaps they are not so wrong in this, for even St. Thomas Aquinas points out the difference between potency and act. Absent the Grace of God and an assiduous cultivation of the virtues, the honorable state of mankind remains mere potential.

This primal insight was also the basis of Augustinian thought which maintains that absent Divine Grace, the mere passage of time will witness only the blossoming of greater depravity, for man is nothing without God. Early Christianity did not conceive of anything resembling universal salvation. Against this tradition of realistic assessment of the unaided powers of mankind we have the drawing room philosophy of Rousseau that states that absent learned social evils, the hearts of man and woman are naturally innocent and pure. No more pernicious doctrine has ever been dreamt-up and I fear that the history of the next hundred years will be a series of attempts to set up various absurd utopias until thinking men come to realize the vanity of all natural virtue and accept the unremitting labor required to achieve even the rudiments of justice and civilization among human beings.

What the French writer, Chateaubriand, once thought to be noble savages were in fact diverse Indian tribes with their own carefully developed social norms and technical craft expertise. They were also not without cruelty as witnessed by the North American Martyrs, Father Isaac Jogues S.J. and his companions. That most practical of spiritual guides, St. Ignatius of Loyola, the founder of the Jesuit Order, understood the need for effort and imagination in spiritual formation by grounding his great work, "The Spiritual Exercises," in the experience of the First Week of the Exercises. Unless a man realizes, as he does in the first week of the traditional thirty day retreat, his utter helplessness and the sheer vacuity of sin, no further spiritual progress may be expected.

The first week of the exercises eliminates any Pelagian presumptions the person making a retreat may entertain. It is senseless to attempt to initiate a Christian life without Christ as our companion. Christianity is not finally a system of ethics, but of relationships. The first task of the professing Christian is always to seek Baptism. This is both a symbol and an efficacious means to regenerate human life at its root. This is why the Church has always taught that outside the Church there is no salvation. Only God of course knows the full parameters of His Church and Baptism may find its way to men and women in ways that a mere ceremonial may not circumscribe. Since God is the agent of Baptism, the Church wisely does not presume to assess the presence of grace in a soul that appears to have lived and died outside the visible community of the Catholic Church. It leaves it to God to round up any stray sheep existing outside the fold while concentrating its energies on the main flock lest its members stray as well.

The Church has found through history that it cannot afford to entertain romantic notions of itself. The same period that witnessed the spires of the great gothic cathedrals rising in city after city throughout Europe witnessed also the reforms of St. Francis of Assisi and the founding of his Order of Friars Minor and the spread of the Cistercian movement in monastic life that advocated a renewal of the simplicity of Jesus. Catholicism is never richer than when it is steeped in poverty and is close to the earth. The best abbeys are not made of marble but of rough-hewn granite drawn from the native soil. What is the harmony of Gregorian chant, but the perfect blending of the voices of the monks where old and young mix their imperfect tones into one common harmony in praise to God so that the combination of their voices cancels out the individual variations and achieves thereby a unity of heart and will in praise of God?

The life of the Catholic Church is that of one great extended family, one overarching unity that cancels and levels the irregularities that stem from self-will in its individual members. Salvation is sought through the abandonment of the desire for individual glory that finds so large a place in romantic thought, even in poets like Shelley. Rousseau always spoke of harmony and natural virtue all the while desiring that the common will would vary in no particular from his own preferences. The greatest democrats and socialists are often so contentious in person that one would find it awkward to share even one peaceful meal in their company. How then shall their thoughts unite all of mankind?

The Catholic Church takes a different course: it makes one man Pope, not because the Church values power as such, but because it despises it. It places one man upon the thrown of St. Peter to follow the admonition of Christ to confirm his brethren in the faith and to feed Christ's sheep, thus liberating the rest of the Church, having done as Christ asked by turning to the voice of St. Peter in every age. The members of the Catholic Church pray for the intentions of the Pope and if they are wise they will rejoice that this particular cup has passed them by.

The history of the Papacy shows how often it has brought suffering and an early death to the one who holds that office. The paucity of Papal canonizations with the exception of the first centuries is ample testimony that the incumbents of the Chair of Peter were not often among the holiest men of their age. The promise of Divine guidance of the Church extends to the office and is not the special prerogative of the man who occupies it. Instead

God chooses his Saints from among the common sea of the faithful the better to demonstrate how different the ways of God are from those of men. Power is often an impediment to personal sanctity and consequently it may take the prayers of the entire Church to intercede for one Pope. Still, for all of this, the helmsman is due the respect of his office and the bark of St. Peter has steered a straight course through the storms of centuries and shall do so until it fetches up upon the shores of eternity on the Last Day.

August 24, 1893
Cork, Ireland

Our boat got into the harbor late last night and I have taken rooms here in a fine old hotel by the docks. Cork, like so many Irish towns, is a mixture of classical pretentions and poverty. The Irish have a deep respect for the classical tradition and it shows in the choices of Irish architecture, particularly in the government buildings. This classical spirit is also apparent in the Irish love of the great bards of the land and no people enjoy more the ability of music to convey the feelings of the human heart. I could easily lose myself in the enjoyment of the culture and the countryside but I must recall that I am here for a specific purpose. I take issue with many of the assertions in Moriarty's letter, primarily with his assumption that God rejoiced in the Fall of Man. Nothing could be more contrary to Scripture. Genesis is uncompromising in its assertion that God looked upon all that he had made and saw that it was all good. Similarly, the message of the New Testament states that God so loved the world that he gave even His only begotten Son, not to condemn the world but that it might be saved. From whence then comes this conviction of Moriarty that God created the world to delight in the torture and death of mankind? I suggest that Moriarty is motivated not be some natural bent towards Zoroastrian Doctrines, but rather from his own dark experience in the Ireland of his youth. The personal often clouds our metaphysics.

Moriarty was deprived early of both his Mother and his

Father, the first by an early death and the second by the darkness of an evil heart. This double loss was such as might well twist the starved and maimed youth, not merely in his body but in his mind as well. Professor Moriarty is ample proof that the fruit does not fall far from the trunk of the tree that bears it. There is no doubt in my mind that the elder Moriarty hated his son because he saw in him a reflection of himself and a daily reminder of his abandonment of the woman he had sworn to love in marriage to the fate of early starvation and death. The lad was then to him like an accusing voice from the grave. I doubt that the elder Moriarty ever saw his son as anything beyond his function as a conduit for the father's own anger and despair.

Of a similar nature is Professor Moriarty's illogical hatred for his mother. It is the product of his sense of abandonment by her, though this was not within her capacity to avoid. She gave him all that she possessed at the time which no doubt only exacerbates his guilt. Caught between his terror as a motherless boy and his anger that she had left him, the young Moriarty was forced in upon his own bereft and empty self where he found only the image of his own father's hatred. Is it surprising then that the very humanity that one usually learns while being nurtured in the bosom of the family is absent in Professor Moriarty? How much of human life is often spent in these internecine struggles in which the parties seem enmeshed with bonds of steel and can only hurt each other as they struggle to break loose.

I have often asked myself why it is that so many of the tragedies of Shakespeare are domestic in plot and in theme. One need only think of the great historical plays but also of King Lear. Is this not because those whom we most love we also most hate and this not only in succession through the generations but concurrently within the immediate domestic unit? The passions of man and of woman are not cancelled by each possessing a complementary nature but are rather accentuated. Each passion is reflected and made greater by being contradicted by the nature of the other so that the end result is one vast confused sea of contradiction in which there is no domestic peace.

I have often said to Watson that the history of mankind is not the history of individuals but of families. Internecine warfare is always the most intractable. Indeed I will go so far as to say that Adam and Eve did not leave Eden in marital bliss and unity but in a state of mutual accusation. Even the first murder was that of a brother by a brother. The fact that marriage is a sacrament then has far more to say about the need of special grace before one dare enter into wedlock so as to be able to endure proximity than it has to do about any natural affinity between the spouses.

I have always taken a grim pleasure in Doctor Johnson's definition of marriage as the triumph of hope over experience. The period of bliss between the sexes is often confined to the period of courtship. A betrothal might then well be more an occasion for mourning than for celebration. Still, the human race would die out were it not for the illusions of youth and that blind groping toward an elusive unity provided by the sexual appetite. It often seems to me that to think at all is to embrace with time a tragic view of human life. The function of comedy is to deflate human pretentions so that our tears may at least on occasion be tempered by our laughter. The great task of the thinking man or woman is to avoid a universal bitterness that begins with hatred of man and ends with the perception that God is foolish to love us, for once having so concluded it is but a step to assume, as does Professor Moriarty, that God has created mankind only out of sport, to laugh at our perplexity and vanity, and to punish our folly and sin eternally in the end. These reflections have caused me to conclude that this bitter letter of Professor Moriarty, sent to me before I left for Ireland, is the best clue that I have yet possessed to tell me how I can reach into his own embittered soul and exorcise the false image of God that he has so long allowed to fester there.

August 25, 1893
Cork, Ireland

I don't know what it is that I specifically hope to find here in Ireland. My chance of ever locating relatives of Professor Moriarty is slim indeed. Yet I felt that I must come to Ireland if only to sense in the people something of what the great famine must have meant to them. Just as the great glaciers sculpt the land leaving moraines and deposits of stone, so do the great events of history leave traces that seep into even the individual soul. Great tragedy leaves traces that manifest over the generations. Such wounds are often not healed after the time of their infliction until the fourth or fifth generation and even then some traces may still remain in occult mental pathologies.

Therefore, I need not find specific relatives of Professor Moriarty to be able to deduce the pressures and fissures that have sculpted his character. It may seem strange, but even eras of optimism leave scars upon the body politic because such times often foment illusions as to the nature of human possibilities. This in turn breeds a bitter but inevitable disappointment in later generations when those same conditions of success and prosperity no longer prevail. It is foolish to expect very much in the order of sustained human good fortune. The scale of our expectations increases with every new level of fulfillment of human needs until for those who are so fortunate as to be well-off even the slightest diminution or delay in their expected gratification becomes an agony to bear. The scale of human happiness is therefore not an absolute but a relative measure. It is the great beauty who notices the first wrinkle upon her formerly unblemished countenance with horror while the shriveled beldame is content if she still has her own teeth in her head. The man of wealth deems it a disgrace if he cannot afford the dues to his club because of a temporary financial reversal, while the pauper rejoices at finding an old pair of discarded shoes that are warmer than those he is currently wearing.

A great advance would be made towards elevating the

general level of human happiness it seems to me if we could only confine human expectations to what is reasonably to be expected. This would prevent many wars, silence domestic altercations, and create that spirit of thanksgiving that turns the mind to God. It seems to me that it would be well for all men to adopt the standard of the cross at the very beginning of life which is to assume that dishonor, contumely, ingratitude, and undeserved pain will be for the most part our lot in life. To assume this in advance would at least prevent the surprise and outrage that most men manifest when these very elements emerge as life progresses. By adapting this approach one might also cause rejoicing when momentary good fortune holds these sufferings in abeyance.

Instead, which man does not feel that he has been ill-used by life? Why has disappointment of so many of his noble dreams dogged his steps and frustrated his hopes? Why does he end life with only shreds of his former strength intact? Why is his youth and vigor leeched away by time? Why are his former triumphs effaced by more recent humbling events? Such a man comes at last to realize that even his very grave will soon enough be marred by the growth of lichens and by moss, the residue of time, and that his great name will fall as others have fallen so that his progeny must begin again at the bottom of the social jumble and begin that long upward climb to the attainment of notice and distinction. Few are the families who hold for long the prerogatives of wealth or nobility. Even the greatest land-owners are often taxed into penury. Great businesses are soon supplanted by their rivals. Those men with athletic or artistic achievements find that their genius is not inherited. The great boiling cauldron of events stirs up many from the bottom and sucks others down into the witch's brew of time. Periods of growth are succeeded by times of savagery when great wars exhaust the surpluses of the sacrifice and savings of generations and all must begin again. A few lost manuscripts may be found in the ruins, men must learn again the practical arts, credit must be restored, and the wasted and shattered land must be cleared of wreckage and the corpses of the dead be buried and forgotten. This is the nature of life. Each generation imagines that life will be different for them only to succumb at last to the realization that human fatality is not mocked, the human condition is non-negotiable, and that human life if it must look only to our few short years of uncertain happiness for fulfillment is a poor bargain. Our very joys mock us with their brevity, while our train of sorrows seems never to end.

I begin to realize that I have fewer illusions about life than Professor Moriarty supposes that I do. I believe that the Professor's plan manifests a desperate effort to escape from the cross of life by making a single great and arbitrary gesture that will only increase the sum total of human pain. His plan is only a symbol and as such it must be attacked as unprofitable and pointless even if it should prove achievable. His plan must be stifled while it remains in the realm of ideas and has yet to be made actual in the order of events. How much human harm might be prevented if such pointless violence could be confined to the human cranium! But then what is the work of the legions of hell but malice that has been partially unchained by God?

The devil foments his plans unhindered, but they must be inevitably strained and filtered through the fabric of the Grace of God that turns even evil toward the service of the good. The Cross of Christ stands triumphant over the powers of this world and the kingdoms of darkness as well. The serpent is always ground down beneath the heel of the Son of Man. The Woman with the Crown of Stars stands in mild triumph over all of human history. These mysteries of the Catholic faith are not mere ideas but are embodied in distinct persons, in the incarnate Christ and in the Blessed Virgin Mary. The salvation of men and women is mediated by the direct action of God achieved through men and women. Even the Church is not an idea but an actual assembly, one so unified as to be a single body united under the headship of Jesus Christ.

I am convinced that to respect the actual is to be saved from the dizzy realm of the mere idea. What seems for us to be the ultimate humiliation, this possession of a single human body that is doomed to die, is in fact the promise of our eventual glory for the individual body itself will share in the resurrection of the dead. The body only assumes its proper stature when it ceases to be a mere idea and becomes an actuality. When it is accepted in all of its limitations and in its transient nature, when the mind's many aspirations and transient opinions are seen for just what they always were, mere fancies after all, when the soft veneers of the flesh wither or grow to a flaccid obesity, and when death finally allows the captive elements to escape and to return to the earth from whence they came; then alone does the individual assume his proper dignity and lasting place in the eyes of God. By relinquishing all things, not in a spirit of stoic fortitude, but rather in Holy Indifference as St. Ignatius Loyola advised his group of spiritual aspirants to do so that they might be restored again in due season at the general resurrection of the dead and according to the purely gratuitous act of God's love for each individual, they might find peace.

In seems to me that to protest against inevitable human fate is little more than a petulant gesture and to resent the reclamation of what one did not instigate, the independent order of things, is absurd and ungrateful to God. Our own being is always derivative; it was never anything else. We are not gods but men and women and our only happiness lies in accepting the confines of our mortality for we shall not escape its strictures. Let us die then not with curses and recriminations but with hope, that having once been we may be restored again, that the God who summons us out of darkness at our birth will call us forth at a later day to the light of eternity where we will live in the Kingdom of God.

August 27, 1893
En Route by rail to County Kerry

I took the train today for the town of Killarney in the west of Ireland. I spent the morning taking my leave of Cork. I spent some time in the pubs where I was able to take advantage of that most dependable of the features of the good Irishman, his love of talk. I was able to make some discrete inquiries regarding the famine years. Though two generations have passed since that horrible time the black legacy of it still arouses a sense of dread and of bitterness in the men of Cork. No Irishman may speak his entire mind openly though for fear of the Black and Tans so the comments were confined to the England of yesteryear and not to the present government policies although I doubt that the England of today would come off any better if the conditions that led to the great famine were to occur again.

The great problem is that England demands that Ireland remain subordinate and subservient, yet England does not desire to undertake any untoward expenses for the maintenance and improvement of the Irish people. For England the fact of Ireland is simply a brute reality and Ireland's perennial poverty one of those great intractable problems that life imposes upon us to be accepted and not changed. So great is the British contempt for the Irish that the mere thought of its self-governance is inconceivable to most Englishmen. Though union with Ireland is in many ways a severe burden, England will never let go of Ireland unless it is forced to do so by a sustained rebellion. Empires do not grow by inviting or tolerating acts of secession. Ireland serves the purpose for the English of providing the point of contrast by its backward and downtrodden state, which every unequal society needs in order to prove to itself that it has a right to rule. The poorest Englishman in the land may at least know that he is not an Irishman and in that regard at least he may feel superior to someone.

The great task for any ruling class is to continue to rule by diffusing lower-class resentments and to justify the existence of an elite class in its own possession of social and economic privilege and rule. The shortest means to achieving these ends is to marshal a fear that the lowest dregs of a subject group aspires to usurp the hard-won position of the class just above them. Anger and fear must always be directed downward to the class just below the one of which one is currently a member. At the same time, the upper classes must hold out some hope, no matter how unrealistic, that with hard work and time some degree of social advancement is still possible. An unequal society must spread the belief that in the few exceptional cases where social advancement actually does occur that this is proof that a similar result is generally attainable by the multitude so that the members of the lower-classes out of the natural optimism that prevails in most of mankind will assume that they are in fact progressing upwards over time.

Of course actual poverty and the threat of the loss of social status are primary motivators for human industry. It is imperative to keep a worker from accumulating sufficient surplus so that the worker may rely more upon it than upon his daily labor for his sustenance. The members of the working classes must remain caught between the twin jaws of unemployment and the marginal satisfaction of needs and wants. In this way wealth remains securely in the middle class made up of shopkeepers and tradesmen while brute labor is disproportionately underpaid and taxed. The teeth of the beast of capital are always turned inwards like those of a snake the better to ensure that the poor man will not escape the specter of debt. Even time works against his advancement. The useful life of the working man is at best fifteen or twenty years under current industrial conditions. Even the most frugal cannot hope in that short time to save enough money to make even marginal gains in personal wealth. This means that each generation must start over again at a predictable point of either penury or indebtedness. Mortality confines the limits of each generation's advancement.

Capital held by the upper class of owners in contrast, which does not suffer from the confines of the flesh, proceeds year by year to grow if it is wisely invested. The systems of law, which are also immortal, have fenced property about with a security that knows neither the limits of age or disease. The result is that actual living people are always subservient to the abstract idea of capital and its rules of augmentation rather than the other way about. The Irish experience is merely an extreme example of the working out of the machine of expropriation of labor by capital. England owns the winepress and Ireland and the Irish people are the grapes.

The Irish people have had only their faith in the Catholic Church to unite them to the rest of Europe and to promise that in heaven some recompense for their squalor and wretchedness on earth under British rule will be rewarded. The pastors of the Church have continually counseled the exercise of patience and Christian forbearance, which has put them in direct contradiction to the justified desire of the Irish to rebel and to shake off the vampire nation that has been battening upon Irish blood for centuries. The Irish people have been forced as perhaps no other people on earth to maintain Christian charity while watching their children starve. They have endured in order to purchase the only realistic comfort that they may ever hope to attain, salvation at last in the next world. For this reason, the Irish Famine of the 1840's manifested in the clearest possible way that sometimes, and perhaps more often than not, survival in this world is impossible to achieve for a Christian.

One of my interlocutors stated, "Could the poor souls have afforded the passage to London, sure they might all have at least died there, until Buckingham Palace was surrounded by a garden of bones! But such is the greed of the British that they would only have carted even these away and boiled them down for the glue to make a profit." I begin to understand the bitterness of the Professor more each day. The astonishing thing, of course, is that my English countrymen are not pagans but are supposed to be Christians while all the while they have been exploiting Ireland. Christianity appears to be for many to be a religion of veneer, all gold trim over plaster and stucco. Christianity should never have left the age of the martyrs behind. To be a true Christian should always be to share the fate of those condemned to early suffering and death by the Prince of this World the devil. To look about Ireland even today one might doubt that Christ had ever come among us as a man.

August 28, 1893
Killarney

I am ensconced tonight at Muckross House which is located just outside of the quaint Irish town of Killarney. No greater contrast to the general Irish poverty can be manifested than that which exists between the comfortable life of the Anglo-Irish landlords and the people that surround them. A habit of good manners and deference though can at times seem to diffuse the underlying inequities and their attendant discontent. County Kerry, I can already see, is perhaps the most beautiful of the counties of Ireland. It is a land of lakes and streams and the ever present and lovely seacoast. The Lord of the manor house has promised to take me about on a drive to see some of the ocean scenery here before I leave in two days for Galway to the north. He was contacted by Mycroft by means of a letter which requested that I should be shown every courtesy on my "diplomatic visit" to Ireland. How wide and far does the influence of my brother reach!

I was picked up at the train station by an ornate carriage and driven past the haggard women and tatterdemalion children who bowed before the carriage as it passed along the road. The manor house is typical of what one might find in England, but here it is exceptional because it stands quite alone and without peer in the neighborhood. The young ladies of the house joined us after dinner and I felt as though they enjoyed entertaining any visitor from the home country. They posed countless questions to me that of course I could not answer about London fashions and what styles the debutantes affect during the season in the town of Bath where high society gathers. I met their polite but disappointed gazes when I explained patiently that as an inveterate bachelor I could not enlighten them on such matters. I did however continue the discussion by informing them that I was lately just returned from a tour of Egypt and a year spent in southern France at which point they perked up like startled deer and posed innumerable new questions to me.

It appears that France is even more exciting to young ladies than stodgy old England. For all of their wealth the members of the female Anglo-aristocracy of Ireland are isolated from the wider world and consequently their existence is insular and provides for them little in the way of urban delights, the primary source of enjoyment for young people. I felt throughout the evening that the inhabitants of the house were more exiled in Ireland than if they had been in Jamaica or Trinidad. I begin to see that one may be involved in certain social evils and still bear not only an air of grace and hospitality, but even of innocence and virtue. This forces me to ask whether certain social systems become over time as inevitable as certain features of the landscape or certain natural atmospheric events and as unchangeable by human ingenuity.

No doubt I am expressing myself poorly here in my choice of analogies, but I simply could not find it in my heart to resent these hopeful young faces. The landlord's daughters dream of attending balls and making a successful marriage some day to one of the young officers of the local British garrison and perhaps being assigned to England. If there is a dark hand of brutality in British rule here in County Kerry, it is less evident than in the discourses that I heard in the public houses of Cork. There is no hint of nascent rebellion here.

Absent the order that is provided by the local constabulary would a state of general chaos break out here if the British were forced to leave? What course would likely follow Irish Home Rule or even complete independence? Would a socialist economic order in Ireland be any wealthier or able to improve the general lot of the people? Does political freedom always result in plentitude? Who would feed the poor of the district if they could not come to the local workhouse or receive their allocation of charitable largess from the denizens of Muckross House on the Sabbath?

I begin to see the intractable nature of economic and social relations that have been centuries in the making. The temptation to undertake poorly thought-out and instantaneous solutions may only exacerbate human suffering here. Perhaps this was why Jesus assured us that the poor we would have always with us. It is more than a mere question of distribution; there is always the question of whether complex societies can exist consistently with equal agency in all their members. Power and talent differentials would appear to be inevitable and to oppose them by force more productive of social evil than to tolerate their existence and the unequal rewards that they produce. Nevertheless the domination of the landlord class in Ireland produces an overleaf of gracious living that cannot disguise the suffering beneath.

August 30, 1893
Enroute to Galway, Ireland

I must return for a moment to a rather esoteric point in my reflections on whether the universe that we inhabit is centered upon and explained by some great and critical past event, "a big-push;" or whether instead everything occurs because of "a big-pull" exerted from God, a call operating from absolute being addressed to nothingness to give birth to a universe. This call would emerge out of some inconceivable future where God dwells. In any case the physics of religion will never be written because religious thought uses an entirely different methodology and language than science.

The need to understand anything properly demands that in order to perceive any object or to discuss any topic it is first necessary to posit a point of view that allows access to the whole. This usually requires that we must abstract ourselves from the element or set of elements to be bracketed by the understanding. No system can be comprehended from within that very system. Unfortunately this is not possible when we live in the very dimension of space and time that we wish to understand; but what if eternity could provide that very outside perspective that would allows us to see every event in our lives as a whole and with perfect simultaneity.

Let us suppose further that the moment of death could be conceived not as the end of life but rather as the source of the entire chain of causes and effects that we consciously experience from a sort of microscopic viewpoint as the course of our lives as we live them. Is it conceivable that the true origin of all that we are and of every happening stems from a point beyond life projected backwards onto a screen of space/time and built of linkages of events that only emerge in all their totality as already assembled and ready to be brought forth as an exhibit before God.

I realize that this is an odd conception and that it violates what our consciousness observes in the pairing of cause and effect where the future is unknown and the past, even though recalled, is no longer assessable in the course of lived time due to the laws of thermodynamics. (Time runs in only one direction; and matter and energy exist in a fixed amount that can neither be created nor destroyed). But, from the point of view of one outside of life the entire assemblage could be imagined as one holistic set of linkages where the directionality of time would be irrelevant. All words referring to succession would suddenly become superfluous and misleading. The sense of passing time requires that we inhabit time; but only abstract consciousness from the dimensions where mundane happenings occur and suddenly various infinities appear. There is no longer a need to speak of origins, of creation, and even of the distance between two points on a line as finite since both space and time may be said to stretch to accommodate anything that we choose to place within them. The role of the perceiver is the key to how the universe not only appears to us, but also how the universe actually is. For me this is merely an intuition and I will have to ask Professor Moriarty if any of his observations or mathematical calculations have led him to the same conclusions.

To continue then along this line of thought eternity has no need of laws, because when faced with infinity all plotting of fixed points necessarily become meaningless. Measurement assumes that the two or more objects to be measured must remain in a stable relationship of constancy to each other so that the act of measurement can occur. Time must be made to stand still. It is the very fluidity and lack of borders when dealing with infinities that make measurement in this sense impossible. Perhaps the real exile from Eden was to leave eternity and to be plunged into the limited dimensions of time and space where causality rules and sins cannot be undone but only forgiven. Redemption and atonement do not alter the rules imposed by cause and effect; they surpass the ordinary limits that they impose and in this sense they are supernatural. Of course ideas as challenging as these make poor dinner-table conversation so I confine them here to my journal.

My time spent in the Kerry region was of necessity cut short since I feel the need to press on in case I am summoned urgently back to London. My train is speeding me onwards even as I write this entry in my journal across the great Irish central plain after passing through Limerick en route to Galway. This is the most fertile region of Ireland. I will soon be leaving the plain behind me since I am heading towards the bleak and stony northwestern part of the country. I have done some research and discovered that the Moriarty family originally came from the Connemara region just north of Galway. If I am to understand the most refined area of Irish poverty I must seek it in the unforgiving land called "the Burren," that bitter place of stone stripped of soil where man and beast alike lie naked to the eyes of God. As I move to the west and north perhaps I will find that the land's harshness will create what I noticed in the deserts of Persia and the Sudan, that the land itself imposes a sense of equality in the few inhabitants that can survive its rigors.

But first I will be spending some time in Galway and its environs which include the famous Cliffs of Moher and the great bay located at the tiny village of Lahinch. Perhaps no land is as one in its relationship with the sea as is Ireland. Yet such is the poverty of its people that it cannot sustain itself on the produce of the sea alone. This fact has made the Irish value land with an almost religious reverence. To the Irish people land means food and warmth. The entire country is heated by turf fires and fed on potatoes; both scrabbled out of the land. If either of these two resources should fail, then death, that other great Irish commodity, will reign supreme. The land often embraces in death what it cannot sustain in a living population. I have seldom seen so many graveyards as in Ireland. In the struggle for life the Irish have precious little time for superfluous beauty, yet beauty is the one thing in Ireland that is free and that could not be stolen by the many invaders of this land for exportation. This ever-present beauty of land and sea has made of the Irish a nation of poets. Even ordinary discourse assumes an air of modulation and grace on an Irish tongue. The Irish rejoice in their musical instruments as well. A fiddle, pipes, and flute and even stamping feet become here the equivalent of an orchestra and bring more joy than one might think that mere sounds could ever produce. The songs of Ireland are the voice of the very soul of the people.

So amidst all their poverty and suffering the Irish possess the gifts of beauty and of music, and last but not least, the Irish have the treasury of memory. Nothing is ever forgotten in Ireland. No spot of land is deprived of its familiar associations so that Irish history has an intricacy and density known by few other people. Before the discovery of America Ireland was already the perfect target for seagoing invaders. The Norsemen came here in their dragon-prowed boats. The Spanish have been here and the Normans from Brittany. Each invasion has left behind a little piece of itself; yet the old Gaelic language has remained and is still spoken. Perhaps only a race that has known so little happiness can value it as highly as do the Irish whenever and wherever it is to be found. Hope has never died within them for the freedom of their nation, the emancipation of their people, and the promise of heaven after death. This gives the Irish their extraordinary cohesion and faith, even when they have been forced to emigrate to other lands. What nation has not been enriched by this lovely people whom their own land could not sustain? Will these faraway wanderers ever return to the land where their hearts still repose?

August 31, 1893
Galway

I arrived at Galway, this most maritime of Irish cities, which still shows some remnant of the legacy left by the Spanish invaders. I took this morning a walk down by the sea-wall and the docks and observed the men mending their nets there. I was amazed at the tiny boats that are used to resist the great power of the sea swells, more like shallow shells or mere feathers floating on the waves. Yet these craft bring in mackerel, cod, and herring every day except during the winter gales.

I returned to my hotel with a selection of this morning's catch and my landlord had his wife fry them up for me making a hearty dinner of them. I am still debating my future course of action. For all their fearsome nature I do not wish to be so close without visiting the famous Cliffs of Moher, those great 700 foot walls of rock that stand guard-duty on the west-central coast of Ireland against the thunderous Atlantic storms. They seem to me to symbolize the resistance and adamantine immovability of a people determined to survive at all costs. Even the famed Rock of Gibraltar will crumble to dust before these cliffs yield to the Atlantic. Tomorrow I plan on taking a room in the nearby village of Lahinch and then returning to Galway after which I will venture north into Connemara. After that I hope to proceed to bordering Sligo and the northern coastlands of Donegal and then to visit the bleak Aran Islands. I hear that there is a venerable Cistercian Monastery located there that I hope to visit before picking my way back by degrees to Dublin, returning to England before the autumn storms set in. I must remember that it has been some time since I faced a winter in England with its fog and rain. I am tempted to return to Italy for the winter or at least to France, but I fear that my time as a Wandervogel, (as the Germans call it) is finally drawing to an end. I am too old to be a mere child of the woodlands playing a reed-pipe like a faun. Casting about vague dreams to recapture the lost pleasures of a resurgent youth is ill-becoming to a man of my mature years. Already the first frosts of age are upon me; the leaves of my life grow sere and pale. I am all too soon plunged into that season where a man must sum up his life, whether he will or not, and face first his own judgment of his days and nights, and then to face that more general and unbiased judgment that must place his life, not in the comfortable context of his own appraisal, but against that of all of humankind. I must then perhaps match my life with an illiterate shepherd in Armenia or with a washerwoman on the banks of the Ganges. Of what use then will be my own tastes and presumptions or my vanity that I am the great detective, Sherlock Holmes, who has dared to attempt the resolution of the problem of good and evil in these pages? Of what use then will be the temerity of my strange journey of discovery with its presumptuous conclusions on life, death, and all that lies between? Yet I must finish what I have begun, if only for the sake of defeating Professor Moriarty at last and saving the British Empire—both of which are tasks that are honorable and worthy of the sacrifices that these years have entailed. But how am I to assemble these diverse observations and insights into a single cohesive vision; this is the task that still stands before me like the great barrier of the Cliffs of Moher.

September 1, 1893
Lahinch, Ireland

What a strange day this has been. I believe that I may have found a place more conducive to clarity of thought and a far better place of resolution of all differences. If I were ever to engage in another dramatic encounter with Professor Moriarty than the famous Falls of Reichenbach, it would be on these majestic sea cliffs. If I am ever to meet a solitary end I would prefer to enter eternity in the presence of this openness of sky and sea that I have found here and not in the claustrophobic confines of a ledge on a mere stream hemmed in by mountains. When one dies infinity should be close at hand to repulse the shadows that will be closing in upon the mind. The edge of life and death should be as clear and sharp as the blade of a knife. Death should be a moment of supreme definition and careful discrimination of degree, not some smudged and non-committal generalization as a summation of a life. I hope when it comes time for me to die that I will not die like a toad beneath a wheel. I am of half a mind to send a telegram to Moriarty and to ask him to join me here for mortal combat. I am not a patient man and the prospect of facing the years that lie before me until 1897 while simply hoping for Moriarty to come round at last to be a trying prospect for the nerves; and my nerves have never been of the best when it comes to the chronic as opposed to the acute. I am much better on the short track than the long course. The place that I speak of is The Cliffs of Moher.

I stood today on those black basalt cliffs while the wind came buffeting about my ears and threatening at any moment to dislodge me from my delicate balance poised over the sea and to cast me outwards into the empty air stretching towards America. I found that I could not venture to the edge without first lying prone like some mere insect upon my belly creeping out to peer over the windy edge to gaze down upon the foam-fretted rocks so far below me. Even to stand up was to risk a state of vertigo for sky and cliff and sea form, as the poet Walt Whitman once said, "O vast rondeur swimming in space."

There is no room to maintain illusions of life or of death in so uncompromising a place. The land ends so abruptly that the very edge of the cliff-face has no gradual slope. I could reach my hand out over the edge and seem to feel eternity in the measure between my thumb and my forefinger as though the entire ocean might be spanned in that tiny space. Just so is death it seems to me, for death divides the land of one's life from the vast ocean that lies beyond and a few sharp minutes serve to efface the recorded slate of a lifetime of efforts and memories.

How sharp an edge is this! Though it may take days for the body to begin to decompose, all that really matters, which is the mind, is dislodged and blackened out by oblivion within minutes and is then irrecoverable by any mortal means. What shall remain for us of the consciousness formed by a lifetime of experience? Will individual memory or loyalty to our past even matter as we merge into something greater than ourselves? Who will cherish then or wish to return to the poor dark life we have known when it is seen from the other side in all the dimensions of unglimpsed and unrealized possibilities? So great perhaps does the distance become from our former selves that only hungry ghosts are said to linger about their former domicile. Perhaps ghosts are not the soul at all but rather are merely dislodged memories that have no place in eternity. These are strained out like so many citrus seeds in the morning of eternity. The Irish of course have always believed in their ghosts and if there are any ghosts at all they must haunt these cliffs that have known so much of storm and gale yet yielded not an inch. I am reminded again of my primary conclusion: that every human life consists of a set of specifics and that Plato was quite wrong in his emphasis upon the universals.

What for instance is the mere idea of a cliff-face when opposed to the actual experience of standing upon one? Metaphor is always folly when applied to actualities such as this. The problem with living is that so much of it is done second-hand. The sheer multiplicity and the clamor of impressions serve to dull our senses until even prayer becomes a dull act of generalized address to our conception of God and not to God as He actually must be. Our lives become rote exercises, mere grammars of life, and life itself becomes only a spelling bee as we try to grasp an unknown word. We are encased in nouns and verbs. Language itself should have all the spontaneity of a baby's cry of pain or longing or outrage. To the newborn infant life is a vast imposition. How dare it ask so much yet give so little and with the need of such effort! Every baby sees Eden fading from its startled gaze and its feeble grasp and laments that this should be so. Only the aged feel the same outrage as time's glass begins to run short so that eventually even the mere grains of sand in an hourglass may be counted as they fall away from us. Surely, each man or woman must reflect at the moment of parting, "If only I could begin again and this time to make a better showing of it?"

But there is no second chance at life and one must gather about oneself the tattered cloak of one's past and enter into the presence of God more naked and alone than even we are at birth, for now each one is deprived of even the time and opportunity that once allowed one the option to err and yet to repent. Then there will ensue only the great nothingness of death, which is the greatest of the Platonic universals, for nothingness knows no specificity or distinction; it is finally and only itself.

The mind of man rebels above all things at the idea of nothingness. To stand where I did today with nothingness within my very grasp as my trembling hand reached out over that dreadful infinity while my whole body clung to the rock beneath me in hope that the earth might not shift upon its axis and spill me over into oblivion was to grasp the fundamental position of every human life. If I might make Moriarty realize this fully I believe there would be no question of his presumptuous will carrying him away on his mad project. Although all of life lies in the specific, no one escapes the great universal solvent of death.

No gesture is adequate to oppose an extinction that is so absolute. The worst of men drag thousands or even millions of men into death behind them through their actions. Does this power serve to build a bridge-head for them alone to pass to safety? Is the chasm of mortality filled by all of those who have died before us so that we need not fear? We die as though no one had ever died before us and all of the light of sun and stars will be eclipsed by our demise. Therefore, it is no comfort that the human condition imposes death upon all men and women.

To have grasped life at all is to rebel against its extinction. It is the image of God within us that protests so vehemently against our fate. The Book of Revelation of St. John tells us that a new heaven and a new earth will replace this present one and that when this happens every tear will be dried and death will be no more. Christianity of all of the world religions addresses the mystery of human sorrow and of death by making these the result of evil and not simply the way that things simply are. More than this, Christianity speaks of the mechanism by which the evils of this present time will be defeated. This present condition ends in replacement by a new order as symbolized by such terms as "the New Jerusalem" and "the Kingdom if Heaven." How can such a radical turning about of all that we know have been accomplished? Can any historical action, even the willing death of Jesus on a cross, change the very nature of being as we know it?

The death of Jesus Christ was necessary precisely for this reason: that the nothingness of death could only be surfeited and satisfied by an infinite life, one whose very essence was to live. For Jesus who is Life Itself to embrace death in a spirit of love was to cancel death. For infinite love to suffer from the works of infinite hatred is to work the redemption of the whole, not in the general order alone, but in all the specificity of every single human life. This gift is extended to each of us in our unique identity and is specific in nature and achieved by the one man Jesus of Nazareth who was the Christ, the Beloved Son of God.

For this reason it is not possible to sever Christianity from the fate of all human lives as though belief in Jesus is only one belief among many. Jesus as the Son of Man sums up all of humanity in His own nature. Thereafter, each of us is encompassed in relation to Jesus Christ. The matter of our collective redemption is not merely functional but structural in nature; St. Paul emphasized this fact by saying, "Now it is not I that lives, but Christ lives in me."

It is impossible even to speak of actual human life as if it might somehow be divorced from its origin as symbolized by Adam and Eve, who were if not individuals (and who may say that they were not) were at least the initiators of a line of descent to us; and also from the signification and centrality to the human condition of the Incarnation of the Second Person of the Blessed Trinity who in his very person redeems each man and woman. The entire human enterprise fails if it is considered apart from Christ.

As for the facile atheist, it is no answer to leave the equation of mortality unsolved, for the terms once posed demand an answer. Human reason itself demands this answer—have we grounds for hope for life eternal or do we not. Professor Moriarty, the man of reason, the great mathematician, must surely understand that even to pose the question of God is already innately and intuitively to know the answer. How does a man as ambitious as the Professor experience himself—as nothingness? I do not believe that even Professor Moriarty is so complacent as to refuse a chance at redemption if it could be made clear to him. To despair of redemption is already to accept nothingness as our own deepest essence; whereas the angel at the tomb said to the questing apostles who came in search of Jesus, "Why do you seek the Living One among the dead?" This might also be said to each of us, "Which do you choose? Life or death lies before you and the choice is yours to make." Faith begins in hope and is sealed in charity; who we are to be is determined by what scope we are willing to allow to the providence of God. If death is near; then the source of life is nearer still.

September 4, 1893
Lahinch, Ireland

I woke today in the little room of my hotel in Lahinch. I was soon dressed and walked up the high street to the village Church to attend Mass before returning to my hotel for a fine breakfast of eggs and oat porridge sweetened with honey. The mists had melted away with the summer sun and I thought that a walk along the bay would be in order.

Lahinch stands at the head of a majestic bay. In any other part of the world the town would be a busy seaside resort but in Ireland the enjoyment of its beauty is confined to the local farmers who come here for Mass, to trade, and to visit the local pub. The path that I took wound down to the water's edge out of the rich surrounding pasture lands covered with herds of sheep. It continued over hillocks and returned at last to the town again and down to the water in the other direction. I paused now and again as I walked to relight my pipe and to gaze out over the blue waters of the bay and to sit upon a stile of rough-hewn rocks and contemplate what yet remains for me in order to draw the strings taut about Professor Moriarty.

My next move has become clear to me. I must find a way to show Moriarty that just as salvation history is predicated upon a unique and specific event, so is the application of that event, the Incarnation and Redemptive Sacrifice of Calvary, applicable to each individual soul in the unique circumstances of his or her life. Grace is infinitely adaptable and takes the soul where it is. The Gospels speak often of the lost sheep and of the effort made by the good shepherd to seek it out and to return with it upon his shoulders. Nothing could be clearer than the fact that God will spare no effort to accomplish, not only the general salvation of mankind, but that also His efforts are directed at each individual soul. Surely such effort by God is not easily thwarted, so that the

Church asks that we pray for all souls, even the most wicked, even after their demise, in hope that the mercy of God might have a universal efficacy.

If this radical hope seems to contradict the Church's admonitions against sins it must be remembered that these admonitions are eminently pragmatic. The pastoral office of the Church is fulfilled by both cautioning against sin as a service to charity and sustaining our hope by being preeminent in prodigality when it speaks confidently of the mercy of God. It is the mark of the vice of presumption that it ignores the former and it is the still greater vice of despair that it ignores the latter. If grace is always operative, then each person's history is so interwoven with grace that even personal sin calls forth from God immediately a particular remedy. Providence acts in such a way that a constant pressure is maintained pushing us away from the cliffs of perdition. Though God does not countermand our freedom, He does use circumstances, even the least salutary, to correct our actions and dispositions and to draw us toward Himself.

What this means for Professor Moriarty is that his early loss of his mother, though a cause of great personal suffering, may have been the ultimate path to his redemption. It has always been Moriarty's desire to be superior to the personal that has condemned him to a life of pride. To what lengths he has gone in life to avoid his pain and to forget the early loss of both mother and country! One often loathes most what one has lost. In order to heal the pain of the irreparable one denies that one has been deprived of anything at all. Moriarty desires above all to be superior to his fate. But no man is superior to his fate. Fatality is in some strange way the shortest path homeward to God!

It is in the incidentals of our lives that we discover who we are and to embrace in our limitations that particular cross, which is ours alone. It is a commonplace for the discontented man or woman to claim that no one knows how much he or she has suffered and strangely each of these is correct in making this assertion. So unique is each man's path that no one knows directly and completely what he has suffered. God alone knows this. God so accompanies each man and woman that only He may judge, as only God ever can, the measure of each man's guilt and culpability and the degree of his cooperation with grace.

God knows us better in fact than we know ourselves and our prayer must always be for greater clarity in our own judgment so that it might more truly approximate that of God. My journey into Connemara is designed then to discover firsthand that land from which the Professor has come. I seek to read his character in that land of barren rock and sturdy horses. Landscape has more to do with the development of character than we realize. Which sailors did not remark the hospitality and peaceful demeanor of the Polynesian peoples? It takes the cold and barren region of Mongolia to produce a Genghis Khan.

After visiting Connemara I shall delay visiting Sligo and Donegal and repair at once to the Cistercian Abbey that I have heard about in the Aran Islands for a month of prayer and reflection. I intend to take seriously Our Lord's admonition that the worst of demons are only driven out by prayer and fasting. It is more likely than not that the world would already have perished were it not for the reparation offered by the contemplative orders of the Church and by the tiny vicarious sacrifices of the poor women and men who kneel after Mass by the altar and offer up their sufferings for the souls of others.

The entire Catholic Church is constituted by a web of prayer forming a great net to catch souls. Foremost of these prayers are the prayers assembled in the magnificent Divine Office of the Hours, which is the very backbone of the universal prayer of the Church, chanted in monasteries and abbeys throughout the world, and second only to the Holy Sacrifice of the Mass in its efficacy for our salvation. The rest of the labors of the Church are in the realm of practical charity. Those who exercise this charity know that though they may not change the world substantially, their works may still bear witness that this world is not to be considered as an end in itself. This final action of mine in retiring to a monastery represents all that I may do in prayer with regard to Professor Moriarty. His final conversion must rest with providence and with any practical action that I must take to thwart his designs should he fail to voluntarily abandon them.

It is time that I returned to my practice as a detective. I can see that now. It is no small matter for a man to know his own proper vocation in life and not to exceed the limits of God's design for him. I have stretched myself these past few years in every direction, yet I find that when all is said and done I remain only Sherlock Holmes at last; I am neither Pope nor Bishop. I am not a monk, nor am I an evangelist. I am only one who by applying observation and deduction may solve those little problems posed to me in my humble lodgings at Baker Street.

It is time that I resumed doing what I know best. It is not my province to change world history, and I may thank God that it is not, for most of the men who have changed history only succeed in adding to the ills of mankind. I may have very few years of active life left before I may need to retire unless my lungs improve more that they have done to date. It is then that I will seek solace in some innocuous pursuit such as beekeeping if I can manage to rid myself of this desire to probe into all things.

Perhaps, if Watson will forgive the lapses of these recent years and my long deception of him (however well motivated this may have been) and return to my side, I may yet do some measure of good by him. I hope to hear again his step upon the stairs as in times gone by and to see him in the old accustomed chair. I may then look forward again to having Mrs. Hudson usher in some distraught citizen with a problem to be solved. I will sit back in my comfortable chair as of old then and gaze laconically through a maze of tobacco smoke as I pick out those facts which are significant from those which are not. I have tried in my way to do the same thing here in my journal. I have tried here to record what I know of the Catholic faith, though I am no theologian, and to call attention to the often forgotten facts so that by seeing the Christian revelations proposed here in a single harmony, through the eyes of a practical detective, some valid conclusions might be drawn. I hope that this journal, if it is ever read, perhaps by no other eyes than those of Doctor John Hamish Watson, may convey something of the thoughts and character of his good friend and assure him of my esteem for his many merits as a doctor and my gratefulness for his friendship.

September 14, 1893

Monastery of Thomas the Apostle

begin a new notebook today. I had hoped that when I returned home I might be delivered from the discipline of keeping a journal having filled the pages of my former notebook, but I find that this habit of keeping a journal and of writing travel accounts under the name of Sigerson like most habits must die slowly if at all. I believe that contrary to most men who have taken a pen in hand to record their thoughts that my deepest aspiration now is to attain the gift of silence. Perhaps the greatest insight of the monks of the great contemplative orders has been the insight that there is vanity in many words and in the sheer multiplicity of life events held in store for the man of action rather than the man of deep mediation and prayer. Perhaps even the greatest writers only continue to write so that they may eventually never need to write again after achieving some signal publication success. What more for instance was there for Dante to say after penning "The Divine Comedy?" The desire of each serious writer is to say everything that exists of importance in his own personal assessment of life and to do so with such accuracy and completeness that everything may be contained in that endeavor once and for all; but such closure and comprehensiveness is never really possible. Not even Balzac could contain all of life in its entirety although he chose as his subject only the bourgeoisie life of France in his own time.

Sacred writings are no exception to this rule. Even the four gospels leave much unsaid of the life of Christ. One evangelist admits as much explicitly when he assures us that if all of the things that Jesus said and did were recorded, then even the whole world could not contain the books that would need to be written. The God who speaks through the Bible brings a message of reassurance and relief in a way that no Deist will ever understand.

At the same time the Bible does nothing to diminish the pain and ethical faults attendant upon life in a physical world. The man or woman who seeks holiness above all else soon finds that Ecclesiastes says best what needs to be said of all human life; this insight is summed up in that shortest and most memorable phrase that, "All is vanity."

The pace and completeness of disillusion and sorrow proceeds inversely to the years that one has attained and the diminishing time that lies ahead; we begin the course of life under the naïve presupposition that now at last all things can be different with the world and that we live in a golden age. Only later do we find that the greatest of human ages may have been those that have left the fewest records. Perhaps the Dark Ages were less dark than they seem to us now simply because during them the mass of Europeans had learned to live comfortably within the brief parameters of a probably short span of life. As our expectations of a long life have increased with time we have come to assume that human happiness and fulfillment can actually be achieved on earth within the short time allotted to us. It therefore seems a tragedy to us to die prematurely in childhood or youth. But where for the true person of faith is the tragedy in an earlier admission to that state that must be our final goal if we are truly to be called Christians? Even as believers we tend to fear death and attempt to preserve the appearance and prerogatives of youth as long as we may do so. The result is that everywhere our eyes are blighted by the vision of superannuated persons among us seeking to preserve the privileges once attendant upon a vanished order of things. The result is that the youth of the world are denied resources so that the aged may flourish in the time of their obsolescence.

What vain hope is this, to believe in an earthly immortality! So many outlive any resemblance to their former selves and become at last only a pile of bones held together by thin muscle and sinew, shaking in a corner, and straining thin soup between their naked jaws. What then is this spark of earthly life that we should seek to preserve it at all costs even if a conflagration of the fire of God's love awaits us beyond the portals of death? Let us then not lament those who die young, those who follow Christ and leave this earth in the full blush of their young powers rather than prolonging the cycle of disappointments that is our life on earth. *Memento mori!*

To be a Christian is to possess the virtue of hope, but that hope does not extend to this world. The fate of this world is to die and to see all things judged in the light of Christ. Jesus has told us that the end of the world that we know will not be an easy one. The daughters of Jerusalem were told by Jesus, not to weep for Him but for themselves:

"For if they do such things when the wood is green, what shall they do when the wood is dry?"

If there is any green wood still left upon this weary earth we will soon have left it behind if the current historical trends persist. Our present age is an age of dry wood and the flames that will kindle it may be nearer than we imagine. To hope for justice in such an age is to deny not only our daily experience but the prophetic witness of the gospels as well. For this reason the wisest men and women have always sought solace behind the walls of monasteries and abbeys. May I find a glimmering of such wisdom during my time here among the monks who have left all things behind in a desperate search to find God; I shall attempt to describe in greater detail here the course of my spiritual journey since my final entry in the preceding notebook that I managed to fill to the very last page.

Jesus once asked the ambitious sons of Zebedee if they would be able to drink from the cup of suffering from which Jesus proposed to drink (of course behind that ironic question posed by Jesus one can hear the narrative voice of the evangelist as well asking the readers of the gospel if in their enthusiasm at first hearing the word of God they would be able to stand by their affirmation of faith until the very end). Many of the early saints of the Catholic Church were termed "confessors;" this exalted affirmation was bestowed upon them in recognition that when persecution came they refused to renounce the faith.

There is a perennial tension between an economy that

exalts the ego (even in spiritual matters) and the humility and strict reliance upon grace that Christianity imposes upon the believer, those who confess the faith. This is why the true Christian abjures honors and glory; because these tend to undermine our reliance upon God and in doing so leave the soul open to the influence of the evil one. The principle of evil is personified because of the dogma that sees evil as not merely an amorphous force but as a legion of spiritual personalities that oppose the rule of God. Experience has shown that the playing field of spiritual growth is not confined to the visible influences of culture, politics, and economic structures but is watched over by a host of angelic beings, invisible but capable of communicating and influencing our perceptions, thoughts, and assessments. Sanctity builds upon the foundation of faith but is not confined to it. The Christian has no choice but to engage with the world while not forgetting that his primary loyalty is to the One whose Kingdom is not of this world. Monasteries provide a special gift to the Church as a whole by the testimony that they offer that the primary task imposed on Christians is to abide in a prayerful attitude of listening.

September 15, 1893
Monastery of St. Thomas the Apostle

After I left the Cliffs of Moher behind me, I took my way back to Galway where I purchased the notebook that I now hold in my hands. It is large and made of Spanish leather and should last me for years to come. I doubt that I shall ever need to buy another. I have written my last published adventures as the explorer Sigerson and I will not need a source book to check for accuracy. Insofar as I ever intended to write anything at all it was to be more in the manner of the *Analects of Confucius*, short sayings and observations that suggest rather than explicate. Wisdom should leave much unsaid but only suggested so that the reader must reach within his own experience to complete the thought or to verify it. To write many books is finally to say the same thing over and over again until one wonders who the author is trying to convince in the end, his readers or himself. Our deepest convictions are those that are said simply. The last reported words of Jesus were short and all-encompassing,

"It is finished. Father, into your hands I commend my spirit."

The volumes of commentary and laborious distinctions of theology only burden the faithful with articulations of the inarticulate. Only God speaks in silence behind these cloistered walls and that silence is sufficient. The task of theology is to articulate what can never be put into adequate words. Yet we do so because our own understanding is too feeble to approach God in any more appropriate manner.

I left Galway the next day for the bleak hills and rock barrens of Connemara. Alas, I found there no memory of the Moriarty's. The great famine had swept all before it like a glacier and even the blurred and primitive gravestones now only weep their names into the earth. The short and sturdy horses though still graze upon the hearty grasses and the sheep and goat herds keep them company. I do not know what I hoped to find. Perhaps I merely needed to make some effort after all so that I could tell Professor Moriarty that I had done so in an attempt to arrive at a concerted narrative of his life and the influences of his heredity.

My failure in my stated purpose for this trip does not mean that I regret this journey to Ireland. I am now at liberty to do as I will since I have done all that I can to trace the roots of the Moriarty clan. I do not know who that poor woman was who gave Moriarty life. She is silent now as are all of the names of the women whose pain and sorrow reach backwards into utter obscurity; yet without them and their most deep and intimate pains out of which they have sustained life throughout the ages, the human race would have long since ended. The stone images found by my friend Dr. Mortimer are a tribute to all of the anonymous mothers since the creation of Eve.

After leaving Connemara I was ferried out to the most bleak of the Aran islands where I have sought refuge at last in this Monastery dedicated to Saint Thomas the Apostle who alone was allowed to probe the wounds of Christ so that all might know that Christ's humanity was neither garb nor illusion but complete fact. God does not deal with airy spirits alone, but with the bitterness of human flesh. Our souls, when absent from our bodies, experience only a transitory condition. Only an eye's blink of eternity will pass before we are reunited with our bodies once again in the General Resurrection of the Dead.

This time before the Second Coming of Christ is the Holy Saturday for the saints of God in which their bodies lie in the tomb. This is why the *Book of the Apocalypse of Saint John* that is also called the *Book of Revelation* ends by saying, "Come swiftly, Lord Jesus!" The early Christians desired this return above all things: that the end might come soon. How long has the twilight of that ancient evening been extended in order to embrace us who now are living on the earth! We are the late workers in the field, those who may labor but a single hour before all are bid to come in from the fields and receive their daily wage. The delay of God allows for a fuller harvest but at what a price!

These entries in my journal represent a selection from my thoughts as I attend daily mass here and listen to the stately Gregorian chant of the monks rising from the great stone church at the specified canonical hours: matins, lauds, prime, terce, sext, none, vespers, and compline. All the rest of my days and nights here will be spent in the simplicity of solitary walks in a silence broken only by the grim and surging echo of the sea. I have been in remote locations before, but in none have I felt this sense that the very earth has fallen away and that only this present place has been left to me. Why do places of desolation have such a subtle attraction for me?

Why else have the wrecks of the human spirit drawn me into the opium dens of East London to hear from the lips of those within those cavernous realms the muttered regrets of a lifetime, confessing sins into the darkness and the incomprehension of their fellow sufferers? Is it because only when the spirit is stripped bare by repeated disappointment that the idolatry of self is quenched.

This stripping away of excess so that all cant and hypocrisy is revealed at last is the function of all ascetic disciplines. But this ascetic activity should only be entered upon by one who is willing to slice into one's own soul and not merely into those of others. How strange that it is the devil who always takes on the role of adversary in order to prosecute our sins while it is God who appears as our defender.

To extrapolate from insight is to understand that it is not God who acts as our judge but rather our own acts that stand condemned by their own objective reality. We do not live in an imaginary universe but one that has a moral valence that we seek to escape at our peril. The subjective element does not alter the hard gravel of experience, but it can orient us once again to our deepest need for love. This is why no act is complete in itself but is added to the total life-mixture, the colloidal product of our lives when seen as a whole.

Poverty, heartbreak, and their dark fruits that result in so much human ruin, are these not the subject of the works of De Maupassant and Baudelaire, the Goncourt Brothers and Emile Zola? We need these "artists of the damned," just as we need the desolate places of the earth in order to set forth in all its wretchedness the cry of the heart of man for his creator. For every Michelangelo there must also be a Toulouse-Lautrec. For every Schoenbrunn Palace there must be a hovel in Whitechapel. It does no honor to mankind to portray only our highest aspirations but also those moments when all unexpected the human arises out of the ashes of its own despair.

The temptation to take up the sword as St. Peter once did, cutting off the ear of the servant of the high priest, is a temptation from which all human beings must suffer at times. No admonition of Jesus has been taken less literally than the injunction to love one's enemies and to do good things to those who persecute us. No single class of cases has caused me as a detective to bend the rules of the law so far as to allow the criminal to go free without any hindrance from me as has been the class of those who have brought a rude and individual justice to bear on undoubted malefactors. Certainly there are men whose very existence has brought so much pain to others that one is tempted to wage a private war against them. Though I cannot justify such a course as a general moral policy I can at least spare its agents the full burden of the sanctions of the law.

Still I am haunted by this partial obeisance to evil; what is it within me, that in spite of my desire to rest everything upon the Cross of Christ, that I can think of any number of circumstances when immediate vengeance would not be beyond my power to exact from a foe? Worse still, I have found that I have on many occasions celebrated that very type of retribution by others although they had acted in the heat of anger, whereas I was reviewing their action after the fact in cold blood and from the comfort of my own armchair at Baker Street. It may be a mere fancy of mine from time to time, but I could easily assemble today a list of persons who exist beyond the reach of the law to punish or even to restrain whom I would gladly dispatch to Pluto's embrace if not to the nether regions of hell. And I am not without the means of doing so!

My knowledge of the methodologies of various great crimes is exceeded I dare say by no one with the possible exception of Professor Moriarty himself. Lest this seem to be an empty boast I can safely speak here of several such mechanisms of death. Among the organic poisons alone there is the case of aconite, one of the strongest poisons known to man. It is derived from the shrub, wolf bane. Then there is an alkaloid from the common castor bean that is truly hideous in its effects if ingested. So caustic are these beans that even to hold them in one's naked hand is to raise welts where they have rested in one's grasp. Nor is the world of the inorganic bereft of its horrors. One need only call to mind the di-methylated form of mercury. A few drops of this compound spilled upon any surface can penetrate any known material within seconds and thereafter the victim is doomed to certain death. Then there is the deadly hydrocyanic acid whose victim no sooner smells the scent of bitter almonds than he succumbs to its fatal embrace.

I have often asked myself why those who plunge their

nations into war by their decisions should not be the first to die in those wars so as to show how necessary indeed was their determination that only war could achieve the necessary ends, the foremost of which is the survival of the nation. Surely war is the least effective of deterrents because once it has been declared the opposing party must fight until victory is achieved. Surely a more efficacious form of the moral blackmail of the wars engaged in by nations could come from a simple demonstration of the relative means of exacting horrific destruction from which no skilful efforts by the victim nation could ever extricate them. Such a device would render the actual fighting of wars superfluous because the likely costs to both nations could be calculated beforehand. Wars would then only be effective to the degree that they did not need to be fought at all because the foreseeable outcome would be both certain and unavoidable except by instant capitulation to the demands of the superior aggressor. Of course even such a victor would need to bear the costs of inheriting a discontented population with all of the inconveniences appertaining thereto.

The best armed nation would, according to this calculus always win. But what if all nations were forced to bear the distributed destruction of a war? Would they perhaps isolate the victorious nation from world trade? Could peace be turned to a more pragmatic use than the consequences following the perennial tides of war? Wars are inefficient by any standard. The perfect weapon would be one that only targeted its effects on its opponent in war with no distributed costs of its destructive potential to non-combatants. Will some future war be fought only with selective agents thus leaving to the victor the emptied cities with no need to clear away the blasted rubble and to rebuild what the victor himself has just destroyed? Will wars no longer be fought by cannon and shot but by carefully contaminated water and food supplies? Will a lens focus the higher forms of electromagnetic waves so that an invisible type of light will poison entire populations while they remain unaware of its harm until they begin to die?

Even with the prospect of such collective horror it is

unlikely that mankind will ever be purged of the hunger for war. There seems to be an inverse ratio between the extent of disaster and our ability to emotionally grasp it. We are most moved by the contemplation of private disaster. I have a secret theory that the charm of the so-called detective story comes less from the means by which the detective solves the crime than from the frisson that the reader feels in contemplating the horror of the individual crime committed in the story by the villain. In all of my talks with Professor Moriarty he has never indicated any desire to escape signing his name to this final crime of his career. Is this a hint that its methodology will be so extensive, clear, and visible that unlike the case of the poisons that I have mentioned above the means that Professor Moriarty has chosen will be visible and even notorious? What is this rhetoric of his that he will destroy the entire British Empire? Can one man alone, even a man like Professor Moriarty, manage such an enormous feat?

But I did not come to this barren rock of an island to meditate upon such unchristian ideas. Yet I must face this propensity for destruction that exists within me and presumably in all men. Perhaps the monks of old fled to the desert not to escape their fellow man but to prevent being enlisted in the ranks of those who kill. Which man or woman does not maintain a hidden list of wrongs from which he or she might at leisure choose several whose death even the most Christian of us would not lament? Resentment is in the last analysis an individual affliction. Which of us is as resentful towards the existence of general wrongs as he does to those that affect him most intimately?

So it is that the successful entrant to the monastic life must strip himself of all the means by which he may be affronted by another. What is the taking of possessions from one who owns nothing? What is sexual jealousy to a man vowed to chastity? How may one feel that his own will has been interfered with when he exists each moment under vowed submission to his religious superiors by a vow of obedience? Thus no grounds remain to serve as a basis for indignant feelings or outrage. But what of we who remain exposed to the great hurly-burly of life, how far must we allow trespass upon our reputation, our property, or our person without seeking retaliation? Are we also asked by God to give our face up to spitting and our chin to those who pluck our beards?

The martyrs went further still, even coveting death if it might mean a martyr's crown in heaven. To fear more for the sin of the agent sinner than for their own involuntary loss of chastity characterized many of the holy women of the early church. These were mocked by a violation that they abhorred committing voluntarily. Today such extremes seem at best ill-advised, and at worst evidence of a disproportionate insistence upon virginity, yet what they demonstrate is an actual adherence to the injunction of Jesus to love our enemies and to sacrifice even one's life as a witness to them of the new life available in Jesus Christ. It was Jesus after all who first of all laid down his life, knowing in faith that he could take it up again, and with Him all who are buried into His death so that they may be certain to rise with Him on the last day. I say this; but in all honesty I am not up to such demands. Am I too prudent to embrace such innocent folly or too lacking in faith to do so? Even if I might accept my own martyrdom, can I make that choice for others? What price must innocence pay in age after age? Surely the time has come when a vindicator of these must arise and say, "Hold! It is enough! The tide has turned at long last; the time of vengeance has arrived."

September 18, 1893—Monastery of St. Thomas the Apostle

As the days pass here the routine and order of life in this monastic community seems to grow upon me. Even time assumes an order and purpose governed by the canonical hours and the alternating day's labor for the monks in the fields or spent fishing at sea in their small scalloped boats. The fish catch is dried and salted for winter use and the turnips and cabbages are pickled in brine while the potatoes are kept cool and dark in the deep stone cellar beneath the side-chapel. There is little physical warmth to be found in the entire monastery and the experience of constant cold is an added cross that the monks must bear in addition to their poverty.

It is strange but with time the body seems to adjust to the

deprivation of all but the essentials of life. There is but little difference between the chill of the outer air and one's own frigid skin. Under these conditions all warmth goes to the center of the body and the heart's every motion becomes the only fire that warms the extremities for it is the only available source of heat beyond the inner fire of God in the souls of the monks. Every motion and act of the day seems to be coordinated with only one goal in view, to create a state of openness for God to enter. There are none of the ambitions that lead one on from day to day and year to year in quest of some illusory happiness or some pageant of display enacted before one's own eyes that flatters the sense of pride within us. There is no social position to maintain here so that the duplicity and hypocrisy of daily life soon falls away and one is left naked before God. One's fellow monks need not be impressed with one's holiness for they know themselves as they are and to do penance in reparation for their own sins is enough to occupy their thoughts.

A common bond of charity and mutual forbearance makes each monk yield to obtain the good of the other for without mutual charity there would be no need for the life that they are leading here and they would be well advised to return to the worldly cares that they knew before seeking refuge here. They know that they are part of the greater Cistercian Order and that not even their own religious community is an end in itself but that it is part of the greater body of the Catholic Church. That greater sense of belonging is the outer limit of their care. Beyond this, their sole earthly desire is to rest quietly in the earth after their death knowing that the life they have known here will be continued by others and that the community will pray for the repose of their souls. They are content to be forgotten, as all will eventually be, and to have their name recorded only in the book of eternal life and not in the annals of history.

As I grow older, the sensibleness of this disposition seems only more worthy of emulation. How much of human misery is created by men who wish not to be forgotten and who are jealous of the ministry of time upon the remembrance of their names! The universality of this fear of ever being forgotten is shown by the reflection that even men renowned for their iniquity desire that they will be remembered even by their infamy. One need only think of the pomp and splendor of military uniforms or the insignia of office in the servants of government to realize the comical side of their pretention, but at the same time to reflect that the pride they take in their honor may lead to the pursuit of evil ends. "To see life fully and to see it whole," in Matthew Arnold's memorable phrase, is to comprehend not merely that one must die but that death is the beginning of that general erasure of the fashions and powers of the age that one has inhabited for a brief time and that history itself grows old and senile as the years pass.

The Catholic Church though is never old in its essential life, for it draws that life from Jesus Christ who lives and is always the same in age after age. Each one discovers anew the perennial nature of this truth which is the truth of the Holy Mass, the truth of the commandments of God, and the perennial need for repentance and for penance. Meanwhile the world adopts ever new programs that promise to sustain human happiness in the face of the losses that occur each day as death winnows its fields. The herd moves along, grazing as it goes, and does not note the fallen ones that will soon be gnawed by the jackals of decay. We keep our horror of death in check by imagining that our might and power as embodied in machine and architecture will hold oblivion at bay. But the race of mankind only appears more foolish to all thinking men by its reliance upon such pretentions.

Better it would be to stand by the never changing might and power of the sea as I have done today and to watch the waves shattered upon the stone cliffs, their great force dispersed among the clinging kelp and mussels there. All is succession; all is subsidence into that brief calm before the next wave hits the rocks as sand fills the fissures that alone are the witness, not to individual waves, but to centuries of their assault upon the land. The clock of earthly time on this island is measured only by the depth of the fissures in the cliffs. Measured against that clock what is a single human life?

We are like mayflies in an orchard seeking sweets and are lucky if we survive a single dusk. The value of the penitential life of the monks is that it makes manifest what actually is the case for us all. It embraces truth because it knows the price of falsehood. It consents to what it cannot in any manner prevent. The monks alone dare to live life in actual prospect of death rather than to follow that path of vanity that is inevitably and suddenly overwhelmed by what was thought always to be a safe distance ahead. Most men live as though they will never die! How much better it would be if facing death squarely they might die to the world even now in order to live fully and openly within the arms of God.

September 21, 1893
Monastery of Saint Thomas the Apostle

Today I walked down again among the basalt cliffs and along the bleak strand and looked back through the mists and fog towards the mainland. I found there a niche to protect me from the wind that drives the mist in great sheets before it. There is a quality in the solitude of the sea that is unique. In a sense one is not alone, for the sea waves themselves are one's companions. Each is allowed, after who knows how long a journey, its moment of expression as it collapses upon the beach. I sit among the hiss and booming of the sea, so I am not alone.

Then there is the mute testimony of the sands. Each grain is a unique product of millennia of such concatenations. I have noticed that the wind itself sorts them according to their weight so that like tends to rest with like. Some is like pea gravel and some so light that the wind carries it about like confectioners sugar even in the lightest airs. Often great drifts are formed and the rocks of yesteryear may be buried when one returns in a year's time. Is all of this seeming labor in vain? Why this constant reassertion of the sands, the drift wood, and the dried skeletons of kelp; all of these seem to return each year? Similarly, what force is it that separates these monks from the wide world and makes them seek refuge on this frail barque of land? Is it to seek a firm grasp on their own transient existence that the monks come here? Or is it rather to find the permanent image of God burning brightly within them?

I spoke to one of the monks today and had the temerity to ask him if he had found yet what he was seeking. He smiled at me and answered by telling me that one of the desert fathers had said that a man of complete recollection could pray in such a manner that fire would flow upward from his finger-tips. He was still seeking that deepest immersion in God that would make such an event possible.

I do not know if he truly believed this or whether the seeming folly of such a statement is meant to be taken as anything other than a metaphor for spiritual perfection. Perhaps the truth is that to a man of complete prayer metaphor becomes real. Can such an event be more fantastic than the fact that I find myself this day sitting among the tiny graves of each grain of sand, myself as transient and tied to time's passage as any of them, doomed in my own final state to be just as reduced to my elemental components? Where then will be the fire of my thoughts? Where then will abide the candle of my soul?

September 24, 1893
Monastery of Saint Thomas the Apostle

It is a peculiarity of my chosen profession that my life has been spent as a righter of wrongs. To do so is to assume a sense of universal personal efficacy that seems to me lately to carry a great danger to the soul. There is a peril in proposing remedies for the lives of other men and women, a peril no less than the assumption of a role that even God appears to spurn. God appears to tolerate a degree of latitude to events that seems ill-suited to His omnipotence. Daily we pray in The Lord's Prayer that God's will be done and yet it never seems to be. Instead history is a witness to the folly of men and women, each pursuing adamantly their own will and vision of happiness.

God has never ceased to allow us the furthest scope of

being like God knowing good and evil by generating evils far in excess of the good we produce. We might well pray that God would be less indulgent of our whims! But would God be God if he acted as willfully as we who are His creatures. God is recognized above all else by His loving forbearance to which we owe the fact that this sorry world of ours has not long since been reduced to ashes by an irate deity. God refuses to comply with our own images of what is appropriate to God. Scope is allowed for us to play at being gods ourselves the better to exhaust evil by showing again and again its vanity.

The multiplication of evils is legion, yet God's own quiet light never ceases to shine in most unexpected places. God is said to be characterized by unity and simplicity. The true good is not a summation or a distributed modification of diversity. No unitary conception of God is adequate. God cannot be comprehended, only apprehended. For this reason God is never closer than when we cast up our hands in discouragement of ever finding Him only to learn that He has been close at hand all the time. We look over and about Him while God is as close to us as our own souls. Human life is characterized by the same desperation as that of a drowning man who would do better simply to take a deep breath and find that he is floating without effort.

How do I know these things? Where is my data? Who am I to speak of the nature of God? The answer it seems to me lies rather in intuition than knowledge. God is not to be grasped by any syllogism but rather in fleeting senses of contradiction. Some have called this manner of approach to God the Via Negativa, to realize God by contrast to our own inadequate summations. My time here at the monastery has bred within me a desire to act as a conservator of the good in the world, to treasure what others treasure and to rejoice in the small things that make them glad and lighten for a time the burden of existence. To see the source of love or of joy in another's life and to nurture that, celebrate that, to let that be, without complacency or interference, or desire to amend it to better fit our own conceptions, surely that would be no mean exercise of charity.

September 25, 1893
Monastery of St. Thomas the Apostle

I have spoken to the little Irish Monk again who I will not name even here to protect that desire for obscurity that has brought him here. He has recently petitioned the Abbot for permission to enter a hermitage on the far end of the island. Since he is a beekeeper we have something in common. I could not help comparing him to his exact opposite, Colonel Sebastian Moran, who is also a contemplative of sorts; but whereas Colonel Moran would consume the entire earth if he might, Father C----- is anxious to strip away as many of the world's distractions as possible so that God might fill the vacuum left behind by his renunciation. Yet his renunciation is not being made in a spirit of fearfulness or sour contempt of the world. He would be willing I am sure to acknowledge the charm of mundane beauty. No grim death's-heads and catacombs fill his conceptions. Instead he is animated by a fire for peace, love, and joy and will settle for nothing less.

Even liturgy to such a one may prove a distraction because of its many added flourishes and superfluities. This seeking for the core meaning beneath all appearances approaches the Zen Koan of the Japanese which is designed to trip up the logical thought processes that we acquire in carrying on with the instrumentalities of everyday life. In such depth of contemplation even language itself is fractured by a prayer beyond prayer so that prayer and daily action become one.

Such is the attitude of perfect recollection in God. It takes great faith to set aside all things for God. Yet is this not what is meant by the first commandment that says that "You shall love the Lord your God with all of your mind and all your heart and with all your strength?" Why then should it be surprising to encounter a man who is willing to do precisely this? Must all others use creatures as stepping stones to God? But what if concern for the creature surpasses that for the creator so that a certain degree of idolatry seems inevitable for the mass of mankind?

Is not my own hunger for the sea more pagan than religious? Perhaps it is Neptune that I seek rather than Yahweh when I go to the sea, not for love and for consolation but for the negation of the human experience of love and longing before the vast majesty and might of the ocean's waves which reduce all things to their elemental forms once again. Perhaps it is not being but non-being that I seek when I come to these desolate places, a legacy of my own despair rather than of my hope.

I am one who has seen too much of the horrors of the world and what I have not seen I have imagined. It is a capital error to follow the paths of knowledge too deeply into the jungle without an adequate guide to show one's way back to innocence. To lose all illusions the better to apprehend truth as a detective must do is to risk falling into an abyss deeper than the one at the Reichenbach Falls.

September 28, 1893
Monastery of Saint Thomas the Apostle

I met with the Abbot of the monastery today. He makes it a point to meet with each of the visitors to the monastery some time during their stay and as I plan to depart before the winter gales make it difficult for the boat to reach the mainland I was running short on time. So it was that I found myself walking along the rough stone corridor shortly after the noon repast in the refectory to meet with the man who must keep this little band of pilgrims together on their road to eternity. He was quite hospitable and did what he could to make me comfortable, even stirring up a small turf blaze in the hearth for he could see that I was cold. I thanked him as we sat over two mugs of weak tea to begin our talk.

"So you are leaving us, Mr. Holmes. Well and so you must unless you plan to spend the winter here. We had a man here a few years ago who delayed too long. Poor man! He never left the island at all. He died in January and is buried with our community here. But then he was ailing a bit when he came. A wealthy man he was or so he told us. His people never came for him although we wrote through his solicitor to his family. They did have the grace though to remit a donation to the monastery that we later used for some new vestments and altar linen. The poor man was a melancholy sort, just such a man as cannot be made happy even with plenty of earthly comforts, those very things that as you can see we are unable to supply."

"But must your life really be so hard?" I asked him. "Surely the God who made the world and has not spared it even such superfluous gifts as orchids and tropical fruits must not intend for men to endure such deprivations as those that you have embraced here."

He answered at once. "But you misunderstand why we are here and not elsewhere. It is not easy to explain, but I will try. We are a place of last resort for what is possible to man. We are aware of the way that the world tends to drift in the direction of luxury for the few at the expense of the many. If humanity can tolerate such pointless extremity in one direction then it only makes sense that some portion of humanity should balance this by going to the opposite extreme in its preferences. It creates a sort of structural balance in the whole of humanity. Our life here is such that it barely sustains us from year to year. Therefore, we excite no envy in our fellow men, but rather awaken in them a sense of thankfulness if they ever become aware of our existence. They can then be happier in possession of their gifts and in the knowledge that that they are not here. Perhaps this whole thing that we are about is foolishness; perhaps even a sort of pride may creep in from time to time at our austerities; but it seems essential to us to show forth all sides of humanity to our Creator. It takes actually living our vocation and not merely entertaining it as a fanciful possibility to achieve the end, which we hope is not trivial when weighed in the final balance. Our prayer is not offered from a point above the human condition, but from within it. We share by this means in the solitude of pain that must beset every man and woman. We are one with the dying, one with the woman lying unattended in child-birth, one with the bereaved who have lost not only a beloved one but one whose very existence was essential for their own survival. We take on as it were the very sufferings of Christ for the world. The philosophers speak of God always from the point of view of God's majesty and from their point of view they are right to do so, but we must find God from within our own condition as men and we find it by entering upon our humanity and not in fleeing from it. We find what is most distinctively human in our way of life here in all its limitations. We have foregone the transitory comforts that hide until the end of life what must finally be faced: that we are finally like a scarecrow in the fields made of sticks and rags. Of what use is it to hide through most of our days from our appointed end? Yet most men cultivate various levels of self-deception only to face in their last days the cascade of their lost powers as old age takes from them all that they once valued with nothing to take its place. It is these that shake their fists at heaven for mocking what was from the beginning a presumption on their part that what was only lent to them was a permanent aspect of their own being."

I hesitated to ask, but I could not forebear putting to him the question, "But if you are wrong?"

"Wrong in believing in God you mean, Mr. Holmes? But in what else shall we believe and still do justice to our nature as human beings. If it was possible to live without memory and to balance always upon the knife-edge of present joys without regret for past happiness or fear for future misfortunes, then a bovine type of happiness might be possible to mankind, but would such an existence be a human form of happiness, one worthy of us as created in the image and likeness of God? I think not, for in that instance one would have forfeited all that makes our nature distinct from the animals. We are balanced over an abyss and know that the bridge across which we must proceed shall fail us after an indefinite course of journeying over it. What matter then if we proceed along it with constant fear and trembling or whether we dance as we go along? We in this place dare all in order to receive all; yet we really risk very little for our fate is already known—we shall certainly die to all that this present world may offer us."

I answered him with this objection, "If our time and resources are of such short duration and beset by such uncertainty and peril should we not rather seek to grasp and hold every enjoyment that is offered to us rather than holding out for an eternal life that may not even exist? What if you awaken to disappointment after all that you have sacrificed in foregoing permissible earthly pleasures?"

The words were no sooner out of my mouth than I realized their absurdity. The dead will never realize that they have been mistaken in placing their faith in God if there is no God to awaken them.

"But then I shall never know shall I," the Father Abbot smiled. "That is God's part; the reaching out to grasp for God is mine. It is my business to cast myself forth in hope. It is all that I as a mere man can do and I have no choice; that is the point."

The Abbot could see that I remained perplexed so he continued. "When the moment of death arrives I cannot tarry indefinitely upon the edge of existing and infinitely prolong that moment, for to do so would to be in possession of eternity by virtue of my own nature and not as a gift from God. Our being is contingent and not absolute in nature. Mortality is the very definition of the human condition and the answer to the conundrum posed by that fact must either be avoided, which is a premature despair of the possibility of eternity; or it must be affirmed in faith and then to leave its resolution in God. We prefer to take the latter course and to take our chances that there is a God and that we matter to Him."

He paused to see if his words had any effect upon me before continuing, "We choose to live our lives in unity with all that we know that is human and to bear as far as we may the pains that we cannot ourselves alleviate through direct charity. Our vocation is an uncommon one, but a vocation and a way of life that must be entered upon by at least some members of the human race in order to recall to the minds of all people the reality of our condition among so many pointless distractions and denials that beset others. Our doing so is the only way that history can be healed from within by those who stand outside of history in the remote and forsaken places of the earth. We ask for ourselves only what no one else desires to claim and as such we exist in peace; we harm none and do not close our doors to the stranger. This was the will of our Holy Father St. Benedict for his sons and daughters: to live apart from the world in order to bear witness, not merely to God but to man of what a human life really consists."

"But so few people are aware of what you are doing or its significance," I objected.

The Abbot smiled, "And because of that very fact we can continue to render our anonymous service unmolested in our folly! So it is always with treasures, my good sir; they are hidden so that perhaps someone will someday think to seek them out. If we trumpeted our labors their very nature would be changed and we would change accordingly. No, Mr. Holmes, it is good that we remain as we are unknown and insignificant."

Our conversation had been a short one, but one sufficient to answer the questions that I had most hoped to pose to him. The sound of the chapel bell came then to our ears to announce the next of the canonical hours for common prayer and our interview came to an end. A short time later I was kneeling in the back of the chapel while from the crude choir stalls the sound of Gregorian chant arose again in praise and thanksgiving to God, a sound that is the nearest human contribution to the choirs of the Cherubim and the Seraphim on high.

October 1, 1893
I leave for the Seacoast of Donegal

Although I could easily wish to remain in this abbey among the monks I realize that each man has his own calling and my mind, always restless though it longs also for peace and stability has not lost its appetite for challenge and for change. I know that I must return to England and take up again my practice as a consulting detective. I feel that my best years lie ahead of me. Travel has shown me the fallacy of a cosmopolitan attitude absent a commitment to a particular time and place. Even the greatest of artists finds that he must be rooted in a technique and a genre if he is to contribute anything worthwhile to a culture. No culture is so poor or shallow that it may be summed up in a simple phrase. There are men who have spent their entire lives upon the study of a few manuscripts or in deciphering the age and origin of glass and pottery fragments found at an archeological site.

My own life has often lacked that special dedication and focus. I have taken as my province diverse fields of endeavor until the shortening years mock my elaborate aspiration for universal knowledge. Shall I then become one of those befuddled gentleman overtaken by death as he potters about in a room littered with half-open books on various tables and chairs? "Just a moment, just a moment," I will say someday in a rattling voice, "I have one last annotation to make to this manuscript before I go."

I do not know where this urge for comprehensiveness comes from. The tides of events soon make every definitive work outdated. Each age reinterprets the past in the light of its particular experience and values. The advantage of non-assertion is that no retraction need be made; an unformed theory cannot be outdated. No apology or explanation need be appended to the last edition of a work that does not exist reminding the reader that everything contained therein is only an essay, an attempt at some definitive truth. Even something as stable as divine revelation is parsed and modified through time as the scales fall from our eyes and we are able to see better. Any general resolution that I attempt to arrive at of the eternal problems of life and death will be outdated as soon as it is made. All such endeavors at a grand synthesis pass swiftly away. Knowledge itself ages, not merely in its transient embodiment in a book or the fleeting transcription of its contents into the cranial vault of individual minds, but even our fundamental categories of perception alter as our focus shifts to bring forth new features of old arguments.

Although I have concluded that I must leave Ireland, I wish before I leave Donegal to walk the path above Slieve League, the site of the highest sea cliffs in all of Ireland, and gaze out over the Atlantic Ocean. After this visit, I will travel onwards to Londonderry and from there catch a train for Dublin. From Dublin I can catch a boat for Holyhead in Wales. The leaves are turning swiftly now on the few trees in the abbey garden and I shiver in the nights as one unused to the full rigor of winter spent on the Aran Islands. The sea seems darker now as the sun's rays, inclining ever lower on the horizon, fail to reach those depths that turn it to the brightest blue or regal purple. Instead the color of the sea alternates between green and gray and my thoughts, fleeing as these late summer days, seem to wish to fly like the hovering sea birds to seek out warmer climes and more familiar places.

So great is my homesickness that I actually long for a meal in a seedy chop-house in Soho or some fish and chips in Camden Town, let alone to sit down to a proper meal at Simpsons. I suppose that I am an Englishman after all. It is no easy matter to foreswear the habits a lifetime and the subtle set of expectation and desire that makes life's prospects sweet and causes the heart to hope again. I am not as unworldly yet as I would like to be. Although my wants are simple they are not easily denied without producing a melancholy that poorly suits one who believes in heaven. But there are innocent joys that enrich the soul and make few unjust demands upon others. I hope to enjoy them again soon and to have dear old Watson again at my side.

My old friend will soon return and I must somehow make my presence known to him. I plan on returning first to my cottage in Devonshire to spend October and November; but by December I hope to be installed again in London. Since to open my rooms in Baker Street to continual occupancy and to receive clients there too precipitately might alert any of my foes who may still remain and wish to make an attempt upon my life, I think the wiser course is to return to London first incognito and to see how things fare. I have always wanted to own a rare-bookseller's establishment and I believe that I can manage to obtain the purchase or lease for an old established concern in Bloomsbury that I visited some months ago with Mycroft. The business was for sale at the time. It possesses space for lodging above the shop that would be quite comfortable for one like me who has learned to adapt to quite Spartan accommodations. It may just suit me and provide me with an entry point to my old life and even provide a small income as well. Ah well, we shall see. My travels have taught me also the advantage of swift adaptation to events and opportunity is often the best indicator of the guiding hand of providence.

October 3, 1893
Dublin, Ireland

If Professor Moriarty and I are ever to decide to settle our differences again over a yawning chasm, I believe that I will suggest Slieve League and not the Falls of Reichenbach. It is a fearful place. The narrow path along the top of the cliffs winds through gorse and heather and opens occasionally to present a most treacherous and fearsome exposure to the wind currents that seem to grasp at one and to pull one forward toward the abyss. The spray from the waves is carried up hundreds of feet and the mists often descend in sheets to clothe the top of the mountains in obscurity. Then suddenly all seems to open up once again and there is an open view of stern rock and sea. The gulls ride the winds and form small white points of reference for the observer like the points of a divider on a nautical chart. Without these points of reference there is only an impression of abysmal depth accompanied by a sense of terror along the spine.

I was quite alone in my walk, for the season is well advanced and the summer visitors that still remain have sought brighter scenes and southern climes. Why is it then I wonder that I take such grim pleasure in the desolation of sky and sea at just such places as Slieve League? Perhaps it is that I am suspicious of comfort, whether those comforts come from nature or from human society. I have lived long among strangers, forced by temperament and circumstance into that solitude that may breed either wisdom or delusion.

Solitude can make the human condition unsupportable, for we were not meant to bear the human condition alone. As I stood on that bleak path, trying to keep my footing, I thought how strange it was to think that one step forward into the air in front of me and I might answer all questions of eternal life once and for all and make faith superfluous. I wonder, was that the nature of the temptation of Christ by the devil when the devil tempted Jesus to cast Himself down from the pinnacle of the temple to see if angels would bear Him up? By refusing to do so Jesus answered not only his own temptation but set an example that man is not meant to know in advance the contours of eternity or to anticipate the designs of God by forcing the inevitable hour of the meeting of God with the soul. We must endure our lives until the end. Just as we may not add a minute to our life, neither may we diminish it. Each heartbeat is counted, each breath measured by the providence of God, so that when the end does come it will in fact be an end and not an intermission. What appear to us as accident or the working out of blind chance that terminates a life early may in fact be a sign that all that was necessary for that unique life has been accomplished and God need wait no longer to embrace this particular soul. It is commonly noticed that evil men tend to live to be old and then to die in their beds, while the innocent and the virtuous often perish young, so perhaps this supposition of mine is true. There are no doubt men who if they lived for five hundred years would never change but only add to the measure of their iniquity.

But salvation is not a matter of time lived in virtue nor is it the fortuitous gift of a momentary impulse of grace, but rather a blend of both, so that each soul is judged on an entire life and also at its state at the hour of death. We are asked to pray that we may not die without final absolution, yet not to despair of those who appear to have died without the suffrages of the Church. Never to despair of any soul's salvation is a sign of the hope that the community maintains even for the souls of those persons who are most wicked among us. How much more should we hope for the salvation of those that though dim at sunset have known moments in their lives of virtue and of cooperation with grace. If my theory is correct and God knows when to pluck the fruit of the soul, then we need not despair of anyone. It is not for us to set limits to the infusion of Divine Grace.

This is fortunate because as I look about me daily I perceive few who seem ready to meet their maker. As I look about me now in Dublin I see how poverty and drink cause much suffering here and make even such a Catholic country appear to be in the grip of the devil. But perhaps even the most degraded may surreptitiously make a sign of the cross from time to time when passing a church. Prayer is never far away for anyone who was raised in the Catholic faith. God dwells in many unusual breasts as Jesus once did in the cold of a manger. He dwells in hearts that we little suppose have granted Him a domicile. If the dying may even conceive as their senses fail what God offers to them, then a final intention of contrition may perhaps be formed. Such a soul may say even as the light of life dies never to be rekindled, "Oh Lord, be merciful to me a sinner!" Even so little may suffice for salvation considering the infinite merits of Christ and be enough to bring one home to God.

October 4, 1893
Irish Sea en Route to Holyhead in Wales

I left today for England, my brief expedition at an end. My impressions of Ireland were in consequence provisional and fleeting. Catholicism sits awkwardly, but still convincingly among such squalor as I observed. The children were hungry and ill-clothed and already showed as in a mirror what they would become with age. Education is pointless when the opportunities for advancement are so limited. The only luck of the Irish was to seek a new home in America or in the Canadian provinces.

I did not choose to tarry overlong in Dublin. I have the horror of all right thinking Englishmen of what we have visited upon the Irish people over the many years of our occupation of that land. I do not blame Professor Moriarty for his indignation and even his anger at the self-righteousness of the English overlords. No doubt I will notice even more clearly the differences of our supposedly united kingdom after my visit to Ireland, but I do condemn the means that the Professor has chosen to avenge Ireland's many wrongs. I hope to be able to convince him that he will become what he loathes in the English if he should share an indifference to the suffering of the innocent. He cannot justly impose a sentence of national guilt upon all and exact a universal punishment. Reason itself should tell him that history grants no absolute point from which an avenger may strike with moral impunity.

All history is muddy and clouded by vagueness and indeterminacy. Normative rules may guide prospective conduct, but never sort out the motivations of past actions in even the individual case let alone parse out the causation and course of history where all is mingled, mixed, and interfused. Thus history has no final summation but is by its nature a set of partial visions. History finally is a series of anecdotes that never reaches an objective point of view but rather resembles those paintings by the French Impressionists that can only suggest through line and color a momentary condition of things passing.

The philosophers presume to find a pattern in historical events or some final goal to all of human aspirations, but still the days and nights pile up like a wave and behind us there lies only the darkness out of which we have emerged. It is not only the individual whose birth suddenly plunges him into life while consciousness arises slowly into the full light of day; the spirit of mankind as manifest in history is also only just beginning to emerge out of its ancestral and reptilian darkness. How can a final pattern be recognized or delineated until all of the data is received and time itself or our residence within it ceases? Until then all is a mere convergence of blind forces marching like the waves today in the Irish Sea outwards toward an unglimpsed horizon.

As we crossed over to Holyhead and I saw the great waves marching rank on rank towards our ship I realized again that proper horror of tempests that each seafaring man must feel. Was this the same quiet sea that bathes the beaches of summer in Dieppe and Deauville? The entire ship seemed to shake as the great roaring breakers assaulted the steel of the ship's side. How lovely did the green fields of Wales appear when we came at last to harbor!

Within an hour I was aboard a train enroute for Somerset and Devon. I must count this landfall as the end of the journey begun so long ago from Genoa. Though the leaves were falling all along our route, I felt the joy incident to all homecomings. Yet withal I felt the same abiding sense of life's transience that I felt when my older brother Sherringford climbed the stairs of the old manor house at Sigerside to our old nursery to inform Mycroft and I that our dear mother had just gone home to God. Our father absented himself for some days and after her burial the light of lives at Sigerside vanished and never returned. The death of a parent leaves a vacuum behind that is not easily filled. Sometimes the death of a spouse can leave the remaining parent maimed as if part of his or her own soul has been ripped away. In the latter case the widow or widower (just as was the case of Queen Victoria after the death of her husband) lives what amounts to a posthumous existence. Peripheral vision is lost and the children that they once shared look in vain for solace in their own bereavement. Weeks passed and no change occurred. It was as though a sheet of ice had encased Sigerside like some glacier grinding everything beneath it into oblivion. The servants one by one drifted away until the staff was unable to care for the daily needs of the estate. It was only then that my father bestirred himself to action. After that Mycroft and I were sent away to school in London.

Book Sixteen

A Resolution of
Many Mysteries

Dr. Watson's Narrative Continues

I closed the journal at this point and looked up to see the eyes of Holmes looking up at me sadly from across the sitting room of the suite in our hotel in Washington. "So you have reached the end at last?" he inquired.

"I have not reached what might be termed a conclusion. Your journal simply breaks off after the entry when you mentioned that you were sent away to London after your mother's death. I felt that this was an opportune moment to lay your journal respectfully aside for a bit. In any case the entries in your notebook ceased abruptly and were followed by blank pages.

A fleeting glance of pain passed across his face and was just as swiftly erased. "That is true, but you as a writer will appreciate the concept of the aesthetic whole. What you have just read in my journal was my spiritual testament insofar as I would wish my thoughts to be preserved for posterity. I place the entire journal into your hands and you may in turn consign it to that old tin dispatch box of yours where it may repose with some of your own manuscripts dealing with our more delicate cases. If you should care to supplement those compositions of yours by a further account utilizing the journal, I think you will have done well by your audience and the whole conglomeration may be published at some time after I retire and Professor Moriarty is dead. By then it can do no harm."

"But Holmes, you forget that I myself am still curious having read thus far. You have yet to connect your narrative of events with my own involvement by filling in the last months of 1893 and the first months of 1894. In addition, there is the whole question of how you managed to bring Moriarty to the point that he did in fact abandon his plans of revenge and came to our aid last year to defeat the schemes of Baron Maupertuis. The whole thing is without proper dramatic closure without further data!" I cried with some exasperation.

"Ah, you are always the aesthete, Watson. Has it never occurred to you that all closure short of death is of necessity incomplete and artificial? I thought that you might appreciate my realism by simply leaving certain essential questions open. But I have no desire to leave a wound open without proper stitches. I assure you that you are not alone in the desire for a closure and summation. Which of us would not like our lives and the world itself to be explicable and contained between the hard covers of a single volume? I fear that will never be the case in this imperfect world. Still, I have no desire to upset you without cause. I have brought along for your perusal my own secret notebook, the third in order of succession. I had intended to keep my own counsel after my trip to Ireland. Journals after all can be so compromising. I have learned as a detective the value of covering one's traces. Still, life escapes us if we do not record a few circumstances to jog our memories from time to time; otherwise the course of our days and nights becomes a blur and life at last in retrospect is a mere shadow in its passing. So you wish more still? Very well old fellow, you are fortunate indeed that when I had filled the previous notebooks I found that the habit of writing had so grown upon me that I could not bear to stop abruptly."

Holmes got up from his chair and walking over placed an elegant leather-bound book into my hands with a small locking mechanism to which he handed me the key.

"This should connect the remaining parts of the puzzle," said he. "But for today I think it imperative that we concentrate our attention upon our present business here in Washington and that you should not while away your time reading of the past."

I thanked him for the confidence that he reposed in me but

could not forebear asking a few questions before getting to the matter at hand. "This lock intrigues me, Holmes. Does this journal volume contain more delicate material than the others?"

Holmes answered with a smile, "Well nothing scandalous, my dear fellow, although your readers seem always to await some salacious revelation where I am concerned. It is just that my speculations after Ireland moved beyond and into realms that challenge the mind even more than anything that I set down prior to the contents of the book that you hold in your hands."

I shook my head, "Well as to that your journal has already been sufficiently complex for a mere medical practitioner. Can you give me an example to make your meaning clear?"

Holmes consented after some little time in reflection, "Very well, you see Watson that I had reached a point where science and religion separate. The Cistercian Monks spend their lives focusing inwards to find God, whereas both Professor Moriarty and I had been engaged in tracing the activity of God in the wider sphere of history even as the philosopher Georg Hegel had done. In contrast the life led by the monks counseled simplicity and trust while I had been engaged in an effort to throw the widest loop possible in an effort to account for all things so as to leave no stone unturned even if it undermined faith and militated against trust in God. I had to find the weak points in religion and to shore them up so that they could bear the weight of the animosity to religion posed by Professor Moriarty. My pious exercise in other words demanded a certain degree of impiety."

"There are certain questions in life that it is better not to ask. Unfortunately science has pressed the perimeter of our prior assumptions and the answers have effectively pressed God to the margins of His own creation. What are we to make of a universe that is billions of years old and of galaxies that make our once familiar stars only the brightest and most evident of unfathomable distances in space and time? Even if we were capable, as we soon no doubt shall be, of tunneling backwards eon after eon to a point where everything that we see might is reduced to a single cohesive point where energy and mass were so condensed that neither space nor time existed to contain them; there would still remain the question of from whence such an incredibly vast potency derived its substance and vitality? Does God stand outside of his creation and simply light the fuse of that great pyrotechnic device?"

"The more that I thought about this problem the more convinced I became that what for us is unimaginably large could very well be infinitesimally small. It is said that God created the universe out of nothing by a simple command; but that is a mere poetic rendition. Larger forces were in play and in comparison to them everything that we are and do are as nothing. Yet our Catholic faith demands that we accord these humble elements of everyday experience meaning and significance to the Being that can work these wonders and to whom no time or space are of consequence however unimaginably huge in extent they may be."

"If I brought this discontinuity of apperception to one of the monks they would simply smile and inquire if I needed anything to make my stay at the monastery more comfortable. Do you see the problem? For these men of God these questions are simply not important! They rise to praise God in choir by night and day. They meditate on the Holy Scriptures and they work around the monastery. Like the eastern practitioners of Zen Buddhism in Japan they attempt to silence the questing mind. They focus their attention on whatever is before them. They live in the present moment with such intensity that they leave time and space behind. What is it to them if some star in a galaxy has ceased to exist even while its light is still traveling towards us? And for that matter what are such matters to God if He prefers to focus His attention upon us? If all that we see in this universe was reduced and contained so that for God it was a mere microscopic particle could we dispute the size? And if other universes were trodden down each day by our footsteps could we maintain that such universes do not exist? Our observations are confined by our own methodologies and perspectives. We cannot even be sure that in some other dimension, one that parallels the four dimensions that we know about everything is altered."

"Shall I give you an example? Assume for a minute that you

were a creature living in two dimensions of space like the surface of this table here. You would have no trouble understanding length and breadth; circles and squares and triangles would make perfect sense to you and even infinite extension would not be beyond your capacities to conceive. But if someone in the third dimension of height were to come down with his pencil and place a dot on a piece of paper before you it would be as if a god had just descended from Mount Olympus!"

"In a similar manner everything that we find appalling in our universe because it reduces the stature of mankind and makes even God appear to be non-existent acts so upon us so that we imagine that our minds should be able to decipher the great questions of existence and assign all values according to our limited perceptions. Therefore I suggest that we are looking for God in the wrong place and time. We are looking backwards in time and outwards in space seeking to draw the infinite energies long dispersed together once again and then to ask how compressed they needed to be without disappearing altogether. Instead we should turn about and ask where all things are tending; time is drawing us towards something; space is making room for new events; new stars are forming even as we speak. We have left our point of departure long behind us; what matters now is our destination!"

What destination indeed awaited us? My introduction by Sherlock Holmes that day to the next volume of his journal ceased at this point. Our discussion raised an interesting point though that I had not sufficiently realized before. By taking a microscopic view in reading Holy Scripture the various branches of Christianity had managed to so closely confine the story related there that that the outer world tended to fade away as though it was an illusion and not also the writing of God not upon parchment but upon the cosmos as a whole.

The consequence of this neglect of creation has been that religion has had no adequate answer to the questions posed as scientific evidence has piled up in physics, geology, and astronomy. This abdication, for I know of no other way to assess it, in turn caused a shift in emphasis so that religion was no longer viewed as the source for a comprehensive knowledge of reality-as-experienced but was instead seen as a mere branch of cultural studies or sociology.

The philosophy of Georg Hegel made a bold attempt to bring God back into history by equating the Spirit of God with the actual course of history. This desperate attempt to a reassert a providential design in history as manifest in events in turn only reduced Christianity to one more thesis among many that would need eventually to be dialectically surpassed by a new synthesis.

The neglect of actual human experience forced philosophy to seek a substitute for religion in the Hegelian dialectic, Bergson's *elan vital,* Nietzsche's overman, Husserl's phenomenological reduction, or the transcendental philosophy of Emerson, Thoreau, and Whitman in their transcendental vision of some all-embracing composite over-soul, whether embraced in the nation or in some other overarching idea of human unification. Others still saw human existence as human to be absolutely inconsequential. Human beings were merely intelligent apes evolved by accident in a universe that could manage quite well without observation or deduction. The order that we perceive, and can even express mathematically, serves no purpose beyond merely being the precondition for the type of universe that could exist completely independent of any observation. Even the most fantastic displays of natural phenomena were not designed to stimulate our curiosity or our sense of wonder let alone to stimulate any attitude of fear or worship regarding a creator standing behind the entire panorama.

All of the above factors led to the emergence of what might be called natural theology as though the world and indeed the wider universe of all possibilities was finally sufficiently important to warrant our inspection and assessment for what they had to tell us, not just about God, but also about our place in the universe, if we had any at all. The key point is that the methodologies employed to assess these phenomena emerged from within the human mind and were not a direct product of divine revelation as consigned to the Bible. The Bible in turn now became a mere owner's manual or guide to ethical living so as to merit heaven and to avoid hell. The Bible had once been so much more! An entire civilization for nearly two-thousand years had rested upon it that was swiftly turning to political and economic theories to order human affairs in the material order (and what else was there) in the dawning world of the 20th century.

Over lunch that day our discussion continued, but was confined to the matter at hand.

"You still believe that we should meet with President McKinley then?" I inquired for in recent days Holmes had said nothing about the purpose of our trip to Washington as we had spent our time sightseeing. We had been caught up in the flow of parties and receptions that is the winter season there and I had seen to my dismay that Holmes had again a feverish air about him and was subject to coughing spells in the late evenings before retiring to bed. "I should quite prefer that if you still intend to meet the President that we do so at once. This damp Washington winter climate is not good for your lungs," I stated with some asperity.

Holmes smiled ruefully before saying, "Ah good old Watson, you are as ever the assiduous physician! You forget my dear fellow that the President has been rather preoccupied of late. A private audience with him is not easy to obtain. But I confess that more is involved in my desire to delay the meeting. I still find my sympathies are with the Speaker of the House of Representatives Thomas Brackett Reed and with that excellent man, Charles Eliot, the President of Harvard. These men abhor the fact of America's advent into the world of colonial struggle. It is the abandonment of traditional American foreign policy and may with time draw America into those very quagmires of history that the brave advent of the new democracy once hoped to avoid. It is the death of the myth of America as a new start for the human race, of America as the New Eden. You have only to read Chateaubriand and a selection of the writings of the early Puritan settlers to see how deeply this conception entered into America's first conception of its destiny. Now, over a mere squabble in the Caribbean all of that tradition has been abandoned, and for what? What if America builds up its naval forces and maintains a standing land army? Will this add to the security of its own citizens? Will it not rather end up by a bleeding of the body politic to fund foreign wars? Is that not what President Washington and his many Presidential successors viewed as the doom of nations? Shall we, my dear fellow, now add our efforts to bringing about that sad end by advocating that America should build a canal, which it must then protect by force of arms? My conscience tells me that what we are doing is wrong. I must confess to you that I wish that we had never come to America. I fear that we are on a fool's errand!"

"Yes Holmes, but if that is so, then Mycroft is the fool. You undertook this mission largely at his request," I stated.

Holmes interjected at once, "You may be surprised then to hear that even Mycroft now has his reservations about urging America to adopt a policy of imperial rule. I have just received this letter from him. I hesitated to show it to you for fear that you would insist that we leave America for England at once. I desire that you should read it now so that you will fully appreciate the nature of the dilemma before us."

I opened the letter that he handed to me and read as follows:

Dear Sherlock,

You have no doubt heard that Her Majesty's expeditionary force under General Kitchener has met and defeated the Sudanese army at Omdurman. Though I am happy to say that the victory was a complete success and that the slave-trading regime of that Moslem pretender the Khalifa is at an end, the victory was such as has brought shame upon our government.

Not only was the entire affair more of a slaughter than a battle, but Lord Kitchener, who was in command of our troops, made no effort to succor the enemy wounded who were left to die in the desert in unspeakable agony. In addition, he went so far as to dig up the body of the Mahdi and to remove the skull, proposing to keep it as a curiosity in his study. The Moslems have very strict rules about the burial of their dead as you know. Her Majesty Queen Victoria was appalled at such a display of savagery by a British serving officer, as was I. How can we hope to turn British occupied territories from savagery if we practice it ourselves? Queen Victoria wrote a letter of admonishment to Kitchener to which I appended my own stern comments of disapproval.

Though the regime of the Khalifa was a threat to the Suez Canal and to our control of Egypt, I cannot but admire the gallantry of the cavalry of the Sudanese forces. They might have attacked at night and improved their chances at victory, but they scorned to do so and rode during the full light of day into our machine gun positions with the cry of Allah Akbar upon their lips. After two hours it was all over and the desert was littered with their colorful pennants and dead camels.

The Commander Kitchener ungallantly summed it all up by calling it "a good dusting." If British pride is such that it must blind us to the bravery shown by other races, however misguided they may be in their choice of rulers, it is we that have left humanity behind us and not those whom we oppose. If Britain is not a force for civilization abroad but only for displays of barbarism such as this, then I fear that I must tender my own resignation.

I am sharing these candid thoughts with you because upon reflection it has occurred to me that I have inadvertently placed you in a precarious moral position by asking you to enlist American resources to build a canal in Central America to prevent the same from being done by the Dutch or the Germans. I now wish to cancel the request that I made of you before you left. You may of course proceed as we discussed earlier if in your own conscience you feel that there is no other way to defeat that beast Baron Maupertuis, but in all honesty I believe that this nation need fear no further instigation of his plan to destroy us by the spread of tropical plague among us. Our ports have been alerted to the danger posed by certain foreign vessels and Scotland Yard has explained the danger of the giant bamboo rats and the plague that they are known to carry. The advantage of surprise is no longer available to the Baron to further his ends. Besides, his interests have shifted now to competition with the Americans over the possible building of a canal. If you abandon your mission now, that abandonment cannot work against the interests of your own nation.

In any case, my reading of events is that the Americans have already made their choice for expansion. After their recent victory against Spain they will annex the Philippines as they have just done with Hawaii. I fear that nothing will now turn America from its desire to dominate the Pacific region. The results of this ambition will be worked out long into the next century. We, my dear brother, will by then be dead. It is quite enough for us to attempt to influence events for the better while we live. I have long endeavored to do so and to keep the peace. But the current trend of competitive imperial ambitions can only lead in the end to war between the great powers. I am now of the opinion that there is no hope for the future to be gained from practical men of affairs but only from literature and religion that alone can span the centuries. You may therefore, in all honor feel that you have done your best for your country, and I am free to tell you that your labors over the past two years for the sake of England by diverting disaster from the spread of the Black Formosa Corruption among us have caused Her Majesty to wish to honor you with a knighthood in recognition of your labors.

I hope that you will return soon to England where we may meet again. Please convey my greetings and esteem to your excellent friend, Dr. Watson, and believe me to be, my very dear brother, yours sincerely,

Mycroft Holmes

I folded the letter after reading it carefully and returned it to Holmes without comment. He returned it to his case before saying to me, "You see then Watson that we are delivered and at the final hour from adding our own efforts to the ruination of America. We may still meet with President McKinley, but my advice shall be to turn aside from his present course, to free the people of the Philippines , to renounce the economic domination of Cuba, and to return to the American tradition of building a just and honorable republic at home."

"A knighthood Holmes!" I exclaimed. "You are to be congratulated. I am happy to see that your efforts for England have at long last been recognized!"

Holmes hesitated before saying firmly, "I am afraid that I must decline it, Watson. If it were offered to me for my life of labor as a detective I would accept it as I accepted the Order of the Legion of Honor from France, but I cannot accept a knighthood that is tainted by my own reports about the Sudan that may have led indirectly to this massacre at The Battle of Omdurman."

"But perhaps it is being offered you for your work in disclosing the scheme of Baron Maupertuis," I objected.

"Nonsense, that entire matter is still hushed in the tightest secrecy. The public will assume that it was my more visible work for England such as our present mission to America that has led to my knighthood. It will send a most equivocal message regarding my true values. In any case my opposition to the Baron was the duty of every Englishman. I will of course communicate my hesitations and scruples through Mycroft to Her Majesty as I do not wish to appear ungracious or to give any unwarranted offense. Besides, what are such titles to me? Would I wish to be saddled with the burdens of my brother Sherringford whose minor peerage has never brought him anything but pain and subjugation? If on the other hand England loses the services of Mycroft ... well then, my own refusal of a knighthood will seem as nothing in comparison. England will lose much if he should feel forced to tender his resignation. In any case we are free now to return to England whenever we wish."

Alas, that was not to be the case, for events soon crowded upon us that prevented our departure for several critical weeks that were to change our lives forever. But I must tell my story in due order. The city of Washington D.C. is unique among the capital cities of the world in exercising only one function, that of governing the nation of America. It is not a great port city like London, nor is it an axis of culture like Paris. It engages in no extensive trade, investment, or commerce. These are instead the province of New York City. It is not even centrally located to provide easy access to most American citizens, such as for instance the city of Saint Louis, Missouri might have been. Instead, it occupies an idealized country of the mind.

The legacy of those very abstractions upon which the nation rests and which are embodied in its Declaration of Independence and its Constitution and laws finds its site of preservation in Washington D.C. It is a city the entire function of which is to exercise power. It is the Versailles of the new world and its order and rituals are in their way as arcane and mysterious as those that once ruled the French aristocracy in their own artful world of obfuscation and deceit. As its influence grows it will also undoubtedly also become the place where the moneychangers of the temple of democracy will come to purchase influence and privilege from the people's delegates. Our time in Washington allowed both Holmes and me to observe the functioning of American government closely and with some degree of immediacy and what we had seen did not leave us sanguine about the prospects for the American democratic order.

Holmes went so far in conversing with me as to call the proceedings that we witnessed analogous to a cattle auction. Not only was there a surprising lack of intelligence in debate, but there was a general air of corruption and venery everywhere that showed how clearly the interests of capital as represented by the great corporations and trusts dictated public policy as the new century approached. It was not that we might not have observed the same corruption at home in Europe, but it was the fact that most Americans still believed, with a remarkably naïve faith, that their own nation was still engaged in the pursuit of the noble ideas of its founders by guarding individual freedoms that we found so sad and discouraging.

Even after the brutality of a civil war, followed by the vile corruption of the Grant administration, and the abdication of the efforts to establish and maintain the former slaves as equal citizens after the war, Americans still believed that the ideas of early America were still intact. With the conclusion of a civil war, waged for the most hypocritical of reasons such as to offend the nostrils of the world, most of the former black slave population had only exchanged their status as property for a new status as oppressed pariahs, frightened away from the exercise of the franchise and in many cases more miserable than they were before the war.

Meanwhile the great industrial cities began to break down the former alliance of most Americans to the land and their ownership of small and independent farms. America was now in the year of 1898 about to embark upon a great quest for empire. Already reports indicated that the local patriots who had sought their freedom by liberating the Philippines from Spanish rule were to be treated as America had already treated the Indians of the great American plains. These Philippine patriots were to be killed to a man if they dared to resist submission to American colonial rule. Reports drifted in that tens of thousands of "rebels" had been killed.

Faced with such appalling news the only redeeming feature of Washington D.C. for both of us during those late autumn months of 1898 was the presence in Washington of Irene Adler. The acting company of which she was a member was staging a delightful musical comedy that was the hit of the winter season there in Washington. She was feted nightly after the show and we were her chosen escorts to those functions. Her fame had preceded her and had opened all doors, so we were able to observe at close-hand the informal aspects of Washington's social life as well as the more formal operations of government that occupied our days.

Miss Adler had arrived at that state of renown that is the goal of every actress where her beauty is only enhanced by experience so that she might be called in all truth, a diva. There are those who assume that a woman's beauty is at its best in her twenties, but what poet can doubt the truth that it is only as she approaches her forth decade that her true beauty shines forth with all of the wisdom gained from her life experience as a woman. It is then that her eye is brightest, her figure refined, and the character of her face shows forth as the excess flesh of youth melts away to reveal the beauty of the bone-structure beneath. She approaches at this season of her life the savor of a fine vintage wine. She is to be contemplated and not merely admired with a passing glance. She leaves behind her at this season the dull uniformity of youth and assumes her full measure of individuality. This was the impression conveyed by Irene Adler in that autumn of 1898.

Her admirers were many of course, but her eyes with their gay and mocking expression always sought out those of Sherlock Holmes wherever he might be in the room. I would look over at Holmes and at such times and see the rare smile of amusement that he reserved for her alone. It was as though each of them was engaged in quiet converse with the other whose burden might have been, "Is not all of this simply too absurd?"

I believe that both of them had arrived at a sense that many of life's rituals are mere gestures, pointless at last to address the actual situations of human existence. They had each by their own unique paths grown disillusioned, but still not become bitter or cynical about life. They could still play the game as it were while never forgetting that it was a game that they played and that real life exceeds its social panoply. What Mr. Thackeray had called "Vanity Fair" was a mere carousel for children, with rings to grasp as the ponies pass, and spun sugar candy to eat betimes. Only the wise may sense beneath and behind it all what Wordsworth the poet called, "that still, sad music of humanity, nor harsh nor grating, but of ample power to chasten and subdue."

Thus were our evenings spent that autumn beneath crystal chandeliers and around tables laden with beef, venison, or pheasants and in libraries drinking bourbon after dinner with portly men, each well-satisfied with his station as a leader of America. Everywhere there was talk of the American victory and its prospects for expansion. America had shown the "little yellow Japanese" that we would not be trifled with in the Pacific and the Russian Bear had been put on notice that any invasion southward into China would be repulsed from American battleships based in the Philippines. The American trade with the orient would now be secure and even the European powers of France and Britain would have to take note that America had arrived at last upon the world stage as a power to be reckoned with.

We even heard talk now and again of building a canal in Central America. It appeared that the Assistant Secretary of the Navy, Theodor Roosevelt, was using every opportunity already to urge the practicability of its construction; that where the French had failed, America, the new America, would succeed! I saw that Holmes had been right after all. Our mission to America had grown to be superfluous. The march of events in a single year had made what had seemed only last year to be a distant and even far-fetched prospect was now a settled expectation requiring only that the details of diplomatic planning with Columbia be completed and execution begun. The northern isthmus of Columbia known as Panama was beginning to be the focus of most intense interest. It was at one of these soirees that we overheard a conversation that was to begin the final sequence of events in our mission to America. I can only recall that it was the conversation of a group near us, and that it had involved some mention of the proposed canal.

Suddenly I felt the grip of Holmes' lean hand upon my arm, for the man who had been speaking had just mentioned that an emissary had already been sent up from Costa Rica to discuss the prospect of the building of a canal there with President McKinley. Holmes and I approached the gentleman later and Holmes addressed him adroitly as follows, "I could not help overhearing your conversation regarding the possible building of a canal through Central America. May I ask if you know the name of the emissary from Costa Rica that you mentioned? I have some acquaintance with that country you see and have a financial interest in the railroad down there. If the canal is built it would certainly affect the value of my shares."

The man accepted the false statements of this clever ruse of Holmes and answered amiably, "Well sir, you might be justly concerned, if a canal ever gets built down there, why then there will be no more need of any railroad to cross the country after the canal is completed. Still, it might be some use getting materials over to the Pacific side during the actual building and no doubt that's why this man has come up, to steal a march on the Mexicans. His name now, let me think, hmmm, I remember now, it was Baskerville, that's right, Baskerville."

Holmes' hand had dropped from my arm then but I saw his jaw tighten with determination. Holmes and I withdrew soon to a corner of the room where Holmes said quietly, "Baskerville again, I should have known; I should have known..."

I spoke up at once earnestly, "What is that to us, Holmes? If as you say the canal will be built in any case, then his advocacy for the interests of Costa Rica and for the railroad there can have no bearing upon our mission, which in any case as you have said, has now become superfluous. Why not let the interests of the worldly powers cancel each other out?"

Holmes looked at me earnestly before replying. "We dare not stand aloof and indifferent in this matter, Watson. The present railroad is but a wedge to divide the people of Costa Rica from their own rightful possession of their land. The profits from bananas and coffee are already diverted to the American investors who own the plantations down there. The building now of a canal will only enhance the depredations visited upon the people of Costa Rica. A man like Baskerville, if he is given power, will only use it to tie the people with bands of steel into peonage and slavery. I had hoped that he might simply retire to a life of decadent luxury when he returned to British Honduras and hence to leave Sir Henry and Lady Beryl in peace. Now I see that I have been wrong. He has evidently left his position in Honduras and returned to Costa Rica. This man's plans must be curtailed. He will evidently never cease to pose a danger. We must at the very least inform President McKinley about the nature and background of the man. I am afraid that we have no other choice."

So it was that we arranged to meet on the following day with the Speaker of the House, Thomas Brackett Reed. We then explained our fears to that most formidable gentleman. He heard us out before raising his ponderous bulk out of his chair and pacing the room nervously.

"You say this man is a scoundrel, Mr. Holmes. Is that surprising? Where the corpse lies the vultures will gather. If it wasn't Baskerville, it would be a man just like him. I have tried to talk to Bill McKinley lately myself and it is no use. He is an example of a man, good in himself, but unable to proceed beyond the possession of a few fixed ideas. He is convinced that the expansion of trade is the key duty of his administration. If the nation is fully employed it will prosper and prosperity will act as a general tide to lift all vessels. This attitude explains everything that he has done recently and every abdication of his own prior wishes and higher principles. The man's greatest weakness is his desire to be liked and esteemed, to be popular among the people. The people meanwhile demonstrate perfectly the weakness of every democracy, the desire of the masses to obtain unpaid benefits by entering into collective national debt. It is always a mistake to give the people exactly what they ask for because short-sightedness is the primary characteristic of the crowd. For instance the nation wanted war, so Bill gave them their war."

"Even I as Speaker of the House could not prevent it and if you will look at my bulk you will see that I am no mean anchor; yet I could not hold back a nation bent on folly. I have seen the President change in the course of this last year in ways that I could not formerly imagine of him. Though he is my friend, I told him to his face that he has embarked upon a course that will sooner rather than later prove fatal for the former ideals of this nation. When American history is written one hundred years from today, it will be the McKinley Administration that will be seen as the one that divided the old America from the new. Some would call that the measure of greatness, to live in a time of change; but what if the present victory is only the beginning of a greater period of dissolution and decline as war debts mount higher and higher? Empires begin their fall from the point of their greatest triumphs. Hubris inevitably brings retribution in its train."

"But to return to your concerns about this Roger Baskerville, this canal, if it is ever built, will bring about immense struggles for influence and profit. Baskerville will meet men like himself in that struggle. If you become involved you may only open a path to victory to a man worse than Baskerville, perhaps that man, Baron Maupertuis, of whom I have heard you speak. But if you still want to meet with the President, I will try and arrange it. I caution you though to consider well your course of action. Every man has his vanity, even a man of principles like William McKinley. Bill likes to think well of himself and will often act foolishly simply for the privilege of gratifying his own good opinion of his actions. It is a fault with which I am all too familiar. It is not easy to accept human failure when it is the fruit of noble motives."

He paused before engaging in reminiscing, "I might have had the Presidency myself you know, but I would not consent to stoop and grovel to obtain the support of my party and buy my way into office. I considered it beneath me and what is the result? Sweet likable Bill McKinley allowed Mark Hanna to push and shove him into the White House. Where will it all end, I wonder? Men like Theodore Roosevelt who love power will always pursue it, but McKinley would have been happier had he been left in peace to attend to his wife who has a weak constitution and to rock in the evenings on his front porch. He has been pushed into history by forces greater than his character can bear. Perhaps history is mindless after all, mere force applied to the weak clay of human nature that erodes beneath the stream of events."

"In any case, I have learned my own limitations during this affair. I have definitely decided not return to the House of Representatives. My influence there is broken and my party has gone its own way in the pursuit of wealth and power. I plan on retiring to Maine where I may read Epictetus and meditate upon the folly of human enterprises; and you, Mr. Holmes, if you are wise, will return now to England and leave this man Baskerville to bring about his own retribution in due season at the hands of others."

It was an unusual spectacle for me to see Sherlock Holmes

receiving advice rather than dispensing it and I could think of no man better qualified to advise us at this point than Mr. Reed. He understood, as did few living men, the ways of power and of practical diplomacy. The sheer intelligence and power of his character and convictions were such that few men would dare to risk his scorn or contempt and he had long wielded these weapons in the House of Representatives to steer his country away from the course it had eventually chosen to pursue at all costs. I saw then before me a man, weary but above all else disappointed, that the nation that he had loved had taken the path of illusion that leads a nation to expand its influence beyond the consent and governance of its own people in order to dominate other nations and to colonize the undeveloped regions of the world.

"Your advice is well taken Sir," answered Holmes, "But I am afraid that in the case at hand I must pose an objection. I have pledged myself to protect my client, Sir Henry Baskerville. If this cousin of his manages to increase his wealth and power by his involvement in this affair of the canal through Central America, he may use that very power to mount a renewed attack upon Sir Henry. In addition, I feel it incumbent upon me to warn the President that this man, in spite of his connections in Costa Rica, is not to be trusted."

"Is any man to be trusted where power is concerned?" asked Mr. Reed with a grim smile. "You must do though as you think best and as your professional sense of ethics demands, but I warn you that you may have a rattlesnake by the tail. Unless you are prepared to kill it, you had best let it return to its den unmolested. There are times, Mr. Holmes, when the man of conscience must be prepared to retire and to let events proceed to their own natural conclusion. I am a great reader of the Greek tragic dramatists: Aeschylus, Sophocles, and Euripides. Fate has within itself its own corrective measures. The shortest way with a fool is to allow him to make his own way. The end of a scoundrel is procured only the more swiftly by granting him his wish of momentary triumph. The greatest sin to the great pagan authors was in overreaching. It is a sin that Bill McKinley is committing even as we speak; but if I told him so, he would draw himself up in his full Presidential dignity and with all the sanctimoniousness of his Methodist convictions assure me that he is only doing his duty as the President of this noble republic by spreading freedom and progress to the benighted natives of Cuba and of the Philippines. No man likes his errors to be pointed out to him while he is engaged in committing them. They are to him like a pair of new boots, all shiny and polished. One must wait until they begin to pinch before saying anything."

"I will contact him though and will let you know if he will see you before you leave Washington. I advise you though to tread lightly when you speak to him, for you will be in competition with his own present high opinion of himself at this hour of triumph when everyone is besieging his doors with their congratulations. American flags are waving at every street corner and America is looking ahead avidly to the challenges of its new position of power in world affairs."

"As for me, well gentlemen, events have proven to me that I am out of step with the times. The poet, John Clare, once wrote these words that I have taken lately to heart, *'And even the dearest, that I loved the best, are strange, nay rather stranger than the rest.'* When a man watches his friends adopt a course of action that seems to him fatal and reason itself fails to convince them of their error, nothing remains to be done. I have opposed these annexations of foreign lands as violating that very principle of self-determination, which is our primary heritage and the basis for our republic: that government may not be imposed from without. This principle was the justification for our own revolution and now we are about to deny that right to others out of some misplaced and self-serving instinct of paternalism. The whole business is tawdry and stinks of hypocrisy. I can no longer serve both my country and my conscience. I will therefore leave the House and return to the private practice of law. It is bitter to me to leave in the hour of my greatest defeat, but so it is. Perhaps it is always thus, for who would wish to retire when he is still effectual and when his most distant goals still seem to be within his reach?

To live is ever to strive and to dream of a better world. I know myself well enough to say that something new would always occur to me, some last stitch to add to the great design, one more daub of the brush to bring out a detail. To one such as I am only defeat, and that a final one, would turn me from my course and cause me to come about. This ill-conceived and vile war has been that defeat for me. I only grow in bitterness by the day and by doing so open myself to the scorn of the vulgar. Those who once fled my gaze over that vast chamber of the hall of Congress now bait me like a bear just to hear me growl. It is enough."

He paused sadly before addressing us once again on the fate to be expected from our own mission, "As for you Mr. Sherlock Holmes, you may try where I have failed if you so wish, but I advise you to leave this pestilential region of Washington and to return to England; not that London is probably any better, but there at least the scar tissue of centuries covers old wounds and injustices multiplied have bred indifference in the people and from indifference more skill in adaptation. The evils of the world are never tolerable, but when they are indulged in long enough, they at least lose their power to surprise us. No one was appalled at the rise of Domitian, wicked though he was; they were simply glad that he was not another Nero or Caligula."

He laughed in a great rumbling manner before saying, "That is my only remaining comfort in contemplating the fate of William McKinley. He begins his reign as a budding emperor still trailing the veil of his former innocence, so perhaps he will still see the light before it is too late. I assure though that far worse men will come after him."

Holmes and I arose then and each of us shook the hand of that noble legislator in farewell before departing. It was the last that we were to see of him. Events were to prove that his advice was wiser and more prescient than we knew at the time.

Holmes said little after our meeting with Mr. Reed until after dinner that night in our hotel when he at last broke his silence. "If one lives long enough, Watson, one must finally face the defeat of one's dearest hopes. We begin life with a sense that all things are possible and that the tide of history will turn in our age to prepare the way for a brighter tomorrow. Experience teaches us otherwise. There is no greater fallacy than the illusion of automatic human moral progress through history. Even the present *Pax Britannica* is an illusion. Though we have avoided during our lifetime so far a major war with France, our traditional enemy, the British soldier has been forced to fight in endless small wars and skirmishes in many remote regions of the empire in order to sustain our domination of those regions."

"Mycroft now informs me that he fully expects war to break out in South Africa with the Boers at any time. Now that we control the Sudan, it only remains for us to control the rich mines and farms of the southern African regions not yet fully governed by England. I look at Thomas Reed and see in him the loss of illusions that even powerful men must retain; I see in him an American version of my brother Mycroft. Both are men who have tried to advance the interests of their respective nations and yet remain men of honor and principle. Both have attained the very summit of influence and power only to find that they are being defeated at the height of their careers and that all of their efforts cannot prevent their respective nations from taking a course that violates the very premises and principles upon which they have staked their own personal lives and honor. The result is that each will soon go his way and retire from the citadels of power and leave the way open to men of narrow vision whose actions to date show the fact that power in the last analysis exists only to gain more power for itself."

"The men who covet power are in the last analysis not men at all, but cogs in an impersonal machine. Power is the idol that knows no surfeit. As the interests of a nation expand so does its sense of entitlement to defend those interests and to protect what was initially stolen by force of arms. The real problem is that America produces too many goods. What then does it do? Does it allow the market to generate lower prices so that the majority of American citizens may afford them or raise wages which would diminish profits for the few? No, instead it seeks out foreign markets for its excess goods, even if it must span the Pacific Ocean to trade with China and Japan to do so. America has already annexed Hawaii and soon it will reduce the Philippines to a territorial status as well in order to protect its extended trade routes. It will then need a bigger navy to protect its merchant ships. Then it must have a canal to make the passage to the east shorter and to service its ports on the western coast of America. Why must it have all of these things when the entire nation once consisted of only thirteen colonies which are quite enough for any one nation to manage? The answer must be because America like England believes in its own moral superiority and right to rule over what each calls the inferior races of the world."

"What has become then of the rhetoric that supposedly led America to undertake a great civil war? Was the purpose of that war to free the black slaves? Are they free today? Are the red men free, those who have been allowed to remain upon the bare remnants of the land left to them, while the rest of the land that was once theirs alone is now flooded with Europeans? What will be the fate then of the people of the Philippines? And we are here to aid America in pursuit of its impious ends. Why? Because Baron Maupertuis is a threat to British rule and Mycroft knows that England will not be able to stand alone against the might of a rising Germany if war shall break out in the coming years. If a man like Thomas Brackett Reed speaks of retirement, shall we who know so little of the ways of government hope to succeed where he has failed? I tell you, Watson, these matters strike very close to home for me. If Mycroft retires, who will take his place? Not I for I have not the capacity nor the temper for such devil's work!"

"What course is left to us then before we leave? To warn the President that he is dealing with a viper named Roger Baskerville? Baskerville is only one viper in a nest of vipers and perhaps soon they will be biting each other if Mycroft is correct in his predictions! Should I tell the President anyway, as I must in honor bound, so that this one snake at least may be turned aside and driven back to his den in Costa Rica? Now I see why direct action so seldom defeats evil and even when it seems to do so it only brings forth greater evils in its train. The devil was most honest when he was asked his name and he answered, "My name is legion," for the armies of hell grow daily in the halls of government. Hell is hydra-headed and multiplies like maggots in the dead body of supposedly free-republics. To be honest with the people is to doom oneself and one's efforts to contumely and ridicule. Even Christ was mocked along the road to His crucifixion. These times already wear a crown of thorns and this world of capital and of greed will not escape what Christ has called the hour that belongs to the Prince of this World without some great deed of destruction breaking out, perhaps even a general war between the great European powers. I begin to understand that St. Paul was right when he wished to be rescued from this body of death."

It was painful for me to hear the disillusionment in Holmes' voice but I found myself agreeing with his sentiments. At last he continued, "I am weary Watson, not in my lungs alone, but in my soul. I feel at times like Childe Roland in Robert Browning's great poem. Have I come so far only to see the Dark Tower squatting upon its plain even if that tower is disguised as the great white city of Washington D.C. in that bright land of so many promises that was America? Perhaps we have been in pursuit all along of Melville's white whale, Moby Dick. I fear that I am like Captain Ahab walking the deck with his leg of whalebone, white as a gravestone. America is going the way that might have been foretold of her before the first Pequod Indian was killed to make way for the Puritan interlopers. That it has taken three centuries to decimate a continent is a tribute not to the energy of the Americans but to the slow progress of the disease of greed. American settlement of these lands has been slow and relentless like the spread of consumption in the lungs of the consumptive and blood shall gush forth at the end. Even if I seek to escape by returning to England, it will be only to return to a nation in a later stage of the same disease. Tell me then Watson, what I should do? Has the time come at last for me to take up the keeping of bees upon the Sussex Downs as you once recommended I should do? I have lived long enough to realize my irrelevance in the great scheme of time and circumstance. My best efforts are like a stone dropped into an empty well. Perhaps John Keats was blessed in dying young of consumption. His poetic words of aspiration are ever present before me lately: to cease upon the midnight with no pain."

As I write these words of reminiscence in 1917, the Great War that such prescient men as Sherlock Holmes had foreseen still rages on unchecked. Each day young lads on both sides are sent over the top into withering gas-shells and machine gun fire only to join a generation of youth that has been plowed into the soils of France and Belgium. Will grass and trees ever grow again upon the scene of such a desecration? There is talk now that President Wilson may order an American mobilization in the wake of the sinking of the Lusitania off the coast of Ireland. Such an intervention may be England's last hope, but it comes too late to save the many young men on both sides who have already died. What is the use of patriotism when it is translated into the dull and repetitive bursts of shells along the trenches? Is this the music of the great new age of progress that seemed to shine just before us at the great world exhibitions from Chicago to Paris in the years before the war? Why could this pointless and horrible destruction not have been anticipated and avoided? Many had felt it coming; among them were men like Mycroft and Sherlock Holmes and Thomas Brackett Reed. Each of these was a man of great power and substance who had throughout their long careers used their unique gifts in pursuit of truth and a more just world and each had lived to witness the triumph of greed and illusion in their respective countries. Whether it was the struggle to possess the diamonds and gold of Africa, as in the case of England, or to control its own hemisphere and reach out beyond the Pacific Ocean as in the case of America, the same motives of pride, racial dominance, and a desire for wealth had come to dictate policy at the highest levels of government.

Both Thomas Reed and Sherlock Holmes could not doubt that ruin must inevitably follow the course of such ignoble aspirations and that war is the final end of such pretentions. Each victory only brings closer the final defeat of the aggressor as the other nations of the earth unite to defeat its claim to hegemony. At first wars of revolt fester in the provinces of empire and the empire decays from within as its substance is bled away to retain its appending dominions; then at the proper time an invisible limit is reached and the empires make war upon themselves from within. In the end it is no comfort to be correct in one's judgments of ruination, if one is still tied by patriotic loyalty to serve the course of the folly. The result is frustration yielding finally to disillusionment and despair. As Holmes' friend and physician I could see at the time of which I speak that the two years of 1897 and 1898, both of them years of ceaseless struggle, had reached their terminus at last. Sherlock Holmes had at least succeeded in preventing the scourge of disease from ravaging England. He had managed to thwart the initial designs of economic gain by Baron Maupertuis. He had even managed to complete the final chapter of that case (one which has yet to see publication) that I have entitled *The Hound of the Baskervilles,* by luring Roger Baskerville away from Devonshire to the Americas.

Surely these triumphs should have been sufficient for Holmes to congratulate himself and to rest assured that he had succeeded in his primary goals of recent years. But this was not to reckon with that side of Holmes' character that could never rest content with even his best efforts. No, he must press on and on even if it might destroy what remained of his precarious health and deprive me at last of his presence and the joy that I always had in his company. I knew at once then what my duty was to Holmes. I knew that I must draw him back from the brink of the present precipice just as I would have wished to do had I been present that day so long ago on the edge of the Falls of Reichenbach.

Was it not enough to have turned Moriarty from his prior scheme and made him an ally against Baron Maupertuis? Was it now necessary to take on once again the wily Roger Baskerville? How could Holmes as a mere private citizen of England hope to defeat him in America? Rodger Baskerville was now again a free citizen of Costa Rica if he had as seemed evident abandoned his arranged post in British Honduras. He now had every right to pursue the interests of that nation by urging the Americans to use the existing railroad that had after all been built though the means of American investment so many years ago to aid in the construction of the soon to be proposed American-built canal project. The building of that canal, whether through Columbia, Costa Rica, or Nicaragua, now seemed to be a necessity to serve American ambitions in the Pacific and would simultaneously frustrate the ambitions of Baron Maupertuis and reduce the value of his shares in the company that he now controlled that was hoping to build a Dutch version of the canal.

I therefore proposed to Holmes that we might return to England in triumph knowing that we had succeeded in our mission and that events had made some of our efforts unnecessary at last. We did not need to fan the flames of American pride and aspiration (as we had once believed we must) for victory over Spain had made the revelation that the published version of the Murillo Papers was false, a moot point. The onward pressure of events had made it irrelevant that American businessmen had aided in the construction of a railroad using slave labor and any perceived libels from abroad would be perceived as nothing in the face of American determination to countenance even greater injustices as national policy if they might now ensure American expansionary goals.

The views of the few men of power and greed were now shared by the many. The indignation that might once have met their conduct was now swallowed up by the complacency of a nation that deemed itself invincible since having come to dominate the Caribbean in a few short months and with the riches of China now beckoning. Distant Hawaii would now be but a stopping point to the harbor of Manila from which American trade would penetrate China and thwart the desires of the Empire of Japan to annex parts of China. The desire for conquest is not confined to any particular race or nation. Such was the condition of the world in that year of 1898 as the last decade of the Victorian era neared its close and the new century was about to begin.

I therefore urged Holmes to abandon any thoughts of a meeting with President McKinley. If Thomas Reed, his erstwhile friend, had not been able to influence the President, then what hope had we to turn America from its current course? "Besides, Holmes," I said at the time, "I do not care to see you risk your health now after making such strides during the course of the summer months. These recent late nights spent at dinners and receptions have done much to undermine the salubrious effects of a summer of sun and sea air. As your Doctor I must advise you to give up this life in Washington and too seek out a warmer and drier climate for the rest of the winter. I suggest that we leave by train for California as soon as you can make your farewells here. We can then return to England by way of ship from San Francisco. I have in the course of my reading of your journal come to wish that I might have shared those travels at your side. I ask you now to journey with me as we might then have done. Let us see those lands of the Pacific: New Zealand and Australia. Let us touch at Ceylon and Cairo. You may even show me the beauty of Montpellier where you did a year of chemical research. Finally, let us cross the channel at last to London where we may resume the life that we once knew in Baker Street and hear again the grate of a hansom cab as it draws up at our door and hear again the hurried step upon the stairs as of old. I urge you to consider that the world is too much for Sherlock Holmes and his friend and associate Doctor John Watson. I do not know how we shall be remembered Holmes, if my little tales of mine will ever be able to adequately display your remarkable gifts and accomplishments, but if we are remembered at all let it be as men who knew when to leave events in the hands of providence and not to tempt fate by attempting solutions in realms beyond our own proper gifts and talents."

I recall that Holmes listened to me in silence and I took comfort from the fact that he did not contradict me at once. It gave me hope that we might soon leave Washington and allow events there to take their own course, but I should have known better. It was unlike Holmes to leave a foe standing unanswered upon the field. It may have been his engrained habit of curiosity or perhaps it was that he could not accept such asymmetry in the world, but Holmes could not leave Washington without meeting with President McKinley. I had no idea what might be in his mind. Surely, he could not hope to turn aside events that were then proceeding headlong, but perhaps he merely needed to know why it is that men so covet their own destruction.

After reading Holmes' own great manuscript, I saw that within and around its many insights there still lurked that fundamental question of why it is that evils, which fail to produce any good, finally come to delight in only their own pain and futility. One wonders if evil remains always in delusion or finally reaches a dreaded clarity regarding its own responsibility for its fate. Even Milton paints Satan as one put upon by God; and by doing so Milton adds nobility to a creature that can never possess it. Evil is always cowardly and seeks always to confuse the issue and to escape the demands of causality and of just retribution, one not visited by God but pregnant within the evil heart itself that brings about its own ruin.

If the devil is a liar, then surely his first lie is to himself. Perhaps the devil is convinced that his way is always better and that God is merely stubborn or tyrannical in maintaining His own essence, for with God to be and to act are one and the same thing. God alone does not need to weigh consequences for with God all is consequential, all must be as it is because God wills it so and in so willing can do no evil because the very idea of God includes by necessity all perfections. Herein is the question that is perhaps unanswerable: is all the pain of creation worth the task of mining virtue? Is all suffering not in excess of its supposed salvific purpose?

Holmes left my plea unanswered. As usual Holmes kept at the time his own counsel after hearing my arguments. A few days later he drew me aside and I was told only this: that he had accepted an invitation when it came from the White House. To refuse would have reflected badly upon those who had aided us. Thomas Brackett Reed must have intervened on our behalf after all, as he had promised to do. So it was that we left our hotel one bright December morning and were driven to that impressive edifice the White House to meet President William McKinley.

A light snow had fallen a few days before but it was already melting beneath the southern winter sun and the grass on the lawns showed through in spots. The air had that delightful freshness though that is born of newly fallen snow and that I recalled from my youth in Scotland when I was at school in Edinburgh as a lad. The morning mists were rising from the lawns as our carriage pulled up before the stately front door entrance where we were met by the head of the household staff and taken, not to the President's office, since we did not formally represent the British government, but rather to a comfortable drawing room. There a short time later we were joined by President William McKinley.

He met with us quite alone and without a secretary to record the minutes of our meeting. He crossed over to us at once and shook each of our hands before bidding us to be seated. He then took a large chair facing us and expressed his apologies for not having received us sooner upon our arrival in Washington.

"I am sorry to have taken so long to make your acquaintance Mr. Holmes and you also Dr. Watson. I had heard of course rumors that you were in Washington after spending the summer in Newport, but I had heard that your primary purpose in coming to America was for reasons of health. It was only when I received a direct communication from my friend, Thomas Reed, that I realized that there was another reason for your presence upon these shores, one of policy and even of diplomacy, in an informal way of speaking. I understand that your position is one of some delicacy as is my own. My office often exceeds my abilities, but I am not allowed to escape my duties as President because of my own awareness of my limitations. I am even forced at times by the events that have rushed upon me to adopt policies that, to speak frankly, some of my friends such as Thomas Reed oppose. But I must brook that opposition with sorrow but with a firm purpose to discharge the duties of my position as I see it, even if that means foregoing the pleasure and assurance of their approval and esteem."

Having in his opening statement and in the most courteous and forthright fashion possible made it clear what the parameters of our discussion would be, the President moved along in his genial fashion to offer is some refreshment and a short time later we were served with a what I believe is called a mint julep, tall and filled with ice. After savoring its taste and the delightful lingering impression of mint on the palate he continued.

"The southerners understand the art of gracious living. My duties are at an end for the day and for once I am spared a banquet for this evening—so I will join you. I need not tell you that as President I usually need all of my wits about me to resist undue influences. These have been busy and trying times gentlemen, as I need not tell you. The exigencies of peace are no less than those of war I assure you and my time has been much in demand. As you must know from the newspapers we have just concluded a peace agreement with Spain signed in Paris. It only remains for it to be approved by the Senate, which I am sure it will be. Our nation has achieved all of its goals. The people of Cuba have been freed from oppressive Spanish rule, the Island of Guam is ours, and we may now set about educating the people of the Philippine Islands for that time when they may be able to sustain the freedom that we have brought to them and set up at that time a democratic government of their own. Until then we will retain the Philippine Islands as a protectorate to guard them against possible invasion and annexation by Japan. My friend, Thomas Reed, through whose agency this happy meeting with you has been arranged, persists in seeing our retention of the Philippines as an act of an imperial nation and in derogation of our principle of self-determination."

The President looked vexed for a moment before continuing as before "He is quite wrong in this characterization I assure you. Thomas Reed is a man of high ideals though somewhat divorced from reality. The Philippine Islands were like low-lying fruit upon the bough. If we had not picked it, then it was sooner or later to be grasped by Japan or even Russia. The Philippine people will do better under our tutelage and control than under the un-Christian and despotic rule of the Japanese, I assure you. We will bring them Christianity and the benefits of trade. The Philippines are the gateway to China and the guarantee of what we call the Open Door Policy. America feels that there are enough prospects of trade with China to satisfy all comers and that it would be a mistake to carve it up into separate economic zones nation by nation. Such action would only bring on needless conflict between the civilized nations of the world, whereas if China remains one, then all will benefit, not least China herself. What we have essentially done is to extend the Monroe Doctrine to the far-east to prevent foreign exploitation and colonial rule there."

"Ah, I see in your eyes some doubt about the truth of that assertion; perhaps you feel that American policy has been extended too far from our native shores. But I ask you gentlemen to consider whether events and the accidents of geography have not forced that exercise upon us for the good of the world. If trade is to be open and free some nation must undertake to see that it remains so."

President McKinley paused to see the effect of his words upon us before continuing. There was a native shrewdness in his gaze.

"Still dubious I see. Perhaps you would object that I am being inconsistent here in light of my belief in protective tariffs to shield our own markets from cheap imports. My answer is that our farmers and newly minted industries are still vulnerable to the European powers that had a head start on us due to our unfortunate civil war. We have no choice but to solve our domestic dilemmas at the same time that we are catching up to the demands of the international arena in order to assume the role that we will need to play in the wider world."

"Even the great Pacific Ocean is less of a barrier than one might think. China is not Africa gentlemen. Its culture, though not brilliant from a political standpoint, has at least made China sufficiently modern that it may sustain production and trade and be allowed to retain semi-independence. Africa on the other hand is only a continent consisting of primitive warring tribes and of a few Moslem despots. I fear that its partition into colonies was inevitable if lamentable from a strictly democratic and maybe even moral point of view."

"Your own nation, Mr. Holmes and Dr. Watson, has led the world in the effort to explore and to bring the benefits of civilized life to that benighted continent and I trust that when you return to England you will tell your government that America is engaged in a similar design in the far-east, to bring stability to the people there. The world is drawing together gentlemen, bound by ship and railroad and even the telephone and electricity. There is no corner where outworn ideas may find shelter from progress. I must say that I am quite at peace with our actions in this great year of 1898, which I trust will be long remembered as a year that advanced the march of human freedom and of Christian civilization."

He then offered each of us a cigar from Havana and lit one himself as he stretched back comfortably in his chair and settled his bulky frame into a more comfortable position after speaking so at length. No doubt he felt that he had set our fears at ease. While he had been speaking I could not but think that his earnest and amiable face and manner had something to do with his popularity. A prospective voter needed only look at the man to see a vision of a well-fed and prosperous America embodied in its President. The man was as sleek and fat as a benevolent sea lion. His piercing eyes seemed to look into one's heart and invited affirmation of all that he said. The large face was innocent of guile and still retained even in middle age the handsome contours of his youth when he had served in the army of the republic in his country's late civil war.

He was evidently a man of thought and deliberation but a man who once having made up his mind about a subject was not to be dislodged by later doubt or recantation of what thereafter became for him a creed. He was not however a man of great imagination; not one apt to be the prey of mere enthusiasm like his choleric friend Theodor Roosevelt. President McKinley was a man who would act only when the force impelling him to do so was sufficient to shift his own ponderous certitudes and convictions, but once in motion he would not stop until his ends had been achieved. He was, in his way, the exact opposite of the Englishman, Sherlock Holmes, who now sat before him.

Holmes always saw the other shadowy side of things. For Holmes truth must always be presented with qualifiers and modifiers, for truth according to Holmes is a dim tunnel through which we try and discern the shape and size of facts. Holmes' very nature was to doubt and to weigh evidence, never to claim as certain more than what science might prove or what faith must affirm. That he was a Roman Catholic was not due to a lack of skepticism in his nature, but because he knew that faith alone might supplement with certainty what no exercise of unaided reason could supply.

In William McKinley on the other hand I was able to discern the result of an earnest protestant mind-set with its desire to do practical good in this world through the exercise of evangelical fervor. President McKinley was a man who would always underestimate man's capacity to do evil in pursuit of goodness. It was that trait that I saw made manifest that morning in his very words to us as the bright winter sun filled the quiet room where he had consented to receive us. I could also see in this speech of his to us that the President was treating us at least as unofficial emissaries of the British government and that he wished us to return to England with a favorable report regarding American intentions and to forestall by his words any check to be made to American ambitions by the leaders of the British Empire.

America's naval fleet was still too small to cavalierly oppose any British objections. Indeed, if British interests were not at the time so focused upon Africa, I doubt that America would have risked war with Spain without more extensive consultation and approval from the British government. No nation at the time could hope to directly oppose Great Britain on the high seas. America's tiny fleet, though adequate to oppose a decadent Spanish opposition force that had bottled itself into the harbors of Manila and Santiago, thus reducing the free-range and firepower of its ships, could not hope to oppose the British navy. Our meeting then was designed to ensure English assent and approval to what had already been accomplished by the force of American arms against Spain. But this was not the purpose that Holmes had in mind when he had requested the meeting. So, to forestall any premature dismissal by the President, Holmes needed to speak up as he then did if he was to be able to address the subject of a canal.

President McKinley clearly believed that the meeting's primary end had been achieved, but retained his courteous manner when Holmes spoke up. "Let me assure you sir that I appreciate that you have taken the time that you have taken today from the many demands made upon you at this time to meet with us. We have as you have mentioned no strict diplomatic role to play, so I beg you to consider any comments that I may make, not as representations of the British government, but as my own. Still, you may have heard something of my reputation as a detective and if I may presume upon my own notoriety, I know something of the affairs of mankind. The first requirement of a detective is to seek to comprehend human nature in all of its permutations. In the period of my first association with my good friend, Dr. Watson, I once scandalized him by pretending to despise what I termed to be worthless areas of knowledge. In point of fact there are none. Many times the solution to an abstruse problem only has come to me because of some obscure bit of information picked up in an idle hour. The detective must in a sense be the universal man. He must be able to see events, not from his own point of view alone, but as they appear to the criminal mind. He must in short seek to trace the threads of evil that wind continuously through life like a strata of clay that appears now and again and then vanishes."

"The detective is in a way a geologist of the soul. He must sift data and assign it weight and classify it according to type and species. Such has been my preparation and experience, which I bring to you today. It is these abilities that I wish to make available to you at this hour. If it is true as you say that events have crowded thick about you, it is also true that your role is central to the outcome of those events. You may feel that you must act in response to those pressures which appear to signal the nation's will, but you must know also that the nation looks to you to either confirm the inchoate aspirations of the crowd or to speak to those very pressures and influences from a higher perspective and with the authority of your exalted office. You are not the mere voice of the people. Your role is to lead and not merely to discern the often ill-considered popular will. You must be the voice of reason that honors the wisdom of the past as well as the demands of the present and the future."

"There is a continuous nature in the office of a chief executive of a nation, whether he is a monarch like Queen Victoria or as in your case only a citizen advanced for a time to office and burdened with being the President of a great republic. It is not a role that I would care personally to assume and I respect your courage in undertaking such a great burden as that presently reposed with you; but having done so I would seek the furthest parameters of my duty and try to rid myself of any temptation to assume that I am spared the necessity of choice by the onward rushing tides of history."

The President nodded at Holmes showing that he had followed him closely thus far. I could see that he appreciated this eloquent prologue and was willing to hear more. Sherlock Holmes could no doubt see this as well because he continued.

"I wish to be specific, sir. America has gone to war and has emerged victorious. In one short year the options for American foreign policy have expanded considerably. In front of you there now lies the prospect of entering into that battle for relative power among nations that never ceases, the method of which often requires the exertion of force. Your own countrymen congratulate you in the hour of your victory. You seem to have given them what men in their collective aspirations always desire, to possess pride of place. What American does not now feel stronger because he is part of a nation that must now be reckoned with in the counsel chambers of the world? But sir, have you not in the process bargained away that one great possession that America once possessed?"

"Distance from European events was that priceless possession. Post-colonial America, guarded by two oceans and separated through a war of independence from the domination of a foreign sovereign and even of an imposed faith was free to choose a new form of government from any existing in the world at that time. Americans were able to choose for themselves both the nature of their government and of how they would pursue collective happiness now and thereafter. But by entering at this time into the maelstrom of the world's struggle for power and for influence and by looking to foreign sources of raw materials and by seeking new markets for your export trade your nation has now bargained away that to which the world once looked with envy, your nation's gift to all who choose to come here for a chance to begin their lives anew, to shake free from the burdens of prior history."

"Why have so many immigrants come to these shores? Did they come only to renew those habits from which they had fled and to re-constitute that way of life that had caused them to emigrate in the first place? No, they came so that might shake off the burdens and shackles of the past and to abandon even those conclusions regarding the iniquity of man so that men might trust one another again and pursue a common dream of change. The literature and the political pronouncements of your government and laws have become the envy of the world's nations, all of which might in time have joined you in a wider vision of world-democracy."

"Your recent civil war was by the will of God a last warning to the world of the folly of taking up a general call to arms. It was a testament to the perennial vanity of bloodshed. But you have now made it a path to gain and to glory. Your armies did not disband after the war but turned their fury upon the ancient and primordial inhabitants of this land and killed them when you might have learned from them of the ways of freedom, for what character did these former inhabitants of the land possess if not freedom? Can anything more majestic be imagined than the great American plains that are now broken by the plow and decimated of the noble beasts that might have been a source of food for generations of Americans and that were adapted to survive the rigors of these open prairies? I speak of course of the American bison."

"Instead what followed the war? Why did not the Emancipation Proclamation of your illustrious predecessor, Abraham Lincoln, extend as well to the native inhabitants of this land? Was their possession any less effective and productive than the current farmers upon the lands taken from them? I speak of the Cherokee of Kentucky and of Tennessee as well as the Navaho of the Western deserts, the Sioux, the Arapahoe of the plains, of the Utes and the Blackfeet of the mountains. Why are these now confined upon lands inadequate to maintain them?"

"But let us not stop there. What of the Americans once brought here in bondage? Was the black slave freed only so that he might now labor for a paltry wage inadequate to obtain for him even the manner of life that he once lived as a slave? And what of the freemen of this country, did the union soldier surrender his arms only to assume the slavery of working in the great factories of the northern states? Where is the dignity of the free man if the very means of his sustenance much be mediated by the whim of his employer?"

"True freedom was last seen among the Indian tribes and is now no more. Instead there is only American power condensed and consolidated into wealth and that national wealth is owned by your new aristocracy. Meanwhile, the so-called free man, as his own personal power has declined and the prospects of his independence diminished, must now take pride not in himself but only in the collective force of arms of his nation while he himself is comparatively powerless to improve his own condition. This sir is not America!"

"I must tell you that you are presiding over the birth of a deformed vision of democracy that will bring sorrow and ruin, not merely to yourselves in time, but to all nations that have ever followed as you are now doing the rule of the sword and the bondage of unfettered capital forged by the laws into instruments of centralized power, of trusts and of great corporations.. Wars only pave the way to further wars and blind mankind to the proper rule of law, which instead takes its inspiration from mutual accommodation and respect for the dignity of each man and woman."

"My words are not confined to the task imposed upon you alone. When I came here, I intended to arouse your people and to engage your national will for the building of a canal connecting the Atlantic and Pacific oceans before a similar canal could be built by the great Dutch financier, Baron Maupertuis. But now I urge you to turn first to the healing of your own land before you give any further thought to national expansion. This is no time to evangelize other nations when your own democratic faith at home has been betrayed! Return to your sources and grasp again what America was and what it might become again if you turn from the perilous course upon which you have staked, not merely your Presidency sir, but the future of your great nation."

"This is my word to you today, Mr. President. I fear that this may be the last hour when such a warning may be heard. I fear less for you than for your successors in this office as they try and sustain a vision that has so far departed from those central tenets upon which America was once based and to which it may never return if you do not act swiftly to reverse the current direction of events among your people. History seldom provides a point where a decided exercise of pressure can determine the course of events for centuries to come. Where for instance would Christianity be today if the Emperor Constantine had not thrown the weight of the Empire behind the strange faith that had emerged from the province of Judea? You sir are in a similar position now."

I had often had occasion to note during my long association with Sherlock Holmes that he was not a man to be impressed with titles or by wealth. His essential dignity was not to be cowed or restrained by granting an indulgence to error or a sanction to mere social position. I had seldom though had occasion to see that characteristic displayed in purer form than when Sherlock Holmes dared to address the head of state of America in the White House and advised President McKinley at the very height of his triumph and acclaim to abandon the very course of conduct that granted had him the almost universal esteem of his countrymen.

I recalled that America was still in the process of extricating itself from the severe economic contraction that had resulted from the financial panic of 1893. The isolationism that had caused his predecessor in office, Grover Cleveland, was seen as weakness and folly and the Republican Party had emerged as the party of decision and of renewed prosperity. Now Holmes was advising that American post-war policy should honor the early rhetoric of mere aid to the rebels in Cuba by foreswearing to fully exploit the spoils of war. Already American businessmen were casting greedy eyes on Cuban resources and the Philippines, which had been a mere backwater of the nation's attention during the hostilities had now proven to be the richest treasure of all, for it was those islands that could provide America with a guarantee of a free port off the coast of China.

So unlikely was the prospect that Holmes' arguments would prevail that I wondered why he was even taking the trouble to attempt to stem the onward tide of events. While he had been speaking I could see President McKinley growing red in the face and the geniality, for which he was famous, that he had displayed at our entry was not to be seen when he spoke up at last after the long silence that had fallen upon the room after the ringing oratory of my friend had ceased.

"If this is a threat from England, Mr. Holmes, I am sorry that they have chosen you to make it, for I had always heard that you were an honorable man and one who recognized the limits of discretion in delicate affairs. Or perhaps you think that I can simply snap my fingers and everyone will come to attention. The power of the American Presidency is not that of an emperor. I serve at the will of the people and each day in office has only added to my appreciation that my power is limited."

Holmes answered at once. "My statement to you is no threat, sir; I speak only in my own capacity. Indeed my first intention upon landing on these shores was to encourage that very enthusiasm that is now so prevalent among your countrymen. I hoped to meet you so as to encourage America to undertake the building of a canal and to challenge Baron Maupertuis and the Greater Dutch Canal Company that he controls by doing so. If now I speak contrary to my own former intentions. It is because I am in honor bound to do so when I see a noble nation treading into a quagmire of entanglements from which it was formerly comparatively immune.”

“Do you not see that once having entered into the colonial struggle there is no retreat? America will become of necessity a martial nation committed to the same series of wars that we have seen in England in order to sustain our power at the periphery of our empire? Or perhaps you believe that our wars could always be successfully characterized to credulous citizens as wars of liberation or national defense in spite of the fact that the fruit of those wars was to advance British economic interests.”

“If so I assure you that it will require a policy of sustained duplicity and delusion for Americans to pursue such an international policy in the future and its own ideals will be betrayed by doing so. Is it not easier then to reverse so perilous a course now in its incipient stage, rather than to wait for that final hour when America will have forfeited both its honor and its substance to pursue the goals of conquest?”

“That hour may be distant, but it is no less inevitable for all of that. The reputation that today is garnished in laurels will then be seen as the critical moment in history when America forfeited its true treasure and witness to the rest of mankind. The way of conquest and of the sword merely forces mankind back into a common penury. When wars cease, they only begin again somewhere else. It is then war itself that is the enemy of mankind. Is the price of human life to be forever so much self-inflicted death? If that is the way of things, then God has no voice in the human soul and we are all only to be counted as among the children of Cain who slew his brother Abel!”

The President was no longer red with indignation but seemingly lost. It was as though what Holmes was saying found an answer in some remote corner of his own Protestant conscience, but it was an answer so at odds with his practical experience of life that he dared not bring it forward into clearer view.

"Therefore he spoke up at once by saying, "Mr. Holmes, you are asking for more than any responsible leader may grant. You may not be aware of this as a private citizen of England, but practical experience has shown that morality has little function in sustaining a nation. The task of the successful leader in a democracy, particularly one made up of as many different constituencies as America, is to say what each of those constituent groups most wish to hear. This can be done in two ways. The first is by being purposely vague and the second is to say different things at different times but with equal fervor."

"A nation is in the last analysis an abstraction, a series of processes sustained often by mere momentum. The tides of events are not the province of even the leadership of a nation to guide. At most a leader may seek to minimize the worst effects of the inevitable by skillful and prudent application of pressure from the perimeter in order to steer events. The broadest current of events may be influenced to a degree in this way, but that current will remain for the most part substantially unchanged. Any major change such as that advocated by revolutionaries will only succeed in disrupting the social fabric beyond repair. Even to change the balance of power prevailing within any given social order is to risk a general dissolution back into chaos."

"From outside it must appear that a mere command by a President as a representative of the people's sovereignty would be sufficient to create greater justice. I assure you that my experience as President has shown me that no command may alter human nature nor may it create wisdom among a people nourished upon only a few poorly grasped fundamental ideas. The task of politics is one not of distortion of course, but of artistry. It is so to display the options of the moment that they may be marginally altered in a direction that does the least possible general harm. More extensive political notions are therefore mere pageantry and poppycock."

"Even the course of the laws is a matter merely of persuasion not command. That is why there is so little that can be recognized as law in the international arena where the threatened force of arms must alone prevail in the councils of nations. If America has chosen to use armed force at this hour, it was simply so that it would not itself be held as an economic hostage someday by the nations of the world with greater power. The recent Financial Panic of 1893 showed how tenuous is the balance prevailing in our own economy. The indignation and restlessness of the anarchists and of the socialist elements has shown how great our own present potential is for renewed civil discord and rebellion."

He paused and then looked up at us with a pleading expressiveness. "If under my Presidency America has left behind its former period of adolescence, it was not because I desired this, but because we are not blind to the present course of events in Europe and the implications that they have for our place in the great scale of relative power in the world."

"How long would we be able to sustain our necessary trade with China or even to retain our possession of Alaska if these were menaced by Japan or Russia without a corresponding ability of this nation to wield an effective counter-strike? Every nation seeking respect from other nations needs to demonstrate periodically its willingness to go to war and to prevail in the conflict when it does so."

"After our civil war there was a natural tendency to desire a period of peace. But without a stronger navy we cannot hope to defend our own new port cities on the west coast. Without a stronger army our own southern border with Mexico would be insecure. The exercise of force in small matters keeps larger conflicts at bay. America will be less likely to risk a conflict with the other great powers in the next century due to my decision to take on the burden of a war with Spain and even Spain well ultimately benefit as well."

"Spain was over-extended and this put its homeland at risk in Europe. By being deprived of its power over its superfluous colonies they will no longer serve to distract it from innovation and industry at home. This will force Spain to stimulate its own productive capacities and no longer rely on imported precious metals to supplement its lethargy. Meanwhile our reward will be a free hand in this continent. Spain will never rise again to threaten us from the south the way that the Spanish Armada once threatened your own England in the 16th century."

"A Spain of reduced power will join those other nations that sustain their dignity like an ancient dowager of diminished means who, no longer courted by suitors for her hand, still insists on riding in a carriage although she has not enough to eat or to properly clothe her person. She will dress in the threadbare velvet of another age and secretly she will be a figure of ridicule even to her servants. But such a diminished condition will serve as a warning that we in America will not brook interference with our position of primacy in the Americas."

"If as you say America has entered upon a path that will only lead to ruin in the end, she may at least have a century of glory ahead of her as a nation and join in her turn those other nations who like great ladies, grown thick about the waist and long of tooth, may remember still the glories of their maidenhood when heads turned as they walked past and hearts yearned to follow wherever she might lead them."

"Nations are in the last analysis no different than the people who embody their dreams collectively within them. Life aspires always to be more than itself. What are the monuments and arches of Rome or of Paris but a record of each nation's history with its triumphs and defeats? Is America alone to be confined to the fate of consisting of only a few rural farms and villages? America also desires to take its place at last among the great nations of the world. Life that does not advance is already in retreat. Did we fight to preserve our union for so small an aim as to be dictated to by countries in Europe that are only a fraction of our size? America's borders have grown of necessity to accommodate the numbers of immigrants to these shores and we will continue to grow as life itself must if it is to avoid death."

"The decision to go to war was not an easy one, but I could see that if America did not take its destiny when it was offered to it, the opportunity to prosper, and yes even to survive, would be offered to another less hesitant nation and that we would be the worse for it. The race of the nations of the world for power and prize is not an option, but the given state of human affairs. I cannot change that fact, nor can you Mr. Sherlock Holmes."

The President now rose to his feet and paced the room as he said solemnly, "When I took this office upon me I vowed to see that the laws were enforced. Among the statutes and treaties there is one law that exceeds all other laws, that a President must act so that the union of our states will be preserved. It was that law that Abraham Lincoln followed, though it meant that the very blood of his own countrymen must be spilled. America you see is not a mere idea, but it is flesh and blood and sinew and the land on which those material things are nurtured. We have taken the land in order to live and have struggled for it as one always must or have it taken away by another more determined to possess it. I, like you Mr. Holmes, long to see a better world and I believe that God will bestow it in due season according to his divine plan and promise, but until that hour arrives I must live in the world as it is and fulfill my duty of office as I have attempted to do in this case."

President McKinley still paced the room as he delivered these final words to us in an address that I felt was given less to Holmes and to myself than to his own soul. It represented perhaps the credo that every man must finally reach to guide his choices and actions. I could sense the sincerity of the man in both his manner and his words and I hoped in my heart that life would not exact from him the penalty of any errors that he had made.

Holmes in his turn had done his best that day to express his own convictions and to warn the President of the danger that always lies in victory. I thought that we had done all that we could hope to do and I was preparing for the interview with President McKinley to end when Holmes spoke up once again.

"You have been most generous sir in speaking so frankly before us. There is another matter however Mr. President that I must bring to your attention. I have come to hear, no matter how, that in the matter of a proposed canal through Central America you have been approached by Roger Baskerville, an Englishman resident in Costa Rica. It is our belief that he has forgotten that he owes a duty to England by his former position in the British consulate in British Honduras and that he may be now engaged in pursuing a private course of action in order to line his own pockets. We have no proof of this however and I will not ask you to divulge any secrets of state implicated by any discussions that you have had with him, but I must warn you that the man has a most unsavory character from all reports that we have received. I will not go into details, but I urge you to exercise every caution in dealing with him. The government of England will of course appreciate any information that may be used in evidence against him should his actions take a criminal turn. At this point to discharge him from his former post, if he has not already abandoned it, would be only to help him effectuate his plans free of any restraint that his position as a British official imposes and to forfeit any cause of action that our government may bring against him for malfeasance in office."

Holmes paused to let this revelation sink in before proceeding further. "I could not leave Washington though without bringing this matter to your attention so that you will be on your guard and to show the sincerity of the goodwill and friendship of the British government to America and for yourself, Mr. President."

Sherlock Holmes' words had a conciliatory effect on President McKinley. His former genial manner returned at once and he offered us some brandy as we talked of more congenial topics for a short while before he escorted us to the door of the sitting room and wished us farewell. He assured us that he would keep the British consulate informed of the future actions and representations of Roger Baskerville whatever these might be. He promised that we would receive every aid and courtesy while we remained in America and we parted in good spirits as a servant led us to the door where a conveyance had been thoughtfully provided for us.

I was only too happy to dismiss Rodger Baskerville from my mind. As we left the grounds of the White House I felt for the first time in months that we might be able at last to resume our travels in peace. I could see that even Holmes felt a certain relief at having at last concluded the commission that had brought him to America. He had been frank and honest with the president and while not betraying faith to England had warned the Americans of their future as the world was about to enter the 20th century with all of its promise and its many dangers.

As we trotted down Pennsylvania Avenue we passed a carriage that was pulled up along the wide street. The traffic was heavy and slow on the grand boulevard. Holmes suddenly grasped my arm as we passed and it fell into position behind us to the annoyance of the drivers of other carriages. When we arrived at our hotel entrance this strange conveyance pulled up behind us and as we alighted I heard a strangely familiar voice as if from some distant dream.

"Ah, Mr. Sherlock Holmes and Doctor Watson of London I believe," it said and we turned to meet the mocking gaze of Roger Baskerville trained upon us. Were it not for the familiarity of his voice I doubt that I would have ever recognized him. He had clearly been ill recently and though his voice and manner showed all of the vigor of a man in the prime of life, I could see that he had aged considerably in body since I had last seen him in 1888. My practice as a physician has given me certain powers of acute observation denied to the layman and my long training under the tutelage of Holmes had taught me to utilize this skill with assiduity until it had became habitual. To the skilled diagnostician there is a unity in the body. For one organ system to be out of balance affects the integrity of the whole. I could see that day in Roger Baskerville that deficiency of balance that is evidence of improper functioning. His eye had a feverish gleam. There was a slight tremor to his hands that he made every effort to conceal. His skin had that drawn and dry appearance that one associates with age and his complexion, even beneath his tropical tan, had a yellowish cast as seen by the color of the palms of the hand. Though I could not say whether he suffered from malaria or jaundice, I could see that before me there stood a man of foreshortened years. Illness did not sit well upon him for I knew him to be an impatient man, one unaccustomed to needing to make allowances to the limits imposed by our humanity. The former spring in his step was now replaced by a heavy shuffle and even to stand evidently caused him some degree of pain that he endeavored to hide from us. His forced familiarity and ease betrayed an underlying anxiety and ill-temper and even perhaps a degree of fear.

"Imagine me meeting you here, so far from Baker Street. I had no idea that your practice was so extensive or have you retired at last? Dear me, that circumstance if true would leave the criminal classes of England rather at liberty would it not? Or perhaps you are here for some purpose on a case? Your detective practice may have at long last left behind its humble domestic phase and have entered upon an international stage? If so you have my congratulations, Mr. Holmes. I always thought your efforts were wasted on governesses and chasing geese in pursuit of hidden jewels concealed within their crops. The tales published of your exploits by your friend here make charming reading, but surely are of no real consequence in the outer world of great events. The swarm of humanity has little time for the quaintness of individual tragedy. You do not agree? Ah well, then perhaps you should return to London and carry on with the good work after all."

Holmes ignored this attempt at light banter and answered, "I am just as surprised to see you, Mr. Baskerville. I have rather lost track of you in recent years. I imagined you quietly moldering away in the depths of the Great Grimpen Mire. Tell me, do you still keep a kennel?"

Roger Baskerville shook his head. "Tut tut, I am sorry to see you resorting to mendacity. It so contradicts that upright and earnest demeanor that you always like to display. You must know that during the last years since 1888 I have seen the evidence of your hand raised against me clearly more than once. I did not imagine that Sir Henry would not consult you with any difficulties that he might have. I admit that I have been guilty once again of underestimating your abilities. Take that matter of the letters of Don Juan Murillo. I had to sell them for a fraction of their anticipated value to a mere purveyor of second-hand information, one Charles Augustus Milverton to be exact. The name is no doubt familiar to you; he is a very seedy fellow with aristocratic tastes. I had hoped to sell the papers in America to some of the rich members of an American railroad syndicate, but I needed funds immediately at the time and of course once I discovered that I had been given forgeries rather than the actual copies after I had dealt in such good faith with my cousin ... but then one never knows where one will find a scoundrel does one? After that business with the hound you left me without prospects you see. I am not a man who likes to live without some extravagant end in view. Even the money that I received for the Murillo papers only served to cancel my debts and I was soon again in need. I sought out old friends then, but to no avail. No, do not ask me for their names, their names are of no consequence ... unless that is you already know them. It would not surprise me if you did. You do seem to have taken an inordinate interest in my affairs if you will forgive me this little criticism. Was it not strange that as if out of the blue when my affairs seemed to have reached a crisis, I found myself suddenly appointed to a minor government post in British Honduras? Was that not remarkable? Forgive me if I suspect that your hand was once again in evidence, Mr. Sherlock Holmes. Still, I was in no position at the time to refuse a benefit even at your hands. So off I went to assume a dull diplomatic posting in a minor colony when everything of interest is happening in Africa and no doubt I might have so remained but ...”

He paused in his speech and his face took on a diabolical look as he asked, “Tell me was it Sir Henry who was paying my salary? I do not want his filthy money, which should have in any case been mine. I would have known how to use it better than he has done. I should much prefer to have been paid by the fat British government. In any case, I have not been content to welter away in the heat of British Honduras sheltering beneath the banana leaves. I am a man of great ideas and projects as you know. I soon came to realize that my real vocation lay in serving the coming power in my old country of Costa Rica; so I took this little trip to Washington to see if my services and connections there might be of help to the Americans as they were once before when a railroad needed to be built. And imagine my surprise and concern when I arrived and learned that you had preceded me! Who should I hear was in Washington also but the great detective, Sherlock Holmes? Do you blame me for drawing the natural inference that you were again upon my track?"

He spoke lightly, but I could see that the man was quite angry, and was made no less so by seeing the cool contempt with which Holmes regarded him.

"The good doctor and I were about to take an early dinner," said Holmes. "No doubt you have other matters to attend to so we need not delay you any further."

His manner changed in an instant and all pretense of light familiarity vanished. "Do not try and put me off, Holmes! I demand to know what business you have just had with McKinley," he fulminated. "I warn you that I will not tolerate being interfered with. I have my own ends in view on this visit to America and they are substantial. I represent many important men in Costa Rica who have allowed me to present their interests to important men here in Washington."

"Is that so Rodger? Well, I believe that you are already under obligations undertaken by oath to the British government," said Holmes calmly. "No doubt you have forgotten the duties attendant upon your posting and the consequences attendant upon any breach of trust in your official capacities sworn to the British government."

Baskerville answered insolently, "I resigned that vile and tawdry position a month ago before sailing for Baltimore or perhaps you were unaware of that fact. I now represent an association of mine-operators and plantation-owners who are in fact the very crème de la crème of the present Costa Rican nobility, so do not assume that I am a mere independent agent groveling to the Americans. The good will of the Costa Rican government and the important men in that country are essential if America is to build a canal there."

"Well I believe other routes are available," said Holmes mildly.

"Bah, that will never be," he cried. "There are mountains to contend with and the route is too long in Nicaragua. The expense will be prohibitive."

"The Panama region of Columbia perhaps?" answered Holmes.

"As a region that is part of Columbia it will not be sacrificed for such a project; the Columbians have no wish to invite American dominance into such close proximity to the homeland. They are a proud people and have no wish to share the present fate of the people of Cuba. The canal must be in Costa Rica, which alone has an adequate rail system to support the building of the canal."

"Well, that is as you say your own concern. Dr, Watson and I have concluded our business in Washington and I must soon as you have pointed out return to my London practice after this little holiday in America. We must in any case await the coming years to see what route the Americans choose if they even persist with their plan of building a canal in Central America. And now I must really bid you good-day, amusing as this little contretemps has been."

Rodger Baskerville ground his teeth at this. "I warn you, Holmes, that you have crossed my path for the last time,"

Holmes turned to face him and looked him up and down before speaking. "I believe Watson that a sedative might be of use to Mr. Baskerville, he is looking quite ghastly is he not? Perhaps you could recommend some useful chemical preparation in preference to the laudanum he is currently using."

With that Holmes turned on his heel and we left Roger Baskerville upon the street, still clutching his walking stick in his pale and emaciated fingers. I had thought for a moment that he might strike Holmes and was prepared to intervene, but I saw that Holmes had a firm grasp of his own walking-stick and was prepared to parry any attack. Roger Baskerville stepped back just in time to prevent a spray of dirty snow from the gutter from washing up and over his shoes as a cab passed. I looked back as we entered the hotel to see his twisted, yellow face still glaring after us. After a time as we waited for the elevator Holmes spoke. "You recognize the symptoms of course, Watson. It is a case of acute laudanum intoxication and perhaps evidence of secondary syphilis, with the resulting mental unbalance and paranoia; very sad, very sad indeed."

I said nothing to Holmes at the time, but I was troubled by the meeting that we had just had with Roger Baskerville. To assume that the meeting was a matter of chance alone was inconceivable to me. I recalled how Roger Baskerville had shadowed Sir Henry upon his first arrival in London to claim his inheritance in 1888 when Holmes and I had first met Sir Henry when he was still fresh from the wilds of Canada, little realizing that the dangers that he had faced from wolves upon the prairie were as nothing to the dangers that lay before him in desolate Devonshire on his own family estate. If Roger Baskerville could lie in wait for Sir Henry as he had done at that time, then he could do the same now in regard to us. How long had he known of our presence in America? Did he even now have a plan or design to exact retribution and revenge for Holmes' role in defeating his aspirations time and time again?

We had completed our task in Washington. There was no urgent reason then for us to remain longer. My first instinct was to leave and to leave quickly. What was it to us what plans Rodger Baskerville might have for Costa Rica? If he was successful in obtaining American aid after our earnest warning to President McKinley regarding him, that was beyond our ability to control events. In recent days I had acquired a loathing for the whole business of politics. It seemed to me now that to be a leader of men was to be grimed and contaminated by the process irretrievably. I doubted of I should ever again view statesmanship as a noble profession when compromise and betrayal of the public good was of necessity its stock in trade.

The very idea of order seemed to me now to be unobtainable outside of fiction. Clarity of motive and character seemed to require the multiple perspectives and the formal language of an artist like the great novelist Henry James; only such as these could hope to explain and to capture the complexities of modern life. Meanwhile, I still wished that the romances of Sir Walter Scott could still be acted out in this new and complex age. What were Holmes and I really but only two absurd knights who had blundered into an age that could no longer perceive them as anything but vainglorious and weary pilgrims from another age, engaged in a hopeless quest that exceeded their powers? Sherlock Holmes was, as it seemed to me at the time, only another Don Quixote; while I in turn was only his poor retainer, Sancho Panza, so it was time now I felt to summon aid from the official police. I left Holmes to take his afternoon rest in his room at the hotel, while I proceeded to the front desk to leave a message for Inspector Stanley Hopkins. I requested in it that he would join us immediately upon his return to the hotel. I then took up my station in our sitting room with my old service revolver at my side to await his arrival.

As the urgency of the Maupertuis affair had now been placed in hands other than ours, I was then most concerned with the threat presently posed by the proximity of Roger Baskerville. During our time spent in Washington I no longer felt that Baron Maupertuis or his agents posed any direct threat to us. His initial purge of his closest contacts in the affair of the giant bamboo rats had broken any direct evidentiary links to the Baron with the single exception of Professor Moriarty; but his continued silence since the return of his racehorse, Silver Star, when added to the fact that any confession that Moriarty might make to Scotland Yard would only serve to implicate him at the same time in that nefarious plot of the Baron, had no doubt convinced the him that he was quite safe from any exposure from that quarter. In addition there was the consideration of the protection likely to be offered by his citizenship in Holland, which would be unlikely to grant extradition of one of its foremost bankers and shipping magnates to answer to what would appear to be a fanciful charge even if the full facts were ever disclosed to the authorities.

Still there was at least some evidence that an effort had been made to keep us under some degree of surveillance perhaps to remind Holmes that he might easily be killed if he should ever pursue too close an inquiry into the Baron's affairs. The posture of events at the close of 1898 therefore seemed to be one of stalemate. The Baron had found a more lucrative avenue for expansion and profit in the Americas rather than in England.

It is also essential here to confess that it had always been Holmes' opinion that Baron Maupertuis had not acted alone in the plan that had initially been developed by Professor Moriarty. Holmes was of the opinion that the German high command had also been involved. Anything that would hurt England could only aid the Germans in their ambition to rival the British Empire in its colonial possessions and to enhance the German presence on the high seas with an expanded imperial navy. To cripple the British economy would help to achieve both ends.

All of Holmes' suspicions though were of little use in the international arena where obscurantism is the rule and where events are shrouded in the fog of vague intentions and secrecy. The greatest international criminals, the arms manufacturers, the advisors and sycophants that seek to influence government policy for their own ends, and all those whose business thrives on conflict and human misery are never prosecuted, for what they do is not seen as a series of crimes but rather as the advancement of the highest aspirations of nation-states and the glory of monarchs.

The immediate threat posed by Roger Baskerville was of another order entirely. It was direct and personal. If Roger Baskerville was indeed a man at the end of his rope, he would behave with the desperation inherent in his position as he perceived it to be. It was then my immediate desire to get Holmes away from Washington at once and by doing so to reassure Roger

Baskerville that he might if he wished importune the Americans to choose Costa Rica as the site for their proposed canal.

Quite honestly, it appeared to me that compared to his prior schemes, Roger Baskerville might have finally found a task that was not on its face an exercise in villainy. I did not of course imagine that he had grown honest in his later years. He would no doubt find ways to line his own pockets with money through some sort of embezzlement or chicanery and come at last to a bad end, but he was at least playing his game with men not easy to be fooled and manipulated. He would have to be on his guard. All of this convinced me that he would have little time to think of seeking revenge for past plots of his that had not succeeded. He would be quite busy enough with his present project and whatever time remained would be spent in that artificial paradise provided by the drug to which he had now become a slave. I could not find it in my heart to pity him and any question of insight and conversion in a case like his seemed unlikely.

This had been the train of my thoughts when Inspector Hopkins knocked on our door. I was quite prepared to tell him of both my fears and conclusions, but I was prevented from doing either by the first words that came out of his mouth.

"Dr. Watson, I received your message and came up directly. I hope that nothing has happened here at least. Is Mr. Holmes with you?"

I stared at him in surprise and told him that I was quite alone but that Holmes was sleeping in the adjoining room.

"Have you checked on him? Then we must both do so now. The concierge told me when I arrived just now and made inquiry that he had seen Mr. Holmes leave the hotel within the last hour. He then handed me your message and I came up to see if he had possibly returned unobserved."

We both raced to the door to Holmes' bedroom which I flung open immediately. I saw with dismay that the room was quite empty. Holmes had evidently used the outer door to the hallway to slip quietly away during my vigil in the drawing room for some purpose of his own.

"We must find him at once," I cried and grabbing my hat and coat in the drawing room I ran down to the lobby with Inspector Hopkins at my side. As we ran out of the grand entrance of the hotel the doorman approached us and asked if he could summon a cab for us. I immediately asked him if he had seen Mr. Holmes leave.

"Why yes suh," he answered. "I had jest come on duty when he run out of de hotel an set off like blazes foh de grand theater. I heard him tell de driver. I don know why he was in sich a hurry cause de aft noon performance was done over an de evenen don start till eight tonight so as people can git dere dinner foh de pofomance. Here is yo cab genelmen. You can be dere in fifteen minutes if de traffic ain't too bad."

We thanked him and shouted our destination at the cabby and urged him to make all haste. We pulled out into the early evening throng of cabs and carriages. Our progress through the busy city streets was slow, but I took comfort from the fact that the cab that Holmes had taken must have been similarly impeded. We could not of course hope to overtake him, but we might be on hand as soon as possible to render any necessary assistance. Why, I asked had he set off in such a hurry and why alone? Try as I might to apply his own methods to the case I could come up with nothing. Had he set up a meeting with Roger Baskerville without informing me? Perhaps Holmes realized that such an unpredictable man would always pose a hazard and it was time to force a confrontation or final duel between them. But that was preposterous! Holmes was not one to engage in an appeal to force where reason and the law might provide a remedy. So great was my concern for Holmes himself that it was not until Inspector Hopkins snapped his fingers and cried out that I was able to entertain an alternative possibility.

"By Jove he has gone to warn Miss Adler!" shouted the inspector. "This meeting with Roger Baskerville today that you mentioned has put Holmes on his guard to prevent another kidnapping, one committed to ensure Holmes' silence!"

I realized at once that the Inspector must be correct. Holmes must have brooded alone in his room while resting about our earlier meeting with Roger Baskerville. If he was aware of our meeting with President McKinley, he might also be aware of what our habits in Washington had been. He might have shadowed us for some time as we went about Washington attending various social functions and noticed that we were often accompanied by the famous actress. Roger Baskerville would no doubt have deduced that Sherlock Holmes and Miss Adler shared a unique and particular friendship. If so, then he might have concluded that he could get to Holmes through her. Engaging in further thought after this supposition I realized that it was no easy matter to kidnap a famous theater personality. The theater is accustomed to the presence of fans who forgetting that the actress is not herself the character that she portrays imagine themselves to be in love with her and often carry unwelcome suits for her favors behind the curtain when it falls upon the play or opera in which she has just appeared. These obstreperous fans often seek her out in the privacy of her dressing room and for this reason certain precautions are made and guards are provided to gently but firmly eject the worst and most persistent of these vain suitors. A successful plot to kidnap Irene Adler would be improbable considering these difficulties.

As I came to that hopeful conclusion I sat back with greater comfort against the seat cushions. Holmes' haste in leaving the hotel without informing me might be attributable then less to panic that his worst fears might have been realized, than to his desire to inform Irene Adler at once of the danger that she might face from Roger Baskerville or his agents before she left the theater that night so that she might be on her guard. I was about to share these thoughts with the Inspector when he reached out and grabbed my arm. The traffic had come to a standstill and we were waiting to proceed again when suddenly behind us we heard the shrill bell of an ambulance from the local hospital approaching and fighting its way through the obstructing vehicles. The sound of that bell brought all of my former fears back upon me with a rush. We could not be more than a quarter of a mile from the theater. I glanced over at the Inspector and saw the same fear in his eyes that was in mine.

We reached the same decision simultaneously. Immediately we both leaped from the cab and pursued our way on foot through the jostling crowds. When we arrived at the elaborately sculpted outside of the theater building the crowd only grew thicker about us. The wildest rumors were already circulating through the crowd. We soon gathered that one of the principles of the show had been shot. Inspector Hopkins managed to locate a police officer who was trying his best to restore order and we were soon being ushered through the crowd to a side entrance where we were admitted by a pale stagehand.

The heavy door closed behind us and the sudden hush of the darkened theater embraced us. We were then led swiftly back along the labyrinthine maze of corridors to the backstage part of the theater which is always so much larger than what the public ever imagines. Ghostly images of props and backdrops reared up before us only to be left behind as we rushed on. At last we came to a larger dressing-room area and were shown through a smaller crowd consisting mainly of the members of the theater company. Many of the women actresses, dressers, and wardrobe assistants were crying softly. Inspector Hopkins left me for a moment and made some discrete inquiries to the stage manager before returning to me with a serious but somewhat relieved expression upon his face.

"One of the actresses was shot, but it was not Miss Adler," said he.

The manager of the theater then came over to us, visibly upset by these unusual events. "I understand that you are an inspector from Scotland Yard, sir. If you will accompany me now I will take you back to where the young woman is being treated. Mr. Sherlock Holmes of London is already in attendance there, but as to how he knew of this tragic occurrence so quickly, I cannot say. He was engaged in seeking admittance at the entrance just before the shots were fired."

"Is the assassin in police custody?" I enquired at once.

He turned to me, "Are you with the police as well sir? You are not a reporter I hope. Oh dear we have had such a successful run and now this!"

I explained that I was a doctor and that my name was Watson, that I was an associate of Mr. Sherlock Holmes.

"Ah Dr. Watson, please excuse my initial hesitation; your name is known to me of course. No sir, I am sorry to say that he escaped in the confusion following upon this dreadful event. Our first concern was not to waste time in pursuit, but to see to the needs of the young woman whom he has wounded."

"You are quite sure that Miss Adler is all right?" I asked.

The stage manager answered at once, "She was not wounded, but this entire affair has been a great shock to her. She was standing by the side of the young woman who is her understudy when the shots rang out. Both women fell instantly to the ground, a circumstance alone that may have saved them both from further injury. Oh, what madman would do such a thing? And things were going so well this season. We are not accustomed to such violence in Washington; this is not New York after all. But if you will both be so good as to follow me gentlemen, I will take you to where Mr. Holmes is attending to Miss Adler."

We were led further down the passage where after a discrete knock we were admitted by a uniformed police officer to a cozy dressing-room. The room was well lit and a team of doctors was laboring over a pale young woman who had been sedated with chloroform the heady fumes of which had filled the room. In another corner of the room a single doctor was aiding Miss Adler. Holmes sat on the velvet divan beside her and was holding her hand when we entered.

He looked up immediately and saw us. His expression was as grave as I had ever seen it. Anger, shock, and concern were written upon the features that I knew so well. He slowly relinquished Miss Adler's hand and pointed out to her our entrance. She nodded to him and I saw that she had been weeping. She looked pale and older in the unforgiving light of the well-lit room, yet she looked simultaneously young and lost and deprived of the sureness and decision of her usual demeanor. Gone was the ironic smile that usually touched the corners of her lips and her eyes seemed to seek for a remembered sense of personal security that had forever flown away at the first sound of the gunfire that rang out in such close proximity to her person.

Holmes took Inspector Hopkins and me over to an unoccupied corner of the room that evidently served as a lounge area kept backstage for the actors before speaking. "I was not here in time! My wits have grown dim through this period of indulgence. The result you see before you. The girl may now die. I blame myself severely."

"Nonsense Holmes," I remonstrated. "Even now I am at a loss how you knew that such an event was in the offing."

"Thank you, Watson, but it won't wash. In any case I have at least arrived in time to witness the intended result as I was meant to do. This was Roger Baskerville's work of course."

"And the target was Miss Adler?" inquired the Inspector.

Holmes turned to him before replying. "No, Hopkins, or else she would be lying where that poor girl is lying now. The target is me or rather my own choice of action. Roger Baskerville was merely showing me that he can take from me at any time one who I hold most dear. If he had done so tonight he knows that he would have thrown away his only power over me and that no power on earth could hide him from my pursuit. Considering its lamentable result it may seem inappropriate to refer to this as a mere warning; but technically that is what it was. I have been put on notice that if I should thwart his future plans in any way that he will exact a measure of revenge to mirror his desperation. Evidently he did not believe me today when I attempted in the most blasé way possible to assure him that it is a matter of indifference to me whether this damned canal is ever built or where the Americans decide to build it. But the man is supremely selfish and sees all events solely in reference to his own interests. He is a perfect example of the megalomaniac. I have always known this about him, yet today I forgot it. I was lying in my bed at the hotel and thinking how glad I shall be to quit Washington with its intrigues and venality and to leave it to such men as Baskerville when suddenly I realized that to men such as he is, the possession of power is everything! They cannot imagine a world in which each individual is free. Such men desire to orient the world about them as a magnet orients iron filings when held beneath a paper cup. My indifference was therefore an insult to his *amour propre.* How dared I simply leave Washington when in his own fevered mind he imagined that my presence here was solely because of him when in fact I had no prior idea that he had even come to Washington from Costa Rica until I heard his name mentioned by accident? Imagining that I am here in order to oppose him, as now I surely shall, he decided to strike first and to put me on notice that he is not to be ignored. He refused to believe my protestations, which I instinctually made to reassure him that I intend to leave soon. He no doubt recalled that once before I had pretended to leave Dartmoor only to return at the final hour and so to prevent his designed murder of Sir Henry Baskerville."

Holmes continued, "When I realized all of this as I lay in my bed at the hotel, I saw at once what he would do and of how I had left Irene alone to face him though my own blindness regarding his motives as they must appear in his own twisted mind. I lost not a moment then but rushed from the room. There was no time to explain even to you, Watson, what was afoot. Seconds might count. I rushed from the hotel, only barely clad as you see me, and caught the first cab I could find hoping that I might arrive before the event that now assumed the most dreadful prospect in my mind's eye. I arrived only minutes after the event; too late to apprehend the man, but in time to rush over to the fallen girl and to Irene as she stooped over the wounded girl trying to apply some assistance and calling for help. I then rushed to the darkened stage and summoned aid with my police whistle. Had I wasted less time at the entrance to the dressing-room where we conveyed the victim explaining my errand and instead rushed to the back entrance at once where Baskerville evidently made his escape ... ah well, it is too late now and regret serves no purpose, but I shall soon bring this man to justice; he shall not escape me again."

Inspector Hopkins then spoke up, "I will of course add my efforts to those of the official police. We shall trace him if he is to be found anywhere within the city."

Holmes raised his hand in remonstrance. "Spare yourself the trouble, Hopkins. Of course he will be found; but he will be found at the embassy of Costa Rica. He would not have come to America without providing himself with a shield. He has no doubt joined that nation's embassy. He will be therefore protected by diplomatic immunity. In any case we cannot prove that he was behind this evening's event. I have already enquired about a description of the assailant. There were no witnesses that could give a coherent account. The side street where the theater exit is located is quiet, deliberately so in order that the actors may leave undisturbed. The shots came from a darkened area of the theater as the actors exited after making their curtain calls. During the confusion no one witnessed the figure of the man as he escaped. Irene had directed all of her attentions to her stricken friend and was herself in a state of shock. No gentlemen, I fear that this set belongs to our opponent. He is no doubt drinking brandy at the embassy as we speak and perhaps playing a game of cribbage. If we are to take him then it must be through the use of unconventional means. He may not be arrested while he remains in Washington. His efforts to sway the Americans to build the canal in his home country may take some time though. His only desire is that I not interfere while he presses his suit with the Americans."

Holmes paused before intoning as if to himself, "If I do interfere, then I must clearly risk the life of her whose affection and trust mean everything to me. He knows perhaps as does his mentor, the devil himself, that there is no greater task for love than to risk the beloved. Our Lord has said that no man shows greater love than the one who will lay down his life for his friends. That is the summit of human love; but divine love is greater still, for God gave even His own beloved Son into the hands of sinners. The devil must have counted upon it that God would never do so. The devil's own certitude in his rebellion was that God's love for man must finally fail when put to that ultimate test. The truth of Calvary lies in the fact that God took up the devil's bargain on the devil's own terms and by doing so defeated him forever..."

"But Holmes," I cried. "Surely you will not risk your own life to bring this man down!"

Knowing Holmes as I did, particularly after reading his journal, I saw at once where his comments were leading. Holmes had arrived at last at the peculiar belief (for so it seemed to me at the time) that evil propagates itself by inviting retaliation in kind. Even if Holmes had been so lucky as to turn Moriarty from his evil ways (by what means I was not myself clear to that very day) could he hope to be so lucky a second time and with a man as callous and unprincipled as Roger Baskerville?

Holmes did not answer me at the time, but only grasped my hand for a moment to acknowledge my fears and to reassure me before returning to the divan to convey what comfort he could to his dear friend, Irene Adler. It was well that he did so for as they sat thus together the doctors informed her and after her all of us who stood helplessly in that silent room that the poor wounded girl had just succumbed to her injuries and died.

The killing of the young actress and the resultant closing of the play, until further notice, cast a dark pall over the citizens of Washington. The spirit of triumph and revelry that had thus far characterized the winter season gave way to an unwonted spirit of reflection but one mixed with anxiety and fear. As if overnight a rumor began to spread that the event had been perpetrated by Spanish Loyalists or by anarchists. The Spanish embassy was attacked by a mob throwing refuse and shouting abuse. For a time it appeared that the peace accords signed in Paris would not be ratified by the Senate. Soon the whole country had picked up the story from news accounts in the major newspapers. At last the President himself was forced to make a conciliatory speech to ward off further acts of demonstration and public outrage. The event was finally attributed to the madness of the anarchists who as always were held to merely await any opportunity to obstruct the national spirit of prosperity that had returned with the election of William McKinley.

After the presidential victory of the Republican candidate, William McKinley, following the uncertain leadership of the Democrats under the former Democratic President Grover Cleveland the now discredited Free-silver Movement of William Jennings Bryan was soon forgotten. The plight of the rural farmers of the west was set aside in the national consciousness by the wave of renewed success of the great manufacturing cities in the east.

The tragedy at the theater in Washington was seen as a portent of what would happen if the Democrats were ever to return to office with their outmoded policies that tolerated or even encouraged trade unionism, a movement now portrayed not as the solace and path to justice for the working man and his family, but as a hidden refuge of anarchists and communists. The organization of labor and its tool of collective bargaining was now seen as a brake upon the nation's gathering speed of economic growth as the new century was about to dawn. Throughout that period of debate and the search for an answer for a new America our little group alone knew the truth: that the real perpetrator of the crime was an Englishman named Roger Baskerville and that the gesture was personal and directed so as to influence the mind and will of Sherlock Holmes.

The very night of the murder Holmes brought Irene Adler back with us to our hotel where she was soon installed in a suite of rooms on the same floor as our own. Her usual lodgings with the theater company in a respectable boarding-house that catered to theater people would not offer adequate protection for her. Holmes requested that a full-time police presence be maintained on our floor of the hotel both night and day. His request had been granted as a gesture of respect to the great detective. Meanwhile we continued our preparations for an early departure from Washington D.C.

Miss Adler hesitated at first to leave her company in the

lurch, so she requested that we remain until various contract matters resolved themselves; we were thus forced to stay on as well despite the danger entailed by that decision. I could only reflect upon the strange irony that Roger Baskerville's own impetuous act had drawn us back to renewed pursuit at a time when Holmes had hoped to leave him to pursue his negotiations with the Americans unimpeded.

I was kept in utter darkness when it came to the present intentions of Holmes now that we were forced to remain. My first fear had been that he would hunt the blackguard down and dispatch him personally and had Irene been killed I have no doubt that he would have done so. But as the days passed I realized that I had wronged Holmes and that my assumption that he would exact an immediate revenge ignored his first comments made in the dressing room regarding the crime. Clearly for Holmes, retribution lies with God alone. As the days passed I thought often of this ethical question of the permissibility of exacting private vengeance for wrongs committed. The evidence is that God does not wish to condemn the soul that consents to evil but rather laments that His grace may not follow a soul that has willfully abandoned it.

I came at last to realize that the real punishment of evil stems from the evil act itself. Roger Baskerville was the source and nurturer of his own evil. There is though no corresponding maleficent anti-grace to correspond to God's action within the soul. The devil can only trick and suggest, while God not only counsels but nourishes the soul from within, for God alone has access to the soul directly.

I knew as much from the doctrines of the Church of which I was now a member, but that Holmes would allow the dogmas of His faith to determine his policy and actions when the danger pressed so close upon him impressed me with the sincerity of all that he had said in his journal regarding Professor Moriarty. At last I began to understand that for Holmes his faith was not mere metaphysical speculation but in all things the practical guide to moral conduct and the end and purpose of his every action. Holmes was convinced that God does not deal with the world as one way among many, but that every action of God in salvation history is in the last degree final and definitive both for the salvation of the individual and for the final destiny of history itself.

Christianity claims nothing less than absolute truth. It is not a mere collection of aphorisms, no mere manual of ethics by Epictetus, but a revelation of the end and purpose of all things. The entire material universe exists to serve this plan of salvation. No dim corner of the most distant stars or dark cinder upon a burned-out asteroid but manifests and advances some tiny inarticulate part of the redemption of mankind. If this seems disproportionate and absurd it is far less so than the divinity and death of the Second Person of the Holy Trinity on a cross in Judea two thousand years ago. Both Holmes and I had come to embrace that very absurdity by our profession of faith in the Roman Catholic Church. It was this very faith that Holmes turned to now to guide his actions.

I was to learn that his willingness to do so at this particular time, was in fulfillment of a secret vow that he had made to Professor Moriarty, a vow that had played no small role in the abandonment by the Professor of his pending plan to revenge himself upon England through the agency of the Black Formosa Corruption, a disease carried by the giant rats of China and of the Indonesian archipelago. That Holmes did not pursue direct retaliation in kind did not mean that he had no intention at all of dealing with the issue of Roger Baskerville that had been thrust again upon us. Evil that cannot be eliminated may at least be contained within bounds to minimize its harm.

Holmes thought that by returning Baskerville to British Honduras that he had provided those bounds. Now it appeared that even the salary and respectability of a position with the British government could not contain that man's ambitions and that he would still use any means to gain and hold onto power. Age had not dulled the early greed and cupidity of his nature, but only caused it to grow and fester in his dark soul. As painful as it was to Holmes to use his full powers against a kinsman of his friend, Sir Henry, he had been finally brought to the conclusion that the dark curse of Sir Hugo Baskerville had in Roger Baskerville again asserted itself. Whatever had been boyish and charming within him was now twisted into that deformation of soul that leads to eternal damnation.

There was a time when I could not speak intelligently on topics such as these. But now as I write these words in 1917 I have a more enlightened knowledge of theology than that which I possessed at the time of the events that I am recounting here. I will therefore include an extract from a contribution that I once made to a theological journal:

It should be noted that whether in such extreme cases these souls may be turned back in their final hour or perhaps even within the very shades of death itself is an undecided and hence a vexed question for the theologian. The Catholic Church offers its suffrages and prayers for all souls with hope of their salvation, but in the final analysis such a soul is beyond both the teaching and the ministry of the Church and must be assigned solely to its creator.

The mission of the Church is not to condemn but to offer its prayers and the sacraments entrusted to its care, while the community of the Church may be of aid through prayer and sacrifice. Its mission is that of the Communion of Saints, which embraces even the souls in Purgatory. At the gates of hell its mission is at an end, for it may not traverse and emerge unscathed from that grim region, one guarded not by Cerberus, but by the even more fearful demons that usher into their own dark realm the souls of the eternally lost.

Even God cannot alter the nature of hell (for it is a condition not of His making) but insofar as it is a region and a place, no effective bar can exclude God's presence even there. It is this which is the fire of hell to the devil and those who live under his dominion. These have lost all freedom, having chosen to lose it in bondage to the continuing torture of the acceptance of a limited good as their final end. That limited good once deprived of God as its source and destination can no longer return each element of existence to God in gratitude and praise.

Instead, that limited good, in whatsoever form it may manifest and until set in its proper relation to God, grows sullen and withered until it becomes the nothingness out of which it was summoned into being by the breath of life, which is the Holy Spirit of God. The lost soul then is left finally with only a shadow of its misguided aspirations. It looks about itself and finds only creatures similarly deluded gazing in puzzlement and rage at the paltry and dusty skins now empty of both wine and joy.

There reigns in hell a bitter laughter at each soul's plight in which mercy and compassion are excluded. Each soul scorns the other as a greater fool than itself. Yet it will not turn back to God, but turns instead to what has been lost of its former pleasures. Even more is this true for a nature that was once angelic. As the nature of an angel is greater than that of human nature, the lost souls fear the fallen angels because of the shadow of what they once were. It is that fear which leads them to obey the devil and his minions and to join their efforts to his; not in community, for only love can bind souls together into community, but instead in a great choir of cacophony and absurdity, which is the music of hell. The outer edges of hell must resemble a ragged wound with souls not so much wicked as trivial: gossipmongers, proud society matrons, selfish employers, women whose beauty leads only to a sour rule over the passions of men, and men who use their money to debauch just such women. These are less wicked than they are foul, like a film floating upon a stagnant pool. But then all talk of hell must of necessity be metaphorical and the prudent soul desires no further acquaintance with it the better to describe or paint his subject. The prudent soul behaves as St. Philip Neri advised: that in the presence of evil one is well advised simply to run away.

Sherlock Holmes however had not run away in obedience to this wise counsel. He had instead spent his life and professional career confronting evil and his great journal had even attempted to describe its confines and to find a true solution to the problem of evil in the light of Christian doctrine. I had also in my own way addressed evil in its more physical manifestations as a doctor treating microbes and the twisted flesh that the presence of physical disease often leaves behind.

I believe that each of us learned that we could not hope to see the end of evil in our lives. Each of us knew finally that it is the task of every man and woman to fight against evil, but with the knowledge that only God may adequately deal with it and even then only through the final efficacy of the suffering and death of Jesus Christ.

It is not that evil may ever hope to rival God in power (as the Zoroastrians and the Manicheans believe) but that God's goodness is seen precisely in the manner with which He deals with evil. As Christians we are taught to deal with evil along similar lines with Jesus Christ; for this reason it is natural for a Christian to die a martyr's death. The Emperor Nero fed Christians to the beasts in the Roman arena. Christians will always be fed to one beast or another, for the devil goes about like a roaring lion seeking someone to devour, even while Jesus Christ and His Church go about like a shepherd looking for the lost sheep. These divergent activities comprise the entire course of world history and the soul must choose in which camp to abide forever.

I return now to a transcription of the journal, a journal of secret revelations, a probing into the dark soul and hidden motivations of Professor Moriarty and of the surprising revelation of how Holmes prepared for a reunion with me, a meeting as gradual and as unexpected as any ever thrown in my way by Sherlock Holmes.

From the Journal of Sherlock Holmes

October 6, 1893
Home again at Grimpen

I am home, yet I have contacted no one. I need to assemble my thoughts after witnessing first the quiet of monastic life and then being plunged into the rabbit warren of the poverty ridden streets of Dublin. My cottage here in Grimpen more than ever seems to resemble a ship sailing on the sea of the moors. After my recent crossing of the Irish Sea to Holyhead I seem still to feel the surge of the waves rising beneath me and it is surely something more than fancy that makes me think that the ridges of the moorland will soon break into motion and come crashing down upon me.

Watson once compared the workings of my mind to the delicate machinery of an intricate timepiece or a delicate optical instrument. I believe that his comparison was an apt one. It is a peculiarity of any such finally tuned mechanism that the conditions under which it is employed are narrow and specific. In my own case I knew early on in life that I require a freedom from supervision and oversight in order to reach judgments that might contradict the general expectations of mankind and the chaos of the public clamor that surrounds me. I am jealous not only of my time but of my location and the freedom to alter it at will.

It may therefore seem a strange claim to make, but I believe that I am essentially invisible at my lodgings in Baker

Street. The reading public may consider me to be a hopeless cocaine addict and be aware that I am in the habit of keeping my tobacco in the toe of a Persian slipper, and my personal correspondence affixed by a knife to the mantelpiece, but I dare say that many of my inner dispositions have escaped notice. By concentrating upon colorful but minute elements Watson has created a smokescreen of irrelevant detail behind which I can maintain the personal privacy that is a passion with me. At the same time Watson has made me appear sufficiently formidable that few people care to invite my own inquiry by keeping too close a watch upon my private affairs. Thus even my comings and goings in disguises of various sorts through the years have not drawn undue attention to me. I prefer my life to be like a polarized glass which admits light in only one direction.

My assumed *nom de plume* of Sigerson during my recent travels is an example of my passion to maintain the scope necessary for a private life. It is a dictum of mine that the best way to hide an object is to place it in plain sight but to alter some aspect of its presentation so that viewed out of its normal context it is essentially unidentifiable. The skill of the selection and placement of facts after all is my métier as a detective. A corollary of this is that one who does not know how to hide things well will not find it easy to find things that are hidden by others. My observations of life make it quite evident that as life becomes more intricate, the zone of privacy allowed one by society becomes proportionately diminished. I find the prospect of this to be appalling. Though social control and hence civilization may appear to grow more certain under the impact of compulsory disclosure, the question remains as to whether the social order will not then so predominate over the realm allotted to the personal that no room will remain to lead a quiet and unobstructed life according to one's own beliefs and standards.

Since I have always believed that genius must exceed the prevailing standard of the times in which we live I believe also that innovation is stifled by conformity. What better way could ever be devised to ensure conformity than to demand a comprehensive and continual disclosure of one's thoughts, values, and commitments as they unfold over time? What engine can hope to pull so long a train? The old adage that he travels fastest who travels alone is *a propos* here. I prefer not to have a curious public situated in imagination behind my armchair. I prefer to listen to the tales of distraught clients without imagining how my subsequent actions may be reduced later and transformed or dramatized to make an entertaining story. What could be a greater distraction or source of bias in the mind of a detective than to have Watson constantly about taking notes? Nor do I need public applause for any successes that I may have achieved as a detective.

For these reasons I have kept Watson's discretion severely limited and only allowed him to publicize my more arcane and bizarre cases. I have hidden whatever real talents I possess beneath an outward mask of being a brilliant but essentially harmless eccentric, one who is ready to dash off at any hour of the day or night in order to pursue the few cases that come my way from governesses and commissionaires. The astonishing thing is that the public has come to believe that I am exactly as I have been portrayed by Watson. What upon reflection could be more absurd? After all one does not find a blue carbuncle in the crop of every goose that one meets waddling down the country roads! By appearing so unique and specialized my general utility to Scotland Yard has been masked by the convenient fiction that the various inspectors do not respect me or I them. Thus I am assumed to have been free to take on cases of greater moment from time to time, but only at the cost of the assumption that I seldom work for a client who can afford to pay me anything. It is my profound hope that when I return to practice that I will take on more cases with an international scope that will have an impact upon public events. Of course these cases are precisely the very ones that must be hushed up. No doubt the public will always presume that I am ill-paid and live off what Watson can make as a writer or that I receive the wherewithal of living from some other source perhaps even less flattering. At times I have received word of various speculations as embarrassing as they were unfounded. My penchant for disguise has at times only added fuel to the fire.

It has therefore been an unaccustomed benefit of my present hermetic existence that I have been able to live beyond scrutiny. I am so satisfied with my present retreat here that I can well imagine remaining here indefinitely; to heave-to so to speak and to ride these waves of quiet moorland has a definite appeal to me at this time of my life. I do not wish to be ground up in the grist-mill of everyday events. The habit of silent thought followed by reflection in the quiet pages of this journal has grown upon me with the years. What philosopher has ever prospered in the cacophony of the public square? Such philosophers sooner or later share the fate of Socrates. Having been so long a peripatetic wanderer across the face of the earth, how much do I long now to rest, to stand still, and to find that stable point of my own certitude, the Greenwich Mean Time of my own solitary soul.

My long hiatus from London is ended, but was there ever any point to it after all? What is any human life but a series of observations, each as transient as the last, yet each deflecting and changing the pattern that might be woven by events in a different manner had fate decreed otherwise. What if this long series of journeys had never occurred? In my youth I imagined that my life would assume an order and a structure consisting of various certitudes with no time spent in detours. The road ahead would lie straight before me and each minor goal would be able to sustain a larger overall purpose. Each day would add a marginal increment to what had been already done and the whole would display that remarkable symmetry of function and proportion that we call beauty. I could not imagine then that what I would discover in my middle years was that I had built a structure composed of partially attained objects and that the only unifying concept of my life has been my faith in the Catholic Church.

Yet at times I wonder if a center point can even be found there. What is the history of the Church but a visible sign of the resistance of mankind to God even within the Church? In the dance of changing circumstances the Church has often been led whither it would not go. Emperors, Kings, and Barons have pushed and prodded for Papal sanction of their schemes to attain and preserve power. In the course of this many popes have succumbed as victims of poison and intrigue. At times it has only been the bare promise of God not to abandon the Church that has called the Church in time back to itself.

If the Roman Catholic Church is the Bride of Christ she has not always been one that any spouse would care to take into His home. The Church has not been immune to struggles for power and worldly honors. Many have been scandalized by the acquisition of riches and the splendor with which the cathedrals are encrusted. But would any material redistribution of the Church's resources end forever the problem of civic want? Is that not finally the business of nations and of economics to achieve? The business of the Catholic Church is to govern the spiritual order of mankind and conform it to Christ and to awaken a general charity in mankind. If the Church was co-extensive with the temporal order would it not soon be caught up in the struggles between nations? Where then would be its political neutrality and its universal call to the many diverse opinions of mankind to be reconciled in Christ?

How then should my life display an order and perfection denied even to the Catholic Church? Yet I would still have it so. I would lay all things down before the bar of reason and hold court there and my own mind would decipher the drifts and flows and ebbs of time and trace causation backwards to that divine simplicity and perfection that only needed to say, *"Let there be light, and there was light."* Why, I now ask myself, should I be allowed such great power over all things as to judge and weigh them in the scale of my own intellect? Perhaps these pages carry more of heresy than of pious reflections.

It was in the temerity of my youth that I first thought that God demanded that I should be certain about all things. This has made of my life a prolegomenon to actually living until I find in my middle years that I have barely begun to live an individualized and actual existence. I feel that I am a mere library and compendium of the actions of others. Even my sins are more the sins of omission than of commission. Even my follies are at second hand. My mind is like a dusty attic or a collector's museum filled with neglected monuments. My grand synthesis forever eludes me so that each year I add on to my collection of facts and assemble a few more partial chains with links that seem strong enough; but how to connect them into one uninterrupted chain that leads back to God and forward to the realization of all things eludes me still. So I am left in the end with no general solution to the problem of human existence.

Even my faith leaves so much unexplained and I know that I will cross the threshold of death without certainty but only hope that there is a God after all and that my life will be judged kindly by Him. I have always feared that God might say to me at the fin al judgment that there was a parallel life that I might have led and that by missing an initial turning point I never found my way back to that one original life existing in the mind of God that alone was assigned to me and upon which my salvation rested. But then, perhaps God desires only that we strive onwards and that it is God Himself that weaves whatever perfection is to be ours from the imperfect strands of events. In any case it is my present desire that I may play a role and find a favored place in God's design for my life so that even my sins may have served some purpose.

Each year, but mostly during these last years of my wandering, I have realized more deeply that the mind of man cannot conceive a general solution to the problem posed by its own existence. Even Immanuel Kant was distinguished above all else by his frank admission of what cannot be known by human reason. We live in a spot of light, surrounded by darkness, seeking purpose behind the phantasmagoria of circumstance. Even the everyday men guided by their senses seem more honest than men like Professor Moriarty and me, men who demand a solution to all things. This pride is surely our downfall.

Perhaps this is why each of us understands the other. Perhaps each of us hopes that if he should fail to solve the great puzzle of human destiny, then he might turn for a solution to the other. If this is so, then my own conclusions may be ones that he may be brought to share at last, for I see no other source where we will find common ground. My conclusion is that we are doomed to the particular and that men make their greatest errors when they pursue generalities. True virtue, it seems to me, is to accept the limitations of one's particular existence in time and place and to accept as well that strange conglomeration of thought and passion that sets each of us apart from our fellows. We are condemned to solitude and uniqueness so that our witness to others must be ours alone. Perhaps it was with this reason in mind that Jesus queried his disciples by asking them, *"But you; who do you say that I am?"* This question shows decisively that any relationship to God demands some individual action of affirmation on our part, that God can only be God-for-us if we choose to make Him so. God allows us to determine our own eternal fate by choosing either to enter into relation with him or not to do so. Heaven is described as a wedding feast for the reason that it involves a betrothal of the soul to God. In the end it all comes down to love and not to causation and links of chains such as the physicist believes. Religion is not physics but a matter of relationship from the within to the within.

This was what that brilliant Danish philosopher, Soren Kierkegaard, realized when he said that "truth is subjectivity." Man attains his own proper end only in relationship to God and he realizes that end only within his own awareness of his aloneness without God. Our very structure as humans lies in our contingent will! God is not an object to be known, but a subject to whom we choose to relate! For this reason, I should not lament now that my life is incomplete and that I judge it now to be inadequate for any purpose that I once intended.

What after all was my jejune intention but a legacy of the desire to be like God knowing good and evil, to be the one after all who is to approve or to disapprove of the pattern of my life. The truth lies elsewhere, for is God alone who has the right to validate the soul. God does this by seeing in each soul a participation in Jesus Christ the Beloved through whom and for whom all things came into being. It is Christ alone who restores what was lost and would be forever lost without the intervention of the Trinity.

It has been the belief that each of us must complete himself without God and to be his own source and destination that has made of history one vast nightmare. Again and again we see the universal refusal to see the world and ourselves as God sees us. Our tiny cinder of power snatched from the blaze of divinity is coveted and contained within our own miniscule darkness. We blow upon the ember and attempt to illumine the world with our science, our arts, and our governing structures, but we are like an ape grimacing into a bit of mirror and all we see at last is only a reflection of ourselves. If we truly wish to find God, we must look behind that bit of mirror that blocks and monopolizes the scope of our view. We shall then find God at our side where he has always remained only waiting for us to turn to Him again who alone is worthy of our contemplation.

October 7, 1893
Grimpen

esterday I hinted at the motive for my excursion to Ireland. I had hoped to find there some particular thing upon which to base my approach to Professor Moriarty. Unfortunately I found only Ireland in its perennial condition still bearing witness to the policies applied there by the ruling English government. Ireland represents above all things the particularity of the human condition when stripped down to its bare essentials. Ireland may be said to define poverty just as the desert defines Arabia. The condition of human life when stripped bare of the accoutrements of gentility and the technical devices that increase the value of exports is one of extreme vulnerability. The so-called natural life as the philosopher Thomas Hobbes once said is Indeed what we refer to as the problem of physical evil is simply the resistance of nature to be subservient to our will and convenience. That this resistance is sometimes violent and horrific in nature and extent has been a source of scandal to many thinkers such as Voltaire who wrote of the great Lisbon earthquake.

Is nature explained as the result of a fallen world occasioned by human sinfulness? If not then why is our will so unlike that of God? For God to will a thing is to see it accomplished. There is no intervening labor, no gradual accretion over time. Why then does not God simply set all things right by fiat? Is human freedom so valuable that the forces of nature should be allowed to provide such extreme and arbitrary resistance to the instantaneous and complete realization of any larger plan that God might entertain as a reward for our moral development? Or is such physical resistance merely an alternative setting for some larger drama taking place on an entirely different level of existence? (The Book of Job hints as much). Why is our nature not nearer to that of the angels, possessing merely a disembodied spiritual nature? Why force human beings to encounter so many trials rather than simply balancing the moral account books in heaven in some less onerous and messy manner? Of course this is precisely the position that St. Peter adopted when he urged Jesus to avoid His coming death in Jerusalem and was promptly and even harshly corrected.

Still we dream of an earthly paradise. If all that we observe is a product of mind, then why should God burden creation with the physical at all? Why these planets and suns at the further end of the universe from us? For God of course all is immediacy, while for us even the light from distant suns may have been traveling since before the pyramids were ever built. What relations have such vast spaces to us who are dwarfed by mere mountains upon the earth? If the seas are unplumbed how much more must the vast spaces between galaxies be unfathomable to the mind of man; why then do they exist? If we are already dwarfed by the domestic why import these distant testimonials to our insignificance? If a mere microbe can lay us low then why bury us in volcanic ash or shake the earth beneath our feet or send the cyclone to draw us up into its hideous vortex? Surely the proportionate punishment of whatever original sin we may have committed seems disproportionate to our infantile and groping minds. Or were we once more enlightened beings closer to the angels? If angelic sin plunged so many angels into hell, then perhaps we chose or were allowed by God to plunge into matter as some sort of intermediate stage to perdition. Perhaps the entire material world is only a narrow ledge separating us from a darker fate that might have been ours. Perhaps we are balanced above unknown and depthless abysses of darkness or are floating upon a tiny fragment of a shattered universe with yawning abysses of nothingness just waiting to claim us once again if we are not saved by God. Is what we call the problem of physical evil then really a remarkable mercy shown to us to stem the onward course of our initial folly in seeking to be like God knowing good and evil?

Is what the German philosopher Leibniz once called the best of all possible worlds not a world at all but instead a rope thrown across an infinite space to reach us where we hang suspended above eternal ruin? What do we know of our pre-existence? Perhaps the story of the Garden of Eden was really an extrapolation into the inaccessible past of what must have occurred to account for our present state. If so is that tale better read as a matter of intuition rather than of actual history? I have no answer to this, nor perhaps has anyone. The Catholic Church inherited the Old Testament and construed it as best it could when no other data was available. The New Testament emerges in intimate relation with all that went before.

As for other religions they must take the human condition as they find it without explanation. Philosophy is more removed still; it is quite enough for the philosopher to deal with our own evils, those that are attributable to the darkness of our own hearts and to leave unanswered the question of the nature of reality as we find it. Philosophy must discern some purpose to make us depend upon one another for the aid that heaven scorns to offer.

In the absence of more ready comforts, the great spiritual seekers of the soul have always sought out, not the beautiful places of the earth, but rather have gone out into the desert to seek God. The great religions do not seem to originate in the fertile regions of the earth but from desert places where man is forced to confront his condition without the soothing balm of the beneficent earth, places where the bounty of nature is confined to only a few meager date palms. The Irish had no date palms but only the humble potato for sustenance and the dried turf of the bog-lands to provide warmth for the hearth. They have had little else than these and their volubility in poetry and song as a national heritage to give them joy.

The particular poverty of the people of Ireland is why they have always been a religious people. They share this disposition with the suffering people of Russia. The comfort of the Irish has always been in their possession of the Catholic faith. Nothing, the cynic would imply, so disposes mankind to religion as dissatisfaction with its present state. But perhaps it is the Irish hunger for a state of plentitude and grace and beauty that leads them to value what the Church has always promised in its reliance upon God. I hope to show Moriarty that the very source of his great anger against England is perhaps also the path to his own happiness. Yes, even Professor Moriarty could be made happy!

His hooded eyes, his stooped shoulders, his entire physical being has always shown me that he labors beneath a great burden. That burden was the early loss of perhaps the only love that he has ever known, that of his dear mother who has been dead these many years. If I might recall to his mind that love, I might show him that love forgives all things and asks for no vengeance. Vengeance actually re-commits the original sin that leads to the death of the beloved Son of God. The message of the gospel is that God seeks no vengeance, but surrenders even the Beloved Second Person of The Trinity to the vengeance of sinners so that they might be saved. The forgiveness of sin asks only that one love God more than one loves one's sin since all sin is actually misappropriated love.

Sin is best conceived as sin-for-us, for what sin in itself does is to block out the action of God in our lives. Sin is then a false absolute. The objective and the subjective components of sin cannot be separated except analytically. Every action is a composite and can be perceived as a whole yet that action is composed of elements. If any element is lacking, then the complete evil effect cannot be realized. Nor can individual sins be seen as distinct events, but in themselves constitute a larger complex or field, which determines future actions. In this manner of speaking a pastor of souls is more engaged in diagnosis rather than accountancy. Sins are not so much counted as weighed in the balance and found wanting in their corresponding deprivation of the good that might have been present but was not.

I believe that this is the key to reach Professor Moriarty. He loves his vengeance; yet it poisons him from within himself! Moriarty is his own disease! Shall Moriarty become then another man like the infamous Trevelyan who considered that the great famine was a solution to the Irish problem? He rejoiced that the rebellious Irish were finally being weeded out by a visitation that he thought was sent by God to work that benefit for the English people. I do not know which condition of soul is more deplorable; to possess a faith like Trevelyan's faith or to possess Moriarty's professed atheism. In practice they are one and the same; both yield evil. Each begins with a generality that allows the soul to avoid the particular. Great evils always overlook the harm that they do to individuals and in that they show their evil design. There is nothing is as predictive of evil in the end as the desire to do great things at the cost of what it regards as little things!

October 10, 1893
Grimpen

I have just re-read my last line in the previous entry of my journal. The desire to great things, is that not the entire purpose and motive of one of the greatest religious orders in the Church, the Society of Jesus, commonly called the Jesuits? If I condemn the desire to do great things, do I not doom not only that order but all Christians to mediocrity? The realization of the problem of Christian ambition does not preclude great actions, but instead focuses the mind upon the action of grace, what St. Ignatius calls in his great book, *"The Spiritual Exercises,"* The Rules for the Discernment of Spirits. The individual soul does not exist in untrammeled freedom in this world. At each moment of one's life one is beset by multiple possibilities, suggestions, dispositions, and actions mediated by the spiritual realm. While God alone has direct access to the soul, the Evil One is allowed some measure of freedom over the mind and the senses and can influence and propose things from outside the human will. This measured activity of the enemy of our human nature may not compromise the fact of human freedom, which proceeds from within the soul, but it may besiege the soul with illusions and seductions.

Realizing this power of evil over each soul, St. Ignatius included in his book of spiritual exercises, means that might be employed to distinguish between the impulses of the soul so as to adhere to the will of God and to resist the suggestions of the Evil One. One of those rules explains how the Evil One begins by proposing something under the aegis of the good so that the well-motivated soul seems justified in choosing it; but then the Evil One gradually leads the soul astray into vanity and ambition, not for the glory of God, but for itself.

The greater glory of God alone must always be the goal of our actions in both small and large affairs, but particularly when the prospect exists of public acclaim or in cases where complex actions with unpredictable effects are involved. In attempting great things the soul is apt to forget its own propensity for evil and to lose itself in illusions of self-sufficiency. For this reason all schemes to produce a better world that proceed without reliance upon and final reference to God as their inspiration and end only tend to add to the burden of human confusion and misery in this life. I appeal to history as the best testimony to support this assertion.

So it is that I pray that I may be spared the burden of history in my own actions. In my dealings with clients I am allowed to focus on what may be called the particularity of evil. Often I am presented with a unique situation where the equities may be balanced apart from the crudity of mere legal norms. I for one have never assumed that legal recognition bestows legitimacy, for too often the civil authority has long since forgotten the primacy of

God. Positive law must be in accord with the revealed laws of God and with natural law if it is to be valid, as Thomas Aquinas so rightly observes. Even the power of Kings is predicated on the fact of anointing by the will of God and an absolute duty of the monarch to exercise his power for the common good. Without that distinction power is simply the rule of force, mindless and cruel, and as apt to destroy the giver of laws as the people whom he oppresses by his arbitrary conduct. All conduct must therefore be termed arbitrary that does not find sanction in the objective order of truth whose very source is God.

The concept of the people as the source of sovereignty, which has been adopted by the Americans is correct insofar as it recognizes the common good as the directive of sovereigns; but it is metaphysically speaking in error because it assumes that the amorphous mass of the populace can ever determine its own good. The common good is not equivalent to the common will, even when the latter may be ascertained, for the mass of men may will whatever violates the good and the true as determined by God just as may any individual. Evil may often govern mass movements precisely because there is no locus of reflection and responsibility in the mass. Mass movements are usually exercises in simplification in which distinctions are obscured in order to serve a mythological pseudo-God or a temporary idol of the people. For this reason, just as ambition is to be forsworn by individual souls who wish to avoid evil, so should nations avoid ambition as well, for out of that ambition flow the evils of war and the desire for conquest and domination.

I will venture so far as to say that all rulers should approach the throne of power on their knees and beating their breasts because it will not be long until the possession of power alters them before their very eyes and they will seem to themselves to cease to be what they in fact are at last: poor weak flesh that is prone to the continuing legacy of Original Sin. To flee from power then is not cowardice but the exercise of prudence for one's own salvation. Even spiritual power has this danger about it and no man would dare to accept the Keys of St. Peter and become Pope if he did not know that the entire Church prays for him in daily mass so that he may discharge the burdens of his office without imperiling his own immortal soul.

All that I have said of course was said by Jesus when he warned his disciples: from the one to whom much is given much will be required. I am content to follow the further advice of our Lord to take the lowest place at the table of salvation as long as I may be included in the Wedding Feast of Heaven at last. If I should be the last admitted through the portals of the Divine King before they close forever, it is enough for me. If I am to be anything more, let it be solely as God wills and no more.

Yet I do not wish to fall into the parallel heresy of Quietism by stating this. The soul is obliged to follow where God leads and to accept a higher place if one is led there. Salvation is not the fruit of mere inertia and self-abnegation. Thus spiritual discernment is of the very essence of human life and for this reason the life of prayer is the *sine qua non* for very thought and action throughout the day and even at the final hour of Compline when the weary soul prays along with the whole Catholic Church:

"Brethren, be sober be watchful for your adversary the devil goeth about like a roaring lion seeking someone to devour. Resist him steadfast in the faith. Now oh Lord you may dismiss your servant in peace for my eyes have seen the glory that is Israel.

May no nightly fears or fantasies come to trouble our slumbers; may we watch with Christ and rest in peace, and may all the souls of the faithful departed through the mercy of God rest in peace,

Amen."

October 11, 1893
Grimpen

The question of sufficiency for salvation is one that must trouble the hearts of all thinking men and women. What is this perennial drive that leads some men to an excess of accumulation and the others to an equally perennial sense of their own inadequacy? Why has slavery and servitude, not only of the body but of the spirit, played such a role in human societies throughout all of history? Do not some seek out servitude merely to escape the burden of decision, of quarrying forth out of their own mind, heart, and spirit some measure of the values by which to live?

Perhaps happiness is only found by filtering our perceptions through the mind of another by receiving good spiritual counsel. Until then our deepest thoughts and convictions remain mere fleeting phantoms within our own bottomless solitude. Nothing in man is sufficient to ground us in our own being without God. The common oath, "As God is my witness," says more than it intends. Perhaps God alone is an adequate witness of the efforts of each man to make something of himself— to seek and to find something adequate to redeem the vanity of his days and hours. Man is obsessed by nothingness, the certain knowledge that after death (and even in many cases before death) all that he has ever owned or been will dissolve back into their primal elements and be dispersed to sustain and enable other uses. What are monuments to supposed heroes but the statuary of our collective vanity?

As I review my own life, I see how much of what I have been has been determined by my father's life. He was a man from that post-revolutionary era now called the age of the great romantics, the heirs of the optimism of the French Enlightenment. He could only consent to accept life on his own terms. When he wed my mother he believed that she, in her beauty and nobility, would be the perfect matriarch, the source of his dynasty. He was both a builder and a collector. It was he who brought investors together to build a railroad south from Northumberland to the halt at Sigerside and on across the empty moors to Whitby. It was he who rejoiced in producing three sons to carry on his name. All that he accomplished was laid in tribute at my mother's feet. Everything seemed possible to them as a couple and then she became ill and died before her time.

Daily he had watched her fading from his sight. The sound of her coughing became torture to him and he fled his own home on horseback to seek the solitude of the empty moors as his only comfort. His frightened three sons remained at home, afraid to speak, not knowing what to say. We were isolated from each of our parents, from our mother lest we contract her illness and from our father by his own stubborn refusal to admit that life was not cooperating with his great plans.

Then one winter she simply died. The light went out of our lives. Sherringford was sent off to university first and soon after Mycroft was sent to Harrow. But it was my fate to remain in that great and empty house. I cannot count the times that I sought out my father's gaze at dinner, the times that I sought some recognition for the little puzzles that I had managed to solve, or to approve one of those constructions that so occupy young boys. At last I grew to feel that I was like a ghost wandering alone along those cold and empty halls with only the few remaining servants to keep me company and lend an encouraging smile to my little enterprises.

So it was that when I left home at last it was as one who flees from a legacy of cold and death. Yet I could not leave England and flee to France or Italy immediately though I often dreamed of doing so. I was condemned to remain year after year and to seek my father's approval before anything that I accomplished had any substance in my own eyes. Only gradually did I come to see that his disapproval was in an inverse proportion to my need of his esteem. My demonstrations of affection were mere parlor games to him. Indeed it was not until Watson came into my life that I found anyone who was able to see the full measure of what I had prepared myself to be. It is for that reason that Watson has always been invaluable to me and why I have quietly resented this ridiculous predilection of his for marriage. Undoubtedly I have been selfish in this regard, but in my own defense and in the blessed solitude of this journal I can confess my terror of admitting my need. Yes terror, for what else can one term the gnawing pain that pursues me night and day. It is a pain of the inner spirit of man that seeks redemption now, not behind the sable curtains of death, but now this very day. We seek ultimately the approval of our God, but will settle for the esteem of men and women if that is the best that we can attain. Such an excess of need is felt as shame. At times nothing will do for me but to be off, to feel like Melville's Ishmael the sea wind in my face, but ever with relentless tread I feel my own insufficiency like a great hound baying at my heels!

Can anything be enough to sate its ghastly maw? The mind alone has been for me an anodyne for such pain. So it is that I have sought in the horrors and tragedies of other people's lives some reminder that my own experience of life is not peculiar to myself. Yet at times I am beset with a global contempt for my own image in the glass and, God forgive me, unable to see the dignity and worth of those who are about me in the great crowds of London. At such times I see in my fellow human beings only the dull lowing of cattle rather than human pain. Life seems unworthy at such times of even taking another breath. If ever any eyes other than my own shall read these words, they will know the force that has driven me abroad these past three years seeking I know not what.

Is it God that I have been seeking or simply a version of myself that I can accept at last? Watson once said of me that when I took up the study of crime, the stage had lost a great actor. Alas, if he but knew I have never ceased to act! My life is the story of one fleeing into the personae of other's lives. The secret of my method is my ability to so infuse my own self into the mind of the criminal that I can see how he must have acted. The secret of detection lies within the imagination. More than that it lies in the ability to suspend all prior conceptions and prejudices, to see that multiple worlds surround us and that each man or woman is perhaps like me condemned to his or her own dark island of solitude and pain. We inhabit adjoining cells in the prison of this earth and only in the occasional brief intersection of human sympathy do we feel the touch of charity and the relief of compassion. Beyond this we have only the all-embracing silence of the spheres, the mute heavens, and the occasional touch of God to heal the great wound of our being.

October 12, 1893
Grimpen

My post-return solitude is ended. Sir Henry heard that I have returned so he sent his man over to invite me to a homecoming reception at Baskerville Hall to be held in my honor. It was a small affair with just a few friends, but it was festive for all of that. The guests consisted of Dr. Mortimer, Mr. Franklin and his daughter, and the Baskervilles. After the Spartan fare I enjoyed at the monastery it was a real joy to partake of some proper English cheeses, roast venison, a savory pork pie, and even a plum pudding for dessert. We all adjourned after our meal to the drawing room, ladies as well as gentlemen.

There over glasses filled with Madeira I told them that I planned soon to leave Devonshire and to resume my practice as a detective in London. The dangers that once made it imperative that I seek refuge abroad were no longer to be feared and such was the state of my finances that renewed labor was imperative if I would restore my fortunes to their former state. I declined the kind offer of Sir Henry for me to act as the manager of the Baskerville estate. I assured him that my own particular gifts did not include the skills of a manager and that I required the unusual and unexpected problems that presented themselves for solution in my practice as a detective to keep my own nervous temperament in balance.

I also need the companionship of my good friend, Dr. John H. Watson, to be again at my side as I trust he soon shall be. Mycroft has made inquiries and has informed me that the good Doctor will be home by Christmas. He will no doubt take over again his medical practice in Kensington, but I trust that he will still have time to aid me in my own cases for I can hardly imagine proceeding without him. It is in anticipation of laying the facts before him that I am led to overlook nothing of importance. He is an essential part of my own mental methods. I have vowed to tell him so, though such confidences are embarrassing to me and perhaps to him also. We have always retained a certain formality in our relations as master and pupil, which I trust I may soon remedy as a partial penance for my neglect of the dear fellow in recent years. If I can only prevail upon him to see how necessary has been this quest of mine, I know that his own good heart will forgive me for not taking him into my confidence until the most pressing matters were resolved.

I have one duty still which must be completed before I return to London. I must beg one final audience with Professor Moriarty and tell him of my Irish venture on his behalf. Though he may not be grateful, he may at least grant me a hearing and I trust that my final formulation may, with God's help, penetrate even his own adamantine soul at last. After that I will see what the coming years may bring.

I know that I shall miss Devonshire when I leave, but I may return for the holidays and perhaps introduce Watson to the domestic joys of Devon and of Cornwall. I think often of how pleasant it would be to be able to live a life of placid scholarship here and to go about with the pick and brushes of the archeologist with Dr. Mortimer, who as ever is filled with talk of barrows, tombs, and excavations. But life's joys must often be delayed in the name of duty and I must take solace at being again in London to enjoy the offerings of the London winter season, with its plays and concerts. Then there is the excellent bill of fare at Simpsons. Ah well, I must soon bid my friends farewell for a time. I took my dog-cart home tonight after our celebration through the falling leaves. The scent of the burning logs in the great fireplaces at the hall had infused the late evening air with that peculiar incense that always awakens in me more of joy than of sadness. The first line of Shelley's "Ode to the West Wind," kept echoing in my mind. "Oh wild west wind, thou breath of autumn's being." Are my own leaves, like the poet's, "falling like thy own?" I write this entry by my own fireside looking deep into the flames and embers and wondering what the future may bring.

October 13, 1893
Grimpen

My autumnal mood of last night has persisted today. The year is waning quickly and harvest time has come. I am seeing Devon at its most beautiful season when the furze grows rich and golden and the leaves on the poplars turn into yellow flames while the oaks turn red or copper colored and shake in the autumn winds. The gales of winter have not yet arrived to send the leaves flying to their winter sleep so the entire landscape is peaceful as though a painting was being shown consisting of a great garden of bog and rock and tor. My walks take me over the moorlands that are, thank God, no longer fearfully haunted by the great hound that once spread dread and fear to the neighboring hamlets. It has passed as all legends do when seen in the clear light of day. But all legends are based upon some underlying fact. Perhaps even the fairy-folk said to dwell beneath the burial mounds of Devon were the ancient Celts and Druids who held sway here before the Romans and the Normans made colonies of these lands.

England like Ireland has known the presence of many invaders. What nation has ever known a course of long uninterrupted freedom? The history of the world is the history of the subjugation of peoples. The desire to exact vengeance upon the oppressor lies deep within us all. In this regard Professor Moriarty is not different from the rest of men. His only difference lies in the unique power of his intellect that may be designing a truly fiendish act of retribution. If I cannot get him to abandon his course of action my one great clue will be to look for a means of destroying England that will entail the maximum of pain and suffering for the English people. The blow when it falls will no doubt be sudden and terrifying so that dread and panic will accompany the destruction.

I have written and heard back from Professor Moriarty. He has agreed to see me once more before I return to London to resume my long interrupted life. I shall go over tomorrow and spend the day at least with him and hopefully return soon. I must make what I fear will be my closing argument to him, for in all honesty I cannot think of any stone that I have left unturned. I begin to doubt that I may hope to convince him on the grounds of religion, though I hope to do so, but I may at least prevail by using the argument of our common humanity.

God leaves his writing on our hearts so that all men must feel that within the natural law there is a dim reflection of revealed morality. If no man is a mere beast (and I still trust that he is not), then he must be able to at least intuit a realm of the transcendent in human affairs, which makes sacrifice and compassion to be integral parts of the definition of man. Yet am I haunted still by his physical demeanor that I observed during my last visit. He does not look well. His health was never robust and it seems already that the cold hand of death has placed its hand upon his shoulder.

It is always the presence of death that is the great scandal in human affairs. If the moral man and the immoral man must share the same fate and fade even as the insentient leaves of autumn into a common earth and if time itself effaces even the memory of their actions for good or for ill, then where lies the essential difference between them? Justice demands judgment so that even the pagan mind must desire some code of human actions. Even the atheist must desire some new Code of Hammurabi to govern the coming socialist order of human justice dispensed by human means. But may unaided humans ever discover let alone dispense justice? Is not every legal order only a temporary truce between warring factions within the state? Even the reasoning processes of the law are only a tenuous chain of analogies and often ungrounded assumptions so that the entire legal order, as intricate as it is, is finally like a castle built in the air.

One does not need to be Descartes to doubt all things. Experience of life finally shows us that power is usually the deciding factor in all events and power alas is often possessed not by the wise or virtuous but only by the most ruthless and cunning among us. Is it nay wonder then that a man like Moriarty, convinced of the righteousness of his own cause, will pursue his end in spite of laws and whatever dim sanction of conscience can come from the long and irresolute debate as to the nature of man?

If Professor Moriarty knew that at times I am in sympathy with him and that I share his indignation towards human life itself, would he accept me as just another Colonel Moran and ask me to do his bidding. Watson once remarked that had I wished, I might have been among the first of criminals. Many saints have claimed that had they not been saints, then they would have been among the most deadly foes of God. Even the devil was once an archangel! So perhaps good and evil are in such close relationship as to be interfused so that only God may separate them at last. I have said often in my journal that man can never be like God, knowing good and evil, for the simple reason that as a contingent being he may not determine absolute good and evil, even when they are weighed in the smallest and most accurate scale. Each quality of course will be finally divided at the final judgment and each is to eventually be segregated from each. The entire universe and the course of history is then a great ripping apart of creation. Already the apocalypse is upon us. What is the Holy Mass itself but a great prayer of deliverance from evil and the reception of Christ in the act of communion is the means by which that deliverance takes place. Grace is the universal solvent of the temporal. It is a reagent that reveals all things in the light of God. Yet the world that must receive grace is as stubborn and slow as a recalcitrant donkey led by a stick and the anticipation or memory of its hay in the manger. How to reconcile these two within the portals of eternity! The Final Judgment, when it comes, will no doubt resemble a great cattle fair with souls milling about to find the herd to which they belong, unless that is judgment itself is such as to reveal all things so that the soul must make its own decision in the light of its many life-choices, seen in the context of the choices of all other men and women.

The final legacy of our freedom is to make the choice of heaven or hell. Whatever choice that may be it must require better eyes than those that we possess now. Are all of our present actions then merely indicative of an underlying disposition, or do our acts adhere to us like so much tar or clay so that only in the fires of purgatory may they be removed by the gentle ministrations of God and of the Communion of Saints that joins us to all of humankind? These things exceed our present knowledge, but we may trust that some such order may prevail between God and each individual soul.

October 14, 1893
Grimpen

St. John states that God is love and the one who abides in love abides in God and God in him. This assertion might be the most significant in the gospels. It seems to indicate that for the one who loves that a bridge into heaven has been established, even in this present life. Love prepares a place where God can abide and by the same token God is driven out of the soul that does not love. The Roman Catholic doctrine of sanctifying grace finds its source in this assertion of St. John. Without the presence of God within us we are dependent entirely upon our own nature which is inadequate to sustain us in eternity. The entire concept of eternal damnation is similarly predicated on this lack of divine life in the soul of those who perish in mortal sin. But that any contingent choice can become frozen into an eternal attitude of heart seems to imply that eternity is static and unchangeable. It is far too simplistic to translate a theological insight into the realm of human actions where mixed motives and incomplete cognition call any absolute formula of salvation into question. Can such a non-dynamic vision of eternity be sustained? Is no further light granted to us as our earthly life fails so that the soul may escape from the last lingering illusions that have made sin disproportionately attractive? The merging into eternity may be more gradual than we suppose. The four last things: death, judgment, heaven, and hell that the Catholic Church has insisted we should keep always before our eyes may have overlapping edges in what amounts to a single process of clarification in our ultimate relationship with God. Perhaps the infusion or at least the clear offer of love increases and is most perceptible at precisely the moment when love's eternal denial by the recalcitrant sinner seems to be immanent?

This assumption is not the fruit of our merits or deserts but rather is predicated on the very nature of God who wishes that no one shall be eternally lost. Still a correlative realty must be born in mind: sin hardens the heart, so that the soul can voluntarily weaken its own capacity to appropriate love and to take it within the soul when it is found. Much of theology has gone aground on precisely this issue of just how far a soul may succeed in resisting what is called prevenient grace, a debate that once threatened to divide the Catholic Church.

From a purely psychological point of view this question also poses the problem of what Edgar Allen Poe once termed "the imp of the perverse." That imp is the strange desire present in some individuals, to bring about their own destruction and sometimes the destruction of all who surround them. For such individuals love itself becomes a deadly poison. They flee from what alone may ameliorate their pain. It is not that they do not suffer, but that they seem able in some fashion to become simultaneously both persecutor and victim of their own persecution. They are in this manner able to express their scorn and hatred of the very being that they are as though an aspect of the self were severable and could stand glowering above the one who cowers beneath the lash—yet both are aspects of a single person. What mad delusion is this? Yet what condition is more commonly observed in bars, brothels, and the prison house. At the furthest extreme such madness or alienation from the true self is the phenomenon termed demonic possession. Who can say that such things are not possible? If there exists, as I believe there do, disembodied beings that have become merged in the vast chain of darkness that once termed itself Legion, then why may not a soul become enmeshed and welded to that negativity and hatred even while it still lives on earth so as to be in effect an earthly resident of hell?

This kind of human aberration exceeds the reach of mere argument and appeals to reason, for such people do not seek happiness by any ordinary meaning of that term. Instead their delight is in experiencing and being a conduit for evil and pain.

The soul is stifled beneath suffocating layers of prior experience that have at last corrupted the very appetites of the soul for goodness, truth, and beauty. Instead they are enamored to what brings them only an increase of their agony. The poet John Clare says, *"They flee me that sometimes did me seek."* Perhaps he speaks of the isolation that must finally envelop such souls that seek out with the impetuousness of a lover their own destruction. So dreadful is their aspect that others flee from them. It is then that they construct out of their own desired abandonment a deeper resentment and desire for revenge until even human forgiveness becomes too great an effort for most to exercise in their behalf. Such people finally have only God alone, yet so great is their despair at this point that they turn from even Him. If there is a path to hell, then this is that path and the stages that I have described are its signposts.

It is often lamented that life is as short as it is. But who can look into the faces that one so often meets in the streets of the great cities and not maintain that life is too extended in duration to be endured by many people such as I have just described. Considering the repeated heartache and disappointment that so many of these people are subjected to, how could the human spirit within them survive if it was forced to bear a greater load of memories through extended years of life.

It would be enough if the general indifference of humankind was all that afflicted such a one, but for those whom a misguided apprehension of love may have instilled some primordial suspicion of any efforts made on their behalf, love would be perceived as a flaming sword to which they react with heartlessness, pointless malice, and ingratitude. Hence one need not search far through the asylums or the prisons to find examples of a viciousness and spite that would shame the devil. What are the familiar entertainments of the various lower social strata but those that manifest cruelty, exile, and oversight, each designed to deny the ever-present pain of existence?

It is this truth that leads me to believe that the only ones who can celebrate human nature are those who are never exposed to its actual workings. There are wounds to the spirit that still fester and bleed decades after the initial injury. To harm another willfully where the only advantage to be gained is to imagine the avalanche of sorrow that one has unleashed in another human breast; is that not the greatest of sins? It is when evil becomes an imaginary stairway out of which we attempt to escape our own doubts and feelings of inadequacy that it seems to take on its most salient substance and form. These then become the false treasures of debased and soured natures, which feed like spiders upon us leaving only the desiccated bodies of their victims behind. For these vampires repentance would deny their own natures, nourished as they are by these crimes of the spirit. They resemble murderers and the expression that they wear is identical to those who approach the shadow of the gallows with mockery in their hearts and a hunger for the first embrace of Dante's frigid hell!

Is the Professor one of these? That is not for me to say. I have assumed from the beginning that some dim flame of charity still burns within that benighted frame. I have rested everything upon our shared devotion to reason. Have I been wrong in this assumption? Can reason only lead us to the tall gate of faith yet fail to carry us over the gap at that threshold be it ever so narrow or wide? Perhaps some must plumb in this life the very dregs of suffering before what seems so obvious to most will ever appeal to them, the belief in love and happiness. Here I have come up against the final and ungraspable mystery of evil that perhaps startles even the primordial innocence of God so that all that He can do in the face of it is to suffer with us under its inscrutable influence present in beings that were created in all goodness and for eternity.

October 17, 1893
Grimpen

I have met with the Professor and returned home again! I will try and set down here the course of our conversation and my impressions. It took me a day upon my return simply to allow matters to settle in my own mind, for as in the case of any meeting with such a formidable intellect the experience is one of such intensity that there follows a period of decompression as though one were a miner ascending from the depths of a mineshaft. Professor Moriarty met me as before in his library, a huge room with bookshelves that reached from floor to ceiling. Even a cursory glance informed me that it included volumes on all manner of subjects, particularly on science and philosophy, but also works of theology so that I need not fear that any comments that I might make would take him into regions unknown to him.

"I had thought we had concluded these meetings, Holmes," began the Professor. "It is not that I am averse to seeing you again, but I must advise you that you are on the wrong tack if you intend to dissuade me from my plans by converting me to superstition. It has taken the Roman Church two thousand years to assemble its many doctrines into a loosely connected whole only to run into truth at last and have the whole thing exposed as an embroidery of rationalizations resting upon unverifiable occurrences. It begins with the improbable and ends with the impossible. But for your edification let me sum it all up as I see it before you begin so as to save time."

"The belief in any beings called gods is quite evidently a universal human preoccupation since every culture tends to create them at some stage of their development. The collective psyche goes through predictable stages of development just as is the case in individual development. Just as the child must believe in some benevolent parental figure to allay its anxieties and to supply its needs, the social fabric is similarly inclined toward belief in some superior lawgiver or protector to provide a base for social development. Since this process is universal why should we believe that the peculiar god of the Jews is an exception and that this god alone actually exists?"

"Even the concept of a single God as a unifying concept and source for all other things requires a leap from the known order of things into the transcendent with no reason to suppose that such a leap is even necessary, but in any case the mere fact that it is transcendent means that it is also unknowable to an intellect schooled in what is not transcendent. If then god in Himself is unknowable, then any supposed revelation about that god, to the degree that it makes sense to us at all, must be by its very nature mythological. The mere fact that anything about god could be stated in human words as infallible doctrine is an indication that it requires the presence of threats to back up its innate credibility. For anything as limited as the human mind, one that does not have direct access to god's own nature, no definitive statement can be made. Everything predicated of the Israelite God is then a mere extrapolation from perfectly comprehensible ideas into the realm of the incomprehensible! God becomes merely the sum total of various superlatives. He is spoken of as great, as good, as beautiful, as all-knowing, and as powerful. Bosh! What an absurd cacophony of definitions!"

"If I were to define God in a manner so that I might at least find it desirable to believe in Him it would be as follows—God is the being that is immune from all human analogies and attributions whatsoever. I would in other words prefer an inhuman God. When you bring forth your God-in-history therefore you only alienate me further. A God who cares for the human race would be a God of the monkeys, for that is what we are, a particularly nasty species of monkey. It is often said that the other animals fear us. Not so! In reality they see within us what we cannot see in ourselves: that we are separated from the company of all other animals by our absurd pretentions. The animals do not fear us; they scorn us for our pretentions. Even lions loathe human flesh and will eat anything in preference to it. In fact man is only wonderful when his knowledge precludes himself as knower. The truths of mathematics admit no human component. They are true per se and would be true even if no man had ever scrawled numerical symbols down upon paper because numbers inhere to the very nature of things."

"What you therefore insist on calling 'God' is mere shorthand for the human desire that our existence have some perpetual meaning in a universe of transient conditions. The concept of God, unlike mathematics, is incomprehensible and meaningless to the universe that proceeds without Him and is indifferent to human struggles and aspirations and even to our existence. All human life is therefore meaningless precisely insofar as it is 'human.' Religion like all meaning structures exists wholly within ourselves as human and has no outer referent whatsoever."

"Let me give you an example: we say that it is a beautiful spring day; the beauty exists in us, not in the day. It is beautiful merely because we find it so, not because it is beautiful in fact. Humans love to see the universe in terms of human utility and to exercise our limited powers over it. What is the concept of God then, but a human effort to manipulate the entire cosmos to serve our own interests? Why should there be a god then except because we desire that one should exist so that He can serve us. You will object that it is God that we fear and that therefore we exist to serve God. Is that not so? But even that is a veiled form of service; we focalize our fears the better to contain them in acts of worship. The whole matter is degrading to the human species. Let us for a change imagine a religion the primary tenet of which is that God will have nothing to do with us. Better still one that is not even aware of our existence."

"Nay, I will go further still, let us imagine a God who has delegated the creation of all things to some feebleminded servant on condition that He, God, never be informed of what has been created. I would find it easier to believe in that sort of arrangement, because at least it would allow God to be God and not soil him with doctrines, rituals, sacrifices, and the thousand-fold absurdities of hymns, Bible societies, and servile women muttering prayers over their beads. If you can provide me with such a god, then we can at least talk intelligently with each other. We can feel the fresh air of divine indifference once again and not be confined to the meddlesome God of the Jews, or worse still, the alternately sugar-coated and bitter God of the Christians. The same God that promises heaven reserves a hell for those who fail to follow the very laws that St. Paul once claimed had been superseded by the sacrifice of Christ on a cross. The Bible is an awkward anthology of contradictions; thus the many heresies of the first centuries while Christianity began assembling a coherent religion around its vanished savior!"

"If you doubt any element of what I am saying, you need only consider what we find grand in this world of ours, the great mountains, the might of storm and sea! Why do we respect and even revere them? It is not because they care about man and woman, but because they do not. We know that the terrible and the sublime are unconscious of us and that is why they are magnificent. I for one have always been scandalized that Jesus Christ walked upon the sea. He had no business doing so. It shows the typical lack of good taste in Judaic writing. Imagine any God going to the trouble to command anything; the sea should have simply recoiled at His approach in terror saying in effect, 'Who is this gentle God that I the sea should obey him?'

"Why should God care about such minusciae as to elaborate the Torah? Why should God care about dead pigeons or turtle doves and burnt offerings of lambs or oxen? Why should God even care about sin itself? What is it to God if we sin? Can He expect anything more of nasty little monkeys? But you Christian believers will insist upon going further still; you say that God Himself became such a monkey and tried to change human nature by doing so! Two thousand years of Christian history disproves that surely. Has human nature ever changed? Are we not in fact growing worse by the day? Even the exceptions, the Saints, only go to prove the rule. They were holy because they were powerless to change their condition. Their endurance and patience was merely the measure of their incompetence to change their lot in life."

"And the great and powerful of this world are no better! Virtue becomes rarer as power increases, so that I will go so far as to say that honor and high office are the proof of nothing so much as that humans are always likely to become depraved when granted the ability to become so. Only the weak show any signs of virtue, because being deprived of all chance of human happiness by the exertion of powers that they do not possess, they turn in desperation to the indifferent universe, which if it does not love them, at least does not harbor any ill-intent in their regard, unlike their fellow human beings. What is human life but a parade of jealousy and envy? The poor are left to possess holiness unimpeded, because everyone knows in his heart that holiness is an illusion. Who envies the madman or the madwoman? They are allowed to mutter their prayers unmolested; unless that is they seek power, for then they become a threat to the sane but greedy masses that far outnumber them!"

"Why are religions persecuted and also persecutors if not because even illusion finally becomes a source of power in this world. Once a religion develops a following, it becomes a threat to other religions. Thus you have the absurd spectacle of men killing each other over belief in their various gods. Are their gods then so powerless that they cannot defend themselves? You see, Holmes, how it is with religions: men are jealous above all else that their pet delusions shall not be upset. That which allows us to think well of ourselves and to imagine an eternal destiny is worth fighting to maintain. But it is pointless, pointless really, for we are what we are, mere pinpricks in the web and weft of time."

Professor Moriarty could tell that I was growing impatient but he gave a sign that I should allow him to complete his diatribe on religion. "Before you speak, Holmes, I make no exception in these sentiments for my own case. Even my great plot against England is nothing really, a mere futile gesture toward justice, that is all. If you had really wished me to abandon my plan to destroy England you would have pointed out to me the futility of the whole thing and perhaps in sheer boredom I would have already given the whole thing up. Instead you have come at me with religion of all things! Why is this? Is it not because by doing so you can believe in your own virtue and significance? Ladies and gentlemen, in the center ring we have the noble Sherlock Holmes doing battle with the growling and grimacing Professor Moriarty! Honestly Holmes, you might have spared yourself the trouble. Let the public believe that I died at the Falls of Reichenbach. You then emerge as a hero and I am allowed to rest in the crevasse in Switzerland. But if you resurrect me you only serve to embarrass us both: you by being defeated in your attempt to stop me, and me because if the truth be told I am forced to admit that I delight in the prospect of defeating you and I scorn my own pleasure at such an insignificant accomplishment."

"Yes, Holmes, I have enjoyed seeing you struggle over this affair. You have no idea how much I enjoyed the occasional missive from Colonel Moran describing you pushing onwards through dust storms, nursing blisters from camel riding, and visiting all those monolithic sites of the world religions, while I sat comfortably at home reading Renan and Darwin and Nietsche and sipping brandy."

Here the Professor laughed his dry and wheezy laugh as though one was turning the wheel of an old and rusty machine.

"You see Holmes, I admit my faults. I may care for very few things upon this earth, but I do care about you; and even those equally ridiculous brothers of yours who are if anything more proud and self-righteous! To defeat the three Holmes brothers has always been my desire. Why do you think that your father chose me to educate if not to show his sons that they could never hope to compete with even an Irish stable-boy? Your father knew you see the folly of love after your mother died. He married your mother, Violet, in one of the few romantic occlusions of his enlightened life. You boys were always a reminder to him of what he had lost and he grew to hate in you the youth that he could never reclaim for himself. Your very abilities became a reproach to him, so to put you in your place he sought out me, yes unworthy me, to show that your supposed nobility of blood was nothing after all, that we are all a product of accident and chance and that virtue and beauty come to nothing in the end."

"You see what I am now revealing, the true secret of Sherlock Holmes, that it is you were the orphan not I! I am his true son, a son in his own spirit and mind, not you, for it was I who share his deepest beliefs."

He regained his feet, arose, and stood swaying before me at this last statement. He was clasping and unclasping his hands as he spoke. His great hooded eyes glared down upon me where I sat by the fire and his stooped shoulders quivered with the passion of his disclosure.

I said nothing at first. At last he walked unsteadily over to the sideboard and poured himself another brandy before returning to settle back like a recoiling snake into his great chair by the fire.

At last he said, "Have you nothing to say to me then, Holmes? Ah well, that is understandable, quite understandable. Still I thought that such an audacious claim made by a mere stable-boy might draw your wrath."

At last I spoke up. "Well, Professor," said I. "Confession is good for the soul, but I am surprised to see you growing so animated about a matter that I have in any case long suspected. I knew of your antagonism to Sherringford and Mycroft, but I had always hoped that we had an understanding of sorts. I had thought you were above petty revenge. Surely a man who hungers for an impersonal universe of mere force and counterforce is not so personal as to maintain lifelong grudges. You surprise me Professor."

"Evidently you think of me only as a scientist, Mr. Sherlock Holmes," he said with a sneer. "I assure you that I have not neglected the other areas of human knowledge. It may surprise you to hear that I maintain a correspondence with William James, the greatest psychologist of the age. I am well acquainted with the theories of human motivation and I have a substantial knowledge of Shakespeare and of Robert Burton as well. See here, my own copy of his *Anatomy of Melancholy;* carefully annotated I assure you. I mentioned what I did just now because I thought you should know the kind of man your father was. It would be a pity if you spent your own declining years seeking to please a man who would have scorned your every effort."

"I believe that I knew him at least as well as you, Professor," I replied. "He was a man tied to the land by primogeniture when his ultimate wish was to have been a Cambridge Professor. He was a disciple of Godwin and Spencer and one of the few of his class to support the French Revolution, even long after the defeat and exile of Napoleon. You were no doubt a republican experiment of his, a chance to see if education makes the man. You were his own version of Emile by Rousseau or the educational agenda forced upon John Stuart Mill by his own peculiar father. Sigurd Holmes knowledge of your own vile father must have made you the perfect candidate for him, would you later take to drink and waste all the advantages that you were given?"

"My father died before witnessing your descent into a life of crime. Had he witnessed it, he might have given up his striving to join the atheists of his age in setting up an ideal of human reason as a substitute for the moral struggle of sinful man. It is an essential dogma you see of the Enlightment thinkers that man is perfectible through reason alone, which of course he isn't. We are beset with passions and the man who denies it only blinds himself to the source of his own commitments."

"My mother as a French Catholic begged him from her deathbed to believe and to join the Church, but he refused. His own pride was such that he would not admit that the love of his life was dying before him. He must prove himself to be the great stoic after all and dismiss her passing as though it did not eclipse the sun from his life. He felt that he must accept death as simply an adjunct to life and no real bother to the man who accepts life as it is. But you see, Professor, it is really Christianity that accepts life as it is. The Christian knows that death is the pathway to eternal life, but he loathes it all the same and he weeps for the dead, for he knows that sin brought death into the world and sin is always a matter over which we should weep. God does not relish the means of our salvation. If the Son of God wished in the garden that the cup of His suffering might pass him by (and there is no greater proof of the humanity of Christ than the fact of that request), the Father wished it also. The Agony in the Garden was a dialogue and not a monologue. Christ desired that the cup of suffering might pass be avoided because Jesus alone knew the cost of such a sacrifice to the Father! It is not the Divine Son alone who died on the Cross that afternoon but also something of the Father as well, for where there is love there is always the possibility of pain. Creation is always a great risk. To attempt anything great is to risk failure. It may be said that the mere existence of evil shows the fallibility of God, for He did not will it so nor did he prevent it. That God allows evil then is not the scandal it is supposed to be, but rather proof that God will risk everything out of love for us. He will even twist His own being into a knot for us, for God is love and cannot do otherwise than He does and still be true to His own nature."

I paused to let this unaccustomed perspective on the Passion and Death of Jesus Christ sink in before continuing on a more personal note, "My own Father failed his own test in the end because he could not endure the heartbreak of my mother's loss while still believing that such a loss is beyond remedy in this life. He felt that he must carry on with a stiff upper lip, even if to do so was a lie, a lie to his grieving children, and yes even a lie to you Professor Moriarty, for you admired his stoic persona and have made it your own ever since. I tell you that you will not be free until you acknowledge your own loss, one that is equally terrible and irremediable ... the loss of your own Mother. It is she, who you have fled all the days of your life, but she pursues you still and she always will until you turn and recognize that it is she who gave you life and she alone who will lead you home at last."

Moriarty leapt to his feet and stood before me with his fists clenched so that for a moment I feared that the violence that did not take place between us at the Falls of Reichenbach was to take place here in the Professor's sedate library. I did not arise from my chair though, so the Professor, finally realizing the absurdity of the situation, turned aside at last and walked back to the fire.

Eventually he spoke after a considerable interval, "You have upset me Holmes. I cannot recall a similar occasion when I have found myself temporarily without resources and beyond my depth. You realize of course that our domestic affairs have no impact upon the world outside of us. What does it matter if our parents should or should not love us? It is a mere matter of internal chemistry! Each of us is a tiny experiment in the infinite laboratory of the universe, a brief blaze of fire and one soon to be extinguished. I have made it my business to care nothing for the personal."

"Is that so," I retorted, "Then your admission that you have long hoped to succeed to the place of my brothers and I as our father's spiritual heir, what was that if not personal?"

He scowled at this and paused for several minutes more before replying with an assumed air of indifference. "Very well, I admit it; why should I not? Could anyone be expected to face life under the curse and contumely of my own father, the drunken brute, the coward who left my mother to perish? It was he who should have died, not her."

Again he paused, for an even longer time, it seemed to me.

"Nor should I have survived. We should have stayed to nurse her through the typhus and if necessary died with her, but we fled from her and from the horror of her illness. Her last moments were spent alone. She gave us all the food that she had and blessed us as we abandoned her to catch a cattle-boat to England. Her final feeble words to me still echo in my head and have so echoed all of these many years. They will not be silenced! She would have done better to curse me, for then I would not need to carry the infinite obligation of her life infused into mine. Why do you think that I am trying to avenge her now? It is so that her voice may be finally still at last, that voice that follows me night and day like a banshee. Her love is my condemnation, don't you see? For how can I go on, knowing what I did in leaving her that day?"

I then witnessed a most extraordinary thing, the Professor seemed to dissolve before me and the aged man was again the emaciated youth who had come to us so many years before, whom I had met when I was just a lad myself. Even his low and ominous voice was different. The French speak of the *Cri de Coeur*, the cry of the heart, those moments when all of life is concentrated into a single utterance, and that was what I heard in the library from the man who seemed to fold in then upon himself before me like a dry leaf thrown into a fire.

For a moment I feared that he had suffered some sort of

horrible attack or seizure. I leaped up and grasped the flask of brandy from the sideboard. I loosened his collar and forced some brandy down his throat when he showed some signs of recovery. At last his eyes opened again and I saw that his face was now wet with tears. After some minutes I helped him to his feet and strange to say he accepted my help.

I rang at once for a servant and explained that the Professor was indisposed. He and I helped Moriarty to his bed and I have not seen him since. A doctor was called in who diagnosed some sort of brain-fever and I made the difficult decision to return home to Grimpen. I could see no point in remaining. There are times when the soul must exist in its solitude, when every effort to reach it only strengthens its own defenses against grace. I have done all that I can do and said all that I can say to him. The rest is in the hands of providence. It may take days; it may take years; I cannot say, but I hope that the Professor will see in time that the words of Christ to the woman taken in adultery are applicable to us all: *"Woman, has no one condemned you? Then neither do I condemn you. Your sins are forgiven you, but from now on sin no more."*

Such total forgiveness is perhaps the most blessed gift that the Catholic Church possesses and the testimony that it is a Church made up of sinners. When Jesus gave the visible power of the forgiveness of sins to those in Holy Orders of the Catholic Church it was with full consciousness that the Church would see in the plight of the sinner its own plight, so that its mercy would be no less than the mercy of God. It is in exercising that ministry of mercy that the Catholic Church fulfils its purpose and its mission to mankind. *"Whose sins you forgive are forgiven them and whose sins you hold bound they are held bound."* If even a Church of sinners holds sins bound, if the entire community, conscious of its own manifold iniquities and enlightened by the Holy Spirit of love that forgives all sin and restores life can find no way to reach the sinner, then indeed he is held bound, for he has bound himself to his sin forevermore. The task of the Church then is not to bring condemnation to sinners, but to exercise the mercy of God and to act as an advocate for the sinner to the extent that the entire communion of Saints lends its prayers to intercede for those who are most lost, yes even at the very gates of hell itself!

If the Holy Spirit that dwells within us supplements our prayers with unspeakable groaning, as St. Paul assures us, and if it is true that if God is for us, then no one can be against us, then there is always ground for hope, yes hope even for such a one as Professor Moriarty, and also for the cynical Colonel Sebastian Moran, hope as well for the often arrogant, Sherlock Holmes.

October 20, 1893
Grimpen

$\mathfrak{I}$ have received no subsequent communication from the Professor nor did I really expect any. Whatever happens now will not be the work of a day or the reflection of an hour. The battle to be waged must be waged within the Professor's own soul. I have dared to risk all by reliance on the particular. The story of each man's moral struggle is not the simple application of generalities to his unique situation, but is rather the search of the individual for some relation to a world order and to God. We begin in isolation and only by the labors of a lifetime do we enter again into relation with the world rejected at the Garden of Eden when both man and woman wished to be as God or rather as they supposed God to be, splendid in power and in isolation. Our primal parents missed in their ambition the primal quality of God which is holiness. Holiness implies a purity and perfection of intent to which the mind of man may only relate by imitation. We may point to it, but we shall never comprehend it or be equal to it. If even the Seraphim and Cherubim must "veil their faces before the Presence," then what must be our attitude toward the holiness of God! Yet the gospel records that Jesus said to Philip, *"Have I been so long among you and you still do not know me, Philip? He who sees me sees the Father or do you not know that I am in the Father and the Father is in me."*

To relate to each of the Divine Persons of the Blessed

Trinity is a mysterious matter, but to do so is to relate to all of the Godhead, for God is one. Yet each Divine Person manifests certain unique qualities that do not subtract from the Divine Unity, but allow us to receive those particular aspects of the composite plan of God for our redemption that in some mysterious fashion are particular to each of the Divine Persons.

By analogy each man and woman manifests a unique aspect of humanity yet is part of the entire human family. It is the desire of God, based on revelation, to reunite all of humanity to Himself, yet the redemption of each man and woman in this shattered world of individuality is to find in his own particular situation the will of God and to follow it. Each of us feels his own loneliness and isolation most intensely in the prospect of our individual death, but also in every other aspect of our lives. We clothe ourselves with our own particular concept of goodness through our own choices, yet we are haunted by the idea of a general good in which what benefits one need not subtract in some measure from others.

Our world of scarcity and competition sets us at war with each other so that even our closest relationships assume the aspect of bargains struck between temporary allies. One need only witness the domestic battles between spouses and between parents and children to know how often love fails, even where it might be most expected to thrive. How much more alienation must then exist between nations, races, and even religions. We are born into a world of enmity and strife, yet we hunger for peace, not least within those warring aspects of our own passions and to hope for eventual happiness. We are not spared the burden of maintaining our particular path through life; yet (and this is the wonder of it all) God speaks to us through our particular situation, by those who love us and even by those against whom we sin!

Human conflict is the path of obstacles that leads to God. Thus penitence is not a mere occasion, but should be a daily occupation for us. Our every thought should contain some element of discernment of spirits. We grope about like men who are both blind and drunk in the midst of manifold afflictions and yet for all of that we are held to the dignity of our impaired freedom and our nature remains one that is made in the image and likeness of God. So close and yet so far is the definition of man in relation to God. We exist in paradox. How comforting it might seem then to be only a happy animal and to foreswear any eternal destiny or to go to the other extreme and be, as Moriarty has tried to become, an end unto himself by dictating even to God!

Anger at God has its beginning in the assumption that this fissure in our very souls is the product of God's choice and not ours. We have since the beginning, collectively and as individuals, chosen our own way. God is surfeited daily with a cacophony of demands so that even prayer is often not really the worship of God but the attempted sanctification of our own intentions. God alas (and think of the paradox in this statement) can only be God. He cannot redeem us according to our own vision of what redemption should entail, but only in that way which alone leads to Truth, the cross of Christ. Even God as Father is not spared the Cross! How then shall we escape it? How then will we collectively and as individuals be spared the pain of losing all in order to receive all things restored in God in its primal perfection?

If I knew another way to speak to Professor Moriarty than by reminding him of his own history I would have done so in order that he might abandon his intention to destroy, the final act of his own personal vendetta against not merely England but against existence as he has known it. It is not then to generalities that I have appealed, but have rather called him to face his own individual life, to face that unique pattern of pain and loss that has twisted him in both body and soul. Will he abandon his plan in the years ahead before it is executed? Ah, that only the future will reveal.

October 28, 1893
Grimpen

It is now that late season of mists and mellow fruitfulness celebrated by the poets when the harvest is in and the granaries are full. Oat bread is baking in the village and the yellow squashes deck the market stalls. Fresh lamb and pork sausage are sold there as well and great barrels of cider are tapped. It is a time of leisure after great labors and of rejoicing in village and in town. Watson would be pleased to see that I am eating well again and even putting on a bit of weight. I take a daily walk over the moors to the village which maintains a small reading library. I sit in a nook and gaze out into the garden now bare of roses and zinnias.

The weather has changed abruptly in recent days and the frosts of late autumn cannot be far behind. Still there are clear days when the wind strips the poplars and oaks bare, revealing the great clumps of mistletoe that reside within their oaken hosts. The few chestnut trees are beginning to drop their treasures to the ground and I think back upon time spent long ago on my first trip to the continent when I would leave a string concert in Vienna and purchase roasted chestnuts on the street corner from a vendor before retiring to a Gasthof for a glass of the pale Riesling before seeking a good night of sleep. I thought in those days that I might remain abroad permanently and leave the cares of the estate to Sherringford and Mycroft. The best chemists were in Germany and I could take my holidays in Vienna or in Budapest. I hungered for the deep cultural roots and cross-fertilization of ideas amidst the polyglot peoples of Central Europe. I found the British Isles to be stuffy in their complacency and the Church of England to be so rooted in the social assumptions of Britain as to be a mere ally to state policy. But then I was young and rebellion was in my blood.

All too soon these hopes were quashed. I was summoned home because my father had died suddenly. He was found out on the moors after his saddled horse returned to the stable alone. Sherringford had thereafter assumed the role of head of the estate and with his typical frugality was conserving our liquid resources and bringing the tenants to heel. I was informed that my further education in chemistry should be at the University of London, "with no more foreign nonsense," if I was bound and determined to take up chemistry and not to assume a proper role as a manager upon the estate. Mycroft after all was already in London and pursuing a career in diplomacy so that a place was ready for me in Yorkshire if I chose to accept it. I could not reconcile myself though to the isolation of the moors having known the great cities of Europe, so I refused and from that hour Sherringford, for whom there was always only the land, resented my decision to strike out and pursue my own fanciful vision of a life.

Perhaps it was fanciful after all. Even now I wonder how I can hope to resume my tangential relations with Scotland Yard and earn a living by the few strange cases that find their way to my door. Perhaps I may aid the foreign police and turn my practice into an international affair. I have not heard of anyone who applies my own particular methods there and perhaps they are after all non-transferable to others. But am I really so unique in my art of detection? Maybe even my few monographs, if supplemented and completed in a general volume called *"The Art and Science of Criminal Detection"* would be inadequate to explain exactly what it is that I do to other students of crime? Perhaps one must always be a bit mad to be a philosopher or a detective. Is it not madness to think that the complete truth can ever be known about anything? No, I shall leave it to Watson to form what synthesis he can of my exploits and shall confine my ramblings to my journals. I am relieved of the need to compose a system in these entries, which are little more than the crystallization process from the solutions in the flask of my own speculations.

I am relieved here of the need to consult the expectations of an audience constantly expecting method and order rather than the free-flow of ideas. Instead what have I composed here in my journal is only my own tale of myself in the style of a new *Tristram Shandy*? But I know that these idle days of autumn must soon pass. I have received news from Mycroft that an old bookseller's establishment is available for purchase in London. It is just the place I have long had in mind, dusty with old volumes, a veritable rabbit-warren of obscure scholarship. I may take up residence in the garret above the store and gradually merge again with the life of the great city of London. Mycroft will act as a sort of silent partner as it is his funds that must provide the initial capital for our joint venture.

Mycroft has few weaknesses but good food and good reading are among them. What could be more natural then than for the brothers Holmes but to own a bookshop? We shall of course not tell Sherringford that we have gone into trade as that might be a final blow to the family pretentions of the poor chap. I doubt that we will enlarge our savings from the establishment which will be lucky to provide a small income and a return of the initial investment over time. It will be a sort of joint library though for Mycroft and for me and I will be spared the unsightly prospect of climbing about over boxes of books in my already cluttered rooms at Baker Street where I hope that Watson will soon consent to join me once again. By this strange and round-about way I hope to resume my life in England. As for my home here upon the moor, Sir Henry will rent it out for me until such time as I have need of it once again. I shall enjoy the last of these mellow days here then as best I may because the opportunity for rest and reflection will be lost soon enough in the clamor and noise of London.

The mellow buzzing of the hornets gathered about the apples that have fallen in the yard will give way to the shouts of cabbies and the noise of trains at Paddington and at Kings Cross. The clear air of the moors will be lost and replaced by the choking coal dust and fog of a London winter. But perhaps I shall soon adapt like an old horse put again into its harness and though I shall no doubt stamp about for a bit I shall reconcile myself at last and begin to pull the load forwards. Devonshire farewell!

November 6, 1893
London

I came up to London two days ago to sign the requisite papers to purchase the old bookshop. Before I left Devonshire I was able to spend All Hallows Eve out on the moors and to observe the festivities in Grimpen. Fires were lit upon the hills as at Midsummer and the children of the village heard tales of goblins, fairies, and of course of the ancient, legendary Hound of the Baskervilles. Many people in the village and surrounding farms continue to believe in that particular bogey in spite of its more mundane incarnation several years ago in Stapleton's fantastic attempt upon the life of his cousin, Sir Henry.

Legends are not easily upset in this part of the world. Only the braver lads and their fearful but game young ladies ventured out then upon the moors by moonlight to kindle the fires of All Hallows Eve. Their songs and dance could be heard from Baskerville Hall where I had gone to pay my respects and to enjoy a last meal at the ancient manor house. We had pheasant, steak and kidney pie, and squash served with treacle and butter.

I did not tarry long after dinner because I needed to be up early to attend Mass on All Saints Day in the village before catching my train for London at Coombe Tracy. High Mass in the chapel at Grimpen with the few Catholic tradesmen and women and farmers of the district in attendance reminded me once again of the reach of the Church. Even our tiny village may participate in the triumph and majesty of the Church Triumphant which in this great feast celebrates the many diverse souls, who responding to the call of their Lord have entered into the Kingdom of Heaven. The feast is a feast of hope to strengthen us who remain in our great period of affliction and trial. It is a comfort to know that the prayers of the dead are united in intercession for us and that those whom we have known and lost are, by God's good grace, hopefully among the saints though unnamed, for the number of actual saints far surpasses those whom the Church has honored for our emulation by raising them to the honors of the altar by their canonization.

The old Pastor met me after mass and blessed me as I begin my journey back into the world from what has been to all outward observation my early retirement. One of the village elders drove me to Coombe Tracy in my dog-cart. My horse will hereafter be kept at Sir Henry's stables and be well looked after there. My house will be rented as soon as my more personal belongings are sent up to London. I closed my door for what may be the last time for many years. My packed trunk already lay in the stone hallway.

The fire was out and the hearth cold, the larder empty but for a few cold victuals that my charwoman will receive along with the gift of a few sovereigns and a note expressing my thanks for her excellent care during my residency.

I caught the train just as the fog was lifting after pacing the platform in the early afternoon chill in my great coat and hunting cap. Long before reaching Exeter the fog had risen and I was able to enjoy the delightful Devon landscape for a last time before glimpsing the spires of Exeter ahead. From Exeter I caught the train that passes through Bath and then Oxford to London. The moors gradually were succeeded by lush pastures and forests as I approached Oxford but dusk had long settled before I reached London.

I met Mycroft yesterday for dinner at the Diogenes Club and was able to tell him about my summer spent in Ireland. I have put up for a few days at the Northumberland Hotel so as not to burden Mycroft. I hope to be able to take up residence above the bookstore some time next week. Mycroft informed me that he has heard from Watson by letter and that he will return to England before the end of the month. I trust that he will escape in his crossing the worst of the Atlantic winter gales.

While it would be too much to say that Mycroft is excited by our purchase of the old book chandler's shop, he was at least pleased at the prospect of acquiring such a vast collection of books and folios as those that are to be found there. He has already scavenged a few select volumes by having them set aside prior to my arrival. We will meet with the solicitor tomorrow and I trust the last dry formalities may be soon completed. So it is that my new life, which is rather a return than a beginning, commences: the return of Sherlock Holmes.

November 12, 1893
London

I have been too busy in recent days to write in this journal. Each day has carried its own burdens which have also been a joy in taking over the occupancy of my own business in the city. Even Mycroft has come by in the evenings to lend a hand, but his great bulk usually only manages to knock over a stack of volumes or to scare the resident cat who keeps the mouse and rat populations down. The documents of transfer have been signed and the final payment made so that I can truly say that the brothers Holmes have title to a bona fide London enterprise. I have hired a clerk, one of my old Baker Street Irregulars, who was the second in command after Cartwright of my own unofficial police force. He is a quiet chap but possessed of an excellent and orderly mind and he shall do quite well I am sure. His presence at the counter will allow me the time necessary to catalogue the more unique and costly volumes and put them in order. I am afraid that the recent owner followed a method of categorization peculiar to his own notions and shared as far as I can see by no other human being on earth.

I am happy to say at least that the place seems free of mice and rats thanks to a fat tabby cat named Byron who came with the premises. He watches me intently as I go about my labors before excusing himself to engage in one of his silent patrols. I have set up a workroom and bindery in one of the back rooms so that repairs can be made to certain volumes and my clerk who has been trained as a printer and bookbinder often stays late after the shop has been closed to work at these dusty treasures. Meanwhile Mycroft and I have settled down to survey our hoard at our leisure. He is quite as pleased as I have been by what we have found. We are rather like boys in a toy shop calling each other over to inspect each new find. My only fear has been that we will become so attached to our stock in trade that he will not wish to part with any of them. I am afraid that our business may hence become only a private library with two patrons, Mycroft and I. I wonder if Watson might soon make up a third.

Physically the place consists of eight connected rooms of various levels, an assorted rabbit-warren indeed, but there is at least a central room with a fireplace and we have installed some comfortable old chairs and a divan there as well as a sturdy sideboard with tea things for a few favored early patrons. I have scones brought in every day at four and do the honors to the gentlemen who drop in to see how we progress. It is a custom that I may continue when we open in December for general business. I hope then to be able to shorten our working hours and to develop a proper clientele of connoisseurs of fine books. If all goes well I should be able to hire on another two helpers and resume my proper practice as a detective in Baker Street by March or April of next year. The interim period will allow me to make inquiries and to be sure that none of my old enemies are still at large, or at least none who will pose any immediate threat. After that I must see if Watson will throw together a few tales for the Strand Magazine to inform the public that I am hale and hearty and clients will no doubt begin to trickle again into Baker Street.

I trust that I am not entirely forgotten. In any case, the last of my Sigerson dispatches have now been published and I have collected some much welcome royalties recently to tide me over until my detective practice is flourishing again. This has been a bad year for business on both sides of the Atlantic and many are in desperate need. Though I know human nature too well to trust in any prospect for the success of socialism here, I am afraid that unfettered capitalism is simply too unstable to provide an economic mechanism to ensure the common good. Some new system will have to be devised to prevent the excesses and the resultant contractions of the present system. We are after all one human community, all children of God, one vast family of humanity.

Human suffering brings violence in its wake and violence is always more expensive in the long haul than the minor levies on the rich that it takes to ensure some measure of justice and equity among the masses if not strict material equality. No doubt the poor will always be with us, but we may at least eliminate destitution. For the present we must wait for things to improve and I at least am grateful to have this universe of books about me. I wake each day and go across the street for my oatmeal, bangers, eggs, and crumpets before setting in to work. At the end of each day I can see shelves stacked neatly and in order and the lesser books set aside for sale to the local book barrow chaps who buy the books by weight and not by title. These in turn go about the streets of the West-end selling their adventures and romances to the servant lads and lasses who run down to purchase them. Literature does not fail simply because it amuses, but it is better still if a book instructs as well.

Whether much truth may be conveyed without the burden of experience in which all truth is rooted, I cannot say. Books seem to me rather to be companions on the quest of life; they do not relieve us of the burden of living, but they make life more tolerable for us by their company. They remind us that no mind exists in absolute isolation and that even the most arcane experiences have sometime been shared by others. They save us the labor of re-discovering the world again in each generation. Yet they in turn (or most of them) have their own mortality. How many books that were once read by all have fallen into eclipse! As the poet Fitzgerald says, *"The moving finger writes and having writ, moves on: nor all thy piety and wit shall lure it back to cancel half a line, nor all thy tears wash out a word of it."* But then he is writing not of the words of men in books but of the indelible recording of events along the imperishable record of time whose scroll unrolls to the very borders of eternity. But enough of this; to work Sherlock!

November 15, 1893
London

The quotation in my last entry spoke of the moving finger that records all of our actions in time. I have been meditating on this during these past days. How jagged and abrupt must seem our actions from the perspective of the smooth and regular orbits of the spheres! Our most determined course is deflected by a thousand accidents. It is no small part of human suffering and fate that a harsh word, a gratuitous insult, or a senseless cruelty may turn the entire course of a relationship aside so that the original course is lost and finally abandoned. At what point may one justifiably take offense and withdraw from another person? We are told that one must forgive an offense not seven times but seven times seven times. Which of us reaches the first decade of that string of beads that adds up to forty-nine? Are even the most seemingly deliberate actions only accidents motivated by subtle and unknown forces in another's soul? Who is in control of every source of hidden malice? I am inclined to doubt the human capacity to see beyond the emotion of the moment and the misguided constructions of another person's intentions. I could wish for a full hearing before the inner tribunal of each soul before any irrevocable act is taken to sever relations and to abandon hope. But we exist every day in a welter of alternative courses for our lives. Bitter separations are often not healed by subsequent events and thus they are to be avoided at all costs. The edges once torn and wrenched asunder soon become adaptable to other uses so that even a poor fit with an alien piece may substitute for the original that is now lost forever.

November 21, 1893
London

Progress is now visible everywhere at our bookshop! Each day I have been working from morning until past dusk when I customarily meet Mycroft for a late dinner at the Diogenes Club. I have separated certain volumes and placed them in what I call the Mycroft room. I know as only a brother may those primary areas of interest that are his. Similarly, I have set aside a room for myself with books and manuscripts that are not for sale to the public. It is not that I may live long enough to hope to peruse them all. Their function is one of mere availability. The world is too much for any one of us to comprehend even a small fraction of the available source material. Similarly our lives are too short to cultivate more than a small acquaintance with people and with places. We are confined to the tiniest circle of local illumination and our zone of familiarity is by its nature insular. Our horizon is the breadth of a compass-drawn circle or the tracing of a teacup. The world beckons and mocks us in doing so for our furthest journeys seem barely to span a stone's throw. The earth itself is lost in the great dark template of the heavens. The light of distant orbs is but a testimony of events from long ago whose point of origin may in the interim have ceased to be.

Where is God in all of this? Why offer infinity to a being content with a glass of cider at the end of a day's toil? For this reason St. John says in all honesty, *"Beloved, we are God's children now; what we shall be has not yet been revealed."* We step into eternity having known only time, and even that not in its totality but in the measured fragments of our days and hours. So much of religion is only indicative. "There." says faith, "Follow that path!" But where it leads at last? Ah religion, if it be worthy of its claims, is silent.

What we know of God is not comprehensive, not even to the extent of providing an outline that is to be filled in later. We are provided with a direction only. The greatest part is hidden from our eyes and to attempt to imagine the totality is itself a blasphemy. We must be content that God is love and let it go at that. Our task on earth is to deal as best we may with the transcendental values of beauty, justice, and wisdom. To that end I have furnished my library with the works of the great thinkers who have pushed human knowledge as far as it may proceed, so that I might follow the paths outlined at least for some small distance in their illustrious company.

There are books that explore my own peculiar interests. They are a varied lot. There are copies of old English charters that show the gradual spread of democratic principles among our people. There are volumes about beekeeping and the brewing of mead. I even possess some books of folklore, tales of the druids and the Celtic peoples with stories of tree worship in oaken groves. I have an oriental section that is well stocked with commentaries on Confucius and Lao Tsu and also the poems of Li Po and the other great poets of the Tang Dynasty. Then there are complete leather-bound sets of the works of John Donne, Robert Burton, Thomas Carlyle, and Sir Thomas Browne. I also have a selection of the great poets of our own age: Tennyson, Browning, Arnold, and even Swinburne and Dowson.

My collection includes a first edition of Francis Thompson's, *"The Hound of Heaven,"* a poem that has said in a few lines what many men have spent a lifetime trying to capture. There are also works by John Clare, Percy Bysshe Shelley, George Gordon Lord Byron, William Wordsworth, and John Keats, each among the most immortal poets of our English tongue, as well as dear melancholy Herman Melville and Nathaniel Hawthorne from among the great men of letters of our American cousins.

Then there are various musical manuscripts, collections of madrigals and motets, Gregorian Chants, and English medieval melodies. There is an excellent translation of the works of St. John of the Cross and of Teresa of Avila. Daily our stock in trade is diverted to my own use so that I fear that between Mycroft and I we are assembling not a book chandlery at all but a mere depository for our own instruction, and all of this at a period in our lives when there is little time to read, for I will soon be again at work finding lost jewels and advising governesses whether to accept positions in country houses!

Ah well, I am not immune to the vanity that imagines that there will be endless days ahead to pursue one's particular interests. Even Sherringford has his hounds and Moriarty his racing-stable. Our interests and passion offer some anodyne to the pain of living. There are many who find no end of happiness in chasing a little ball across a meadow with golf sticks. Others lie on their backs in opium dens dreaming fantastic dreams or like Coleridge with his laudanum. Even many philosophers have had their only true joy in wine or spirits. Then there are those who must be trotting about all day from various social gatherings, while others wall themselves off from their fellows through excess shyness or fear. The human spectrum is more than a mere catalogue of virtues and vices, it is one long scroll of diverse human possibilities and perhaps even God may wish it to be so. After all, the Hasidic Rabbis say that God made man because He loves stories. How strange to think that it is we who amuse God rather than God who promises to entertain us at the Wedding Feast of Heaven, but perhaps it is so. Perhaps God does take delight in His creation after all, for did He not look upon it, as Genesis bears witness, and pronounce that it was all very good indeed?

December 1, 1893
London

The last of the rooms is now completed with the various subjects separated and the titles recorded. We open our doors to the public today and I expect that word will soon get about among the various scholars and collectors who will be our clientele. Mycroft will be over later and we will celebrate with a dinner at Simpsons. Events are moving swiftly now. Watson's boat is expected within the week. I plan on traveling down to Southampton to meet it, although I will go in disguise. I am at a loss as to how and when to disclose myself to Watson. My long silence now seems less necessary since the many dangers that I feared here in London seem to have been much exaggerated. I have made inquiries by name through Mycroft as to the status of certain men who might have designs upon my life and find that they are either in prison or have been hung. The men of Scotland Yard have apparently not been idle during my absence.

For the ordinary class of criminal, men like Gregson and Lestrade eventually get their man. As for those unusual classes of crime that require my particular methods, the very fact that they remain unsolved dooms them to obscurity, for what remains shrouded in mystery is soon forgotten. Events tend over time to heal themselves. All of this of course is not flattering to my vanity. I find that I have been dispensable after all and that England can get along fine without me. Perhaps even Watson has found life better without being forced to adjust to my constant demands for his company on my cases. He no longer needs to look for the tobacco, stuffed into a Persian slipper rather than kept in a proper humidor, or to listen to my violin wailing in the night when I find that I cannot sleep. If Watson has any fault, it is perhaps his long sufferance of my peculiar habits.

I do not mean to be inconsiderate of him, but I possess to an excessive degree that quality of concentration that so loses itself in a train of thought that all exterior considerations seem to vanish. I am rather like a sight-hound that once upon the trail will burst its heart rather than give up the chase. How often have I dragged Watson along with me into danger! Now I must have some sign from him that he desires a renewal of our old partnership before I disclose to him that I am still alive!

December 8, 1893
Southampton

Today Watson's boat will be docking in the afternoon. I came down here yesterday and put up at the Lion's Rest, a comfortable middle-class hotel near the waterfront. I was up early for mass at the Cathedral since today is the Feast-day of the Immaculate Conception of the Virgin Mary who alone of all human beings was conceived without the stain of Original Sin. This unique privilege of grace did not remove her from the fallen world in which she lived her life nor was her sinless and Divine Son spared the result of sin in the world. To endure the trials of the flesh when one is sinless is then by its very nature a redemptive act. The Church honors this fact by recognizing the Sacred Heart of Jesus and the Immaculate Heart of Mary as twin devotions, the first encircled by thorns and the second pierced by a sword. These images in turn are meant to convey the pain of sin visited upon the innocent. Without the willing assent of Mary to God, the redemption of the world could not have taken place. The consent of the Blessed Virgin Mary removes forever the stain of Eve, but at what a price!

The Virgin Mary alone of all humanity knows the price of redemption to God in her very being. Only from the perspective of her sinlessness can she alone have from the beginning complete knowledge of the Divine Will for man and for woman and for the universe that was meant to minister to their needs. For this reason she is honored by the Church as the Mother of God and it is she who alone who shall crush the Ancient Serpent at last beneath her feet.

Even Jesus, though he is God, made Himself subject to her in life. Their twin wills are one by the mutual assent of love. It is in the Virgin Mary that the Church celebrates the particularity of good and of evil, that these are not mere disembodied forces. It is always the intense personalism of Christianity that is a scandal to the Moslems. It is impossible for them to imagine Allah's will being accomplished within history by the mystery of the Incarnation of Christ through the assent of the Virgin Mary. It is easier instead to believe that the Koran was penned by God in heaven and delivered to Mohammed.

Islam represents the triumph of the spirit of the letter of the law. It is a last upwelling of human desire to save itself by adherence to a code of conduct, no matter how demanding. But God is not encased by any codification. God breaks out of all categories and definitions. *God is the personal, acting upon the personal!* If God wished to order human affairs to perfection he might have done so by simple fiat. That he does not so command explains everything about God. God does not act by compulsion but by invitation. Even the course and fate of salvation for the entire human race was submitted to the will of a mere unlettered girl! For one brief moment the fate of the universe was held in suspense and creation invited to pronounce upon the will of the creator!

The most startling fact of time and space depended upon this new beginning. When Mary said to the angel, *"Be it done unto me according to your word,"* the universe from that moment turned upon its axis and resumed its direction towards God and not away from Him. All of the law and of the prophets and every obscure motion of human desire for God found its fulfillment in those few words and the heart that embraced not its fate but its gift. The assent of Mary is the perfect correlative to God's gratuitous act of creation. From nothing proceeds something! From the humble girl comes an opening to the Divine action of redemption. This story is too beautiful to be contained in a book as mere doctrine. No poet or musician may find a means to celebrate it properly! Mysteries such as this require contemplation as the only avenue to their appreciation because they are the very foundation and basis of all further thought and action. On this special day I requested the aid of the Blessed Virgin that she might touch the heart of my dear friend Watson so that he will forgive me for my many transgressions against him and so that she may show me the way to make reparation to him in some way for his many good services to me and for his long and devoted friendship to one Sherlock Holmes.

December 9, 1893
Southampton

I have seen him! I stood in the crowd on the dock dressed as an elderly Italian Priest, just as I had been dressed on the train to Dover so many years ago. I was determined to give him every chance to exercise his powers of observation and to recognize me; but alas it was the same old Watson who disembarked with his eye on the gangplank and his greatcoat collar pulled up high against the chill of the sea wind. His face was brown from the Louisiana sun and he looked rather like he had after first coming to England from Afghanistan so many years ago. He seemed healthy though and his step was sprightly as he saw his baggage delivered to a cab and hopped aboard. I heard him give the cabby the address of the Queens Arms, a hostelry a few doors down from my own hotel. I waited a bit before hailing a cab to follow him. He alighted at his hotel and for a moment I thought of following him in the sheer joy of seeing him once again, but good sense prevailed and I have returned here to my own room. After all it has been three long years since I have seen him. He has lost his dear wife in the interim. Who can say what changes have taken place within him as a result? I must have some sign that he will understand my motives and that he will appreciate that my journey had to be a solitary one as I pursued what each man must, a final and adequate reason for his life.

It is not enough of an explanation for human life that we are simply plunged into existence and then at some future and indefinite date seemingly plucked from life again by death. If one becomes convinced that his own life is totally without meaning or consequence, a mere accident in a world of colliding particles and senseless motion, then what becomes of the moral instinct and the sense that one's choices matter and can be discriminated one from another? The mind of man must reel into madness if there is not some final point to which it may be affixed and tethered so that from that particular vantage point it may assess all things and set them into order. If there are valid criteria for judgment and discrimination in the order of even the smallest things, then surely there must be a point of ultimate order, of ultimate truth, of ultimate beauty in the universe. I went to the east to seek that point.

I had to do so. In the years before 1891 I had come to the point where the probing of my detective mind had caused me to doubt all things. I had even begun to wonder if Moriarty might be right after all and that power alone can be the only means of addressing an opposing power, if violence must be appealed to in order to counter the slow corrosive influence of the great organization of capital and the cynical rule of the multitude present in the so-called democratic republics, let alone the absolute rule of the decadent monarchies of Europe.

I did not have the bitter and sarcastic humor of a Voltaire at my disposal, for I am a romantic at heart and every romantic has a hunger for a faith to which to devote his life. The great religions stem from the comparative innocence of the past, while we live in these latter days when the first hopes of mankind's youth are being vanquished. Just as a man ages and begins at last to know what he can expect from life, so it is with entire civilizations. As a man's expectancy of duration grows shorter, time becomes more precious; the tasks of life grow more numerous and demanding, and the paths of new possibilities become more rare and therefore more insistent. Each new obligation threatens other commitments until a slow confusion begins to build within the man himself. He wakes one day to realize that his life is not only incomplete for all his efforts, but that it is in fact a hodgepodge of partially completed projects; his most sanguine hopes were perhaps always mere exercises in vanity. Such a man begins to suspect that he is a fool after all and that he has been wrong for years in his most tested assumptions but did not know it until the very moment when it has become too late to begin again. Even if he now knows the truth of things, he has not the energy of youth to start again. He doubts whether he might not awaken yet again after spending another decade or so of effort only to find that once again he has been mistaken in his core suppositions about how the world actually works, for are not the mistakes of all mankind more manifold than can be counted? Who is he then to have found the truth at last, even of his own life let alone the world? It is in that hour of desperation that he must call out, like St. Peter when he was sinking into the sea, for a hand to reach out and a comforting voice to murmur, *"Why did you doubt?"*

But I did doubt and in doubting I did what any good Pelagian must, I sought my own answers with redoubled efforts. I thought that I must place all of the world's religions side by side and find a criterion to choose from among them as though they were loaves of bread upon a baker's shelf. But if it is religion that must provide the ultimate criterion for choice, then no other outside standard will suffice to provide a man with the means to discern the best candidate for a valid commitment.

For this reason, it is God who must reach out to us to confirm our partial faith. Until then, even an enlightened choice of a faith must still partake of some degree of doubt so that a man will be tempted to hedge his bets, to keep something in reserve for the next race so that he may make up his losses. But alas, our lives are the final race of the day and we must place all that we have upon one chance and one alone and rest all of our fortunes upon it. Will Watson understand any of this? Will he understand that before I left England three years ago that I was as desperate as Professor Moriarty, that both of us were fleeing London and our own past associations and commitments?

Perhaps, good man that he is, Watson will understand for did he not do as much when he fled to Louisiana after the death of his wife to find himself again? Was it charity alone that motivated him to seek out life among the living dead of a leprosarium? Perhaps it is only when we face the many fears that have haunted us throughout a lifetime: our fear of poverty, disease, and of death itself that we begin at long last to live in the freedom of the Sons of God. At that darkest moment of our lives Jesus turns to us and asks us gently, *"Why did you doubt?"*

December 10, 1893
Southampton

atson has left; I watched his train leave for London without having communicated with him. It is not time yet. It will be enough for him to do as I have done and face being in England again, to go to his home in Kensington and perhaps only now be able to realize that Mrs. Watson is gone and will not return. He must have time to mourn now and mourning such as that must be done alone. Certain losses plunge us into our own essential solitude. There are deaths to bear in life that are far more bitter than our own, for when we die we do not know that we die. Death for the convinced Christian is after all only to be severed from all that was only a dim reflection of God. Death is less a deprivation than an advent into true being, so that to die to the earth is to be born into heaven. But these comforting reflections are of only partial aid when it is another's life that we lose, while we remain behind.

It is not only Edgar Allen Poe who seeks some reply from

the ghastly grim and ancient raven of death, whether in some distant Aiden it shall clasp a sainted maiden named Lenore. Why do the dead not speak to us to allay our fear and our grief? Perhaps it is that the dead may continue to love us, but their love for us is transformed into the universal charity of heaven so that all partial loves seem to bear about them that which perhaps they always possessed, no small admixture of selfishness. We love others so that they may love us in return. To love with complete forgetfulness of self seems the prerogative of divine love alone. Our earthly loves always have about them this bi-polarity, this commoditization in exchange. We cannot imagine God until He is all about us, our all-in-all. When that happens to the soul, all partial illumination melts into the light of the sun which is its source.

Yet (and this is the greatest mystery of the Catholic Faith) we will one day be re-united with our bodies so that we will not say farewell forever to that most particular source of being that is us with all of its partial loves and familiarity. There is no real dissolution forever so that our identity will be lost. Something in us, perhaps the soul, makes us stand forth as individuals through all the permutations of life. But if God, as He will someday, becomes our all-in-all, He does not proceed beyond that first embrace to dissolve us and resolve us into His own being, but will be with us in a similar manner as it is in the case of the Three Persons in the Holy Trinity—although there are three persons are one God, they remain distinct from each other.

As I express this article of faith I realize not for the first time that the language of theology is not mere metaphor but refers to what shall become actual experiential events that will in time resolve the mystery of human existence for us. To say that culture, morality, and religion are mere accidents of history, that they have no more reality than dreams, is to deny their real and ubiquitous nature. Our total realm of experience cannot be reduced to a sequence of brief sensory events. All efforts by materialists to reduce our speculations to the senses and to the raw data of experience deny our capacity to extrapolate from what we know to what is unknown. The human race is always in advance of itself. We may visualize and plan for possibilities beyond our present condition. Is it strange then that our thought may penetrate beyond the arbitrary confines of our own death? If eternity did not exist, then why does it so haunt the thoughts of men? If there were no transcendent values, why do we perceive them as morally or aesthetically normative and why do we feel a duty to recognize and to pursue them if we are ever to realize the true and the good in all things? Though our ceremonials may seem to cheapen and degrade what pertains to God, they must be meaningful to us to be effective in our present state. For this reason we are plunged into metaphor to express what exceeds the dull inadequacy of human language.

Doctrine and dogma in the Catholic Church have the function of preserving truth in vessels that can but partially contain it. Liturgy in turn seeks to attune our minds and hearts to a love that exceeds our own feeble response in return. We have religions then not because they are ideal and complete, but because they are simply the best that we can do to approach the ultimate reality. Even should science grow over time in its descriptive capacity and accuracy, it would still remain a language with which the mind of man communicates with itself. Science would still be confined to our own conception of the meaningful and the significant and for that reason it will always be biased and distorted by our own capacities, which after all are not infinite.

It is good to have faith in human reason as an avenue to the intelligible, but to assume that the human mind may reach a definitive conclusion to all things, all time, and all potency is to assume that the part may contain the whole. So it is that we stand on the shore and throw rocks into the sea of being and marvel at the splash that we make or the skipping of the stone over the sea, but the sea remains the sea for all of that and we remain poor pilgrims along the shore, haunted by the cry of the seabirds that soar over us in the distant air.

I have determined to remain here for a few days in order to prevent all possibility of a fortuitous meeting with Watson. London is not so large a place after all. I will tour the Sussex Coast then for a bit and return to London in time for Christmas. I have set the bookshop in order and our small staff may do their work better without my meddling. I have already set aside those volumes that I intend to retain and Mycroft has done likewise. It is time to resign myself to the loss of many volumes that I shall never have time to peruse. Every life is an exercise in incompleteness. I have perhaps spent too much time already in trying to define the will of God and an inadequate time spent pursuing it by assuming the duties of my state in life.

December 14, 1893
Dover

I proceeded over the Sussex Downs visiting the sea towns along the way. I stopped at several apiaries. The bee-hives are quiet now with the chill of winter filled with the honey stored against the long sleep until spring. Just so it seems to me should a human life be banked full with the honeycomb of virtuous acts, a simile to the oil of the wise virgins of the Gospel whose lamps did not go out before the bridegroom approached. But there are other hives that resemble abandoned refuges of dried wax and empty cells devoid of honey. Can these too find hope in spring? Are the warnings of the gospel only pastoral in nature, meant to strengthen the community by reminding the individual members of their duties, or are these warnings addressed to the individual soul to warn us of the all too likely possibility of eternal exclusion?

The great Dr. Samuel Johnson was one of those who feared that for all of his great labors, his performance did not do justice to the gifts he had received from God. What hope is there then for the average selfish man who has always considered first his own advantage and convenience, whose only regret is that he did not enjoy life more and have more time in which to enjoy it? Is that rich man trying to squeeze through the eye of a needle? Yet we are assured that the mercy of God may accomplish what seems impossible to the human mind. But at what cost is moral neglect of duty to God and to mankind? Is it not better to take our purgatory now rather than to pay a dearer price in the purgative station at the portals of eternity? Does the yoke of virtue grow lighter for us to assume after death? If to do good now is difficult, may it not seem infinitely harder when the means of the exercise of virtue are taken from us and we have only the sodden mess of our guilt hanging about us like a heavy shroud, sodden and foul with the putrid brine of our vices that have at last almost submerged us?

I have stood alongside of sloughs and estuaries and smelled the rot and decay where the land mingles with the sea, or worse still have smelled those vile pilings beneath docks in the Thames where strange hybrid creatures dwell exposed by the retreating tide. The Thames is fouled with the floating refuse of commerce just as life is fouled by the very means that we use to preserve it. How much effort is expended to procure the small profit which is the tiny margin which sustains our lives? This constant pushing and shoving for space on the pilings, would it not be better to fall off at once rather than to be buried beneath layer upon layer of humanity, each afraid that its access to the swampy soup of the tidal flow might be cut off? What is this competition of life amidst the scarcity that determines all economies but a human analogue to this sordid struggle for life on the rotting posts and piles along the Thames estuary? Where is the human equivalent of these grand white cliffs of Dover to be found?

When will human life be worthy of the doctrine of the immortal soul? I do not believe that men and women love ignorance and vice but how many are condemned to just these things by passion and penury? What toothless gin-soaked prostitute is there who was not once as virginal as the dawn that broke over the sea this morning that I viewed from the ramparts of Dover Castle? Why should she lie beaten in a gutter by some brute who has just robbed her of the price exacted from sharing her meager flesh? Can the horrors of life ever balance the moments of peace and plenty known by, alas too few of the total human population? Might it not be better to be among them than to know of their existence and do nothing to alleviate their condition?

December 15, 1893
Dover

$\mathfrak{I}$ stood today on the summit of the chalk sea cliffs with gulls sailing overhead balancing on the light airs blowing over the channel from France. My cloak was warm about me and I felt in the vigor of my step that all things were again possible to me. It was that same air of triumph that I have felt in the laboratory when I have made some new discovery. At such times I am still like the lad I once was in Yorkshire running home to show my mother some treasure that I had found upon the moors. I feel the years ahead of me like some great bank balance or beckoning fertile fields. I count over the coins of my future and dream of triumphs yet to come.

But then like a cloud the habit of critical reflection comes again upon me and I know that these fields have been swept by time's grim sickle before and that only a few paltry decades remain to me of what had once seemed endless plains like those of the American prairies. What have I sown? How little have I reaped! What will I return to in London but only more of the same? Have I not made Professor Moriarty appear so great merely so that I might appear greater still? Have I not made him the Napoleon of Crime simply so that I might equal the stature of my counterpane dreams of Wellington who defeated him at Waterloo?

As I said here, I stood upon the cliffs today and realized how dear to me is my own vanity and how perhaps I hunger for the greatness of God simply out of my greed for the infinite as alone adequate to make life to be a worthy proposition for the living to entertain. I feel the need to be able to affirm at last that life is in fact good and not the ugly and sordid business that Moriarty believes it to be. To love God is finally to love the world that He has made, because in condemning the order of things we only condemn ourselves. We turn to Christ as it were in scorn and say, "Why do you not come down from that Cross?" But, thank God; that He never shall do. God is one with us in our human condition and that alone makes it tolerable and even finally beautiful, as beautiful as the open sea at dawn.

December 16, 1893
Canterbury

I have moved on to Canterbury. My long hiatus is ending at last where it began in that long ago spring of 1891. I have come back to the city of Chaucer's pilgrims, to the great Cathedral of Canterbury, so that my circle can be made complete. My own circle is almost done, but that of Canterbury has yet to be, for the Cathedral is now only English and England is separated from the rest of the Church by its submission to the temporal power of the Kings and Queens of England.

The result is that even in Canterbury my pilgrimage must be celebrated at Mass in the humble Chapel of the Oratory Fathers. I may still visit the Cathedral of Canterbury of course but I cannot in good conscience kneel there. I reserve my submission for Rome, not for its splendor as a city, not even for the majesty of the Basilica of St. Peter, but rather for the living and universal Church present in all of its members in the unity of the Catholic faith throughout the world.

My loyalty is not a product of the often blemished history of the Church; my loyalty is to the promises of Christ who promised to remain with His Church until the consummation of the world. I have no doubt that the world is being consumed by history. I feel that a new dark age is coming upon the world. The pride of English rule will soon come to an end. I feel already that the world is preparing itself for some gigantic struggle for hegemony. A world not unified under Christ is by definition a world at odds with itself. The many partial creeds are nothing else than mankind's attempt to create meaning and to fashion a God to meet our own conceptions. Even Mohammed, political genius that he was, could only create a faith adequate to politically unite the Arab tribes but falling far short of Jesus as the divine redeemer. Its later successes were achieved by forcing its will upon other races by the sword.

Islam will spread its errors throughout the world until its own emptiness and inner divisions cause brother to oppose brother in one final struggle over a vain caliphate like that of the Ottoman sultans.

But to be honest is not even Christianity splintered and in manifest opposition to the final prayer of Christ who prayed, *"That they may be one Father even as you and I are one?"* Will humanity raise its common voice to God only from the embers of this world as it expires in one final conflagration? If I have infinite faith and hope in God, I have little in unaided human reason. It is not that men are sheep without a shepherd; it is that man without God is a wolf, nay rather a shark rending its very flesh in a frenzy of consumption. What is history at last but a tale of snapping jaws? For this reason I seek peace and tranquility above all else.

A gentle snow was falling today as I left the chapel and entered the festive streets of the town. I found as I walked about the old buildings that my melancholy began to lift, for it is after all Christmas time. The year is ending and for a time the peace of the season seems to reign over the hearts of men and women of good will. The English know how to celebrate the season of Christ's birth as well as any people on earth. I am happy to say that in a rare gesture of good will I have heard from Sherringford by way of Mycroft that he will come down to London and celebrate Christmas with us there.

It is a rare gesture of reconciliation and Mycroft also has given his assent to that meeting. Our dear mother would be most pleased. Christmas is the one season when the ancient rule of the Diogenes Club is suspended for a day and the members freely greet each other. Extra tables are brought in and the entire membership shares a sumptuous repast, perhaps more of a Saturnalia than a proper Christmas feast. There is gin-punch sprinkled with citrus fruits, spiced eggnog with rum or brandy, and then when the members are properly thawed-out by drink a Christmas dinner is served. There is salmon, roast venison, Surrey pheasants, beef rib-roasts, and racks of lamb. There are heaping bowls of potatoes and turnips joined by loaves of fresh spiced breads and cheeses.

Dinner is followed later by toasts of port and the service of a flaming Christmas pudding for dessert. The festivities usually end at three o'clock in the morning and soon all will have been cleared away so that the early rising members may enjoy their morning coffee in the renewed silence of the ordinary rules of the club. There may remain still a flush upon the cheek and a small left-over gleam in the eye so that members may so far forget themselves as to nod at one another on the day following Christmas, but soon the members resume what they feel is the best guarantee of peace among men, the rule of silence. The rule of silence descends again upon the denizens of the Diogenes Club and the New Year is celebrated by the expectation that it will be like that which has just passed because the nature of man does not change and even grace will only take it as far as the portals of the mercy of God.

December 20, 1893
London

𝕴 left the town of Canterbury well provisioned for Christmas with bottles of port, sherry, and brandy and with wreaths of the holly that now festoon the old bookshop. The shops were alive with cheerful folk seeking their holiday treasures. Upon returning to London I immediately reserved a suite of rooms for Sherringford at the Northumberland Hotel. I was lucky to succeed in finding a room, but the name of Holmes worked wonders. Sherringford will arrive on Christmas Eve and I shall meet his train at Paddington Station. We shall dine without Mycroft on Christmas Eve.

It will take Sherringford at least a day to get used to the hustle and bustle of London before meeting Mycroft whom he has not seen in many years. Mycroft does not deal well with the posturing and noise present in the Houses of Parliament, so that even when Sherringford used to come to town to represent his district the two brothers did not meet. I am looking forward to the holiday with the enthusiasm for Christmas of my youth and even the coming year seems strangely welcome to me in spite of its many uncertainties. I expect to resume living in my old rooms at Baker Street with the New Year of 1894 and I hope that I will soon be fully engaged again as the world's first consulting detective. If only I might have Watson again by my side then my joy would be complete. But how am I to manage this? How does one emerge like Lazarus from the tomb by one's own efforts?

December 21, 1893
London

I have at long last devised a plan to intercept Watson. I shall assume the role of an elderly and eccentric book-peddler. I know the type well for many such fellows have come to the bookshop during the last month to purchase their stock in trade from the selection of books for which we have found no place upon our shelves. It is characteristic of the type to have set ideas as to the marketability of various obscure volumes dealing with even more various arcane subjects. These opinions are often shared by no one but themselves, but their technique is to stick to a prospective buyer until he will make the purchase simply to be rid of their company. They often provoke laughter in the passers-by who are only too glad that it was not they who were set upon by one of these strange fellows. Their usual garb is a familiar one: an old patched coat, mittens without fingers, a scarf wound several times about the lower part of the face to ward off the chill air, and a battered wide-brimmed hat to top it all off. I shall also don some false whiskers and a pair of ancient tinted spectacles for the occasion. Then there is the voice, which is high, quavering, and penetrating so as to grate upon the ear. Since Watson is a physician, I may bring along a few obscure and outdated medical volumes as well to complete the ensemble. I doubt that I shall reveal myself to him, but this ruse will at least allow me to hear the dear old fellow's voice once again.

I must try and catch him after he closes his dispensary, when he goes out for his dinner. He is a man of regular habits and

I know them all well. He has a veritable passion for fish and chips and at least in the old days he had a particular favorite pub that he frequented with a fish and chips shop just round the corner from it. His other passion is for curries, a legacy of his days in India. For this fare also he had a favorite restaurant that was run by an old Bengali man and his wife, located on the outer borders of Kensington. I much prefer the usual bland British fare of steak and kidney pie if I must make a plebian choice in dining rather than going to Simpsons, but I am willing enough to accommodate his tastes and have dined with him when I cannot persuade him to join me for French cuisine or at Simpsons for the best of what London has to offer the palate. I wonder what surprises this evening shall bring with it.

Later—

It was just as I had suspected the usual publican fare of fish and chips for Watson. But then he has been absent in the American south for some time and this may have been a special treat for him after such a long period of exile. I waited outside his Kensington dispensary having arrived in good time to see that his rooms were still brightly lit. The fog had just begun to rise from the river and dusk was just settling down when I saw the last patient emerge from the dispensary door and hobble away.

A short time later the gas lights inside the dispensary were extinguished and I saw the familiar figure of my friend emerge from the door and descend the few steps to the pavement. The traffic was light on the sidewalk and I soon managed to approach the good doctor and by an awkward side-step managed to place myself directly in his path so that he collided with me causing me to drop my load of books at his feet. I cried out in dismay and bent down to retrieve the precious volumes. Dr. Watson, good fellow that he is, sought to render me immediate aid, which only caused me to drop the few books that I had already retrieved. I shall describe the scene as Watson himself would have done since it proved to be an amusing encounter h my books, my precious books," I cried in the moment after the collision. "If you knew sir the value of these volumes, you would not go charging about like a great bull into a poor man. No doubt you are a rugby player. I have no doubt that you have cracked a binding. Yes, see here, a crack and in as rare a volume as I possess. See, it is *'The Origins of Tree Worship.'* This remarkable carelessness of yours will reduce the price I can get by a pound at least!"

As he tried to hand me the few that he had gathered up I continued as before, "Here now you, handle them carefully please! Do you not see that you are holding a seventeenth century translation of the Roman poet, Catullus? But then what do you young fellows know of books, always charging about on the rugby fields. I tell you sir if you studied a bit more you would go farther in life than you have done heretofore."

Watson attempted a feeble defense, "I beg your pardon, but I assure you I am no rugby player as you suppose, but a physician and a gentleman, and as to my age I am not so very much younger than you."

I answered, "Nonsense Sir! I know a great awkward rugby player when I see one. Look at you, all bronzed over with the sun! I doubt that you received that coloration from days spent in a London dispensary. Now tell the truth young fellow!"

"I am but recently returned from Louisiana in America and I do not work in public hospital. I am in private practice," Watson answered haughtily.

I scoffed at this, "Tosh, Louisiana! The next thing you will tell me is that you have come from Alabama with a banjo on your knee. I warn you sir; the law has ways of dealing with young scamps of rugby players that go charging down the street knocking people about. No doubt you were off after practice on the field to get a bit of dinner for yourself. Ah, I see that you do not deny it! Food and young ladies and rugby! I despair of the fate of the empire if it must depend only upon young fellows like you to sustain it. Who will take up the Professions?"

"I tell you, sir, that I am a doctor!" he repeated with

some asperity.

"You are a doctor? I find that hard to believe." I pretended to adjust my spectacles. "Why dear me, yes you are not quite as young as I took you to be at first. But where pray tell is your medical bag? One can't be a doctor without a medical bag!"

"I was off to get my dinner my good man, not upon a professional call."

"Well that is a pity. I would have had you look at my back doctor. I was just knocked over by a young rugby player! Now where has he gone to? Just like a young cad like that to go running off! But I must thank you for helping me to retrieve my books. Ah there it is, a fine copy of *'British Birds,'* and barely scuffed at all. And here is *'The Holy Wars of the 13th Century,'* also, a most excellent book, all about the Crusaders. Fine fellows those Crusaders, rather like that young rugby player, but they were always rushing about then with swords and maces!" Here I pretended to be having a regular coughing fit. Watson led me over to a nearby stoop where I pretended to collapse. I looked up through half-closed eyes and saw again that look of concern that I have missed these many years. The dear fellow was no doubt convinced by this time that I was more than eccentric and perhaps a little mad.

"I think that you had better rest here a bit," said he. "You are not of an age that can take a fall without upsetting the nervous system. Can I help you home?"

"Nay, nay, I can get about quite well on my own, if you would only be so kind as to help me to my feet. I have a bookshop in Bloomsbury. Perhaps you know it? Ah you must come by and see my full stock." Watson appeared to doubt that I could be an owner of a bookshop considering my disreputable appearance.

"Ah, I see you doubt me sir? As it happens I have come into a bit of money of late. As to my clothes, I am one of humble station and the habits of a lifetime are not to be lost in a short time. All of my money goes to my books, my precious books. You must come by; say that you will! Ah good, excellent! We have quite the medical section there, which you may enjoy, seeing that you are a doctor. You did say that you were a doctor, I believe? Yes? Well may I ask your name sir?"

"My name is Doctor John Watson," he replied kindly.

"Not the Doctor Watson of Baker Street!" I exclaimed. "Why I have read of you in the Strand Magazine. I was sorry to read of the death of your friend Sherlock Holmes. A sad tale that, as sad as any I have ever read."

I saw the look of pain upon the dear fellow's face and it pierced me to the very heart. I could see that even the passing of the years had not altered his sorrow at my passing and I blamed myself again severely for my reticence in his regard. How I longed to tell him at once that I was alive!

"Ah, I see that even now the pain is fresh. You are no doubt a most devoted friend. I must say though that having read the story of his passing there were a few little points in your account that troubled me at the time."

"And what were they?" Watson inquired as if to humor me.

"Well now, from all that I have read of this fellow, Sherlock Holmes, in your other stories he seemed a clever enough chap. Now then, if he knew that this master criminal; I forget his name, was in hot pursuit of him and had even vowed to kill him, now would he be taken by surprise on a rocky ledge and would there have been no final exchange of a volley of gunshots. I trust that he was armed. At the very least he might have used his alpenstock to beat back any attack, yet the account of yours that I read had that very alpenstock used instead to affix a note to your good self. Surely it had a better immediate use! This was followed I understand by some sort of wrestling match or fisticuffs in the course of which both he and his assailant plunged to their deaths. The whole thing makes dramatic reading of course, but you will forgive me if the entire tale does not contradict my entire impression of the resources and abilities of your friend. Why even I would have found a better way to avoid falling backwards to my death, having no end of experience in warding off young rugby players upon the pavements of London!"

"Yet it happened, just as I told it in my account," cried he.

"I was there. I saw all that was to be seen. You were not. I saw the signs of a scuffle. I read the footprints. There could be but one conclusion to be drawn. Both men perished. Or do you imagine that Holmes has been lost these many years without a word of communication to me. Do not play the detective for me sir! Holmes simply met a man who was as resourceful as he was himself. Perhaps he wished in his own gallantry to give this man Moriarty a sporting chance. I see them poised above the falls as though I had been present at the time, with will opposing will, each certain that he would prevail. Their battle had always been such, with mind opposed to mind. Is it any wonder then that they should have died while engaged in an equal struggle?"

I answered him laconically after a bit as his passion subsided, "Ah well, you may be right after all, but the whole thing sounds a bit Manichean to me with its good and evil as equal principles engaged in deadly struggle. For myself, I always assume that goodness will always have the upper hand. But I am a good Christian and not a heathen rugby player like you. It has been my experience in life though that one must never approach a problem with too many fixed ideas. But I have taken enough of your time, doctor. Thank you for helping me with my books. You had best be off to your dinner and I in turn shall return to my bookshop where I trust that you will soon visit me and look over my collection of medical books. Perhaps you will do so before Christmas and I will set aside a little gift for you in order to repay you for your kind services rendered to me this night."

With that I bade the good doctor goodbye. I hobbled off round the corner without looking back until after I had merged with the busy holiday crowds. I turned around at this point and saw that he in turn was off for his fish and chips. Well, they say that fish is good for the brain. If it is so, then I trust that while eating his fare tonight Watson will begin to think about the clues that I provided to him this night and may perhaps revise his premature conviction of my death so that when I do meet him as myself, it will be less of a shock.

I have at least provided some grounds for the exoneration

of my acknowledged guilt in keeping quiet for so long about the events at the Falls of Reichenbach. I will point out if pressed, that Watson should long ago have guessed the truth about the supposed death of Sherlock Holmes by merely applying the very methods that I have so laboriously and repeatedly recommended to his consideration during our long association. He will no doubt still feel that I might have made inquiries or communicated with him, but I will then confide that I was for most of the period of my absence half a world away.

December 23, 1893
London

I had hoped to hear from Watson at once that he had finally solved the puzzle. Our clerk as a former member of the Baker Street Irregulars would of course know him on sight, although since our clerk is now quite grown up, Watson may not recognize him. Besides I gave an address in Bloomsbury not Soho. I spent the day in my rooms above the bookstore in an agony of anticipation, but dusk came and the evening hours drifted by until it was time to close and still there was no sign of Watson. Can it be that with such a broad selection of clues that he still cannot reason himself into believing that I am alive? My heavens, I spoke to the man! Or is it rather that he knows and is angry with me for having deceived him for so long?

The thought that this might be the case freezes my very blood. I would deserve it though. How could I fail to have trusted Watson? But no, it was my fear that he would seek for me on my journey and run risks in doing so. Even now I cannot believe that Colonel Moran and I succeeded in going among so many tribal cultures the people of which have no reason to tolerate the English and yet managed to return safely. I simply could not have concentrated upon my tasks if I had needed to worry about the health and safety of Watson as well. But can he know what my motivations were? Perhaps he thinks that I have simply been playing a game with him or even mocking him. I have an unfortunate compulsion to set up these little show-pieces and can never resist the lure of the theatrical.

I need only think of my spontaneous performance of two days ago to provide an example of this trait. I thought the whole thing up on the spot. I could not simply reveal myself after the first few minutes. So I created a full character that became only the more believable to me as I became him. I almost came to believe that Watson in turn was indeed a young, insolent rugby player. It is no small part of what abilities I possess as a detective that I can imagine myself in the very role of the malefactor, but this skill can lead me at times to lose sight of myself, so that I must cast about later to recover my own senses. The artist is in some measure his own medium, even in the spiritual sense this is true.

The perfect artist is a mere conduit between the real world and its reproduction, using any given medium or technique. Art is at its best when it seems to be not an effort of the will but as though the artist had become transparent. It may be that art creates itself. It may even be that art creates the artist! There are some individuals who seem not to exist unless they are creating something. Perhaps there is so individual self after all. What we are may be but a stream of impressions. What is the activity of the mind if it is not a stream of events deflected now and then by the deposits laid up by past impressions? If this is so, then it may be true that there are thoughts but no thinker, for the thinker is the thought. Try as one might one may not purge the mind of all content and arrive at the mere mind itself. It is impossible to arrive at a state emptied of all of the accidental contents of memory and affection and the bias that these create for present awareness.

Only God can be God prior to any action whatsoever. For man, his actions constitute the self. How many imagine that they may claim to be virtuous, yet never act virtuously. Such men may live an entire life under the delusion that they are one sort of man, when in actuality they are of another type entirely. For this reason providence prepares its traps for us, to jar us loose from such illusions before death, so that we may know ourselves as we are, and be spared that grim introduction of a man to his un-repented sins at the particular judgment of his soul. We must all pray then to see ourselves as God sees us, for God alone sees us with love and asks only that we respond to that love as the practical medium in which we live and breathe. It is for this reason that this careless and brutal world that we see about us is an illusion also in its way.

We never emerge clearly from the mélange of events. Hence the life-world is clearly our own dream-creation and not derivative from the will of God. To one who imagines a world without the effects of moral evil, this observation will become clear. God takes the world as he finds it. God is led to embrace extremes to counter our own evil. Perhaps even the crucifixion of Christ was contingent upon the sin or the rejection of the teachings of Jesus. History is not pre-existent and God adapts to the contingencies of time rather than dictating them.

One question of Jesus shows this clearly. The question is when the Son of Man returns, will He find faith upon the earth? No clearer statement exists that the fate of the earth and of our souls lies in our own hands; creation is entrusted to our care and what we make of it is our responsibility. This is where any thought of predestination fails. God can be aware of contingent events without determining them in that act of divine knowing. God is more audience that player! Yet God is not the disinterested figure that the deists acknowledge but do not think to worship.

God leaves the door open to our doubts and reservations. This is exactly the reticence that allows for events to emerge in their own course and to define themselves under the influence of our free moral actions. It takes constant effort to bridge that silence and absence in prayer and reflection. I could not hand Moriarty the solution to his moral dilemma and I cannot simply sweep away the false conclusion that Watson came to regarding my supposed death. To do either would be to interfere where each man must reach his own unaided conclusions. My task has been only to provide the necessary clues, to raise the probing questions as in the case of any true mystery. When stripped of all clichés the mystery story is a series of questions rather than a recapitulation of old tropes. That is the task that I have been about here and I can only hope that the correct solution is reached at last by all involved, both Doctor Watson and Professor Moriarty.

Dr. Watson's Narrative Continues

ith this transcription of Holmes' journal I must pause for now. I must return to our last days spent in Washington D.C. in 1897...

During those last days before our departure, I was able to spend many hours alone with Irene Adler. It was a revelation to me that when not on stage she was among the most quiet and domestic of women. She still retained her sparkling wit and intelligence, but I could see that she enjoyed her hours of peace and solitude quite as much as Holmes did. She also had her private areas of interest and was well-read in many unique areas. Her knowledge of Italian sculpture was un-excelled and she had spent much time in Florence visiting the Uffizi Gallery. Our talks were always pleasant and informative and the time passed quickly in her company.

Many thoughts possessed me during the long and weary days that followed the loss of the poor girl at the theater. Holmes was absent through most of each day, engaged with Inspector Hopkins and with the Washington police in the search for the murderer. Holmes would return each evening overcome with weariness and retire to bed after giving us a brief summation of the day's activities. I would try and force him to eat something, but as so often before when he was on the scent he ran on nervous energy alone. All of my efforts directed to Holmes that he must take sufficient care of his health were in vain. Instead Holmes merely assigned me the task of guarding Irene Adler and of keeping her company during his absence each day and refusing all offers that I might accompany him. As for Irene Adler she seemed to have an intuitive grasp that any effort to interfere would only prolong this period of investigation. There was no alternative but to allow events to determine their own outcome.

At first our discussions during those days were both sparse and desultory. Each of us knew Holmes well, but in the course of our brief discussions neither of us could fathom what the web might be that Holmes was weaving about Roger Baskerville. We met each day in the drawing room to pursue our own occupations. Irene would read or knit and I returned at long last to those supplemental pages of his journal that Holmes had entrusted to me, which took up where his journal had left off with his visit to Ireland followed by his return to Devonshire. We saw very little of Holmes and of Inspector Hopkins as the days passed. Holmes often returned late in the afternoon with only a shake of the head to dispel any inquiries we might make. Even I who knew his every expression so well could not tell what progress if any had been made in the investigation.

We usually dined in the Hotel at night having surrendered the exhausting social swirl of Washington. During those dinners Holmes did not share anything about the progress of the case at hand, nor did I ask him about how he planned to bring Roger Baskerville to justice. I knew that Holmes would disclose all when the time was appropriate, but not before. Part of living with Holmes entailed the development of patience. It was a virtue that I had acquired long ago without which living with him would have been impossible for anyone possessing premature curiosity; however I could see by his distant gaze that all was not going well. There was a strain in my companion which showed me only too clearly that for some unaccountable reason the villain was still at large in the city and that the authorities evidently were not cooperating as fully as they might have done. English law could not reach him in America and we could not afford to provoke an international episode by taking any direct action on our own.

The Americans have their own way of doing things. Still, I

was surprised. The whole thing seemed like an open and shut case to me, but there were clearly factors in play the nature of which I could only guess. I naturally turned to Irene Adler hoping that she might shed some further light upon the matter, for her intelligence and insight was such that even Holmes had always referred to her as "the woman." So it was that at luncheon one day in the hotel I brought the matter up. I could see that she was as troubled as I was becoming over Holmes' continued silence. Her days of seclusion at the hotel had come to wear upon her. She wished to rejoin her acting company to which she felt she owed some loyalty. It had moved on to Baltimore with a new understudy playing her role. I proceeded then to ask her if she had formed any conclusions of her own regarding the murder of her friend and why some summary arrest of the agents at least had apparently not yet occurred. She seemed only too willing to express her views at last to me.

"To one who has lived in Italy for many years, the solution may be only too evident, Doctor Watson, although I fear to express my fears lest they be proven true by events. Americans tend to believe that the rule of justice may be easily obtained by fiat. They forget that the history of the world is the history of injustice, of bias, of preference, and of the rule of arbitrary power. No mere revolution, even if motivated by the highest of ideals, can change human nature. The Americans are living in the benign afterglow of the ideals of the eighteenth century when men thought that reason might prevail in all things and that a rational religion of man was possible. There followed of course the age of Napoleon where it was discovered that only the despotic rule and military aggression of one man might spread the revolution's ideals to an unwilling Europe. Sadly the rule of absolute monarchs is the background against which all democracies seek to raise their temporary standards only to fall back into the old order with time. Government is always controlled and co-opted by the powerful or by those who have the wealth to purchase favors from compliant and corrupt representatives as is the case with republics."

"You may not guess it but my own sympathies are with the

trade unionists and even to a degree with the anarchists. Only they have realized the central truth that the individual will always be menaced by the nation-state whatever its form of government may be. The nation is always the servant of either the military or of the oligarchs whose property interests will always carry the day. What I expect is happening in this Baskerville matter is simply this: the man is immune from arrest because of his position in a larger affair, an affair of interest to powerful men. These men will protect him as long as it is in their interest to do so. He is no doubt sheltering at the embassy and is visited there by the Americans. What after all is diplomatic immunity but a way that the powerful protect each other while they plot together the destruction of the powerless citizens who know nothing of such matters?"

"But in this case an innocent young girl has been killed," I protested.

"Yes Doctor and she was my friend," she said in a voice that still showed her shock and affliction. After a pause she continued and her voice expressed her anger.

"I ask you not to be shocked by what I must now say. You must know that I resided for many years in Italy. If this event had occurred there, then the course of events would be quite predictable and justice would be served at last. Years might pass, but finally the girl's father or a brother or lover would track down this Baskerville and he would be killed. Such actions may appear primitive, but they rest upon the awareness that the government is not the force to aid the population but to keep it in subservience to the great families. There would never be any expectation that the law would care about an obscure songstress or actress in a traveling company if the man who killed her was important enough."

"Only in America does the pretence survive that the law is not ultimately the servant of the long purse, though even here the evidence is everywhere that the poor man or woman goes to the law at their peril. I have been remaining here in the hotel, not because I have been awaiting justice, but to remove one additional worry from your friend. I assure you, the quest is pointless, but I realize that he feels he must do something. I have remained in seclusion here merely to please Sherlock who feels more at ease knowing that I am safe. The truth is that I have always been safe and the show might have continued the very next night at the theater. I know the mind of men like this Roger Baskerville who have learned to think in the Latin way. Baskerville has made his gesture and unless our friend makes a countermove against him, no further action will be taken."

"You see, Doctor, it is only the desire of Sherlock to protect me that puts me in danger. The death of the girl was tragic and unjustified and it might have been me just as well laying dead, but the motive and the outcome would have been the same. The message that Roger Baskerville intended Holmes to receive was, believe it or not, that he had conferred a favor upon Holmes by not killing me and a true Latin gentleman would have read the message aright and quietly left Washington. But my dear Sherlock with his good and noble Anglo-Saxon mind desires to play the gallant knight and to vindicate his lady fair. By doing this he places me in real danger, for now this man Rodger Baskerville will know that he must strike at Holmes' very heart in order to get him to desist."

"If you believe this, then why do you not tell Holmes?" I inquired.

"Ah there, Doctor, you raise a delicate point. Your friend is one of the last representatives of the medieval mind in a modern age. He is rare, rarer even than you who share many of his unique qualities may ever know. In every age there must remain a few men who believe that they may work their will upon a recalcitrant age and restore the glories that they imagine the world once possessed in a nobler time. There must always be dreamers who imagine that some new system of thought will change men and women and make them disinterested servants of the true and the just. But for those like me, who have lost their husbands in youth ... well we alone know only too well that the human condition both physically and morally is unchangeable and insupportable as well. We live in a vale of silent tears and the prayer of even those of us who are sanguine Christians is to hope that the world may be made better, while secretly knowing that it never will. Jesus Christ will not soon return, even though the Apocalypse of St. John ends with the plea: 'Come quickly Lord Jesus!'"

"I often think that each day should begin with this prayer above all other prayers. What does the day possess for any of us but a tithe of troubles and what does the future contain if not the certainty of death."

I looked over at her in surprise. I saw before me a woman, still beautiful and with the promise of many years ahead, could it be that she already took such a dismal view of life?

She raised her head and smiled although her eyes remained modestly downcast, "I see that I shock you, Doctor Watson. Did I not tell you that you are a romantic, just like Sherlock Holmes? You may well wonder why I am not a romantic as well. Perhaps, it is because I am an actress and because in traveling about as I do I have seen too much of the world. I know that the men and women who pay to see me and cry when I portray figures that call out to their mercy, will soon leave the theater and probably ignore the poor old woman selling flowers at the entrance in order to eke out a meager living. People confine their emotions to the convenient purging function of art and keep for the real world the cold determinism of self-interest. There are exceptions of course; the world will always possess its share of saints, thank God! But the rule holds that the great ocean of mankind is a treacherous place for a drowning man and only the saints are like islands that are all too few on that dark and wintry sea."

We were both silent then for some time. She gazed into the fire and I sought distraction for a moment in the glass of after luncheon brandy at my side. It was not that her comments were strange to me, but rather that I heard in her very tones that same weariness and dignity that I heard in my wife's last days of illness before death claimed her. Women seem to carry about with them a clearer knowledge of the loss of Eden than we men, who still carry about with us something of the innocence of Adam.

Women are reminded daily of what earth's exile really

entails. Deprived as a sex of worldly power, they know how short life is and how dearly purchased new life must always be. As a doctor I have learned how men fear to be present during childbirth. It is too visceral, too lacking in the abstract; it is life itself demanding to be born. Only in those arduous hours of her labor giving birth does any woman, reduced to being a conduit of a power greater than what her strength may by sheer will-power provide, understand the value of life and the close proximity of death. I have often thought that it should be a requirement for the world's generals to spend a day at least in a maternity hospital so that they might know the pain and labor that supplies them with the infantry that they dispose of so readily upon the battlefields of the world.

"But then what are we to do?" I suddenly inquired of her.

Irene shrugged her shoulders. "How can I say? Are you referring to Holmes? Well then, I will say only this; he will do as he always has done. He will attempt to use every method at his disposal, for he is not a man to accept defeat easily. I do not think that he will make a direct attempt on the life of Roger Baskerville or else I would have spoken up by now. What he will do is to try to use all of the forces of the law to discover and extricate the man. He may even make a direct appeal to President McKinley; but he will be disappointed in this should he attempt it."

"No, I fear that we must both be on hand to comfort your noble friend and to draw him away swiftly before his efforts cause a renewal of his old malady. It is time that we all leave this place of the dawning of the America of the next century. My understudy appears to be doing well enough in Baltimore. The role was always better suited to a younger woman. So I plan on going across the country by rail to San Francisco to join a new acting company there. Perhaps both of you may care to come along with me as well. From San Francisco you can both catch a steamship to Yokohama and from there travel home to England. The sea air would do Sherlock good I am sure you will agree and you may still be home by the early part of next year."

She clasped my hand. "You must help him to take up his

practice again in London after this most recent diversion. I of course will remain in San Francisco. I have always wished to live for a time in that exciting western city by the bay. Even an aging actress may find in that delightful climate some last vestige of her former youth and charm for one last bow to her audience of admirers."

She smiled at me with tears in her eyes, "You see my dear Doctor Watson that it is always an actress's vanity that is the last element to pass over into the wisdom of age."

Through the course of the years I have often wondered whether such extraordinarily gifted people like Irene Adler have received a gift or a curse. One can feel too much in life. Most of us learn with time, if we do not already have the ability, how to release attachments when to retain them will work our ruin. This is not bitterness or cynicism; it is the simply recognition that the mind tends to organize itself around and to interweave its joys into the fabric of our being so that when these pet visions are suddenly and without apparent reason taken away from us we are astonished to realize that they were never intended to be permanent. The depth of the resulting wound to our hearts is the measure of our supposition that anything is lasting and eternal rather than merely a brief condensation of chance factors that for a moment form a pattern and as swiftly are dispersed, perhaps to gather again in another time and in another place. We must not follow them or for a time even indulge in memory of them. Yesterday is already light-years away from us; it isn't what was lost that brings us to the edge of despair; it is the size of the empty space left behind and the time that it will take to fill that space once again and the fear that nothing will ever be identical to whatever was lost. No final version of what our lives will become should ever be planned.

L istening to Irene's words with the greatest of care I realized for perhaps the first time how deep was her devotion to Sherlock Holmes. It was a devotion that exceeded the more usual love of a woman for a man. Her devotion was more on the order of a disciple for a master. Yet, there was about her admiration also a protective quality, a desire to guard Holmes from the excesses of his own nature. In many ways it is the women of the world who guard the males, who may be after all the weaker sex. A man's strength is limited to what he may see clearly before him, but a woman's strength is comprehensive. Women seem to have access to a repository of ancient wisdom as old as life itself, whereas men seem always to be engaged in imagining a future that may never come to be. I have always thought that the strength of woman is drawn from the permanence of the earth itself.

So much of a woman's life is centered about the daily necessities of existence that she is curtailed in the scope of her speculations. A man on the other hand seems to wilt beneath necessity and only to become his true self when he is as it were in advance of his present condition. It is this characteristic of men that makes them love power, even if that power in the last analysis betrays them into the service of evil ends. Men fear age and death because it robs them not of beauty but of power. Women give themselves to life as it is without hesitation and for the good of life itself while men are willing to sacrifice life in order to obtain some elusive and shadowy ideal of what life might someday be.

Men may desire perfection but on their own terms. For this reason to humble a man may crush the very life out of his spirit. Men grow only gradually to admit defeat so as not to lose all hope. Irene Adler's words were for me proof of this assessment of the relative strength of the sexes. She knew already, perhaps in those first days in Washington, that Holmes would not be able to vindicate the death of her young friend and bring Roger Baskerville at last to heel by his own unaided efforts when opposed by the inertia of the American government.

Still, I could not believe it. How was it that such duplicity could exist in a nation even if it was to bring about that nation's ruin by sheltering such villains; or was it that the pursuit of power always exacts such concessions from statesmen? Private morality seems to be turned away from the councils of government whose sole interest seems to be the achievement of power at any price.

Knowing this fact of diplomacy may account for the mistrust that prevails among all nations and why even treaties are in the last analysis only temporary concessions meant to achieve larger strategic goals.

The Chinese of course realized this truth long ago. To read Sun Tsu on the Art of War is to comprehend the laws of diplomacy that are finally the art of deception and of compromise. Perhaps this is why government must be conducted in impressive halls and in magnificent council chambers, so that the citizens may imagine that the councils of statesmen are more than mere displays of intimidation, like the growling and the baring of teeth of beasts about a recent kill.

Even the religions of the world are not immune from this competitive spirit. What was the *auto de fe* but a demonstration of power over the consciences of men? Believe or burn! What is the famed jihad of the followers of Mohammed, but this same desire, not so much to vindicate God, for is not each such demonstration a guarantee that God will presumably do this also on the last day to unbelievers? It is men though who kill over their belief systems and not to vindicate God, but to ensure that their own fashion of belief may prevail over all other considerations because they believe that God demands this of them! They kill then for power not for truth. Their indignation in the face of what they call blasphemy is proportionate to their fear that perhaps their own belief system is in vain. Religious violence is most extreme during times of doubt when the rule of faith seems threatened. For this reason also nations become most violent when the core assumptions of the nation are most in doubt.

Would America have gone to war with Spain over the professed ideal of freedom for the Cuban people if the American people were aware that the American ideals (which so many had thought would find a new birth after the war between the American states) were being abandoned by that very act to usher in a new and less democratic order of things? Instead of a renewal of government by the people and for the people, antebellum America was becoming an ugly place of conflict among the emerging industrial classes. Great fortunes had been amassed by trusts and corporate business ventures. Public lands had been conceded to railroad companies that then sold the so-called right of way acres to the new immigrants for farms at a profit for the private interests that owned the railroads. Great speculative schemes plunged the nation into a series of financial panics.

How then best to turn aside the growing mistrust and wrath of the citizens than to seek out an enemy beyond the seas upon which to displace the groundswell of national indignation and sense of betrayal of the public good? What better technique has ever been devised to maintain power in the hands of the few than to flatter national pride by short-lived victories that only lead to new wars?

I saw now how foolish Holmes and I had been to imagine that we as private emissaries of a foreign power might change the course of American policy. America would go on to build the canal, of that I had no doubt, but it would have resolved to do so even had we stayed in England. Why then were we in America at all? Why had I cooperated with Holmes and risked his health by undertaking such a labor at the cost of a year of his life when his detective practice was just beginning to flourish once again? Why had I abandoned my own cherished retirement as well on such a futile errand?

But then thoughts turned to a strange passage in St. Matthew's gospel dealing with John the Baptist. In reference to his illustrious but decidedly odd kinsman Jesus asked his disciples, many of whom had begun their lives as followers of the Baptist, *"What did you go out into the desert to see, a reed shaken by the wind?"* This phrase had always fascinated me. The child Moses was discovered by Pharaoh's daughter hidden in the rushes or reeds growing along the River Nile. But this parallel was not why the passage fascinated me. It was not even the poverty of John the Baptist that Jesus goes on to emphasize that so stimulated my interest in the phrase. It was the naked picture of a single reed standing in mute opposition to the wind, a figure that seems to sum up Christianity.

This is a case where the words of Jesus are perhaps even more suggestive and evocative than the contrast that Jesus is attempting to make before his disciples. It is the raw image of futile resistance that bears testimony; this solitary reed suggests to my mind's eye a single voice caught up in the winds of history. Suddenly a new though comes to me, a thought regarding expectation and preparation for salvation.

After all, who goes out into the desert expecting to see anything? Only one who has already sought salvation in the more usual places makes one last effort in the desert. But what if he finds there only a reed shaken by the wind? It is this message of perseverance despite all odds that Jesus is calling his disciples to recognize. The gospel is always misunderstood at first; the truly spiritual eludes us because we expect it to appear somewhere else. It is the utterly prosaic nature of a reed shaken by the wind that impresses me. Jesus was killed precisely because later Judaism expected a glorious messiah to restore the Jewish nation and free it from Roman rule. Jesus was, for those who expected this, an utter disappointment. This could not possibly be what the people had gone out into the desert to see. This search was after all no idle stroll but an adamant quest and look what it came to—a reed shaken by the wind bearing mute witness of an absent God. (Or so it must have seemed to the early followers of Jesus when the triumphant early experience of Pentecost was itself becoming a distant memory).

The first generation of Christians was dying out and Jesus had not returned as many had expected he would. Those hearing the gospel needed to hear something now, from Jesus himself, to remind them of what their expectation had been when they were first baptized. What were those expectations were now? Could the early communities endure what was to come?

The gospels were written for a specific purpose in a world that had for thirty or more years functioned without them. The Jesus that they present to the reader is already clothed in theological garb. There is already a purpose in these remembrances and quotations. They are meant to be overheard as though they, the new Christians, had been present at these events. The new convert is asked, as every subsequent generation has been asked ever since, *"Who do people say that I am?"* shortly to be followed by, *"But you, who do you say that I am?"*

There is a key distinction here: the Christian is not the same in his or her evaluation of what can be expressed by *"a reed shaken by the wind."* The desert means something entirely different to one who has endured and will endure exile and what might follow, the indefinite delay of the full realization of the Kingdom of God. The greatest cross that the Christian must bear is captured by the futile image of a dried-out and hollow reed, weak and shaken in the wind, but still capable of emitting a tiny whispering sound.

This is not the Church Triumphant anymore than the vision of a man expiring on a cross could match the haughty appellation of Pontius Pilate who in the perfect expression of his contempt (not only for the Jewish people subject to him, but above all for the man that he had just condemned to death) proclaimed in a sign affixed to the cross, *"This is Jesus, the King of the Jews."* From such an unlikely beginning Christianity springs forth in the desert. Thereafter, the parade of souls into heaven has been that of a motley band of unlikely people, the very last candidates that anyone would expect would attain salvation.

This is why Christianity above all other religions is most likely to be true, because it causes us to recalibrate all of our expectations in order to grasp where God just might possibly be found. Of course my reading of this passage comparing the gospel message to a wind-shaken reed is my own idiosyncratic reading of the passage. Jesus in this account while addressing the crowd goes on to emphasize that the religious quest can never be reduced to a mere quest for nature; we seek prophets to convey the divine massage to us. We seek a human meaning and more than that we go into the desert in search of a prophetic message that will lead us to God. But still it is the frailty and nakedness of a reed standing in solitary witness that captures my imagination. I have always preferred the evocative image to the categorical statement.

Symbols resonate with meaning denied to mere nouns and verbs closely tethered to a stake in the ground lest they invoke unintended meanings.

Catholicism as the years have passed has grown ever more jealous of its dogmatic definitions to the point that the message of salvation is contained like a pearl in a jewel box lest someone should steal it without permission of the owner. After sufficient time passes one forgets about the pearl and only sees the box that contains it. How different in symbolic suggestibility is this passage, *"the Kingdom of Heaven suffers violence and the violent bear it away,"* where the message of salvation, even if it should be imperfectly formulated and understood, is grasped for what it offers without proper license or permission, but simply because of its probably innate value. I believe the gospel should remain unguarded and accessible in order to retain its first character as a startling proclamation beyond any prior expectations. At the same time some vagueness should be allowed to remain in order to stimulate interest. In any case God exceeds anything that can be said about God. Correct belief should be less valued than correct action. It is far better (or so it seems to me) that a person should act like a Christian than that he or she should merely hold beliefs that are unimpeachably orthodox, but beyond that bear no resemblance to Jesus Christ. Some people of course manage to attain both unimpeachable belief and virtuous actions based on those beliefs, but I like to believe that Jesus makes up for any deficiencies in our accounting of either qualification on the final day.

Irene seemed to read my very thoughts as Holmes was often wont to do for she suddenly said, "I believe you have a great tolerance for human imperfection, Doctor Watson. Perhaps, I have said too much in my prior comments. Is it possible that you feel that all of this has been in vain? If so then you must listen to me. It is never in vain that we raise objections and resistance to the course of events. It is the task of the good people of the world to bear witness to what we cannot change. What were the prophets after all but witnesses and guides to a better life? They did not change the betrayals of the covenant, nor did they avert the course of Jewish exile. Their task was to keep alive the memory of the law and to promise that present evils would have an end. Their task was to keep hope alive in dark times. That is the function of men like you, Doctor Watson, and of men like our mutual friend Sherlock Holmes. In the end he will have struggled and born witness to the truth and that is enough. That is all that God at times can expect of us."

Her words were a comfort to me both then and now looking back after so many years. We had both been avidly awaiting Holmes' return, but as the hour was growing late and considering that he had been less than communicative of late when he would return, we both decided that we had better place our speculations aside and retire to our respective rooms for the night. Holmes had promised to have breakfast with us at least on the following day, so we would have to wait until the morning at the very least before hearing how he was progressing in the investigation.

So it was that we left the sitting room in the suite that Holmes and I shared and I escorted Irene down the hallway to her own room where she bade me goodnight. I could tell that she was weary of the routine of our days together. She was one who had grown accustomed to a hectic schedule with the demands of rehearsals and performances, so idleness was an added burden to the anxiety she must have felt daily about Holmes. I was also concerned lest this defeat, if such it proved to be, might upset the precarious balance of his mind. It was no easy matter for Holmes to abandon his practice to undertake first an enforced period of convalescence and then to undertake this strange diplomatic errand in America. He had hoped for a speedy recovery from his lung complaint of early 1897 and now here we were about to pass into the New Year of 1899 without a definitive solution to the problems at hand.

It fell to me then to reassure him when the time came that his efforts had after all not been in vain. We had at least forestalled the introduction of a hideous plague that might have been brought to the coast of England and from there have been disseminated through the length and breadth of the country. We had protected Sir Henry and Lady Beryl from a new attack upon their peace and security from a man long supposed to be dead, Rodger Baskerville. We had caused Baron Maupertuis to go to ground for the present and to direct his schemes for financial gain to a project that would put him into direct competition with a similar American effort to build a canal that would unite the two oceans. This review of the course of our labors over the last two years helped me to realize that the world was changing all about us in ways that made the old problems that Holmes and I had once faced in Baker Street seem like exercises in an elementary educational text. Even men like Mycroft Holmes would soon be hard-pressed to keep up with events in the coming century. Yet we alone possessed the skills developed in creating what remained of the old order; surely we must use our final years to avoid the potential hazards that frowned down upon us like great boulders precariously suspended over travelers in the mountain passes of Tibet.

Both Holmes and I had come to America to attempt to caution the leaders there to avoid the path of imperial rule with all of its burdens and dangers to the domestic order of the nation. Most men would have felt nothing but pride in what we (if I may include myself) had accomplished, but it was characteristic of my friend to underrate his own achievements and to hold in contempt his own powers. I have often thought that his ultimate desire was to create a world worthy of the first coming of Christ, rather than to accept that it is mankind's sins, those very innate human characteristics that demand the existence of a redeemer, that had not changed and would never disappear completely and must await the second coming of Christ.

The belief in human moral progression and of cultural evolution occurring simply through the advancement of scientific knowledge and technological innovation is an illusion. The relation of nations is comparative not absolute in nature. Economic competition would always make occasional wars inevitable.

Meanwhile, the logic of capital growth is to increase production without creating an oversupply of available goods and by doing so to lower the unit price that can be obtained in the market so as to increase or even maintain profit margins. This struggle for existence (for it is nothing else) means that new markets for finished goods must constantly be found in order to keep demand steady or to increase it. Alternatively the costs allocated to each unit of production must be reduced. Traditionally the great industrialists have sought to lower unit costs by reducing the growth in wages over time, but of course without adequate wages paid there is no domestic market for finished goods unless they can be exported to reach buyers in other countries who can afford to pay more for the same items than consumers in the country where the goods were originally produced. The delicate task is to increase exports relative to imports without triggering the imposition of tariffs in reprisal. As between nations a balance of trade must be maintained.

An even better solution to this problem is to look to other costs of production than reducing wages by reducing the cost of raw materials. This strategy explains the need for powerful countries to control the economies of colonial possessions where raw materials can be obtained for a fraction of their real value and consumed or utilized at home or in other similarly situated countries that can therefore afford to pay higher wages to their citizens with higher skilled jobs. The task of the property owner, the possessor of capital, who of course is in competition with other firms, is to obtain more labor for less cost and thus gain a greater share of the market or better still to drive his competitors out of business and to obtain a monopoly. Wages will tend to rise with skill levels unless that growth in expertise (called industrial progress) is pirated away to the factory owner rather than remaining with the wage-earner. The demand for higher wages as profits increase must therefore be resisted at all costs. Men like Baron Maupertuis manage this feat by what I will call here "the calculus of fear." The laboring man or woman must be placed in constant fear of losing his or her position. Any rising discontent of labor that might lead to unionization and collective bargaining must be resisted by violent means if necessary. An aura of fear and scarcity must be maintained at all times. The best way to achieve this is to import cheaper foreign labor from the colonies where expectations are lower and where the worker can be readily sent home if the necessity arises.

Problems do occur of course if the domestic labor-pool should suddenly decrease as it does when workers are co-opted by the nation to die in war. Suddenly yesterday's superfluous worker who could be fired at will is replaced by industrial need and it is the employer who must face uncertainty and fear from a hitherto unimportant quarter. This phenomenon alone would seem to make wars unlikely occurrences. They are if nothing else detrimental to industrial growth and lead to an increase in the national debt. Why then do they occur? I suggest that the answer to this question brings the moral dimension of mankind back into play and simultaneously explains why moral progress with technical expansion is an illusion.

The great constant factors of human life come into play here: greed and fear. Mankind is desirous of the Kingdom of Heaven that it forfeited long ago and still seeks to obtain without resorting to virtue; this is the definition of greed. Regarding the other human constant of fear, mankind lives in fear of extinction by his fellow men whether through imposed scarcity or violence and thus is motivated to destroy or to be in turn destroyed. This is the final root of fear. But there is something else, something that exists beneath both greed and fear and something that is more evil than both of them put together; it is something that exists within us. Shall I write down here what I have come to believe that something is? Very well, I will attempt it. This mysterious thing can be distilled out of every religion, but it is most manifest in the Bible and therefore I am and remain a Christian and a Catholic as the most ancient of the many sects that proclaim Jesus Christ to an uncomprehending world, the same world that is just beginning to shake free from a great war of the supposedly most civilized nations of the earth.

The something is this—even if we had everything back again, even if Eve was as fresh and beautiful as she once was when taken from the side of Adam, even if Adam inhabited a paradise where he might enjoy her without fear of a rival spiriting her away through his blandishments, even if God should wake this original couple each day with the song of glorious birds and bid them walk beneath trees filled with fruits of every imaginable delight so that their imaginations could picture and their hands could reach anything that they desired, even then one tree alone would beckon to them and to us and beneath it a serpent would lie in wait for the most recent of these two most precious creatures of God and they would choose it at the cost of everything else (as would we). They would choose it in the same manner that such evil choices are always made ... they would choose evil above all other things even over God because ... they love evil for itself in a way that they could never love God! And a greater miracle still in the story of the Garden of Eden is that God knew this about us and must have always known this choice that they and we after them would make and what it would cost to remedy what they had freely chosen and God created them anyway out of love!

This tale of our moral origin as human beings is replicated in our daily experience of an imperfect world. Christianity differs from all other religions by presenting God in human form and then by historically enacting in the life of a single individual, Jesus Christ, the way of life that Christianity proposes to each of us to adopt if we wish to be considered children of God. The attribute of divine holiness is no longer something existing out here somewhere in another dimension; it is demonstrated for us and then sacramentally instilled into us by "existing no longer for ourselves but for Him." St. Pails uses such visceral phrases as to "put on Jesus Christ" so that anyone who sees us will in effect see God acting within us through grace. The Christian's goal is to become like a transparent window through which God is made present to others.

One last lesson remains to be distilled from this account of our origins. The Tree of Life of course remained neglected and alone and of little immediate appeal amidst such splendor in Eden, a tree scorned by all persons ever since, because it was reserved for only One who would ever eat of its bitter fruit. The Tree of Life is a leafless tree, rough-hewn and splintered, twisted and deformed in the shape of a cross prepared for the hour of our salvation. I will stop here before returning to Holmes' journal in Volume 7. The remaining entrees there finally gave me the clarity I had been seeking since that fatal day at the Falls of Reichenbach. They explaind how even the great Professor Moriarty, who had once been called the Napoleon of Crime, found a path of orbit around the Catholic faith of Sherlock Holmes, a path not unlike one of his own burned-out asteroids circling in an elliptical orbit around a star.

Note From the Author

As one who has always esteemed writers such as Graham Greene, Evelyn Waugh, and George Bernanos (each of whom was Catholic) it has been my hope that my own effort in The Confessions of Sherlock Holmes might be part of a venerable tradition. I would like to point out however that the position of a writer who incidentally is Catholic must be distinguished from that of a Catholic writer whose writings are meant precisely to reflect church teachings as such. There is a tension between these two positions that makes it difficult for a Catholic to be both true to his faith while remaining simultaneously true to the form and literary intent that must accompany any act of composition. It would be awkward and indeed impossible to write a cohesive narrative seeking to capture and comment upon human life and conflict if the writer had to simultaneously ensure that goodness and fidelity always emerged in clarity and triumph while its opposite was equally revealed in all of its inherent malice and folly. Fiction, even when dealing with theological reflection, as is the case with the present work, can never be a substitute for catechesis. The reader is therefore cautioned that in reading the present text no decisive conclusion be drawn that the positions of any of the characters reflect either the final views of the author or the official position of the Catholic Church. Literature embraces life according to its own limited perceptions as it is and even in its suggestions of a better world must always fall short, not only in displaying accurately whatever emerging forces may exist in human history, but in depicting all that has been revealed of a higher purpose and source to illumine us in our beleaguered world.

Thomas Mengert possesses a Masters Degree in English Literature with a special expertise in the complex works of the Irish author, James Joyce. His background in humanities and philosophy are combined in this probing novel. As a final Sherlockian synthesis, The Confessions of Sherlock Holmes is Mengert's attempt to understand the true depths of the best known detective in world literature, a hero to his many fans who find in his character and habits of mind an endless fascination.